Midnight Tales

Midnight Tales

A WOMAN'S JOURNEY
THROUGH THE MIDDLE EAST

by *Rosina-Fawzia Al-Rawi*
translated by *Monique Arav*

OLIVE
BRANCH
PRESS

An imprint of Interlink Publishing Group, Inc.
www.interlinkbooks.com

First American edition published in 2006 by

OLIVE BRANCH PRESS
An imprint of Interlink Publishing Group, Inc.
46 Crosby Street, Northampton, Massachusetts 01060
www.interlinkbooks.com

Library of Congress Cataloging-in-Publication Data

Al-Rawi, Rosina-Fawzia B.
[Tante Fatima kauft eine Teppich. English]
Midnight tales ; translated by Monique Arav. — 1st American ed.
p.cm.
ISBN 1-56656-558-8 (pbk.)
1. Arab countries—Description and travel. 2. Al-Rawi, Rosina-Fawzia B.—Travel—
Arab countries. I. Title.
DS36.65.A4213 2004
956.05'3'082—dc22
2004011349

Cover photograph by George Azar

Printed and bound in Canada by Webcom

CONTENTS

PROLOGUE

However persistent, the difference between past, present, and future is but an illusion.
—Albert Einstein

Childhood is a world of wonders, of amazement at the variety in this world. In each movement, each shape lies our incredible, pulsating, wonderful existence. Youth hardens the heart, an armor is put on, and then later the heart softens again. This is the mystical journey from refusal to compromise and intransigence to compassion that each human being experiences totally individually.

Every encounter, every event, however inconspicuous, carries in it a meaning, and self-knowledge grows from the willingness to accept those encounters and events, and from the ability to change direction spontaneously in order to respond to them. At the end of the way, this is what makes the difference between a rich and a lost human being. To err is human and natural, yet to die without having understood one's mistakes turns life into a meaningless exercise. Compassion and understanding, superficiality and egocentrism have nothing to do with age, but with the life one leads.

Life holds more than the two poles of consciousness, awake and asleep. Whoever only accepts these two misses out on a whole range of tales, blue worlds, and fragrant gardens. Some time along the way, one realizes that even the evil impulse is only present to aid the good. Without darkness there would be no concept of light. If the light is to understand itself, it must know about its antithesis, about darkness. Heavy sweetness, filled with the fragrance of death and spiced with musk. Whoever was subjugated once becomes forever impregnable. Time and time again, we bend further back into the past, drinking from the source of our old songs and dreams. Remembering the time when the voice of our mother healed all the wounds of our soul. A time comes when we turn our backs on lies and approach the truth, without ever quite reaching it.

IRAQ

THE CENTER OF THE EARTH

I was driving with Aunt Fatima along Rashid Street, Baghdad's most famous main street. It goes around the ancient souks and bazaars and as you drive, you can peep into the dark, covered lanes of the souks and catch the last whiff of ancient Baghdad.

In 100 AH[1] (762 CE), al-Mansour, the second Abbasid caliph, ordered that this city be built on the western bank of the Tigris. Within four years, it was built in the shape of a perfect circle. The outer ring featured four gates and in the middle of the inner ring stood the palace, the government buildings, and the Friday mosque. He named it Madinat as-Salam, the City of Peace, and indeed, it stood in a central position: between the Arab peninsula, Egypt, and Syria on the one hand; and Persia, Central Asia, and the Punjab on the other. Boats on the Euphrates and caravans brought food from Egypt and Syria, while tools came over the sea from China and from Byzantium and Mosul on the Tigris. By moving the capital from Damascus to Baghdad, al-Mansour changed the pure Arab quality of the previous dynasty into a general Middle Eastern one. All of the Middle East and Southeast Asia were reflected in this city. Baghdad became the center of the whole Islamic world and, before long, also the wealthiest city on earth.

The famous Arab geographer al-Muqaddasi described it as "too famous for praise, too beautiful for words, and too solemn for fate." He wrote: "Every excellence is hers, every good, and all skills come from her. All elegance is hers and all hearts long for her. All wars will be waged by her, and she will shelter all." And as for the inhabitants of the City of Peace, they "have special qualities and grace, innate affections and kindness. They enjoy a mild climate and precise knowledge."[2]

Al-Mansour had tried to make it so: Before deciding on the city's exact location, he had ordered several men to sleep there during the different seasons in order to find out exactly what the winter, summer, rain, mosquitoes, and air were like. Everything was to be right, for he wanted to build a city that would remain unforgettable in the history of mankind. Beauty, health, and peace were to be its attributes.

Yet it turns out that throughout Baghdad's history the city has experienced very short periods of peace. Even its climate seems to have changed and the mosquitoes multiplied over the centuries, seemingly as a consequence of human beings' inability to live in harmony.

Suddenly Auntie decided that we should get out. "Stop here!" she ordered the driver. In next to no time we were out of the car. A relative in the United States wanted a piece of home, and Auntie felt a carpet would be just right. But before we dived into the souk, Auntie wished to pay an important visit to Abdul Qadir al-Jilani's mausoleum mosque.

Abdul Qadir was a 12th-century mystic whose Sufi teachings remain to this day the most widely spread. He travelled throughout the Far East and had many followers, especially in Pakistan, Java, and Guinea. His spiritual school was very popular, and his knowledge of the soul's stages of development and his experience with healing through color therapy made his teaching very lively. Popular faith describes al-Jilani as the master of the djinns and many eerie caves and holy sites are dedicated to him, especially in the Maghreb.

The front of the mosque was swarming with vendors selling all sorts of incense, scents, and essences. Auntie rushed—she was always in a hurry—to one of them, armed herself with amber and rose, for once without haggling, because it would not do to worry about secular matters in such a holy place, and then all of a sudden she slowed down. Even Aunt Fatima slowed down when she entered a holy place.

It was really amazing how time seemed to stand still as soon as we went into the burial mosque. Inside, we forgot which century we live in, and as soon as people came in, they took off the mad rush of life like a heavy coat. Men sat in the long forecourt of the mosque; women held their *masbahas* (prayer beads), and with every bead that they pushed back with their thumb, they seemed to sink deeper into themselves. The fragrance hanging everywhere like soft mist rocked the restless spirit to sleep and made space for the soul.

We walked slowly past the people to the great master's mausoleum. We were about to enter through the narrow doors when we saw a thin figure moving to and fro on bended knees. When my eyes had become used to the darkness, I realized it was a woman. She had soaked her dress in rose oil and was now using it to carefully wipe the whole room. Very slowly, so as not to miss any stain, she wiped to and fro, moving backward toward the entrance, bowing time and again to let her lips lovingly touch the floor. There was so much reverence and devotion in her movements, so much absorption in her task that she took no notice of anyone or anything around her. She wiped the floor as if it were the last thing that she would do in her life.

She was no Arab, or certainly no Iraqi, for such humility is seldom found among the proud Iraqis. I was utterly bewildered and could not tear my eyes from her—the intensity of her being in her work, her selfless devotion, made her shine like a jewel in the tiny dark room. She was Pakistani, it turned out, and had come all the way from Pakistan to honor and pay respect to the great master.

Abdel Qadir al-Jilani was no teacher of wonders and miracles: He was a mystic of the heart. Although his body had already left this world centuries ago, his *baraka* (spiritual blessing) retained the power to touch and soften the heart. Once the woman was finished, we entered, opened our hands to the sky, spoke the *fatiha* (the opening sura of the Qur'an), brushed our hands over our faces, and walked three times around the mausoleum.

My heart became lighter with each circle, and sweet tears flowed from my eyes. Each drop seemed to nurture my heart, and my head filled with a slight feeling of dizziness. Bathed in a feeling of contentment beyond words, with the ancient knowledge that everything is right, that reality reflects the inner state, a space for peace and confidence grew inside me. May you rest in peace, great soul!

No sooner had Aunt Fatima and I stepped outside than we were embraced by the hectic rush of the present. Still dazed, we wandered toward the souk. I hooked my arm in hers and without a word we went into the carpet merchants' quarter. There Aunt Fatima spotted a wonderful carpet and her senses seemed to awaken. "We'll look at other carpets first, so the merchant can't tell we're interested in this one," she whispered, "otherwise he'll increase the price right away!"

"*Ahlan wa-sahlan, ahlan wa-sahlan*! Welcome! You are now part of the family and may your journey have been easy!" the carpet merchant greeted us. Two stools appeared as if by magic and Auntie relaxed her muscles gratefully.

"Show us what you've got. We'd like to buy a carpet for our house." Of course you don't say that it's a present for a relative who lives abroad, for this too will affect the price.

"Tea or coffee?"

"Don't go to any trouble, young man!" said Aunt Fatima.

"But that won't do, *chalti*, my aunt on my mother's side!" replied the young merchant, "You are my guests!"

"Well then, tea, please, but *toch* (very dark and sweet)!"

In a wink two dark teas were ordered and then the actual ceremony began. The merchant started dancing around his shop. He drew a carpet from under a pile and unrolled it.

"A kilim from the north, colorful and strong like the northern hills, as thick as the northern meadows, and soft as a she-camel's lips. Its colors rejoice the heart and awaken the senses. It was woven by the people of the Kurds," he explained.

"He speaks beautifully, and without any grammatical mistakes," Auntie said, leaning toward me. Auntie was a true child of her culture, and nothing softens an Arab's heart like mastery of the Arabic language. Auntie's body relaxed; she seemed satisfied that her instinct and Allah's will had brought her here.

"Show us the two sisters." She pointed at a deep-hued kilim woven with animals and ornaments.

"Your taste is beautiful, *chala*! The sisters come from the south, from the free Bedouin people. As you can see, *chala*, it has two strips—twin but not identical sisters. Each carries her own personality and love is the link to her sister. Born together, they tell the story of the herds, of the desert's sudden spring blossoming, of life's transience, of the beauty of the moment. You can separate them by untying the wool thread that binds them, and then you have two long pieces, or else leave them next to each other and enjoy them together."

You could tell Auntie liked the merchant. She smiled mischievously and said: "My son, if you can add a poem to the carpet, then I'll pay you the price that you want and we will both be satisfied!"

The young man stared at the floor for a while. He was beautiful, tall and lean, with a striking face. Although he was still young, you could feel that worldly responsibility had been on his shoulders for a long time, but nevertheless his soul beat strongly. He lifted his head and his eyes said that he had accepted the challenge. Suddenly, his voice seemed grow from his belly, much deeper and richer than before:

> As the coat of unity embraced us,
> the longest night went in an instant;
> now that she has gone, my nights have become
> those of a blind man, when no morning awakes.

Auntie blinked thoughtfully, took a deep breath, and replied, "Al-Wasiti, 10th century. You've chosen well and described romantic love. I'll give you a *bayt* (verse) on mystical love:

> The sun never rises nor sets
> without my longing for You.
> Every breath I take, sad or joyful,
> is linked to the remembrance of You.
> I sit with people and can't speak
> without ending my words with You.
> Not a drop of water do I drink, thirsty,
> without finding Your picture in the glass.

"Allah!" answered the young merchant, continuing:

> You run between the heart and its skin,
> like tears run from eyelids,
> and You dwell in awareness in the depths of the heart,
> like the soul dwells in the body.

"Al-Halladj—who else could thus describe the longing for the divine!" he said.

For a while two souls touched—Auntie's old, experienced heart, and his young, big heart had made time stand still. The sharpness of the eye only made out blurred differences in age, appearance, and experience. The carpet was tied, the price settled fairly between them and Auntie was henceforth a regular customer.

Moments later, we were back in a taxi. The carpet, professionally rolled and tied, lay on my lap and we drove through Baghdad's wide, modern streets. Aunt Fatima gazed through the window with heavy eyes. I knew a different mood was coming. Actually there were only two moods in Aunt Fatima's life: delighted and cheerful or mightily depressed, and both were borne by a slightly cynical mind.

"In actual fact, the only thing that matters in life is love," she proclaimed. "Yet the inquisitive mind must be fed a few facts in order not to starve in its misery. Look at Baghdad! Over the centuries, this city has taken on so many faces; it has been shaken by crises and various threats; it has experienced fame and oblivion, the greatest feasts and the bloodiest street battles; it has given birth to great souls and narrow-minded fanatics. Yet time and again it has stood there, decorated anew and full of hope, and over the centuries it has acquired the wisdom that makes life bearable. Whoever lives solely with reason buries the world of wonders, and Baghdad is a unique wonder of heavy melancholy."

The driver took a sharp left turn and went over one of the many bridges that span the Tigris. My eyes lingered on the movements of the water, which seemed to have caught Aunt Fatima's attention too, for she went on philosophizing: "Big old river, see how each drop flows into the next, mirroring the experience of the whole river, just like us human beings. In each of us lies the whole history of mankind, forever repeating itself, yet always different. One people grows through another, building on its knowledge or ignorance, to demonstrate once again that it is unique. The Arab empire, which ruled this earth for 600 years, had fed on the Persian, Greek, and Roman civilizations, growing with their knowledge, expanding, correcting, enriching, the same way as the awakening of the contemporary West drew its knowledge and early culture from the Arabs. Doesn't each drink from the other and sharpen its skill and experience against the other? Everything has its turn in the eternal dancing circle of life. A good circle, which only greed and lying tongues can distort..."

With a sigh, she cloaked herself again in silence. Being with Aunt Fatima was always a strain, but it was never boring.

A BLUE SHOE DAY

Aunt Fatima's shoes always reflected her mood. It seemed sometimes as if her whole attitude to life could be found in her shoes. Whenever she came for a visit, I would first glance unobtrusively at her feet. Black high heels meant dignity, no talking to Auntie today, her ears half closed to the world and its people, the history of mankind swarming too much inside her, the sweeping feelings too strong. Great loves, wars, plagues, tortures, hopes, and tears of joy swayed in her breast.

Only her regal attitude could keep her above water. Her eyebrows would sometimes twitch uncontrollably and a ring of hard, tense muscles would form around her neck, yet except for that, no one could see or seemed to notice anything. Least of all Grandmother, who could dismiss Aunt Fatima's passionate inner world and painful melancholy with a single wave of her hand. Aunt Fatima reacted invariably in the same way: she would wrinkle her forehead, look to the side uncomprehendingly, and retreat inside herself.

Grandmother usually left her there, but then she would pity her and try to draw her out: "Don't take everything so personally! No one wants to upset you."

"Yes, you do, you never care, you're always above such things."

"You live in your own fantasy world, stop representing the whole world to yourself, but finally live in it!" replied my grandmother.

"I'm just different, you'll never understand that."

"You're not different, cousin, just lazy!"

Aunt Fatima usually stayed stuck on my grandmother's negligently thrown bait; all her strength seemed to wrap itself around this word; not a sound came through her lips while she took it into her inner cave, where it would be torn apart, pressed, swallowed, angrily trampled and discussed in a thousand talks to herself.

Several days later, when Grandmother had long forgotten about their brief talk, Aunt Fatima would come out with her answer, at the most inappropriate time, just when Grandmother was concentrating on the schedule for the day: "I'm not lazy, I'm just sensitive."

"What was that, cousin?" Grandmother raises her head, slightly irritated.

And the fleeting, slightly upset expression on Grandmother's face was enough to make Aunt Fatima retreat once more, silent and misunderstood.

I was a frequent witness to this relational game; and it was only love that wove a thread between them and linked them, time and again.

But another day, Aunt Fatima wasn't wearing black shoes, but pale blue, inch-high sandals. Her feet looked handsome and relaxed, with her well-shaped big toe and the others held together by a wide strap. She smiled contentedly and self-confidently from her armchair, and I was delighted to have my happy aunt back.

Aunt Fatima was a history teacher, and no one could tell the history of our people better than she. One of her favorite heroes was Harun al-Rashid, once an inhabitant of Baghdad and the most famous caliph of all times.[1]

"Handsome, clever, strong, and full of bright, brave ideas. It was his grandfather Mansour who founded Baghdad," Auntie explained to me. "Harun was only 22 when he came to the throne and it was his mother who helped him. Indeed she played a major part in his life. Harun wasn't satisfied to sit in his palace and receive news from his people through messengers and informers. No, he kept travelling throughout the kingdom and his popularity came essentially from the many people who had come to know him."

"And do you know how he used to travel?" Auntie asked, her eyes wide-open. "Disguised as a merchant, so the legend goes, he would wander through the streets of Baghdad with his vizier and by listening to all the stories, worries, and complaints, he would gain a lively, vivid picture of his subjects and their lives. He was so well informed that magic powers were ascribed to him. They say that he had a magic powder and he could change into a stork and fly over the roofs of Baghdad so as to watch and hear its people."

How great to fly over Baghdad as a *laqlaq* (stork)! There were plenty of storks in Baghdad; they would build their large nests high up and look down on the world with curiosity. Could they be telling each other the story of Harun?

"You know, my little one, Harun was already past conquests, in a way. He was interested in commerce, exchange, inventions, and culture. Baghdad was the wealthiest and most beautiful city in the world. Only Byzantine Constantinople, the other capital, could rival her. The Arabs traded with China, Indonesia, India, and East Africa. Our ships were the biggest and by far the best oriented in Chinese and Indian waters.

"The merchants no longer wished to carry with them the large quantities of gold coins they needed, so great was the risk of being robbed. This is how a new means of payment came to be devised. The Muslims invented the check, which was lighter and safer than the heavy bags of coins. The word comes from the Arabic *shaqq*. These checks required a highly sophisticated banking system. Through a moneychanger, an Arab merchant could thus cash a check in China from his account in Baghdad."

What a great story, I thought. My aunt's bubbly enthusiasm was infectious!

"There was also another payment system: Merchants made deposits in a bank and the mutual transactions were carried out by means of written instructions. Problem-free worldwide trade demanded that the prices of goods be determined by a contract and made public. This is how the Arabic *ta'rifa* (announcement) became the international tariff."

I admired Aunt Fatima for the knowledge she would always proudly communicate in her stories. It was of utmost importance for her to nurture our Arab awareness and to tell us about this past of ours, because she strongly believed a day would come when the Arab world would again occupy a glorious place in the world, and she wanted to contribute by educating children and telling them as much as possible about their past and their history.

"At that time the Baghdad bazaars flourished," Aunt Fatima went on. "Comfort kept increasing and luxury articles on offer multiplied. The bazaars were covered and while buying and haggling, you could enjoy the beauty of the colorful exotic birds and parrots flying freely, and of the different trees brought here from the whole world."

I gaped: how beautiful it must have been, a true paradise! To walk through the souks with a small, brightly colored parrot sitting on my shoulder...

"With the founding of the Abbasid dynasty in 750, everything flowed from the vast empire into the center, to Baghdad, and the various peoples brought with them their own inheritances — their cultures and civilizations.

"This was when Arabic literature reached its zenith. The great legal codices were formulated; philosophy, science, and medicine were taken from the old cultures and completed with new dimensions and components. All worked together. It was a peaceful and fruitful time. And do you know what else appeared at that time?"

I became fidgety whenever Auntie asked me such a direct question and I could only stare at her mutely, like a big question mark myself.

"This was the time when the *bayt al-hikma* (house of wisdom) was founded.[2] It was the first scientific academy where, in particular, the philosophers Aristotle and Plato and the doctors Hippocrates and Galenius were translated and enriched with new interpretations and insights.[3]

"Research activities reached an unprecedented development and intensity, never before had the range of accessible knowledge been so widely open." Aunt Fatima was so pleased with her own words that she was close to tears.

"The knowledge of the old Eastern cultures joined Greek sciences; all the sources of traditions were transposed into a single language, Arabic, and they could thus become part of a great synthesis."

Auntie paused, leaned back, closed her eyes, and suddenly she was gone. Yet before I could stand up, she snapped out of it and continued to reel off her knowledge: "Just think that this was when they introduced the five-day week; there was free medical care, there were free hospitals, free universities and grants for the students. Human beings had it better then. Unfortunately this wealthy, peaceful period did not last for long."

"Why not, Auntie?"

"You know, trade slowed down, business wasn't so good any more, and instead of saving or stimulating people to work more, the state just went on spending. Taxes increased and money lost value.

"Over 80 years later, the picture had become quite different. A famous historian of that time wrote the following about Iraq." Aunt Fatima's voice changed as she quoted:

> Iraq is home to uprisings and famines. It regresses more with each day and suffers greatly from oppression and high taxes... Baghdad was once a great city, but now it is on the way to ruin.[5]

"Despite this decline, Baghdad did not stop producing great thinkers, philosophers, and mystics who enriched and inspired the Arab-Islamic world, indeed the whole world."

"Let the child play a little!" My nanny Adiba interrupted Aunt Fatima's history lesson. "The girl can't just listen to the past."

"She should be armed for life and waste no time," Aunt Fatima replied. "Now is the best time. Teenagers always immerse themselves in looks and love affairs, and their hearts are closed to whatever happens outside them."

"So listen!" Auntie went on, unperturbed. "The darkest day in the history of Baghdad was February 20, 1258. On that day, after a ten-day siege, the city was destroyed by the Mongols. They plundered and massacred nearly the whole population. More than 800,000 people died."

I pressed my eyes closed and my face contorted at the pictures that suddenly welled up inside me.

"You're frightening the child!" Adiba shouted.

"For over half a millennium, the God-given[4] had been a crossroad for cultures and civilizations, a goal for the seekers of knowledge, research, and spirituality."

Why do adults love destruction and war? Why do they enjoy exercising power and domination so much? Who let them become like that? How little I wanted to have to do with this adult world! But I didn't say a word. I went on listening to Aunt Fatima's story.

"Again Baghdad tried to rise up, again it tried to exist and face history, and to a certain extent it did succeed in building itself up and becoming a famous city. But then came the next blow, and again from Central Asia. This time it happened in the summer, in July 1401. Tamerlane the Terrible was the leader of this army. He was an ugly, lame, and cruel little man who delighted in torture and destruction.

"After defending itself for six weeks, Baghdad was conquered by Tamerlane. One hundred thousand people were massacred. He had 120 towers made out of their severed heads, and rode laughing through the ruins. An Egyptian historian wrote then about Baghdad:

> The word civilization can no longer describe Baghdad. Baghdad stands in ruin and ashes. It has become an ugly provincial city, made of brick houses and brick huts in the middle of the mounds of earth that were once palaces."

The story was nearly too much for me. Baghdad had already seen so much pain. But Auntie went on talking unconcerned. She had to pass on her knowledge to the next generation. That is how she saw her task, and that's what she had in mind.

"In 1534 the land-between-the-rivers became part of the Ottoman Empire. Turkish pashas were put in place by the government in Istanbul to administer the henceforth Ottoman province of Mesopotamia. But these administrators were more interested in exploiting the population through taxes in order to preserve their own standard of living, than in maintaining the thousand-year-old irrigation canals. In the course of time, the canals fell into disrepair and the once fertile fields turned to barren plains.

"The Ottomans ruled for nearly 400 years and when the Ottoman Empire started slowly collapsing, the next conquerors were already in the background, plotting and scheming among themselves. This time they came from the West, and the powers did not hesitate to use Arabs themselves in order to achieve their aims. With the promise that an all-Arab state would be born with the victory against the Ottomans and that the old dream of a united Arabia would come true again, the Arabs sided with the Western powers and fought against the Ottomans. But it was just a mirage."

Aunt Fatima asked for some water, as her throat was parched. She had come to a very painful point in the history of the Arabs, a wound still bleeding.

"You know, at the end of this betrayal of the Arabs came indeed the military defeat of the Ottoman Empire, but also the creation of a Jewish homeland in Palestine. There was no more mention of an Arab state—the big powers had already divided up the Ottoman territory among themselves.

"England took over Iraq, but put in place an administrator from among the Arab elite. This is how Hashemite Emir Faisal, originally from Saudi Arabia, became king of Iraq. King Faisal was a noble man who believed in the pure Bedouin virtues of honor and courage. Yet fate had made him into a plaything in the sad Arab history: first he fought on the side of the Western powers and against the Turks for the dream of a united land of Arabia, and was bitterly deceived, and then he was transferred to Iraq as a king with restricted sovereignty, a puppet.

"You know, my child, people are so diverse in Iraq. There are Arabs, Kurds, and Assyrians; farmers, nomads, and city-dwellers; Sunnis, Shiites, and Yazids.[5] The borders of the new state of Iraq artificially created by the European powers were rather foreign to them. In Faisal's own words: 'There still isn't in Iraq'—and I say this with a sorrowful worried heart—'an Iraqi people, but incredible masses of human beings, removed from any patriotic idea, without any common link.'"[6]

"What is there to link us," Aunt Fatima exclaimed, "when we are a small people who prefer death to bondage, who only want to be ruled by our own moods and ideas, and for whom pride and honor matter nearly more than our daily bread!"

I was tired and hungry, so I leaned my head against my arm. When Aunt Fatima saw me like that, she smiled, forgot about history and conquests, and took me into her soft, plump arms. "Whoever lives solely on reason buries the world of wonders," she said, pressing me lovingly against her before letting go.

SOUL FOOD

"How can I reach God?" asked the seeker.
"The ways to God are as many as His creatures.
Yet the shortest and easiest way is to serve others,
to not harm others,
and to make others happy."
—Abu Said, Sufi master (978–1061)

As children, we had several favorite games when we met at the end of the afternoon. "Forbidden corner" took place at the bottom of the garden, where old stones had been piled up in an abandoned corner when an old room of the house was demolished. We gathered and whispered, choosing one child to go to the pile of stones while the others waited from a safe distance. After slowly drawing close to a stone, all of a sudden the child would knock it over with a quick jerking movement. It was essential to knock the stone over and jump aside at the same time, for that cool pile of stones was home to black, extremely poisonous scorpions. Most of the time, frightened by the earthquake, two or three scorpions would crawl out, their tails raised, and run off.

This nerve-racking game was a test of courage: The idea was to get as close as possible to the scorpions—without getting stung, of course. The game was all the more dangerous and attractive as we always went barefoot everywhere. Some children lost their nerve and started jumping up and down like maniacs, their faces flooded with tears. Hasan and Ali, the two seven-year-old boys from next door, loved to run very close to the scorpions and tease them by making tickling movements in the air. They bent forward so low that their hands moved just in front of the scorpions' bodies. It always scared me because I was worried about them, but at the same time their courage inspired imitation. Yet I preferred observing the scenario full of suspense from a distance and only occasionally did I come close to those dangerous little animals.

The fact that we could not shriek (lest we alert the adults) lent the spectacle even more nervous tension, and all the excitement gathered in our bellies. My friend Buthayna lived two gardens further down and she always came to see us with her little sister. Although neither of them particularly enjoyed this game, they were always counted in and I wondered why they never refused to play.

The little one pulled and tugged on her sister's clothes, lifting her leg as if she wanted to climb on her. And then it happened: a pool spread under her and the fidgeting turned into two straight legs and a confused expression, followed by tears.

"It doesn't matter, Muna (yearning wish), no one will know!" I turned to the other children and looked at them sternly. Hasan stifled an upcoming malicious giggle and the whole matter was quickly solved between ourselves. We removed Muna's underpants, fetched water in a goblet from the clay jug, swiftly poured cool water over her, back and front, pulled the dress straight... and that was the end of the matter.

But something else had happened. Dunja! My little cousin! I had forgotten about Dunja, whose well-being was my responsibility. She was heading clumsily and unruffled toward a scorpion, standing in front of it and observing it with her head inclined, saliva dripping from her mouth. She seemed totally engrossed in her joyful excitement, and she uttered shrill little squeaks. Slowly bending forward, she stretched out her little hand to catch the scorpion. She seemed to fascinate the animals, for all of a sudden a second scorpion hurried over. Dunja seemed to change her mind and started swaying forward and backward, then moving on the tip of the toes, in her usual short steps. The scorpions recognized their victim and rushed after her.

I was seized by panic; frightened for her and frightened of the punishment I might receive, I hurried after the three of them. Dunja ran into the house and the scorpions followed her into the long corridor. Then she turned around, once more, and headed toward them. Utterly fearless, I jumped in the middle, pushed Dunja aside and confronted the scorpions barefoot. I was amazed by my thoughtless courage, but also by my love for my cousin.

At that moment Adiba, our nanny, appeared. She grasped the situation, took a broom from a corner and captured the two scorpions. The baffled animals were taken out of the house and as a reward, my arm was pinched by Dunja so strongly that I had to cry out, and tears of relief ran down my cheeks.

Dunja belonged to a different world, and the laws of that world were always full of surprises. I could never predict how she would react, or what she would do next. She would look through me, recognize some kind of invisible creature and teeter away toward it in her quick, short steps. Dunja provoked two strong feelings in me: fear and, nevertheless, the wish to protect her.

"Be kind with Dunja, you know she can't understand everything, the *miskina* (poor thing)," they would say. Yet she was particularly strong physically, much stronger than I, although I was two years older. Her favorite pastime was to release her inner tension by pinching. When she was near me, I avoided being cornered, afraid that she might block my way and pinch me to death. Thanks to Dunja, I later had a good feel for space.

I learned something else from Dunja: never to fear people who are different.

When Adiba saw me crying, she said calmly, as customary when passing on a piece of wisdom: "Don't expect any reward or praise when you do something good, but see the reward in your very action, and let your soul grow with it. Nothing is ever lost, even when the eye cannot immediately see it!"

In any case, this was the end of our games with the scorpions. I had had enough of scorpions for the rest of my childhood.

I'M THE QUEEN!
CHAYZURAN AND ZUBAYDA

All things in the world are mothers,
only one doesn't know about the others' suffering.
—Maulana Jalaluddin Rumi, Sufi master

Whenever we girls played at dressing-up, our favorite epoch was Harun al-Rashid's. He was not our model, but instead the women around him, in particular his wife and cousin Zubayda, his mother Chayzuran, and his half-sister Ulayya. Since all three women enjoyed ostentatious clothes, we always required vast quantities of fabric and material for our play. We collected all the armchairs available and used them as thrones, places to sleep or lie on, or even as seats for our invisible fellow actors. Someone had to secretly remove the linen basket with all the clothes-pegs from the laundry room so that we could hang the fabric on the clothes-line, making corridors that stood for different rooms, through which we walked majestically.

Zubayda was allowed to sit on the armchairs and obviously required slaves whom she could order around—she never did anything herself. Zubayda had to spend the whole game sitting in the same place giving orders: "Go to the market and fetch me some biscuits!" "I want a glass of water!" "Come here and sing me a song!" "Go and see what is happening in town!"[1] Her wish was our command, provided she remained on her throne, inside our fabric harem.

Although it was fun to order others about, in time I got bored with being Zubayda, even though I had fought for the part, and I was quite happy to swap places with one of the "free" slaves.

The real Zubayda could obviously do nothing of the sort, though she was influential politically and extremely socially involved. Being locked up in a harem did not suit either our child's love of freedom or our Bedouin blood.

In the real Abbasid court, the whole world was indeed turned upside down. Above all, people saw how the Persians ruled and all of a sudden they wanted to govern like the Persian kings in the conquered Sassanid kingdom. A complex court etiquette was introduced, which included the harem system of the great Persian kings. Neither the old tradition of the peer tribe system nor the *umma* (Islamic tribe) held sway any longer. Absolute power changed during the time of the Abbasid caliphs, who were supported by a huge bureaucracy and an army of military slaves dedicated solely to the caliph.

How did these changes affect women? Did they benefit from them? When the Byzantine and Persian peoples merged under Islam to conquer the richer areas on the other side of the Arabic peninsula, they were confronted with luxuriant gardens, bazaars, palaces, and also with ancient civilizations. They took these newly acquired impressions and riches with them, and developed an advanced civilization that reached its full flowering with the caliphate in Baghdad.

Cities started expanding and people from various traditions and different civilizations poured into them. The Arab Muslim women who had followed the conquerors into the new countries were all of a sudden seen as superfluous. Men became more interested in the spoils and the gold of the conquests than in fighting for the honor of their tribe and of Islam. No one cared any longer for socially critical poetesses who appealed to the fighters' consciences. Female poets and warriors were to stay at home.

The enriched men all at once had opportunity to build themselves large houses with many rooms, where they could guard their women against "foreign" influences and thus guarantee their virtue, although such measures had not been necessary during the short period of the early Muslim communities. Veiling and isolation began to be interpreted more strictly, and raised to a new status symbol, reinforced by Persian traditions.[2]

At the beginning, these rules were still relatively flexible in the Muslim community, but with time the verses of the Qur'an that had demanded that the wives of the Prophet Muhammad, the mothers of the believers, should stay at home and speak to men through curtains came to be applied to most women.[3]

Veiling already existed in those countries with which the Muslims were in contact, such as Syria and Palestine. There the veil was a status symbol, just as it had been with the Greeks, the Romans, the Jews, and the Assyrians. But at the time of the Prophet Muhammad only his wives were veiled. How this tradition extended to all women cannot be ascertained with certainty. Nevertheless the conquest of the areas where veiling was customary among the higher classes, the Arabs' increasing wealth, and their ensuing high status, as well as the imitation of the wives of the Prophet, all must have contributed.

Of course women who lived in the country, or poor women of the cities who had to earn their keep or contribute to their family, were less affected by this confinement. It was more the socially privileged, cultivated, and potentially most influential women who were banished from the world around them. Henceforth the life of women from the higher classes was not only shaped by confinement, but by another major factor. With tremendous wealth came vast numbers of slaves, mostly women, so that polygamy and concubinage spread. Zubayda and many other women now had to share their husbands with several concubines.

Men from the elite had at their disposal thousands of beautiful slaves, often of noble origin, whom they increasingly preferred to free women. In the eyes of many men, the slaves' merits must have been essentially related to their forced obsequiousness and to their utter dependence, since they were without family protection and support.

Marrying a free Arab woman meant marrying a woman with legal rights, who benefited from the support of a family and received high compensation in the event of a divorce. It was therefore much easier to buy a beautiful, obedient, and still cultivated woman on the slave-packed market. Since according to Islamic law the descendants of such a marriage were legitimate and not slaves, nothing stood in the way of these unions. This degradation of women, who were treated as sexual "consumer goods" would bury their dignity as human beings for a long time.

Yet Zubayda did not let herself be deprived of the right of decision and she continued her involvement in politics and social life. During her pilgrimage to Mecca, she spent three million dinars to supply the city with water, which was brought from a source nearly fifty kilometers away. She also had wells and inns built along the pilgrimage road from Baghdad to Mecca, thus earning the blessings and praises of the locals and of the pilgrims.

She and her half-sister Ulayya seem to have enjoyed their lives. They started fashion trends, such as shoes and sandals decorated with precious stones, and headbands, which Ulayya invented to cover a birthmark on her forehead. These were adorned with jewelry and often embroidered with suras from the Qur'an or short poetic verses. They soon became highly popular among society ladies. It is said that the following verse was embroidered on the headband of one of Harun's slaves:

> Tyrant, you were cruel in your love to me
> Yet may Allah be the judge between us!

Ulayya's beauty lay in her voice and in her gift of spontaneously composing poems and songs that befitted the moment. Her charm and wit lent much joy and a humorous atmosphere to the court. In the early days, she was the only free woman who mastered this art, which was otherwise practiced by trained female slaves.

When we played queens, Ulayya's part would always be taken by delicate Zaynab. She was a slim little doll-like girl, her face sweetly framed by soft brown curls. She fluttered about like a butterfly between the fabrics, singing la-la-la, and she seemed so engrossed in her role that she was no longer aware of the others.

It is said of Zubayda that she could hardly walk, so heavy were her jewels and sumptuous clothing, and that she introduced much of the splendor and pomp at the Abbasid court. She was a versatile, sharp woman who tried to push back the social limits imposed on her. She did her best to have her beloved son al-Amin succeed Harun, instead of al-Ma'mun, the son of a Persian concubine.

Instead, Harun gave al-Amin the Arab section of his kingdom and al-Ma'mun the Persian share. After the two clashed and al-Amin was killed in 813, Zubayda was asked to avenge her son's death by leading an army, in accordance with the old Bedouin tradition. Yet that much she could not do; lacking her predecessors' courage, she who was better acquainted with the weapons of the weak—manipulation, poison, and deceit—did not wish to act in public, and quietly abandoned herself to her grief.

Something of our views on motherhood were reflected in our idea of how to act the part of that most important woman in Harun's life: Chayzuran, his mother.

"If you want to be Chayzuran, you must tie a pillow around your middle—every mother has a belly!"

Chayzuran actually means "slender, graceful reed," and the original Chayzuran would surely have had us all beheaded for that pillow. But to me, Chayzuran was like Grandmother. They knew about everything that went on and you had the feeling that nothing ever moved without their consent. Who knows?—maybe Chayzuran was Grandmother's secret role model.

Chayzuran arrived at the Baghdad court as a slave from Yemen, and she had managed not only to become the wife of the third caliph, al-Mahdi, but also to exercise a great influence on her husband. She became the *éminence grise* at the Abbasid court and the richest woman in the kingdom. She had three children: Musa, Harun, and a daughter that al-Mahdi loved so much that he took her, disguised as a boy, everywhere with him when she travelled.

When her son, Musa al-Hadi, became caliph and she was besieged by petitioners seeking political advantages, he tried to keep her away from politics. "Women have no right to interfere in the affairs of the state. You should pray, retreat from the world, and obey as it befits women. If I hear that one of my high officials or servants is standing outside your door asking you for a favor, I'll have them decapitated and I'll confiscate their property. What's all this about daily processions in front of your apartments? Don't you have a spindle to keep you busy, or a Qur'an to make you see reason, or a house to protect you? Leave me in peace with your suggestions and don't bother me," he is reported to have informed his mother.

But poor Musa was soon to die a sudden, strange death (he reigned under the name al-Hadi only from 785 to 786), and Chayzuran spun a web of intrigue to make sure that her beloved son Harun (786–809), who happened to be much more open to her wishes, would ascend the throne.

"Chayzuran can do as she pleases, she doesn't have to stay behind the drapes, she's the caliph's mother," argued Hiba, my playmate.

"Okay, but then all the slaves"—we usually had five of them—"must go with her," said Huda. She was the eldest among us, tall for her age and slender as a willow.

"I am Chayzuran, and I don't need a pillow. Don't you know what Chayzuran means?" She strutted around like a billowing peacock, nodding to the right and to the left, moving her hands as if she was talking to hundreds of petitioners and making them promises.

"That's not fair! If all the slaves go with you, then Zubayda won't have anyone to order!" I moaned. At this point either the game ended or we managed to share the slaves, two for me, three for her. Sometimes Zubayda and Chayzuran even succeeded in walking peacefully together in the garden.

Chayzuran had worked hard for her high position. She took lessons with the best teachers of the palace in *fiqh* (Islamic theology and law), in astrology, mathematics, singing, and poetry, and she cultivated her contacts with the most respected and influential members of the harem hierarchy. She recognized that beauty, erotic charm, and wit did not suffice to wield power when competing for the favors of the ruler.

Other female aristocrats followed her example and used the opportunities to educate themselves. This is how many a woman found the meaning of her life as a patron of the arts and sciences and also—as is typical of women—of "practical" spirituality. They read, inspired by Sufism and great souls such as Rabi'a al-Adawiyya;[4] they built convents that offered religious instruction to all women and were used as sanctuaries by divorced and deserted women. Chayzuran even went to great trouble to locate the house where the Prophet Muhammad was born, and she had the Birth Mosque built there.

In those days strict sex segregation reigned, which required educated women to meet the needs of women in the harems where men were not allowed to enter. There were thus women to wash the dead, women to mourn the dead, women bakers, women hairdressers, laundrywomen, harem spies, women who recited the Qur'an, midwives and women doctors who had studied in renowned medical faculties. They often did their apprenticeship with male relatives, since professions—such as carpet-weaving—were usually carried on in family businesses. Religious teachers were trained, mainly to instruct the girls, but some of them succeeded in learning and applying Islamic law as teachers and judges for both sexes.[5]

The most famous among them was Shuda in Baghdad. One of the greatest authorities on the hadith (the sayings and deeds of the Prophet Muhammad and his companions), her lectures were attended by famous men who admired her as "the scholar" and "the pride of women." Amat al-Wahid, the daughter of a judge from Baghdad, studied Islamic law under her father's supervision and was famous as an outstanding judge.

In our harem games, we knew nothing of the intricate and difficult circumstances in which women lived at the time. Our school books merely told us about the glorious early Abbasid era, the Golden Age, as being an epoch of tremendous economic and socio-cultural upswing, a time when philosophy, sciences, and literature reached their full flowering. No one had told us that we owed to this early period the emergence of so many misogynous interpretations of the Qur'an that have survived to this day and been turned into dogma, carried by the patriarchal traditions that arose in Islam and remain today.

WANDERING PAJAMAS

Baghdad is a desert city where sand is always your most faithful companion. Sand in your shoes, sand nesting in every fold of your clothing, even sand in your mouth, during sandstorms. Human rhythm is governed by the climate. You get up with the sun, go to work until eleven, then back home, lunch, afternoon siesta, the holy *qaylula*, wake up around five, and go to work until nine.

Life starts in the evening and it is customary to go to sleep late. In this fashion sleep is divided into two stages: the night and the siesta. Modern technology, in particular air conditioning, has somewhat broken this rhythm and many people work non-stop until around two or three in the afternoon. Then you go home, eat, have a rest, and wake up refreshed around five to have some tea.

This is when the sand sprinkling ritual starts in front of the garden door. Wandering gardeners look after the gardens, but sand sprinkling does more than refresh the atmosphere and quiet the dusty streets. It marks the opening of the evening activities. Young and elderly men stand in front of each house, armed with garden hoses, and the first evening communications can begin.

The traditional sand sprinkling costume consists either of striped pajamas or a light colored *jalaba*. The pajama army also enjoys extending its water hose blessings to passing cyclists or cars that appreciate this refreshment. The children of the neighborhood are particularly fond of these daily rituals and jump contentedly from one jet of water to the next. Then it's time for visits.

The streets fill up with striped pajamas and white *jalabas* and clattering *qubqab* (wooden clogs) or more modern plastic slippers. People consider their neighborhood to be an extension of their home, and comfort takes precedence. Women who stay at home greet their guests wearing a nightshirt and a nightgown, or, when they join the evening walk, their long, wide garments. The doors are open in all the family houses, tea and water pipe ready in hand.

People often sit in the garden, where it is customary to have at least one family swing, made of cast iron and therefore capable of coping with human weights of all sorts. Time is of no importance and this attitude, combined with the climate, make the movements leisurely and soften the thoughts. Aunt Fatima always said, "Allah, in His infinite wisdom, has put the Iraqis is this furnace to allow their fiery nature to be dampened."

Visits usually continue until late in the night. At the end of the evening, parents carry sleeping children home in their arms. And if the adults happen to fall asleep somewhere else—well, they are already properly attired.

SLEEPING ROOFS

Those who have reached the end of their dreams fall asleep.
—Arab proverb

When the nights were hot, a mysterious world appeared in Baghdad, a world that only lived in darkness. The inhabitants of this world carried soft, oblong, pressed-down wool mattresses rolled up under their arms, usually with two large white sheets. Up the stairs they went, fast or leisurely according to their age, into the kingdom of the night.

Once on the roof, they would stand in front of four-legged iron platforms, take deep breaths, and in one strong jerking movement unroll their mattresses and cover them with sheets. They sat on the side, lifted their legs in one swing, leaned their heads back in their new homes and stretched out their legs. This was the traditional position in the kingdom of the night.

Familiar "aah's" "ooh's" and "Allah's" resounded across the roofs, accompanying bodies relaxing and eyes gazing at the stunning sight of the star-filled sky. Nowhere in the world did the stars seem so close, so much within reach, as in Baghdad, except maybe in Babylon. No wonder that astronomy was born here.

After this uplifting star-filled experience and the deep feeling invariably provoked by the beauty of Allah's cosmos, secular giggling would steal into the kingdom of the night. Night greetings would be blown from roof to roof. This takes place either laying back looking up at the sky—since people can hardly see each other in the dark anyway, and everyone recognizes their neighbor's voice—or, in the case of young, active people, in a semi-raised position, resting on one elbow.

Children giggle and talk, old people talk in their usual experienced tones, and teenagers, whether boys or girls, have a special soft and sweet intonation. Aunt Fatima said that it was the love-birds' cooing that overcame one at a certain age.

I loved this kingdom of the night—the darkness made everyone so sensual and delightful, and the edges of the strict norms of the kingdom of the sunlight became blurred in the light of the stars. We children usually enjoyed the additional privilege of a fine, transparent tent shrouding our bed to protect our tender skin from mosquitos.

"Um Yahya, will you come with me to the city to do some shopping tomorrow? I need some fabric for a dress," called Aunt Fatima to her friend on the neighboring roof.

"Yes, I'd like to, *Inshallah*!"

"God willing" was the answer. You always say *inshallah* when you plan to do something, for people plan and God decides what must be.

Aunt Fatima was a cheerful lady endowed with the strongest voice of all Baghdad, and a reputation for being wild, unpredictable, freedom-loving, and utterly loyal. In other words, she was a person who could be counted upon. With her, you could discuss problems not otherwise so easily confided.

She had never married, not that no one had ever asked for her hand, but because destiny had not wanted it to be so. Her younger brother's wife had died in a car accident and left him with two young children. It was obvious to Aunt Fatima that she would bring them up, and in her mind, this left no space in her life for a husband and children of her own. She often jokingly said: "Allah has given me two children without me having to ruin my figure," at which point she always lifted her dress to show her legs, which were indeed very beautiful.

Whenever Aunt Fatima spent the night with us, I would beg her to take the night bed on the roof next to mine. She loved children and could hardly deny us anything.

"Aunt Fatima, please sing us a song, please!"

"Oh, my little one, my heart is empty—how can I sing?"

"Please, Auntie, do it for me!"

With a deep sigh she would fill her heart with the lovers' tears and pain at being separated, and start singing. Her voice became so enchanting that huge tears came out of her eyes and wet her pillow. When Auntie sang, all the roofs around us went quiet, and everybody listened to the lovely wistful nostalgia in her voice. Some of the listeners' ancestors were masters of the sweet melancholy, and every drop of their blood hugged the other, intoxicated with love. I would often fall asleep while she sang. I did not need to worry about Aunt Fatima, for she was always in the best of moods after a song. According to her, singing and crying made space for laughter again.

THE RIVER TIGRIS,
OR THE WORLD OF SOUND

We are not only responsible for what we do,
but also for what we don't do.
— Voltaire

Y ou're not allowed to get too close to the water. You
know that every year the river takes away a couple of
children," Adiba, my nanny and Grandmother's cousin,
kept warning me.

Our house stood in a street perpendicular to the river Tigris,[1]
about 400 meters away. The river exerted a magical attraction
on me. Wide and heavy, it thumped along, ceaselessly flowing
along Baghdad in giant steps.

Adiba's exhortations always left me stubbornly silent,
because it angered me that everyone should always try to
persuade me that the river was a monster. But Adiba knew me
too well, and she only uttered her warnings when she saw a
certain flicker in my eyes.

"Where do you want to go, little Fawzia?" she asked me, her
voice soft and worried.

"I'm going to discover the world, Adiba."

I always called her by her first name, although politeness
should have commanded that I say Auntie to her, but Adiba's
love for me was so great that she indulged me and forgave me
everything.

"It's not the right time now—Grandfather will soon be home and he'll surely want to see you."

I stared angrily at Adiba, guessing that although she was such a good-hearted human being, she had simply never felt such yearning in her breast. I went to the bureau and took out my little bag, put a notebook and a pencil inside, slung it over my shoulder and wanted to leave. I had no time to waste discussing matters with Adiba. Adiba understood. Anxious, she quickly fetched a few dates and biscuits, then nodded knowingly: "I won't tell anyone, but please come back soon!"

Baghdad comprised several quarters, some of them Sunni and others Shiite.[2] We lived in a Sunni neighborhood, with one extended family house next to the other, each surrounded by a garden.[3] All endeavored in their own garden to carry on the tradition of the hanging gardens of Babylon, so that every walled garden offered a small sea of flowers, especially roses.

I went to the front of our house and stood on the empty dusty street. It was shortly before noon, the hottest time of the day, when only those who couldn't avoid doing so ventured outside their homes. I looked around, thinking about the direction I would take. I decided to walk toward the Tigris. Of course I felt a little queasy at the idea of going alone into the world. But it didn't matter: I had made up my mind, so I started walking slowly along the street. I passed one house after another; silence was everywhere as if the houses had not seen one human soul in centuries.

But when I reached the fifth house, I heard some noise. A door was open between two palm trees, and I could hear soft music. I stood there raptly listening, for I had never heard this kind of music. I took a few steps toward the door to listen better. Out of the blue, two dark eyes looked at me, protected by a pair of thick glasses.

"What are you doing here?"

My heart stopped, and I would have loved to end my excursion right then and there and run back to Adiba's familiar arms. I couldn't utter a sound and my feet were stuck on the ground.

The dark pair of eyes came closer and I recognized their owner. She was a shriveled little woman and a hidden bag sat between her shoulders. My throat filled with sounds again and I answered cautiously: "I'm Fawzia...," but before I could continue, the little woman gestured in the air, saying, "Come in if you wish, and sit down!"

I followed her slowly through the tunnel-like corridor, into the living room and toward a small table, and sat in the corner of the sofa that was behind the table. Piles of bundled newspapers and open books dominated the room and unusual music came from one corner, where a black disc went tirelessly round and round, a needle tickling the sounds out of it.

The old woman followed my eager look and said: "Bithuwan (Beethoven). Pure soul music. It was also Abdel Nasser's[4] favorite music!" She giggled and added, "Must have been 'cause he was deaf."

All of a sudden she shook the invisible bag on her shoulders, walked purposefully to a corner, put her hand into the darkness and pulled out an *ud*, a lute-like musical instrument.[5] She sat on a stool, facing me, and nestled the belly of the *ud* against her own. She stroked the strings with her fingers while firmly clasping the neck of the *ud* with her other hand.

"Do you know the *ud*?" Without waiting for an answer, she made the strings vibrate with her wrinkled hands.

"The *ud* is the *amir al-tarab* (the prince of musical delight). Over a thousand years ago there lived in Baghdad a philosopher and musician by the name of al-Kindi.[6] He discovered that the instrument's four strings were linked to the four seasons, to the four elements (fire, water, earth, and wind), to the four human humors[7] and to the various celestial bodies. To play the *ud* is to set out on a big journey. A journey that brings everything into resonance, making the stars above dance with the trees on earth, the wind and the fire, and finally touching the string of your soul and stroking it soothingly."

So this could all be summoned by this little musical instrument! I was impressed. I looked wide-eyed at the *ud*, this magic instrument whose invisible strength filled the whole room.

"Do you know that Caliph al-Mutawakkil[8] used to organize swimming moonlight concerts not far from here, with the musicians on ships on the Tigris? Such was his passion for music. The inhabitants of Baghdad then went out with torches to the riverbank to listen, or else they joined the trip in their own boats. Whenever the *ud* calls, the magic of those moments never fails to awaken."

When the old woman sounded the strings again, the books, the newspapers, even the dust on the furniture, seemed to vibrate in unison and to surrender to the sounds.

The old woman closed her eyes and sang: "I am Zalzal and Abdil Wahhab, I am the prince of delight, I am the soul longing for the voice, the love seeking fulfilment, the songs striving for eternity..."[9]

The old woman stopped unexpectedly, got up and disappeared into the dark. Soon she returned and set a tray in front of me, with two glasses of fruit juice. I took the dates and biscuits from my bag and we ate and drank together in silence.

"You must go now, little girl, and when you next set off on your travels, don't forget to go and visit al-Farabi's[10] memorial on the western bank of the river. He was the one who discovered all of Pythagoras's tones—the quarter tones, the great and the small third, and he was the first to recognize the relationship between music and mathematics, thereby offering the world the most significant Arab contribution to the theory of music. His favorite instrument was the flute—that he mastered brilliantly—and if you go to his tomb and you are very quiet, you'll hear him play!"

I stood up and suddenly felt very tired. There was a buzzing in my head. In actual fact the whole room seemed to be uttering tones and I felt happy to be back in the open air. I tottered slowly back home, my eyes fixed to the ground so that I would not stagger amidst the sounds of the universe.

"Welcome, welcome home!" shouted Adiba when she saw me, as if I had really been away for years. "Praised be Allah that you are back. Tell me, what happened to you, then?" But I had only one wish: to go to bed. Before I closed my eyes, I think I must have muttered: "You too are buzzing with the world!"[11]

SINDBAD'S HERITAGE

Travelling is the most beautiful way to learn.
—Arab proverb

I was walking in the souk with my father when we stopped by a small shop. Two elderly men were sitting on typical Iraqi stools, about ten inches high, four-legged, with seats made of woven palm branches. Father and the two men greeted each other warmly, kissing and embracing. I was received with a friendly smile and that particular handshake that old people often give the young, each time seeming to be sentimentally greeting their own erstwhile youth. I felt instantly at ease with them.

Two stools were brought and instinctively a *farrash*[1] appeared at the same time.

"Bring us two teas, my boy!" He vanished as amazingly as he had materialized.

I looked around the shop, which was more like a niche than a proper store. It was difficult to tell what the two men actually sold. Was it the few bales of cloth on the shelves or the scrap iron stacked up in a corner? Or maybe the fairy tales they told their visitors? Both men were widowers: from their somewhat neglected clothes and from that rhythm of movements that belongs to those who no longer have any worldly obligations, you could tell that their wives had already passed on.

My father and the two men exchanged the usual information about health, food supply, and news in the papers.

One old man sighed: "You know, Basil"—that was my father's name— "we can cope with everything, food and clothes don't really matter much at our age, even security is no longer so important once you are this close to the gates of death. The only thing that's really bad is that since they closed the borders, we haven't been able to enjoy Allah's big wide country like we used to, and we can no longer admire His magnificence through our senses. Before the war [the Iran–Iraq war, 1980–1988] we worked hard, but once a year, we would load the car with everything we needed, everything including the *babbur* (stove), the teapot and even the *istikans* (small tea glasses), blankets, and a little money. We'd get in and drive leisurely through different countries, as far as it was enjoyable and the money was enough. This was how we tried to learn to understand and enjoy life."

The old man's eyes suddenly became very soft as he went on: "May Allah open the borders again soon! What wouldn't I give to be able to travel once more before the last goodbye!"

"You know how we Iraqis love travelling," added the other. "Our whole history is a testimony to the fact that we enjoy nothing more than to discover other cultures and countries. Isn't Sindbad the Sailor our ancestor?"

Although we all had to laugh, my heart had grown heavy with his words and I wanted so much to be able to fulfill the old men's dearest wish. How terrible for a human being not to be free to travel, to look around and get to know other people and cultures. Is it not a fundamental right of every human being to spread his wings and enjoy the beauty of this earth?

"Father," I called, "let's go and drive around the country for a while."

"Oh, yes!"—the old men's eyes lit up a little—"let's drive to Hilla. They have the best water buffalo cream in all of Iraq!"

We stood up right away, called to the shop next door: "Abu Khaled, mind the shop!"

And off we went! When the rulers' laws close the borders, we human beings favor the cravings and laws of the belly.

KARBALA' AND NAJAF

A human being's true vocation is to find himself or herself.
—Sufi wisdom

We were driving with the car on one of the serpentine roads that wind through the desert, surrounded left and right by flat rock country stretching as far as the eye could see. Father once explained to me his theory about the Iraqis' love of travelling.

"You know, Fawzia, we Iraqis are a melancholy folk. Up one minute, down the next. From one moment to the next, we can be on top of the world and then down in the dumps. We either love people or can't stand them, and everything is decided in the first few moments of an encounter. When you are so constantly shaken by your emotions, you need space, you need to be free to go to and fro, and to find a balance through adventures and the discovery of new worlds. Only in this way can you then return to yourself and understand yourself."

My Bedouin blood could only agree, and in my thoughts our car changed into a galloping horse, his mane floating freely in the wind. My body bent forward to feel the warm body of my horse and breathe in his lively wild fragrance.

"What are you looking for?"

I was abruptly called out of my ancestral reverie and found myself with my head leaning on the dashboard.

"Nothing, Father, I'm just a little tired from the heat!" Stupid, seductive, and oh-so-comfortable technology, this car.

In the back were seated Um Ali (my uncle's wife), her friend Salwa, and my aunt Lahib (my father's sister). I loved to be around Aunt Lahib. Whenever I looked at her face, I could guess what I would look like in twenty years.

"Did you bring your *abaya*? You know you have to wear it in Karbala'," Lahib reminded me.

Of course I had brought it. It was an old *abaya* that belonged to my grandmother, and the only item I had wanted of hers after her sudden death.

Iraq is made of several different worlds, and you abide by different ethnic and traditional rules according to your destination. The south is ruled by the Shiite world, the north by the Kurdish world, and the center by the Sunni world, with Baghdad at the heart of the country. In the same way as people assemble in different family, tribal, ethnic, and religious groups, the country itself takes on different faces. The south is desert, the north mountainous and fertile green, and the center flat, fruity, and salty. The Baath party, after taking over in 1968, was the first to create through a program of state development a state and a loyalty to that state and to the party, instead of the prevailing patriarchal loyalty.

We drew nearer to Karbala' and were welcomed by an uncommon sight for such a lively city: a whole sea of tombs. At the back of the car Salwa started reciting the opening sura of the Qur'an, the *fatiha*, for the souls of the dead. Her mother and father were buried here. My aunt handed her a handkerchief. All of a sudden a group of some thirty men appeared. Each one wore a beige *dishdasha* (*jalaba* in Iraq) with a leather belt and flowing sand-colored *bisht* (a cape for men made of camel's hair). On their upright heads, they wore the traditional Arab headgear, *kufiya* with *igal*.[1] They looked manly and proud.

"What is the gathering for?" I asked.

"Farewell to a soul," Um Ali answered briefly.

Father stopped and we went down to the tombs. We followed Salwa to her parents' tomb and spoke once more the *fatiha* for them and for all the dead. All at once and without saying a word, we spread out between the tombs. We all took a different direction, lost in our thoughts. I started reading the names of the dead, calculating their lifespans. A human being by the name of Fatima al-Baghdadi had spent 70 years on this earth. Many more recent tombs sheltered young bodies, victims of the last war between Iraq and Iran. A warm wind stroked my face and I let my eyes glide over the sandy sea of tombs. There was nothing threatening about this place. On the contrary, I thought it was beautiful and appeasing to have one's last resting place in the dry, warm sand. May Allah have also predestined for me the desert as my last resting place.

Karbala' is a little town of some 85,000 inhabitants. When you drive off from the main road into the heart of Karbala', you get to a big square and you find yourself taken in at once by the atmosphere of this holy place. One side of the square leads to the impressive and magnificent mosque and mausoleum of Hussein, the Prophet's grandson (May Allah's blessings and peace be upon him), son of the Prophet's daughter Fatima and his nephew Ali (May Allah grant them peace). The golden dome of the mosque with its golden minarets seemed to catch all the surrounding light. On the other side of the square is the mausoleum of Abbas,[2] Hussein's brother, which is also crowned with a golden dome. Hussein and nearly all his family met their deaths during the battle of Karbala', in 50 AH (680 CE). Karbala' is a holy place and, together with Najaf, which holds Ali's tomb, a pilgrimage center for the Shiites. Hussein is considered by the Shiites to be the first Muslim martyr. To this date, his martyrdom has remained the highlight of the religious calendar. Every year the Shiites celebrate the memory of Hussein and the events of Karbala' in many popular plays called *ashura*.

The holy places were governed by the families of the local scholars, *'ulama'*, who held the hereditary right to be the guardians of the shrines. We parked the car near the main square, pulled on our black *abayas,* and stepped out. We fell instantly under the spell of this lively square, and the warm wind kept us women, who were unaccustomed to such things, immediately busy with the flapping *abayas*. These fluttering provocations were overcome by pressing both sides firmly together, leaving only a thin slit open through which our faces could peep out. And so we headed toward the mosque. The square swarmed with people, many from far away, carrying suitcases, bags, and prayer stones. Unlike the Sunnis, the Shiites touch a block of clay from Karbala' with their forehead when they pray. It is the sign of their eternal connection with that place and with the family of Ali and Fatima (Peace be upon them).

The mosque was extremely overcrowded. Women and men prayed side by side and if you wanted to go through, you had to skillfully balance on the tip of your toes in the narrow free spaces and hope that no one changed position at that moment, for that meant the end of your carefully calculated hope not to disturb anyone. I felt deeply touched by the mass formed by the many bodies pressing together. The place was filled with the prayers of supplication, the wishes, the longings, the tears— everything that lay in the hearts of those people. I squeezed between two praying women and disappeared instantly in the praying mass. It is a warm feeling of intimacy, when the self recedes into the background, together with all its wishes, demands, and desires, and one's own outlines melt with the surrounding people.

Yet all of a sudden my ego reclaimed very concretely the center of my attention: I was hungry. We crossed the big square again and found a small restaurant. Kebab skewers were lined up in the window, surrounded by various salads. The white-tiled restaurant was fitted with simple, plain iron tables and chairs. It was clean so we sat down and ordered several dishes with salad.

The owner was Egyptian. We were amused by the way he spoke because he had attempted the almost impossible—namely to combine the Egyptian and Iraqi dialects.

"I've been living in Iraq for five years and I have a good life here. Iraqis are a noble, generous people and I have found a second home."

During the Gulf war between Iraq and Iran, some two million Egyptians had come to Iraq. Most of them worked in the service sector or in farming, replacing Iraqis who were busy fighting. Many of them remained after the war ended, and many an Iraqi widow was now married to an Egyptian.

We decided to drive on toward Najaf.

We stopped near the great mosque that held Ali's mausoleum (May Allah's blessings be upon him). The atmosphere was quite different from the one in Karbala', much softer, calmer, and humbler. We turned to one of the *sayyids* and followed him to the mausoleum. The title of *sayyid* is borne by

49

the descendants of Fatima and Ali. The *sayyid* with the green turban stood in front of the mausoleum and started reciting the suras from the Qur'an for the soul of this great companion of the Prophet. This place radiated something noble and calm, and tears flooded down our faces. I was still dazed when we decided to drive to the house where Ali (Peace be upon him) had lived.

This house, in which the fourth caliph and ruler of all Muslims had lived with his family, was in Kufa, next to the mosque where he was murdered in January 661. Dim light filtered through the small openings in the walls, and in the biggest room a water fountain kept the house pleasantly cool. People flocked in and out of the house, which was amazingly modest, especially compared to the homes of contemporary rulers of Islamic countries. Simplicity, humility, deep knowledge, and faith in God had been this man's riches.

We entered the nearby mosque and Lahib's unfamiliar *abaya* slipped from her head. A guard came and reprimanded her. "You are in a mosque here, a holy place, cover your head," he said forcefully and self-righteously. Lahib—never at a loss for words—replied immediately: "If your heart is as hard as your tongue, then I am more covered without a veil than you are!" The man's mouth sharpened to a disapproving point and he threw her a dirty look before turning back. Lahib covered her head again.

We decided to tour the little town of Kufa.

"They're building a new university here. They're planning to have the most important faculty of medicine of the whole south of the country, with state-of-the-art equipment. All the instruments are imported from Germany," Father explained to me. "Saddam wants Kufa to blossom into a new scientific center."

"Let's go home, Father. Our eyes and our hearts have had our fill for today."

They all agreed. We bought boiled corn from a little cart with a big steaming pot and went back to Baghdad nibbling happily.

NONE OF OUR WOMEN SIT AT HOME

Every woman has the right to grow into the professional world
that suits her.
—Louise Hay

None of our women sit at home!" thundered Grandmother when my father explained to her that my mother wished to stay at home for a while. "Your sister works, your sister-in-law works, and your mother works. Why then should your wife stay at home and demoralize the other women? She is an educated woman!" she argued.

Since Grandmother was a school head and historically aware, she went on soothingly: "As early as in the 12th century there were women lawyers, women doctors, women civil servants and women university teachers in Baghdad."[1] In Grandmother's view, the world was divided into women who stay at home and women who go out into the world and take an active part in the building of the country. In that sense, she was a typical representative of her time.

When the Baath party came to power in 1968, it started a program for the building of the state. This aimed to restrict the links between individuals and their extended family, and ethnic and tribal reference groups, and to replace them by intensified loyalty toward and identification with the state. Women were given a key role in this program to centralize power. On the one hand, the long-term industrialization and growth strategy based on oil income had an urgent need for women as a workforce. On the other, the creation of state-controlled women's organizations resulted in an alternative form of social organization for women, outside family ties, which tended to functionally weaken and transform the traditional loyalty ties. Fighting illiteracy in the country, especially among women, as well as providing an extensive education and welfare program, was part of what would stir women into taking an active part in the development of the state. Women were encouraged to participate in social, cultural, political, and economic activities initiated by the state. They were given equal rights with men in the workplace, and in 1980 they were granted active and passive voting rights.

"Every woman must be able to read and write—it's part of her human rights," Grandmother explained when a Bedouin woman from southern Iraq visited us, whose husband forbade her to take part in the free evening classes designed to fight illiteracy.

"Should I report him?" she asked her visitor.

But the latter waved her anxiously aside: "If you report him, he is threatened by two years in prison, and who will then feed my five children? No, no—what good is it to me if I can read and write, and I'm starving! He'll see reason."

"Send him to me," Grandmother replied, "I'll speak to him! The transition from one conception of life to another is always difficult and we have to support each other in the process."

Grandmother was an authoritarian person and like many women from prosperous households, she had learned to exercise authority well. When she started working, she simply applied this experience to the outside world, without getting into a conflict with her identity as a woman, or having to apologize to men or seek their acceptance. To her, authority was never the antithesis to femininity.

The Iraqi state was rich, with 87 percent of its income originating from oil, which granted it extensive economic and social independence from the local social classes and communities. The government offered its citizens a comprehensive social program, free education, free healthcare, free school meals, and a social security system for working women, including generous maternity leave and childcare in the workplace. These advantages, however, were not seen as rights to be legitimately claimed, but rather as favors in return for one's loyalty toward the leader of the party and the state.

Grandmother was not interested in such details. To her education was simply the most important element in the development of the personality—it paved the way to independent thinking and therefore to independence, and she was happy to see her life philosophy supported by the state. She had absolutely no understanding for women who didn't seize the opportunity offered with both hands and take an active part in the development of the country.

She interpreted cigarette-smoking, her great weakness, as an act of liberation, and couldn't care less about other people's opinions when she smoked in public. In her school, she was even stricter with the girls than with the boys, for she took great pains to make it possible for all her protégés to have a good higher education. This meant achieving good A-level grades, for they determined which further education would be offered by the state.

Grandmother was loved and feared in equal parts by teachers and pupils, and she represented absolute authority within her model school. She was also very much in favor of birth control and never tired in her repeated preaching: "I have three children. Had I had more, I would never have become headmistress!" She believed that education and birth control went hand in hand.[2] Grandmother only had two taboos: extra-marital sexual relationships and alcohol.

"We don't want to throw our Muslim Middle-Eastern ethics and culture overboard; we don't want chaos in society, but a society in which men and women can develop according to their capacities." She kept telling her sons: "Mothers and fathers should educate each of their daughters well, put the Qur'an in one of her hands and education in the other, and together they'll build her backbone and shape her understanding of herself; then she can set off into the world reassured, and there's no need to lock her up at home for fear of the family honor."

UNEVEN SISTERS: BASRA AND KUFA

The one and the many are different, yet mysteriously linked.
—Ibn al-Arabi

Basra and Kufa are sister cities at whose mention the body of every Arab straightens in pride. They are the old symbols of the Islamic mind and knowledge and of the Arabic language. They were founded at the time of the second caliph Umar (634–644) in 17 AH (638 CE), originally as fortified army camps.

Kufa was built not far from old Babylon and it became the capital of Ali, the fourth caliph (656–661). Throughout the generations, it would remain the center of Ali's party, the Shiites.[1]

During the Umayyad dynasty (661–750) these two cities grew prosperous and densely populated, thanks to their propitious locations, intensive trade, and the immigration of numerous scholars. By 50 AH (670 CE), there were 300,000 inhabitants in Basra and this "Venice of the South" counted 120 canals.

Basra and Kufa played a major role before the rise of Baghdad. Basra, in particular, was as much the melting-pot of the most varied scientific and philosophical schools as the sphere of activity of manifold religious groups.

Yet Basra and Kufa had also developed into spiritual centers. This is where, in the middle of the 8th century, Hasan al-Basri lived, a man who the descendants of a whole range of spiritual families saw unanimously as the great model of deep, moderate, and reasonable piety. Most religious branches in Islam trace their origins back to him. His goal was to live an honest and decent life and to lead his friends to lives that were pleasing to God. He had seen the great conquests of the Arabs and in his sober clarity he felt the dangers that threaten a society solely interested in multiplying conquests and accumulating riches. He warned his fellow human beings to live according to the Qur'an so that they would not be shamed at the Last Judgment: "O human child, you will die alone, and you alone will be called to account!" Hasan was deeply wrapped up in that sadness and fear that is so typical of the ascetics of all religions. He was so loved by the whole population that on the day he died, October 10, 728, a Friday, the whole population joined the procession and no one was left to lead, or participate in, the Friday prayer in the mosque.

Of the problems discussed in Basra and Kufa, two became more and more significant: the question of the creation or non-creation of God's revealed word, and the question of the relationship between belief and action in the face of divine justice. In other words: Is there space for human free will in the face of divine omnipotence? Such were the most prominent preoccupations of religious and spiritual people at that time, which then led to various interpretations and movements. From those cities, in the course of a few generations, came many of the ideas that would later spread worldwide.

Arabs and Iranians lived side by side in Basra: Arabs, who were intent on upholding their ancestors' glory as well as the tradition of the Prophet, and Iranians, who preserved their own culture while at the same time attempting to gain a new and appropriate position under the Islam that they had adopted.

It was also in Basra and Kufa that the explanations of the Qur'an were collected, especially the ancient literature written in the traditional language of Higaz, which was spoken in the area of Mecca and Medina. The norms of pure Arabic were elaborated on that basis, thus creating a model of "classical" Arabic for the present and the future. The need arose essentially in order to bring the Arabic language closer to non-Arabs and to protect it, on the basis of the Qur'an, from the foreign influences of Syrian, Persian, and other languages. This process was initiated and duly completed by Abu al-Aswad al-Duali (d. 688), inspired by the words of the caliph Ali: "The language consists of three elements: names, verbs, and particles. So take this as a basis for a treatise on the Arabic language!"

He was followed by al-Khalil ibn-Ahmad, another scholar from Basra (d. 786), who compiled the first Arabic dictionary *kitab al-ayn* (the book of the source) and invented the Arabic prosody that is still valid today. He collected words and classified them and to do that, as was customary in those days among scholars, he went to the marketplaces to meet Bedouin people, for they had mastered the purest Arabic language.

His pupil, the Iranian Sibawayhi of Basra (d. 793), had been the first to record systematically the structure of Arabic in his work called *al-kitab* (the book). As a non-Arab, he must have felt strongly the need for a systematic study of a language that was not his mother tongue.

Those were turbulent and complex times. Although many different peoples took part in the construction of this new civilization, it can nevertheless be described as Arab civilization; although people had been separated by their languages, civilization was now built on the common basis of Arabic. During the 8th century, the codification of Arabic was therefore led by the two great rival grammatical schools in Kufa and Basra, whose results were then summarized by Baghdad scholars in the 9th century.

Kufa was the stronghold of the Alids and it was in Kufa that the new Abbasid dynasty originated, although the city had drawn its strength from Chorasan with Persian tribes.

Kufa was also home to Abu Hanifa (699–767), one of the founders of Sunni law. That school was the most closely linked to the Abbasid regime. Hanifa had some wealth, from which he lived modestly and which enabled him to dedicate all his strength to social science, without holding a public post.

By the 10th century, four Sunni law schools had found their final form. Their founders had each brought the legal precepts of the Qur'an into a systematic form and now four different legal interpretations appeared, in which Qur'anic laws mixed with elements from each respective regional and cultural tradition.[2]

At first sight, these four schools—the Hanafites, the Malikites, the Shafiites, and the Hanbalites[3]—only differ in small details, but these variations are nevertheless significant for women. Whereas all schools agree that the marriage can be brought to an end unilaterally by the husband, Malikite law differs from the other three inasmuch as the woman has the legal right to obtain a divorce. For its part, the Hanafite school recognizes that a woman has the right to define various clauses in the marriage contract, for instance to the effect that the husband may not marry a second wife. To prevent or end a pregnancy prior to the fourth month is allowed in all schools, but according to the Hanafite school, a woman who wishes to have an abortion does not even need to inform her husband. According to that school, the husband must match his wife's family in social standing.

The fact that Islam was tied to the traditions of the various regions—in particular with respect to the relationship between the sexes—and that the implementation of the strongly egalitarian ideas of the Qur'an was not enforced must have contributed significantly to its rapid expansion. In particular, the cultural traditions restrictive toward women that existed in the conquered Byzantine and Persian regions, where the limitation and control of women had been comprehensively legally codified and secured through the state, contributed to shaping the interpretation and canonization of religious texts.

Kufa was also home to people who were keen to experiment, such as Jabir ibn-Hayyar (known in the West as Geber). Around 776 he was one of the great alchemists. He was convinced that metals like iron, copper, lead, and tin could be changed into gold or silver through special substances, and he devoted his whole strength to searching for them. He acknowledged the importance of experiments and thus contributed greatly to the theoretical and practical development of chemistry.

Basra and Kufa, the two sisters, thus nurtured and protected great thoughts, bold experiments, and deep longings of the soul. My own love for Basra grew through two people who have found an eternal place in my soul and in my imagination: Rabi'a al-Adawiyya, the great mystic, and Sindbad the Sailor.

On sultry afternoons, lying on mattresses, Grandfather would tell me about Sindbad's courageous adventures, which took him on his boat to the most faraway countries, to enormous birds and one-eyed giants, to powerful sea queens and greedy *djinns*. Time and again, Sindbad's cunning and wit would free him from danger, and he would return home crowned with treasures. Could I have inherited my love of travelling from his stories?

Rabi'a's stories were totally different. Rabi'a introduced the element of selfless love into the austere teachings of the early ascetics, thereby transforming Sufism into true mysticism.[4]

"Once upon a time," Grandmother began, "there was a very poor man, who had a wife and three daughters who he could barely feed, so poor was he. When his wife became pregnant once more and once more gave life to a daughter, he was in such despair that he even contemplated killing her. But he came to his senses at the very last moment and remembered Allah's words, that every child brings its food, and he abandoned the thought. Not knowing how he should name her, he simply called her Rabi'a (the fourth). And it is true that soon after she was born things improved slightly in the family. The days passed and Rabi'a grew up. Things were still bad, so her father sold her to a man to be his slave. One night the man came to Rabi'a and his eyes opened wide when he saw a ray of light around her head. In his confusion and fear, he set her free.

"Rabi'a decided to go into the desert. She spent many nights there—no one knows how many—and when she returned to the city, she started playing the bamboo flute and thus earned her keep. She was not interested in the world. She simply played her flute and whoever heard her was touched and gave her a coin, so beautiful sounded her soul through the *nay*, the bamboo flute. Her soul fed on her love for Allah, and there was no space left for anything but this absolute love. Rabi'a started preaching this love of God, and people came to her to drink from that love. She spoke of love for the sake of love, not out of fear or hope for a reward.

"Many men and women who also walked the way of Allah came and listened to her. Many a man asked for her hand. But she was not interested in marriage or children. She wanted to remain free without tying herself to worldly duties and oppressions. She lived alone with her attendant, and only owned a brick on which she lay her tired head, a prayer mat, and a bowl from which she ate. In her, there was room for nothing but her absolute love for God.

"One day Hasan al-Basri, the great mystic, came to Rabi'a who was meditating with others on the beach. To impress her and the others with his spiritual powers, he threw his praying mat on the sea, sat on it and invited Rabi'a to come and sit next to him. She understood his plan, threw her mat in the air, flew up, sat on it and said: 'O Hasan, come to me. People can see us better up here!' Hasan remained silent for flying was beyond his spiritual power. Then she said: 'Hasan, what you have done, any fish can do, and what I'm doing here, any fly can do. True spiritual work is beyond such deeds!'"

I was deeply impressed by Rabi'a's deeds, especially by her modesty and her clarity and how, unimpressed by apparent strengths, she would shed them as weaknesses.

The Qur'anic verse: "He loves them and they love Him" (sura 5/59), in which God's love precedes the love of human beings, was explained as follows by Rabi'a: "Love has come from all eternity and it goes into eternity, and no one in the seventy thousand worlds could drink a single drop from it without finally returning to God; this is why we say 'He loves them and they love Him.'"

Whenever I watched the wonders of the sky, delighting in the stars, which I felt were my special protectors, I would remember that Rabi'a hadn't looked up to the sky for thirty years out of respect, out of love for God. The stars did not matter to her, but He who had created them. And nothing could or should distract her from Him.

I remember the time when my grandmother told me the famous story of Rabi'a for the first time: "Rabi'a was going through the streets of Basra carrying a torch in one hand and a bucket full of water in the other. When people asked her why, she answered: 'With the torch, I would like to set the Paradise on fire, and with the water extinguish the fires of hell, so that people only worship God for His beauty, because He deserves worshipping, without any fear of punishment nor hope for reward!'"

The simplicity of that story had touched me very deeply and I kept retreating to mull it over. It left a strange trembling in my breast while opening my heart to a new world. I kept running back to Grandmother to hear the story anew. It calmed me and at the same time it confused me. Yet when I look back, many years later, it was Rabi'a's story that for the first time embedded the feeling of divine love in my heart.

Another time Rabi'a's behavior confused my vision of the world. We had a neighbor in Baghdad who lived across the street from us, and my grandmother often visited her. She very much liked this rather pale, thin woman, who chatted quietly about her everyday stories and whose whole attitude was extremely modest, although she held a high position at the Ministry of Education. I paid little attention to her until I found out one day that she was a vegetarian.

This was the first time I had set eyes on a human being who fed solely on plants. The Arabic word for vegetarian is *nabatiyya*, literally "plant-eater." Suddenly my whole perception of this neighbor changed. I stared at her, trying to make out something extraordinary in her appearance. Was there really a greenish gleam on her face or was the light deceiving me? Little plants seemed to look out shyly from her ears... No, I shook my head: it was only her hair, which she had tucked behind her ears. She didn't eat any lamb, beef, chicken, or fish. She let them all live and was only a danger to those beings endowed with roots. All that fascinated and confused me, for I and everyone around me ate animals as a matter of course.

After that discovery I sat for days in our garden under my favorite date-palm, engrossed in the scrutiny of the industrious blades of grass, strenuously wrinkling my forehead and waiting for my soul to understand this new discovery and the many thoughts that kept buzzing in my head. Every so often I looked again at our neighbor's house across the street. Was she a better human being than were all the others around me because she didn't eat any animals? But hadn't Allah allowed us human beings to feed from the living beings on this earth, whether plant or animal?

I didn't feel well, and I suddenly lost all appetite. Everything seemed alive to me, and to the despair of my whole family, I couldn't eat a thing apart from sweets for I felt that they were neither one nor the other. As often in my life, my ever-watchful grandmother recognized my restless state, and as often before, she let me ferment and examine my inner questions before intervening.

"Do you know that the great holy woman of Islam, Rabi'a Al-Adawiyya never ate animal products?"

I lifted my head and looked at Grandmother wide-eyed. Why was she telling me this, how did she know?

"She did that so that animals would no longer flee from her, because animals can smell what human beings feed on. There are many human beings and peoples on this earth who are vegetarians, but this doesn't necessarily mean that they are better beings. In our religion we are allowed to eat animals, but what matters is how.

"When an animal is sacrificed, the human being must wait for the moment when it surrenders and lays there very calmly, and no other animal should witness that. When the moment has come, the divine formula is pronounced, which takes everything back to divine unity and which means that everything on this earth has come to be in the name of this unity."

"*Bismillah ar-rahman ar-rahim*," I whispered, and Grandmother nodded.

"Then, with a single, sharp move the windpipe and gullet are cut through and the blood flows back into the earth. When you eat this meat, again you say this formula, aware that a living being has surrendered so that you may enjoy it and become stronger. In that way it is honorable and your responsibility and awareness grow so that you too are a part of the circle of giving and taking."

I was very grateful to her for those explanations, but what touched me most was what she had said about Rabi'a not eating any meat so that animals wouldn't flee from her. In Iraq, Rabi'a had brought about a new, creative period in the development of mystical love. In me she awoke the awareness and sense of responsibility that go with eating meat. Her immortal, love-soaked soul lives in the conscience of many people, and to this date it is customary to describe a particularly pious woman as a "second Rabi'a."

The Persian poet Jami, a man otherwise not too well-disposed toward the feminine, wrote the following verses on Rabi'a:

> If all women were like her, the one we mentioned,
> Then women should indeed be preferred to men.
> Femininity does not harm the sun,
> Nor does masculinity serve to honor the moon.[5]

OFF WE GO

*Be the daughter of the moment—*bint ul-waqt—
for peace lies in the eternal present.
—Sufi wisdom

Father rushed into the room and cried out: "We're travelling! I got the job!" We were eating. Grandfather looked up, and when I saw his face I noticed that it had shrunk suddenly and become pale. The words that came out of his mouth belied the pain his body silently showed: "Congratulations, my son. I'm happy that your wish has come true!"

In his joy Father didn't notice what went on with Grandfather, but I could see it, and it filled me with great fear to see my beloved grandfather so sad. Something very bad would happen now—this journey must be awful or at least very dangerous, otherwise my courageous grandfather wouldn't react this way.

"That's great!" Uncle Mazin cried out. "Beirut is a wonderful city. I would give a lot to be able to come with you!"

So Beirut is the name of this dangerous place, and Uncle Mazin finds that great. I'd always felt that Uncle Mazin was a little bit strange and his comment was just another confirmation. He was in the army and everybody there somehow seemed to have a strange understanding of the world.

Grandmother, wanting to lighten the situation by saying something nice, said: "People speak differently there. You'll say *kifik* (how are you) and *shu badik* (what do you want) instead of *shlonic* and *shtirdin*, little Hanan!"

She was speaking to me and I really felt that this was too much. I could take a dangerous country — after all we Iraqis have a reputation for courage — but now a strange language too! Tears started pouring silently down my cheeks and the food in front of me lost all its taste and meaning.

Only Grandfather and I seemed to recognize the real truth of this journey — he because of his knowledge of life and me out of an intuition that only children or the wise carry inside themselves.

"You will learn the new language very fast," Aunt Lahib said soothingly. "There's a sea and beautiful green landscape over there," my mother added.

Oh, you grown-ups! As if the language or the attraction of the sea were the problem! It is leaving home, where the familiar and loved faces live. It is the leaving behind of the roses that greet me every morning. It is the knowledge that once you leave a place, even if you come back later, you no longer really belong there. It is the fact that from now on you will be a stranger, no matter what happens — that is what tightens the heart in sorrow. Grandfather knew, and the worry in his eyes at that decisive moment is forever engraved in my heart and soul.

We were off and a traveller I would remain my whole life long.

LEBANON

THE LAND OF INFINITE POTENTIAL

Beirut, the capital on the Mediterranean coast. I had never set eyes on such a place. From the plane, I could see soft, green mountains, dotted with houses and their pointed red tiled roofs. They lay peacefully in the folds of the mountains, isolated or huddled together, and everywhere the wonderful green of the trees and bushes. I had never seen so much green in my entire life. Was this what Paradise looked like? And out the other window stretched the endless sea. Soft and tireless water rose to greet the coast and surrender to the sand, like a baby surrendering to its mother's breast. How beautiful, I thought. I could have watched these hypnotic movements for hours.

Proud Beirut stands exactly midway between mountains and sea, its many high-rise buildings confidently exposed to the wind. Beirut hugged the coast—or was it the other way around?—before stretching toward the mountains. It seemed so beautiful, so noble, from above, and our first encounter on the ground only confirmed this initial impression. Newcomers were met by a wide, perfectly straight avenue, surrounded by palm trees and flower beds. Everywhere signs proclaimed: "Welcome to Beirut!"

Although I had hardly seen the city, I could already feel myself bewitched by its Mediterranean charm. The taxi driver chatted happily away, and indeed he spoke the funny Arabic dialect of which my grandmother had already given me a sample. When we turned right off the avenue, the official reception was over, and the city showed its everyday face. My God, how the Lebanese could drive! They didn't miss the slightest gap, didn't spare any horn or politely stifle any swear word, while alternating brakes and accelerations were mastered by gifted drivers' feet as if by virtuoso pianists. Now that was fun!

We drove through a very busy area, mostly inhabited by Muslims. Here Shiites and Sunnis lived together.

"Here, please," Father tapped on the driver's shoulder, asking him to stop next to a five-story house.

We got out and I examined the building from the bottom up.

"We'll be living in a flat on the third floor," my father said.

So high up, I thought to myself. Were we somehow related to the other people who lived in this high tower, even if they were only distant relatives?

We went in and despite the flight of stairs on the right, my parents walked to an iron door with a little glass window. They pushed a button, which lit up instantly. But nothing else happened. Yet we all stood there doggedly, hearing strange noises, until a narrow beam of light appeared out of the blue. It grew wider and wider, then it went "yeeeem" and everything was quiet. Father picked up the suitcases and asked us all to take one step back. And that's when the light suddenly went off.

I was so busy observing everything that I simply couldn't think. Mother opened the door, the light came on, and behind it was actually nothing but a small room, no bigger than our earth closets in Baghdad. No one seemed to mind—my father, my brother, and my mother all went inside, so I followed, excited to discover what kind of game this was. We were now all standing inside, the door closed by itself, the grownups turned left and right, apparently looking for something, found it, pressed another button and the little room started moving. In my feet and in my stomach I could feel it going up.

It was strange to be standing so close together, and the grownups grinned at each other in a strangely friendly way, which was, I would later find out, the traditional little-room-grin, a mixture of politeness and embarrassment. One light came on after the other and suddenly we stopped with a jerk of the stomach.

"Here we are!" Father shouted. He opened the door and we

were really somewhere else. We stood in a small corridor opening onto three doors, and there was a little sign on each door. The door opposite the lift was ours. Father opened it and we all followed him.

Our flat consisted of a hall, two bedrooms, two living rooms, a dining room, a kitchen, and a bathroom. There were also three balconies. One stretched along the kitchen and the adjacent bedroom, the second was next to one of the living rooms, and the third in front of the second bedroom. Everyone seemed excited. Such nice light, and big, my mother said, and my brother too seemed to feel comfortable here. Of course Father liked it too— after all, he had chosen it during his last visit.

I was the only one who disliked it. It was so much like a box, so far away from the earth and anyhow, what would life be like without Grandfather, Grandmother, my aunts and uncles? I whizzed around the room, secretly hoping to chance upon one of them. It was so hard to imagine life without them. My brother and I were given the bedroom next to the kitchen and we spent the next few days cleaning, tidying, and furnishing the flat.

Our neighbors soon came to visit us. They were an extremely diverse group of people. On the first floor lived a Christian family. The mother came with her two young daughters and her four-year-old son. She brought a bouquet of flowers. I was all excited at the idea of being given a bouquet. The daughters were very pretty and wore short skirts and tight-fitting blouses, but they seemed a little blasé. They sat next to each other on our new sofas and let their eyes glide over our furniture as if the furnishings would tell them more about their owners.

Sitt Suzan (*Sitt* is Mrs. in Lebanon), a very thin and apparently self-confident woman, was particularly interested in my mother. She was delighted to hear my mother, a European, speak such good Arabic, and she seemed to relate her talent essentially to her religion; this was apparently the way of the Lebanese. Everything here was connected to religion and judged accordingly.

"I'm sure you know that the educated class in Lebanon are mainly Christians. We have the best schools in the whole country!"

Mother smiled at her, yet against all expectations she did not respond on the subject.

Sitt Suzan was disappointed, but she made one further

advance: "We travel at least once a year to France. It's so important for the children to know Europe well and to master the language!"

Mother agreed and said that travelling was one of the most beautiful ways to further one's education, but she didn't continue on the subject of Europe.

Poor Sitt Suzan—she thought she'd found a new sympathizer, but this one didn't really seem to understand her hints. The visit ended abruptly because George, the little boy, had to go to bed at the same time every day.

Soon after, the family from the second floor came to visit us. Um Isam[1] (literally, mother of Isam) came with her two daughters, one seventeen and the other six years old. Um Isam wore a transparent white veil on her head, loosely draped around her shoulder. She brought homemade pastry filled with spinach and goat's cheese. Her older daughter wore a knee-length skirt and little Samia sat, well-behaved and shy, next to her mother.

"*Ahlan wa-sahlan*, welcome," my mother said, "*tfaddalu*, please sit down!"

Um Isam was a plump little woman who radiated a deep calm. The calm of a woman who knows how to carry out her duties in life.

"I have five sons and two daughters," she said nobly and softly.

"*Ma shallah*, what Allah wills happens, *allah ichallilik yahum*, may Allah keep them in good health," my mother answered.

Um Isam's heart had been won! In the Middle East, people simply go over the moon whenever a foreigner speaks their language and knows their customs.

Like her husband (who was her cousin), Um Isam came from a prosperous Shiite clan from South Lebanon. As with most Shiite families, their wealth came from the trade of sheep and goats. But her husband had chosen a different path and, after many ambitious sacrifices, he had made a successful career in the army and become a colonel, an unusually high position for a Shiite in the Lebanese army. Since Muslims in general and Shiites in particular were the poorer and less educated class in the country, this family had started sending the children to the better Christian schools. They also planned to send them later to university in France. The parents' favored studies were, of course, medicine.

"Isam will, if Allah wills, become a doctor—it's good to have a doctor in the family."

What Isam himself wanted was not a priority; he had to accommodate to the plans of the extended family. "My husband's parents live with us and they are very weak already. You always need medical care. Besides, doctors are needed the world over."

There seemed to be no end to visitors on that day. Now was the turn of the Druze family from the top floor.

"We travel to Syria to our relatives every summer," Um Walid said. They had only been living in Beirut for a few years and came from Beit ed-Din, the Druze stronghold in the south of Lebanon.[2]

"You really have to come and visit us one day. Beit ed-Din is a dream of a village—high up in the mountain, amid luxuriant vineyards, fragrant trees, and olive orchards."

Um Walid seemed to miss her home, for her voice became softer.

"Isn't there in Beit ed-Din one of the most beautiful Arab castles in the whole region, near Der el-Qamar?" Mother said.[3] She loved history and archaeology and her knowledge never failed to impress those around her.

"Oh, so you know Beit ed-Din!"

Fine, Um Walid, too, had taken my mother into her heart. I was proud of my mother and of how she always managed to win people's hearts with her charm and knowledge.

Mother felt at ease in this multicolored country, whose many different ethnic and religious groups made it possible to wander from one group to the next, picking from this and that one, and creating one's own pleasant and free world.

So we lived in Shiyyah, a Shiite suburb with many immigrants from the south and east of the country. And we had been given a television. A funny square thing. You pressed a button—only my parents were allowed to press the button—and then a light appeared in the middle, which suddenly stretched and changed into a moving picture. In that world, all beings came in shades of black, gray, and white. They moved, they talked, and they had their own problems, which they shared with us. Some days, on children's programs, drawings of characters moved at the speed of lightning, and fell off cliffs and immediately got up unharmed. They banged on each other's heads with a hammer and nothing happened—apart from stars and a couple of chirpy birds flying around for a moment. A strange, fast world!

Once I was visiting our neighbors on the top floor, who had two daughters who were the same age as I was—and I discovered that they had the same box. My thoughts raced: What if they see the same in their box as we do downstairs? I had to know, at all costs. So I looked closely at the scene and hurried away, running down the stairs as fast as I could to our flat. I rang the bell impatiently and as soon as the door opened, rushed to the living room and looked. The scene was different; the box on the top floor showed something else! Or was it my mistake?

I ran upstairs again, arriving at the top panting, and charged into the neighbors' flat. The grown-ups looked at me, puzzled.

"What's the matter with you? What are you looking for?"

But I had neither breath nor time to answer them. I had to end my research first. The pictures had changed again. How about downstairs, at home...?

I ran downstairs once more. I could hear someone calling after me: "Do you need to go to the toilet?"

These grown-ups—they always have to find such profane reasons for everything!

I stood in front of our television again, and again, a new scene awaited me. Now I was totally confused, as well as exhausted.

Did all human beings see the same thing or did each box show something different? I sat down, feeling depressed. Would I ever find out? The subject kept me busy for the whole evening, but I didn't dare to ask. I couldn't have taken it if a grown-up had answered me with a typical adult-to-little-unexperienced-being smile, generously drawing from their all-knowing pot of experience.

The following day, I relented slightly.

"Mother, when I sleep, is the whole world asleep too?"

Mother looked at me. "What do you mean?"

"Well, are all people always doing the same thing? When I'm sad, is the whole world sad?"

Mother seemed to reflect. "No, my daughter, there are very many people on this earth and when some of them are sad, others are happy. When you sleep, other people are awake, and maybe they're working or driving a car or reading a book at that very moment."

"Does that mean that each person can do something else, each can think something else, each can watch something else on television?"

Mother looked at me and inclined her head slightly. Grown-ups do that when they think hard.

"Yes," Mother finally said. "But on television there are only two channels."

I simply couldn't imagine billions of things happening at the same time in this world, each human being busy with his own little world. It was somehow beyond me. But I would soon be presented with a very vivid example.

A couple of days later, I heard voices shouting and crying. I ran to the balcony and discovered a procession. A huge crowd followed a coffin carried by young men. The top was off and I looked straight at the dead body of a young man. He seemed quiet and unconcerned amid the hustle and bustle of crying people clad in black.

So much pain and grief radiated from the crowd. A few women cried loudest and walked directly behind the coffin. The eldest, supported by two younger women, must have been the mother; the others may have been sisters or cousins. The big procession caused a traffic jam. Some drivers came out to pay their last respects to the dead. No one seemed capable of escaping this strong feeling of grief. In order to get a better view, I ran into the house and went to another balcony.

I pressed my body against the railing and my attention was caught by another scene. Near an old stone house, I saw a group of women preparing giant unleavened breads. The small balls of pastry were separated, and then skillfully thrown up in the air and whirled from one hand to the other until they became paper-thin and as large as a tray. They laid the bread on a large round cushion and stretched it even more, then removed it from the cushion and slapped it on the domed oven.[4]

The women chatted and laughed, and they seemed to have a good time. I was totally confused. Didn't they know that a few yards away their sisters were taking a son to his grave? Couldn't they feel it? I was exhausted by those two different scenes. So it was true: every human being lived in his own world and actually didn't catch much from the others. My God, how this world was big and diverse!

REBELLIOUS NADJA

The only betrayal in life is fear.
Unclaimed freedom is in reality a prison,
and love unfelt in reality fear.
—Gibran Khalil Gibran

The porter Abu Hasan sent my mother a helper who came with her mother. She was a pretty young woman, about seventeen, and her name was Nadja. She had long black, smooth hair and I liked her at first sight. Nadja lived nearby, in one of the poorest Shiite neighborhoods. She was the eldest daughter in a family with seven children. I instantly felt a rebel hiding behind a shell of shyness, which made Nadja very interesting to me. At the beginning her mother, a small, delicate woman with a prominent belly, always came with her daughter. Every morning at half past seven sharp the doorbell rang and in came Um Ali and Nadja.

Um Ali always wore a headscarf that she tied at the back of her neck; Nadja refused. And her mother was constantly in a dilemma: on the one hand she wanted her daughter to cover her head demurely, but on the other hand she was proud of her daughter's beautiful long hair, and secretly shared her rebellious ways, which she herself could never have put into practice.

When it came to family rows she always sided with her daughter and most of the time Abu Ali would end the argument by saying: "You'll see, one day you'll be sorry to have given your daughter so much freedom!"

Um Ali confided her worries to my mother. She told her about her problems as she cleaned.

"What can I do?—I would so much like to give her the possibility to fulfill her dreams. I'd like her to have a better life. I'd like her to have her own way, lead her own life and find a good husband."

Mother understood her preoccupations very well. Lebanon was indeed a country where everything could be found...

To strike a balance between tradition and new, individual ways was a difficult walk along a tightrope where only brave, intelligent beings gifted with inner poise could succeed. Nadja was brave, and she also had dreams.

"I'd like to be a hairdresser and have my own business. All the society ladies would come to me for their hair care. I'd buy myself a car, which I'd park outside my door and whenever I felt like it, I'd put on my high heels, take my handbag in one hand and swing my car key in the other, and then I'd slowly go down the stairs and walk to my car like a lady, and in front of everybody I'd confidently open the door, glide onto the seat, and drive wherever I pleased!"

Her dreams reminded me strongly of those Egyptian film scenes where frail, beautiful, upper-middle-class young women behaved exactly that way. They were pretty enough, but didn't those slushy film heroines always meet with tragic, dramatic ends?

Nadja claimed my attention. I enjoyed watching her walk from one room to the other with a spring in her step. She had a bouncy walk; with every step her thin hips took in the whole space right and left. Time and time again, she shook her head softly so that her hair stroked her face gently. She never came near a mirror without looking at it to see her youthful beauty confirmed.

I caught myself copying her movements, strolling through the flat, stopping here and there, shaking my head before moving on, busy. Um Ali moved totally differently: she rushed from one task to the next, she bent down strongly with a jerk, and when she picked something up, she grabbed it and gripped it tightly. She scrubbed the floor with all her muscles and when she wrung out the floor cloth, it seemed as if she were taking the last breath out of its fibers. Practical, efficient, and swift was her basic attitude to work. She didn't allow her body any weakness and even during the breaks when she had tea with my mother, she would stay standing, her eyes roaming for the next task.

"Do sit down, Um Ali," Mother would say. "Life comes to an end, but work never does!"

Um Ali would gently smile, allow herself a light sigh, glance at her daughter and mutter something like, "She'll have a better life..."

To grip tightly, to treat herself to nothing, and to earn money was how she would make this possible. At two o'clock the cleaning came to an end. Um Ali tightened the scarf around her head, and Nadja ran to the mirror, took her comb out of her bag, threw her head forward so that all her hair fell down, brushed it, and then threw her head back in one elegant, strong move. She observed herself once more mischievously in the mirror before the odd couple left us.

"Poor Um Ali," said my mother, "she's such a good and honest soul. I wonder what will become of the two of them?"

THE BITE

Homes in the air had no gardens and so it was customary for all children in the building to meet downstairs and play in front of the building. After making ourselves reasonably at home, once everything had found its place in the house, my elder brother decided one day to go down and have a look around. I followed him and together we stood outside the entrance to our building. Next door stood a small grocer's shop on the right and on the left stretched out a garden that belonged to an old dilapidated house. A giant mulberry tree grew in the middle of the garden, its branches stretched peacefully in all directions, confidently withstanding the test of time.

A few children were downstairs already, some older than my brother, some his age. When they saw us, they came closer and asked my brother: "Who are you?"

"We belong to the tribe of the Rawas, one of the largest and most famous tribes of Iraq!" I would have answered solemnly.

But my brother answered modestly, "I'm Manou and this is my little sister Fawzia."

I was speechless: was that all? Here it seemed to be enough, and the others also introduced themselves with their first names only. The children decided to include my brother in their game, but they ignored me. Strangely enough, my brother didn't seem to notice this—apparently he was so happy to have been accepted in the new group that he didn't mind exchanging his little sister for it. I watched them play from a distance.

One of the boys had a ball and they divided into two groups. One team stood on the left, the other on the right, and in the middle were children from both teams. While the ball was thrown from one side to the other, the children in the middle had to catch it and throw it back to their team. This was how you scored points, and the first team to score ten won. My brother was in the middle field, happy and concentrated, he jumped as high as he could when the ball came, eager to demonstrate his competence and prove himself to be an honorable new member.

My brother and an older boy from the other team jumped, collided, and my brother caught the ball. Suddenly all the children stood still. The elder boy took the ball from my brother, billowed his chest, and rammed my brother.

"Hey, I'm the leader here and if I catch the ball, then you don't interfere!"

Two younger boys came next to him and started intimidating my brother. They kept pushing him further back and I saw my brother go paler and paler and lose confidence.

The Lebanese dialect spoken by the youngsters was a little foreign to us, which only made him even more insecure, and I noticed that his silence came mostly from the fact that he couldn't communicate in their dialect. But they seemed to interpret this as weakness and they enjoyed their power. Fists were raised and threatening gestures made at my brother's face. Manou seemed close to tears, but I would not allow them this triumph. Not one drop of the water of life would they get for their mean ways. Small as I was, I crawled on my knees in the middle of a commotion of excited child-legs, until I reached the leader. I calmly lifted his trouser leg and bit into his calf with all the strength of a healthy child's teeth.

Now that was a loud shout! All the children jumped back in horror and their leader tried to shake me off by desperately kicking his leg.

I too wanted to let go, but my bite had taken a life of its own, and only when he stood still and in tears did I let go. Isn't it amazing how quickly the balance of power can shift among human beings!

They looked wide-eyed at Manou and his beastly sister and a respectful distance appeared, especially around me.

"*Magnuna*! She's crazy!" shouted Hisham, their leader. "You've destroyed my leg!"

Interestingly enough, I suddenly understood the Lebanese dialect perfectly. "Who are you actually?"

The moment seemed right: "I am Fawzia, Manou's little sister, from the tribes of the Rawas! We... " I wanted to add a few noble explanations, but it seemed enough.

We were quickly adopted into the community of children and Hisham and I became good friends. He admired me and henceforth I became quite famous. Whenever a new child arrived, we were introduced as follows: "Here are Manou and Fawzia!" And they added softly: "Be careful, the little one's dangerous—she bites!"

I'M A CHRISTIAN, WHO ARE YOU?

*Yet without greeting life as a whole, you can only live within
the limited world of your own understanding...*
—Unknown

In Beirut I went to a mixed private school that had developed the interesting concept of joining two school systems into one, integrating Arab and foreign (mostly European) pupils. The project had been developed by the German government especially for Lebanon. Four languages were taught in that school: Arabic, German, English, and French. Latin and Spanish were secondary subjects.

Two systems coexisted: the Arabic–Lebanese and the German–European. Arab pupils were required to complete both systems, whereas European pupils only needed to complete one. In the German system lessons were taught in German. Biology, physics, mathematics, geography, and history were therefore taught according to the German European concept. We Arab pupils followed this teaching, in addition to which we also had to learn the whole Arabic program taught in Arab schools. We thus had classes in Arab geography, history, mathematics, and of course in Arabic—grammar, literature, and so on. This is how the Arab pupils came to taste and work hard in both systems.

Not surprisingly, I often envied the "Europeans" because they had much more free time, and I could hear them playing in the yard while we declined our Arabic sentences. But sometimes we would also feel slightly superior because we learned more. The general atmosphere at school was balanced and pleasant, and the pupils' varied socio-cultural backgrounds were an enrichment. Looking back, they also had a positive influence on our attitude to life. A black-and-white picture of life was hardly possible given the multicolored ethnic and religious mix of pupils.

This was no small miracle, especially in Lebanon, where ethnic and social heterogeneity determined so much. From shoe-cleaner to minister, all were identified by their religious beliefs. In Lebanon in the 1970s, there were fifteen—later came another three—officially recognized religious communities, and all issues, all decisions, were dealt with on the basis of their respective rules. Ascertaining everyone's religion was therefore of utmost importance. The Lebanese had developed a quick sense for this: from the first moment, they could tell to which community you belonged, from your posture, movements, pronunciation and choice of words, from the expression of your eyes, and of course from your clothes. An interesting game, and new to me.

Unlike Iraq, the weak Lebanese state, which had scant resources, made this ethnic and religious social division into a ruling formula: the stronger the division of society into various small communities, the better the control over the society. All civil matters such as marriage, divorce, and inheritance were ruled and controlled by the respective religious communities.

The Lebanese were an ingenious and efficient folk with a great talent for trade, which they have enjoyed ever since the time of the Phoenicians. Their sense for life's pleasures reflected most intensely in the capital: Beirut pulsated with the light of seductive glamour, sensual pleasures, and winking eyes. This place was definitely paradise on earth for the rich, the young, and the beautiful.

Most of the country's economic opportunities were in private hands, which admittedly led to exploitation and corruption, but also to quick money. And the Lebanese—men and women—seemed quite willing to sacrifice a lot for prestige and looks.

I loved sitting in the back of my parents' car, driving through the streets of Beirut, because it was like attending a live fashion show. Male or female, no one with any pride would venture into the streets without adequate preparation and the latest fashion.

This was no game but a matter of honor, since in Beirut you were judged more on appearances than on personality. If you also happened to belong to an influential family, the picture was just perfect.

Yet Beirut had more to offer. It was ostentatious, but also cultivated; while symbolizing insatiability, it also stood for intellectual cosmopolitanism and Mediterranean charm. Despite the contemporary veneer of French *pénétration culturelle* and the imitation of the American way of life, Phoenician, Hellenic, and Levantine classical antiquity and civilization flowed through the veins of the city and its people.

Beirut had many different faces and energies, which were reflected in the different districts. Shiyyah, for instance, a poorer, conservative, Shiite quarter, was dominated by Islamic customs, and extended families and clan structures represented the major institutions. The Shiite population was at a social, financial, and educational disadvantage in Lebanon, so the family structure was the individual's main social security network.

The steep quarter of Ashrafiyye, on the other hand, was a conservative Christian stronghold. There too, family ties and clan thinking played an important part, but also education and trends were adopted and copied from the Christian West. Although the various Christian factions lived next to each other, one was expected to marry within one's own religious community.

All women could work or go into business, as long as they abided by the rules of the extended family and conformed to its social and political clan structures. The motto was that individual strength is the group's strength. The clan's hierarchical structure provided protection and support, while demanding loyalty and obedience. It was not only a social institution, but played a vital part in the economy. Individual loyalty meant, for instance, supporting the patron, *za'im*, during parliamentary elections by campaigning and voting for him. Extraordinarily, women could even become head of the family.

People would socialize, send their children to the same schools, go to the same restaurants and theaters, discuss the same new publications. Occasionally they even married outside the limits of their own community. In this district, one could watch the evolution that would gradually spread to the whole country, with the emergence of a secular society, despite the opposition of the political and religious elite.

Ras Beirut was also home to many intellectuals who had a different point of view: "They want to convince us that the basic problem of Lebanese society comes from the split into ethnic and religious groups, but that's not quite true," a friend explained to my mother. "This society is actually divided in classes, just like all other Middle-Eastern societies. The Maronite small farmer identifies more with the Shiite small farmer than with the Maronite bourgeois city dweller. Their similar situations create a strong bond. Those at the top fight for power and people are being persuaded that it's an ethnic and religious debate. Isn't Ras Beirut living proof that the different religious groups have more in common when they belong to the same class? You're a Christian and I'm a Muslim, yet the language we speak and our vision of life are closer than those of the same religion who belong to different classes. But this threatens the very existence of those in power because it would mean the collapse of their clever 'divide and rule' system."

Ras Beirut was Mother's favorite neighborhood and it was indeed particularly beautiful, right by the seaside, where the eye could see all the way to the horizon. Could it be that this openness influences people's views?

A few months later, we too moved into this quarter. We lived on the third floor, which was fine, because I had come to enjoy living "on the heights." Here, the view from the sitting and dining rooms was breathtaking. Every day I was greeted by the sea and the majesty of its eternal, leisurely movements. It became my best friend in Lebanon. Upon waking, the first thing I did was to go to the window and say good morning, and in the evening I would let my eyes glide on the dark mass and go to bed with the warm feeling of eternity. How similar were the desert and the sea! Both filled my soul with a longing that burned inside me and warmed my heart.

I had always enjoyed observing people and listening to grownups carefully while they discussed their plans and worries, or analyzed world events (one of Middle-Eastern people's favorite pastimes), but I had never really felt a part of it. The wind caressing my cheeks when I stood on the balcony, softly whispering secrets into my ear, the sea rising up against the cliffs and revealing its foam, the dead bird in whose entrails maggots refreshed themselves—all those felt closer to me than beautifully clad adults who could sit for hours, ceaselessly talking without ever changing position. They did their best to keep the flow of words going, as if silence were the big people's greatest *faux-pas*.

Father loved company. He loved people so much that he often forgot himself and his family for their sake. To my mother's dismay and quite against her will, he would often turn up for lunch unexpectedly—with five or six friends in tow. I understood him well—it was his way of making up for the extended family he missed. But I didn't have to do all the cooking!

In Ras Beirut, too, our neighbors were a mixture, but different from the ones in Shiyyah. Opposite us lived a young Japanese family, with their three-year-old son Takau. Below us lived a famous Palestinian painter, Joumana al-Husseini, with her son Samir. I took an instant shine to him, but since I was only eleven and he sixteen, he didn't take too much notice of me. Diagonally below us lived a Sunni family, very nice people according to my mother, but I hardly ever saw them. I only used to see the father, a lawyer, when he left in his big car in the morning and came back in the late afternoon.

Opposite them lived an Englishwoman who was married to a Lebanese surgeon and had two sweet daughters. Above us lived a newlywed couple. She was half-Lebanese, half-Qatari. This young woman was so beautiful that I was happy whenever my mother went upstairs for a coffee, because I could go with her and admire her shyly from a corner. She had huge velvet, peaceful eyes, thick kohl-black hair, and in the color of her skin played the most beautiful hues of a Levantine and a Bedouin. The movements of her willowy body and her delicate hands resembled more those of a gazelle than a human being.

The building's caretaker and his family were Palestinian. They regularly visited their relatives who lived in one of the Palestinian camps, and they saw it as a special privilege to be able to live and work here in the house, outside the camp. They had three children who always played downstairs in the garden and whose big eyes would follow every passerby as if they were on their guard. The caretaker next door was a Kurd. People whispered he was a communist, whatever that meant. I couldn't find out despite careful observation, except that his children were particularly clean and polite.

Mother was extremely sociable and curious about life. She was not in the least concerned by ethnic and social differences, and so we were in contact with all the people around us.

Unfortunately, she had another major weakness, which she inflicted upon us children: she loved old stones, indeed everything dead and old. The older the more interesting and the further away she was willing to travel. Those stone-people are usually called archaeologists, but when they happen to be your mother, you just call them tiring. Over the next couple of years in Lebanon, we would get to know every single old stone in the country. The biggest one, in Balbek, near the fertile Beqaa plain, even did something for me. I don't know how many hours of my life I have spent sleeping in the back of the car on one of our "today-we'll-make-an-interesting-and-absolutely-major-discovery" weekend expeditions.

At the end of the 1960s, Lebanon coasted along on a period of growth and prosperity. It was dubbed the "Switzerland of the Middle East" and visitors from all over the world enjoyed the relative economic and political openness that reigned here. Indeed, Lebanon had much to offer. You could enjoy the sea and its countless bathing clubs in the morning; in less than an hour's drive, you could be skiing in the mountains, and in the evening, you could enjoy yourself until dawn in the many bars and nightclubs. Lebanon was also strewn with sights: Balbek in the Beqaa plain, with its Greek pillars soaring into the sky and the many ruins of the Roman Empire, 6000-year-old Byblos with its Phoenician harbor, King Ahiram's mausoleum, and the Roman amphitheater, a favorite Sunday excursion for many Lebanese, with pleasant fish restaurants along the harbor.

The Lebanese were culinary masters. Not only did their food taste wonderful, it was also balanced and healthy. When you ate out, it was customary to order a *mezze* (appetizers); the table was then decorated with different starters laid on small plates: *tabouleh*, served with fresh green lettuce, *hummus*, *baba ghanoush*, to name but a few typical dishes.

The *mezze* are actually used for entertainment: people sit together and chat, while reaching every now and again for the plates with a piece of unleavened bread to scoop a morsel. The choice seemed limitless and once you had nearly eaten to your heart's content, then came the main dish, usually grilled fish, meat, or chicken. After the meal came invariably the water pipe with honey-soaked tobacco, which was enjoyed by men and women alike, and the wonderful cardamom-scented Arabic coffee. The Lebanese really knew about enjoyment!

85

But as far as I was concerned, my favorite food was *mna'ish* which, eaten with a cup of sweet tea, made the most succulent breakfast. This is because *mna'ish* taste best soon after sunrise. Luckily for me, our bus driver was also a fanatic of the *mna'ish* culture. When the bus picked me up at 6:20 in the morning—I was first on the route and it took an hour to drive to school and collect all the pupils—and I looked particularly tired, Abu Ali, the driver, would cheer me up by saying, "How about some *mna'ish*?" Those words never failed to curl my lips into a sweet smile. We even had our favorite baker, whose shop was on the way, thank God.

"*Sabah il-cher, ya'tik il-afiye*! Good morning, may Allah give you vitality and good health, five *mna'ish*, ya Abu Mahmoud! One more round and I'll pick them up!"

Soon after we were back, and the heavenly scented, paper-wrapped warm *mna'ish* were pressed into our hands.

"The art of the *mna'ish* isn't just in the dough, my child," Abu Ali philosophized, "it comes from the proper mix of *za'tar*. You take a big handful of finely ground thyme leaves, add one and a half tablespoons of *sumak*, carob bean, two tablespoons of roasted sesame seeds, one teaspoon of salt, one teaspoon of red pepper, and a cup of olive oil. Some people add a small, finely chopped onion. This is how my mother prepared it, and my wife has learned it from her."

As long as I could chew on a *mna'ish*, Abu Ali could talk as much as he wanted. It was a long drive to school, but never boring. I always kept the back row in the bus for my friends and every day we'd make up new games—music orchestra was top on the list—or we would quickly write the forgotten homework or rehearse the Arabic poems we had to learn by heart. Our school was outside the city, in Doha. It was located on a wonderfully empty hill, overlooking the sea. Only bushes and cliffs surrounded it and, in the distance, a few scattered houses. You could see the sea from the classroom and this open landscape somehow turned the entire time at school into a time for the muses.

NO ONE SHALL STEAL THIS DREAM
FROM ME

The lover sees with the heart,
so leave to the heart what it has chosen.
Not with the eyes does one see in love,
and through the heart only the ears can hear.
—Bashar Ibn Burd, an Arab poet

My father worked with a young man who often visited us at home. He was nice and tall, and he had dark hair and a friendly smile. I noticed that whenever he came to visit, Nadja went through a sudden metamorphosis. Her face turned a silky red and her otherwise very soft movements became nervous and slightly uncontrolled. Her voice softened and a shy giggle ended her whispered sentences.

I also realized that she took no notice of me and that my questions went unheard. But she jumped all the faster when Mother called her, thus giving her an opportunity to go into the living room and see Isa, the young man. Isa was very friendly to her, but I could not see any change in him when Nadja appeared. With time, things worsened and Nadja seemed to remain in this confused state even when he was not present.

One day Mother called Nadja. I followed her because I knew from Mother's voice that the talk would be about some serious matter. Unfortunately I was sent away and soon after Nadja came out, too, with tears in her eyes and anger in her belly.

"What's the matter?" I asked.

But no one would tell me anything, and only after overhearing several snatches of conversation between my parents and after much observing did I grasp the whole issue. Nadja, a young Shiite woman from a humble background, had fallen in love with Isa, a Christian who enjoyed a better social position.

Her love had driven her to disguise herself and follow him, with a dark pair of sunglasses and a headscarf. But Isa had recognized her all the same. After she had followed him several times, he had spoken to her. He felt flattered and inviting her for a drink meant nothing special to him. This happened a few times and Nadja was spotted by acquaintances who told my mother. Nadja was lucky that they had been so tactful and not brought the news to Nadja's father.

Mother and Father questioned Isa who acknowledged meeting Nadja.

"I find her pretty and she's a nice girl," he admitted.

"Are your intentions serious?" came the next question.

"Marriage? No. It would be far too complicated to marry a woman from another faith, and even if my parents agreed, hers would certainly never agree."

He was quite right. Conservative, Shiite Lebanese would not agree to such a wedding.

"Anyhow, I'd like to enjoy my life, not complicate it. I already have my eyes on a girl who comes from the same social background as I do. She is educated and we can build something together. She too is a Christian and our families would complete each other nicely. I feel a bit sorry for Nadja — I only wanted to make her a little happy, nothing more. I haven't raised her hopes!"

All this was passed on to Nadja and her whole world collapsed. But she wouldn't give up so easily. At home with us she became moody and her beautiful dark eyes blazed angrily while thoughts circled almost visibly in her head. She saw Isa as her hero, the one who could offer her a better, freer, more open life. A good-looking man she could look up to, who treated her pleasantly, who owned a car, at whose side she could at last be free and break out of her narrow world.

No one would steal this dream from her! Everyone was just jealous, they wouldn't allow her this love. All of them were liars, she was sure of that.

"I am Nadja—I don't always want to be this one's daughter, that one's sister, the other's niece, and the other's neighbor's daughter! I don't need the shelter of the family. The family protects me but it also takes the air away from me. I don't want to be always hemmed in, I don't want to be always part of a herd! I'm not afraid, I'm not afraid!"

It was total chaos at home. Mother sympathized with her. She could understand her and her longings, yet she also knew that it was hard for girls like Nadja, who came from a poor and conservative background, to break free. The price would be the bitter pill of loneliness and isolation, which could be exploited by others. Mother was ready to help her within the bounds of her family, to talk with her father, to enable her to train as a hairdresser or in another profession. She was willing to offer her a free space within her home, in which she could collect her thoughts and express her wishes, but she could not and would not be responsible for more. I didn't understand much of all that went on, but I felt the tension and saw Nadja become thinner and thinner. I saw her sink deeper into despair and retreat into herself before bursting out in tears.

Um Ali suffered most. She tried to talk to her daughter in her simple way, but Nadja would not listen. In her despair, Um Ali would then hit her: "You harlot, you only think about yourself. What kind of example are you to your sisters. No one will ask for your hand if you destroy the reputation of the family. Where am I to turn my face if word goes around that you go out with strange men! Why can't you come to reason, why can't you come to reason!"

Nadja let her strike her and pull her hair. She was willing to accept everything except giving up on her dream, giving up on Isa.

"Not like this, Um Ali, leave the poor child!" Mother stepped in and Um Ali collapsed.

"What shall I do? What shall I do with this girl?" she mumbled.

Nadja stood up, ran to the door and disappeared with a bang. She was gone for two whole days. No one knew where she was. On the third day, Father and Mother drove to Isa. Had he seen her? Isa was a little embarrassed. Yes, Nadja had come to him. She had thrown herself into his arms, she had offered herself to him.

It had been difficult for him to resist, but he had been reasonable enough to send her away. He explained to her that he wouldn't marry her, that he had someone else. Nadja had then disappeared again, in tears. He did not know where she was.

"I hope she hasn't come to any harm!" Mother was deeply worried. She felt partly responsible.

In the evening the phone rang. Nadja had been found at her aunt's. Everyone was relieved.

Several months went by and we didn't hear anything from Nadja. My thoughts kept returning to her. She was my friend, wasn't she, so why didn't she come? Mother didn't speak about Nadja either and when Um Ali came, they discussed everything but her, as if she had never existed, and I didn't dare ask about her.

Time passed. Nadja and Um Ali had long left our life when I suddenly heard my name called out on the street. I turned around and there she was, with a huge confident smile.

"*Kifik habibti*, how are you, my love?" I looked at her wide-eyed and when my eyes came to rest on her round belly, she laughed.

"My third belly, I have two daughters!"

I was totally confused. Isa came instantly to my mind. Could it be him?

"Come, you must have coffee with me at home, I live just here." She waved to the back. Nadja's outward appearance had hardly changed, she still wore her hair long and uncovered, and even her figure was the same, as far down as her protruding belly. She looked so beautiful!

"I'm sorry, I can't."

But that was not true, I had only said so out of politeness, to give her the possibility to repeat her invitation twice more, as custom dictates, so that I could be sure she really meant it. My curiosity was far too great for me not to have the time.

She led me to a three-story house. Once we had reached it, she called out: "Hasan, Hasan, come, we have a visitor!"

A very nice man came out of the electrical shop. His skin was a warm shade of brown, his eyes sparkled with life, and his smile was inviting.

"*Ahlan, ahlan*! Nadja's friends are always welcome!"

Nadja explained to him quickly who I was and he repeated his friendly invitation. I liked him even better than Isa. A heavy weight fell from my heart. Nadja had struck it lucky after all. From the way he spoke and his attitude to her I immediately realized that he was politically educated, most probably liberal left.

"Go upstairs, I'll be right with you! Take good care of our guest."

"But of course!"

Nadja was beaming. She seemed happy and content, and it warmed my heart.

"Can you still remember what happened at your place?"

And how I could remember! I had carried the despair and pain she felt at the time to that very day. Maybe that was why fate had wanted us to meet, so that I could be free of the burden.

"Hasan is a Palestinian. He is very active and I help him change our society. We can talk about everything and he shares everything with me. He is a good man and a wonderful father. My daughters are lucky!"

She smiled again, "I'm very happy that it turned out this way. But without my first experience maybe I wouldn't have had the courage to associate with such a man, and my parents wouldn't have agreed. But they were happy that I married at least, albeit a Palestinian and a Sunni, but all the same!"

Hasan came and we had coffee and exchanged a few words before I excused myself. It was nice to have seen Nadja. The rebel had changed into a self-confident woman and it felt good to know that she had found her way and that she hadn't given up on her dream.

THE ETERNAL FLOW OF THE OCEAN

The drop: "How far I am from the ocean!"
The world ocean laughs: "Your sorrow is in vain!
Aren't we all one, all God...
Only the smallest dot separates us... time!"
—Omar Khayyam

Indifferent to the confusion and errors of human beings, the sea moved in its eternal rhythm. As was my habit, I stood on the balcony and watched the waves. The sea felt like my own breathing: unwavering, pulsating, detached from the moods and thoughts crowding my body, my breast rose and fell. If human beings paid greater attention to those inner wonders, to the devotion with which our hearts work and pump for us day and night, we would recognize more what we have in common than what differences divide us. But who wastes time on such things?

Screeching tires—a car spins out, but the driver manages to regain control at the very last minute. The road that separated us from the ocean was also the scene of countless car accidents, which suddenly seemed symbolic to me. Why are those many people always rushing? What pushes them to hurry all the time, to hoot, to flee? Always running into the future, where happiness lies, always carefully carrying with them the bundle of the past.

The ocean rises and falls like breathing, an eternal beat. What is that rhythm, great sister, and why isn't anyone listening?

"Get ready, we're going riding!" my mother's voice rang out.

In an instant, gone were my thoughts! I ran inside, dressed in no time, and moments later we were in the car, driving to the stables. Here too, you could choose. If you were into prestige and glamour, you went riding in the "Horse Club"; if not, you went to another club, a little further away. That one was near the two Palestinian camps of Sabra and Shatila.

Whenever we arrived, I often saw children my age, marching barefoot two by two, with a stick on the right shoulder, shouting *idbah al-aduh*, "kill the enemy." It was clear who the enemy was! The camps consisted mainly of barracks and patched up crates, with women endlessly washing in large buckets in front of the huts.

"Mummy, why don't they build better houses for these people?"

"They do it on purpose, so that they won't forget their homeland, Palestine. If they had a good life here, they might forget."

Well, if you wait four, five, or six years, it may be good, but these people had been waiting for over thirty years! Their longing, their common goal forged the bond between them. I suddenly saw them differently. Yes, Lebanon was indeed a very confusing country, with its Druze, Maronites, Armenians, Shiites, Kurds, and Palestinians, and somehow they didn't seem to like each other. Had it always been that way? The wonderful, God-given Lebanese scenery stood in sharp contrast to all this human confusion.

Injustice and the resulting clashes between the various faith and clan organizations started for many with the French occupation. When the French Levantine army seized the Syrian mandate, it proclaimed Lebanon as home to the oriental Christians[1] under the effective leadership of the Maronites,[2] without taking into consideration the fact that nearly 70 percent of the population were Muslim and Druze. This unjust distribution of power laid the foundation for ceaseless tides of violence and anger.

The religious communities quarrelled steadily every ten years and a new civil war eventually erupted in the history of

Lebanon. In 1958 the Druze and Muslim opposition rebelled against the ruling Christians and in the 1970s a new wave of violence seemed to take shape, this time with a new actor: the Palestinians, whose Palestinian Liberation Organization (PLO) was officially created in 1964.

The Palestinians needed a base, a country from where they could carry out their goal to recapture Palestine. They had tried to convert Jordan into a platform for their military clashes against Israel. But once they had become a political force within the country and they developed into a threat to the regime, King Hussein replied in 1970 with a fierce and bloody counterstroke.

In order to gather the *fedayeen* (freedom fighters) scattered throughout the country, King Hussein offered Yasir Arafat the region of Jerash as headquarters. Arafat accepted, thereby falling into the trap that had been laid for him. Once they had all gathered there, King Hussein arranged a bloodbath with his tanks and Bedouin fighters. Since the PLO often operated from refugee camps, Palestinian civilians suffered greatly. Many of them were among the over 3,000 dead of "Black September," the name under which this event was written in the tragic history of the Palestinians. The remaining Palestinian refugees were submitted to rigorous governmental control and the surviving partisans of Yasir Arafat had no choice but to flee, mostly to Lebanon. There they would be greeted by a Palestinian population that had been living since 1948 in "temporary" refugee camps, where in the meantime the third generation was being raised.

The political explosive had accumulated in the "Oriental Switzerland" since the 1958 civil war. Muslims and Druze, pan-Arabs, left-wing extremists, all had felt inferior to the Christian commanding armed forces. When the PLO appeared they hoped to gain an ally with whom they could gain their political rights. The PLO's political power increased speedily. They demanded the right to a say in decisions and soon became a state within the state that stood up to the Lebanese police and army.

Neighboring Israel did not watch idly, and Israeli air raids on Palestinian villages and camps became part of our everyday life. Those raids sometimes caught us on our way to school. The school bus driver would then shout: "Duck and hold tight, children!" while we rushed home among falling bombs. It was always the bus driver's nerves that couldn't take any more—we children found it rather, well, frightening and exciting at the same time.

The Christian Maronites felt not only their privileges but their very existence threatened. All the conditions for civil war were ripe when they called up their militias in order to meet that threat, which was lethal to them, by force of arms. In Ain Rumanieh, a suburb of Beirut, the straw broke the camel's back when a bus full of armed Palestinians on the road to Damascus fell into a Phalangist ambush and was massacred. Then the Muslims, the left-wing groups, and the PLO fighters lined up against the Christian right-wing militias.

LEBANESE DEATH DANCE

Better to live under the wing of a fly
than to lie dead in the graveyard.
—Arab proverb

The events that took place in Beirut in the following years were truly the most absurd, surreal scene of human activity that I have ever experienced, for it included all the facets of human existence. Beirut was torn to pieces, crushed and raped by its people, re-awoken to life, only to be scornfully knocked down again, while amid the whole deadly tangle and the dreadful massacres an animal celebration of life took place: dancing with corpses, dining quietly and fashionably. The delicate skin tanned on the beach and the heart was roughly pushed back into the unconscious.

Valium to numb the senses and quiet the nerves now stood on every bedside table. People turned gray overnight and the fruit of decades of work disappeared in an instant under an exploding bomb. Fronts shifted, Beirut was split into East and West and human hearts began to harden from inside, as is always the case when the "enemy" is pushed back into the invisible and the abstract. The Lebanese now spoke about "we" and "those over there," meaning the Muslims on one side and the Christians on the other, but of course it was all much more complicated and confused and oriental than that.

There were two main corridors that could be used to dive into the other "world," if one had the courage and an inborn liking for risk, a measure of gambling spirit, or a certain God-given ingenuousness like I did, which I believe I inherited from my mother. One crossing followed the race-track alongside the Lebanese national museum and the other, even crazier, went through the harbor.

Mother refused to have anything to do with all these stupid politics, as she called it. She didn't see why, all of a sudden, she should stop going to visit her Christian, Armenian, or Kurdish friends, the poor ones being now exactly on the border of the no man's land. And we children always went with her. I believe courage is handed down from mother to daughter. My father kept tearing his hair out, but what can a man do against a determined woman?

Mother sat behind the wheel, in her casually brave style, and we drove through Mazra'a, once a mixed neighborhood of upper-middle-class Sunnis, well-to-do Shiites, old established Christians, and a few Kurds. The so-called no man's land started right next to Mazra'a. You became an outlaw once you were there, and when times were very bad, those who had been shot down by snipers were only carried away after several hours, or even several days.

The back of Mother's neck tensed up and I noticed how her head sought protection between her shoulders, but she did not let it show and went on driving at the same speed. The eastern part of Beirut was controlled by Christian Phalangists. Once we were there, my brother was no longer called Bilal, a Muslim name, but "Dudu," as my younger sister always called him.

"Better to be on the safe side, we don't want to get into unnecessary trouble," was my mother's comment on this change of name.

I kept having to repeat it to myself because I felt confused with all these adjustments. The world of grownups was really a strain. Mother was actually quite right because there were road blocks, whether Muslim or Christian, where one's religion meant at least kidnapping, or even death. The devastating civil war had taken on numerous macabre and confusing forms. Religious identity became political, and everybody turned into a walking political conviction, evinced by increasingly bigger crosses worn on the breast or suddenly strictly-enforced Islamic regulations. Some stuck even more to the family as the institution of social support, while others used the civil war chaos to relinquish all taboos and morals, and finally to live as free individuals.

Small groups of young people emerged who created their own worlds within the social ruins. They lived according to their own ideas, had sexual relationships with each other, philosophized, and took drugs. They simply did everything that occurred to them, because they did not know whether they would still be alive the next day or what the whole scene would look like in the end.

"A friend of mine meets a clique. She has a friend, his name is Rami," whispered Rosa excitedly. "She's sleeping with him," her voice went even softer with those words. "Can you imagine, when I asked her if she wasn't afraid of her family, she only said mockingly: 'Who cares about virginity in this chaos! I have no idea whether I'll ever marry, let alone whether I'll survive! All I know is that I'm alive now!'"

Rosa's mother was a very capable businesswoman. She owned an exclusive shoe shop in the old shopping district, close to the former Jewish quarter. After the old city was torn apart in the war, like many other Christians she moved to Jounieh, a small port that had developed into a miniature Maronite state, and opened a shoe shop there. I liked this small, self-confident woman very much—she seemed to know exactly what she wanted from life. There was nothing motherly or sentimental about her and she treated all family members as responsible individuals. She travelled twice a year with her husband to Italy to bring back the latest fashions, and she had some of the models copied in Lebanon. Her husband helped her but she was clearly the boss. He had a small textile firm with ten seamstresses, and manufactured mainly men's shirts and women's night-shirts.

Rosa's mother had been able to build up her business thanks to the children's nanny, Wafa'. Wafa' means "the faithful one," and she was truly a loyal soul. She would look after the four children and whenever problems arose, she was the one the children first went to for advice. "Wafa' has been with us for over twenty years already. She never started her own family, and we have become her children," Rosa would say. Every two months she visited her brothers, but the rest of the time she lived in Rosa's family.

Rosa enjoyed much freedom. Her mother trusted her and saw her as the heiress to her business and she wanted to pass on to her the connections she had worked hard to make. They had an agreement: Rosa was totally free but she had to make one promise.

"As long as you are a virgin, you can come and go, study, get a job, meet your friends. Should anyone say anything, I can answer back and say that you are an honorable girl. But without this proof, which will come out sooner or later, we lose face!"

Rosa stuck strictly to the agreement. Her family's reputation and good name mattered more to her than any adventures or own wishes.

In that sad civil war, the Christians seemed to lose the battle against Palestinian and left-wing Muslim fighters. Then the Syrian army came into the picture. It defended the Christians, and fierce battles erupted between the Syrians and the Palestinians. In order to restore the peace, following protracted negotiations, an Arab peacekeeping force was sent to Lebanon, the so-called Arab deterrent force, which was made up of Saudis, Libyans, Sudanese, and Syrians.

The checkpoints had become even more colorful. The funniest were the Saudis. If a woman drove by, they stopped her, but although they asked for her identification, they did not look at it because they were too shy even to look at the picture of an unveiled woman. I felt sorry for them, those poor peace defenders. They were as ill-suited to this confusing Lebanese scene as their desert-colored camouflage suits.

There was a Sudanese checkpoint next to our house and on a mild afternoon one of the soldiers was sitting on the hill right next to my favorite field. I sat down a little ways behind and observed him. He looked old to me, but he couldn't have been over forty. He stared at the sea, motionless, and seemed lonely, lost, and nauseated. I crept toward him, determined to take a closer look at his dark face. Without noticing, I stepped right into a swarm of giant locusts. They came from Africa and visited Lebanon every year. Overcome by horror and fear, I shouted, jumped up and ran away, exactly toward the soldier.

"What's up, my child?" he asked in Arabic.

But I could not speak a word—somehow I hadn't expected him to speak Arabic.

"Where do you come from?" was the first spontaneous

question I asked. Not very polite, I thought to myself, quickly adding a *salamu alaykum*.

"Peace be with you too," he answered with a smile. "I have a daughter who's about your age. I belong to the peace-keeping force, which isn't one, and I come from Sudan."

A peace-keeping force which isn't one—what could that mean?

He must have read my mind, because, looking at the sea, he went on: "They think we're naive and we don't know what's going on. Poor Lebanon, this country will have to put up with many years of war. I will long be gone home and there will still be war here. The peacekeeping force will go, the Syrians will stay. Neither the Syrians nor the Israelis want peace in this country."

What the soldier said couldn't be right. Back home, they kept saying it would all be over in a couple of months. In a couple of months, everything would be built up and normal life could start again.

But how right he was! The peacekeeping force left, the Syrians stayed (and they are still here today) and ruled according the famous motto "divide and conquer"! Once the Palestinians and the "progressivists" had been crushed, it was the Maronites' turn.

Israel, whose obvious interference in Lebanon had started with the presence of the PLO, had planned to take the Christians under its wing and to deliver arms to them. But when Jounieh was caught in the Syrian pincers' grip, they watched and did nothing.

Their true aim was not to help the Maronites but to get involved in the Lebanese tangle and above all to keep the Palestinians under control. When South Lebanon, which the Palestinians had built into a base for an attack against Israel, was invaded in 1978, not only Palestinians but also many Lebanese were killed.

After the invasion, Israel built a 40-kilometer (25-mi) long protection zone, which they have occupied to this date with their allies of the so-called South-Lebanese army.[1] One of the most obvious reasons was of course the large water reserves of this region, which Israel wanted to tap quietly.

One morning we were awakened by the sound of landing missiles. Mother ran to the window and to her horror she saw Israeli ships bombing the coast. "The Israelis are here!"

She needed to say no more: we all jumped out of our beds, quickly dressed, ran down the stairs and to the neighbors' who had a cellar. The only cellar in the whole area. We were greeted by screaming children and nervous, sweating adults. Some had thought of bringing water bottles, which they passed around in a friendly way.

It was hot and sticky in that June of 1982. We stayed in the cellar for a couple of hours, then most of us chose to go up again, preferring to die outside in the fresh air rather than suffocate in the cellar, which had turned into a sauna. So we went back home or rather back to what remained of home. A missile had totally destroyed the top floor, but thank God our flat was still there. We spent the following two and a half months in the most intense war.

The Israelis bombed Beirut from the coast and from the air, and at the same time the Israeli army moved into West Beirut. Street after street, the Israelis fought with tanks and heavy artillery against the Palestinian *fedayeen*. Mother was determined not to watch idly and she demanded the same from us children. We provided the freedom fighters with bread and water, and Mother drove the wounded to the hospitals nearby. She also put her car at their disposal and when it was returned at the end of the day, it was always with more bullet holes. Soon there were more holes than metal to be seen, but our Subaru held out.

The Israeli checkpoints multiplied and it became more and more difficult to take food, water, and information from one checkpoint to another. The whole population suffered from food and water shortages because both were being held back by the Israeli troops.

"Can you imagine?—yesterday I managed to get a cucumber," Sami, one of my brother's friends, explained. "I started eating it with relish when two small children and a pregnant woman ran after me, shouting: 'Give us a piece, too!' I felt so sorry for them, the bite stuck in my throat and I shared the cucumber between the four of us!"

Sami had lost his parents and three brothers and sisters in the war, after a bomb destroyed their house while he was out. He now lived on the streets and had banished all fear of death from his heart. He wanted to go over to his uncle who lived in another quarter of Beirut, but because he was a Palestinian, he was afraid to be caught by the Israelis.

"We'll help you!" my brother and I decided. Without telling anyone, we took Mother's car. I sat at the wheel, my brother next to me, and Sami lay down on the floor at the back of the car, where he could peep between our seats.

Sami knew his way around perfectly and he guided us well through back streets and alleys, but suddenly an Israeli checkpoint was in front of us. Sami quickly ducked under the towel we had taken with us and I drove on with a pounding heart. "Where are you heading?" he asked in Arabic. I decided to speak English and to pretend to be naive.

"We want to go to my girlfriend in Mazra'a—she's leaving for America tomorrow and we wanted to say goodbye."

The Israeli soldier looked at me sternly. I smiled stupidly.

"Who's this?"

"My brother."

"Open the boot!"

I pulled the lever and he went to the back to take a look. I decided to act conceited and to stay in the car. In an emergency, I would accelerate. He walked slowly to the front and looked at the backseat.

"Hello," I shouted quickly, "is there a quick way to Mazra'a?"

The soldier turned and looked at me searchingly.

"Straight on," he answered casually. He slapped his hand on the car and we could go.

Sami removed the towel laughing and the three of us felt like heroes. We reached Mazra'a without further incidents.

"Thank you—you have been a great help. If they had caught us, they would have murdered the three of us, because I have important documents for the head office!"

Impudent, those Palestinians were indeed! But it would not help them much. Under Israeli and international pressure, 8,000 Palestinian fighters and with them Yasir Arafat left Lebanese soil in August for Tunisia and other Arab countries. The PLO said it was retreating in order to spare the Lebanese population any further sufferings. After this period, a new phase started in the history of Lebanon, with Western, in particular American, influence spreading.

The American Marines positioned themselves around Beirut's airport, an Italian contingent was posted around the

Palestinian camps, a French contingent patrolled the city, and a British contingent positioned itself south of the city, not far from an Israeli post. The whole unit went by the name of MNF, or Multinational Force.

In their free time the soldiers visited Hamra, West Beirut's animated shopping street. It was apparent here that this commericial metropolis had a tenacious will to survive. Between war ruins and piled up bags of sand, one could still find every conceivable luxury product. The boutiques with their brand-name goods and newest world creations were mostly visited by the Italians.

With their manly Ray Ban glasses, they were the ones the Lebanese liked best. One could haggle with them, make a little business on the side, and they understood Lebanese wit and charm better than the sterner French or the reserved British. The Americans supported the Lebanese government and helped build up the Lebanese army by providing training and weapons. A period of relief and hope began.

"It will get better—the war is over. Everything will be all right!" people said at home and in the streets.

But to live in Lebanon means to trust one's instinct and there were enough people who knew that it was not over yet. The real problem had not been solved: to achieve a fair distribution of political power and representation among all the Lebanese communities.

In April 1983 the American embassy was blown up. Under pressure from the Americans, Lebanon and Israel had started negotiating to obtain the retreat of the Israelis. The agreement was signed on May 17. It was met with anger by many Muslims, by some Christians, and by the Syrians because they felt that it only served American and Israeli interests.

And so the fights resumed between the Muslim and Christian militias. The Lebanese army was called upon several times by the government to bomb the Shiite quarters of Beirut. Such orders again led to a split in the army since the Shiite soldiers were not willing to obey. The MNF retreated and only the French remained. Once more it came to fights between the Muslim militias who were against the Israeli–American agreement and the Christian militias who were loyal to the president.

The Syrians' influence in Lebanon increased while the decay of the Lebanese army and government accelerated. This also marked the end of Israel's and America's efforts to build a Lebanese government favorable to them. Under pressure from the Syrians and the Muslim leaders, the then President Gemayel was forced to revoke the agreement to withdraw the troops that had been signed one year before.

The Shiite communities started focusing their energy against the Israeli army. They managed several times to inflict severe losses on the Israeli army, thereby undermining for the first time its reputation for invincibility. The Shiites were fed up with being the eternally oppressed and they were ready to die for their rights and their freedom. The Lebanese leaders met several times to discuss political reforms and to grant the Muslim communities their rights. But the Christians feared that this would further weaken their already diminished position and that it would give the Syrians even more influence. Everyone knew that extensive political reforms were needed to build a united, strong, independent Lebanon; yet instead of instituting change, they were all busy with their own strategies and power games.

"Many believe that once the foreign powers finally stop interfering with Lebanon, we won't have any problems and there will be peace. Unfortunately, this is only wishful thinking. It will probably never happen. Lebanon's strategic position is too important. Now the Syrians are here, but they too will sink in the Lebanese marsh. Apart from death and destruction, the war hasn't achieved anything. In terms of reforms, nothing has changed, nothing at all," said the greengrocer in a fatalistic, tired voice.

The Lebanese were very politically aware and during the war switching from one news broadcaster to the next had developed into a national sport. Many Lebanese were sick and tired of the violence, the constant insecurity, the ceaseless closing of schools and universities, the nearly daily power failures, the water shortage, and the permanent worry about family members whenever a new bomb exploded. Those who could afford it looked for a new life abroad. During the summer holidays, they would come for a visit to see what had changed. Most of the time, they would leave after a pleasant summer, for despite everything entertainment, games, discos, and swimming clubs were still plentiful, and they would wait for another year.

"You can live anywhere in the world, but there's nowhere more beautiful than Lebanon!"

Everyone longed to come back and those who stayed behind felt more and more depressed. The devastated economy of the country, the collapse of the Lebanese lira, and the escape of Lebanese capital made life hell for the poor and middle class. Only those who had changed their savings to US dollars, who were supported by family members outside the country, or who belonged to the *nouveaux riches* of the war or to the ruling class, went on living in their oases between the ruins.

Was Lebanon to be built on the divisions between its various religious and ethnic communities, or would it grant men and women a more autonomous life, so that people could contribute to the country and to its future, beyond the constraints of sectarianism?

In March 1998, for the first time in Lebanese history, Lebanese President Hrawi proposed to legitimize the voluntary choice of a civil marriage. Though the bill didn't pass, it was meant to bridge the huge gaps that had formed between the various religious communities during the civil war, and to herald a new era of understanding and tolerance. The Muslim and Christian leaders rejected the proposal vehemently and it was suggested that this new direction be adopted as the nineteenth "faith" group or party. This and similar modern bills would have weakened the clan and family organizations and reinforced the state. Time will tell whether this is the right way for the Lebanese.

LEBANON'S COLORFUL WOMEN

He who takes a wife for her beauty will be deceived;
He who marries a woman for her wealth is greedy;
But he who chooses her for her understanding
can say that he is happily married.
—Arab proverb

Lebanese women are as varied as the country's politics and ethnic groups. You find women sunbathing in small bikinis on the beach of Jounieh, while a few kilometers away, another woman walks the street of Baalbek wearing a *hijab* (head veil). As in so many Arab countries, it is the women who highlight most clearly the different characters and contrasts. The Lebanese government seems to have an interest in preserving these differences and reinforcing them through various patriarchal and sectarian laws.

In 1953 Lebanese women were granted the right to vote and since then many feminist movements have fought for women's rights. In 1996, they succeeded in eliminating all discrimination against women from the Lebanese conventions, with the exception of family law and transmission of Lebanese citizenship through the wife to a non-Lebanese husband, or to her children. In Arab societies, children take on their father's religion and since his faith could be different from the Lebanese mother's, this was seen as potentially disturbing the sectarian balance, since belonging to a religious movement also means belonging to a party.

Despite all the achievements, many legal, mostly sectarian, hurdles remain, which prevent not only equality between women and men, but also among women. This is especially apparent in civil law and in matrimonial law. Since 1959, non-Muslim women are entitled to the same share of the inheritance as their brothers, while most Muslim women only inherit half of that share. The tendency toward social division is particularly marked in matrimonial law: a woman and a man of different confessions can only marry if one of them converts to the other's faith.

Yet ironically, Lebanese law acknowledges civil marriages contracted outside the country. Many couples of different faiths therefore fly to Greece or Cyprus to marry. However, according to Lebanese law, they are still seen as living "in sin," given the absence of a religious marriage. In the case of divorce, the Lebanese court will apply the law of the country in which the marriage was contracted. This is why women's organizations demand that civil marriages be recognized as one more form of marriage in Lebanon, pointing out that this is already the case in two Muslim countries—Tunisia and Turkey—as well as in the greatest part of Christian Europe. But this proposal was not only rejected by the religious leaders, but also by the politicians who draw their power from the fragmented Lebanese communities.

Lebanese women are active participants in all spheres of public life. They represent 27 percent of the country's labor force, but the high positions are nearly exclusively reserved for men, although 50 percent of university graduates are women.[1] It is interesting to note that only 2 percent of the 128 members of parliament are women. The absence of women in high and important positions is in contradiction with their advance in the fields of work and education. Once more, this dichotomy is rooted in the patriarchal and sectarian system of the country.

The strong patriarchal system does not encourage women to participate in politics; male leaders generally hand over their positions to their sons. Only a few Lebanese leaders managed to create power bases in another way. But no sooner did they reach an important political position then they participated in the existing structure instead of continuing to fight it. This is why many women see the creation of a secular state as the only possibility for the granting of equal rights to all Lebanese citizens and for the transition from an archaic political system to a modern state, in which women will have the opportunity to shape the future of Lebanon alongside with men.

"I've always wondered at the assurance and self-confidence with which women move through life in Lebanon. Most of the well-off women remind me of childlike women, spoiled and egocentric, always a hint of boredom around their lips—and yet I envy them that self-confidence and their carefree attitude to the world around them and its many problems. Emotional and intellectual children, they only seem preoccupied by themselves and those close to them. Be beautiful, fresh as a child, demanding in a sweet-moody way, and naive, you need do no more!" said Suha cynically.

She was an ambitious, extremely talented young woman, an active member of a women's organization, but there too she was critical: "Most Lebanese women's organizations only perpetuate the split through their sectarian membership. We have Maronite, Greek Orthodox, and Shiite women's charitable organizations, but we need a nationwide union. People should at last get it into their hearts and minds that we are all Lebanese women!" Suha leaned back in her chair and made an inscrutable face.

She habitually ran her hand through her hair, grasping it, as if this could keep her from fully sliding down the terrible slope of disillusion. Her sharp analytical eye enabled her to see events without sentimentality.

She went on: "Lebanese history always requires a crisis before any reforms of this sectarian system are suggested. In the 1970s, the economic and political situation worsened once more. The progressive, left-wing movements demanded that ta'ifiya (denominationalism) be eliminated and asked for 'almaniya (secularization) of the state machine, as well as improved social conditions for workers and farmers. In my opinion it is a mistake to believe that the Lebanese social and ideological divergences originate in creeds. Lebanon's ruling circles, the US and Israel, and also Saudi Arabia and other governments in the Arab world, saw in the bloodshed one last chance to maintain the artificial barriers between the various sections of the population, the socio-economic relationships of dependence within the population and Lebanon's position as a strategic control center for US political interests, and at the same time to weaken the increasingly strong political presence of the Palestinians.

"Nevertheless in 1976 the patriotic forces managed to reach an agreement and present the Lebanese parliament with a document for a constitutional reform,[2] as well as obtain a cease-fire. Unfortunately, as we already know, this hope was short-lived." She closed her eyes and I felt the pain well up in her heart. She must have seen much suffering during the war.

"Today, after the war massacres, we are once more faced with demands for reforms and I believe we women should take an active part in carrying them through. So many among our Lebanese women thinkers and writers have shown us the disadvantages of sectarianism and of the strict patriarchal system. Layla Baalbaki advocates individual and political freedoms; Ghada Samman demonstrates in her works the importance of self-realization; Hanan al-Shaykh focuses on specific women's issues in the Arab world; and Emily Nasrallah promotes in her works the awareness of feminist-political themes and points out that the development of society cannot take place without changing the situation of women. We are a new generation of women and we will no longer play the old game of Christians and Muslims. Neither will we let ourselves be oppressed by patriarchal structures."

SYRIA

GREAT SYRIA

Syria lies at the junction of three continents. Geographically and historically, it is an extremely varied country: a coastal mountain range, valleys, the Lebanon mountains, highlands, plains, and the Syrian desert ending in the lowland plain between the rivers Euphrates and Tigris. The population is equally varied from both the ethnic and religious viewpoint. Muslims—both Sunnis and Shiites—are in the majority, and there are also Nusairians or Alavites (who revere Ali, the Prophet's cousin, as an incarnation of the Divine), Druze (who revere the enraptured Fatimid ruler al-Hakim[1] in a religious system that entails mystical and pantheist elements), Jews, Maronites, Catholics of the Syrian Church, Greek Orthodox, and other Christian minorities. This colorful crowd lives in cities, on the land, or as nomads or half-nomads.

The way from Lebanon to Damascus goes over a nearly deadly mountain road, which most taxi drivers travel as if they wanted to test whether Allah has granted them an extension of life. So if you manage to reach Damascus safe and sound, once your fingers have relaxed and you feel grateful to be alive, you can open your eyes and look curiously at the throng of the city.

The next minute you find yourself in a different state, your nose itching with the stench of gasoline, and your head slightly muzzy. Funny how gas doesn't seem to be properly filtered in this country. Visitors to Damascus are first drawn to the overflowing souks and at the heart of the souks is the famous Umayyad mosque, built from 706 to 715. Both the great mosque and the markets are typical of Muslim cities.

The Umayyads, the first caliphate outside the Arabian peninsula, had chosen Damascus as capital and seat of the caliphate. The founder of the dynasty was the famous caliph Mu'awiya.[2] He was a gifted statesman who described his diplomacy as follows: "There is a silk thread between me and my people. If they pull, I give in, and if they give in, I pull!" He was not liked, however, because he was made responsible for splitting the Muslim community into Sunnis and Shiites. His favorite dish was *molokhiyya*, which for this reason, to this very day, no Shiite will ever eat.[3] To find out whether someone is a Sunni or a Shiite, people often ask: "Do you eat *molokhiyya*?" If the answer is no, then they think, "Aha, this one's a Shiite!"

After countless conquests, the Umayyads were suddenly faced with the problem of administering a huge empire and turning Bedouin life into settled life.[4] They started accepting compromises and thus became suspect of acting according to their own interests and worldly concerns, in contrast to the previous caliphs in Mecca, who had solely pursued the spreading of Islam.[5] From the very beginning, they were criticized by men and women who blamed them for giving up the pious simplicity of Medina for the new luxuries of empire.

Yet from a diplomatic viewpoint, the Umayyads' achievement was no small feat since they succeeded in securing the cohesion of the state. Their first priority was to control and administer the new empire. They put the responsibility of preserving the *sharia* into the hands of individual *qadis* (judges). Those judges ruled legal issues on a case by case basis. Whenever they were faced with a new situation, they tried to refer to precedents from previous Muslim generations, in particular the Qur'an and the *hadith*. The encoding of the *sharia*—the Divine law and the systematization of the teachings regarding every aspect of life—only started with the arrival of the next dynasty, the Abbasids. From that time on, the caliphate became virtually hereditary and it ceased to represent the chosen leadership of the Muslim community, as was customary in the first three decades following the death of the Prophet Muhammad. The Bedouin idea of choice only survived in the ceremony of the *bay'a* (literally, purchase). In this ceremony the new caliph takes the hand of the preceding caliph as a sign of his tribute. Although the tribe leader still required official confirmation, power was clearly in the hands of the clan of the Umayyads.

Those who had once been sons of the desert turned into city-dwellers with settled ways of life, and the traditions and ceremonies that developed were largely after the fashion of the Byzantine kings. This period saw the beginning of the development of an urban culture and of other forms of centralization and organization. For instance, the original, tribe-oriented Arab armies were replaced by salaried, permanent ones, which became the first regular and disciplined Muslim army.

With all this came change also in the situation of women. It was no longer fitting for them to go about freely and without supervision. The luckiest were offered gardens and bazaars, every conceivable luxury and sumptuous castle walls. They no longer needed to fight, to weave tents, or look after the land and the herds, since the number of slaves was constantly rising as a result of the many conquests, but women had also lost their freedom and to a large extent their voice and active role in the shaping of the community.

"Be beautiful and bear sons—everything else is taken care of!" was the message. Of course the poorer women remained on the streets, but their educated, influential sisters disappeared gradually, albeit not without protest, behind the scenes. The control system the Abbasids elaborated for women had already started under the Umayyads, only the Abbasids drew their inspiration more from the Persians and the Umayyads from the Byzantines.

Yet the longing for the original Bedouin women's free desert life remained. Mu'awiya's favorite wife, Maysun, expressed her nostalgia for the free life of the past and her protest against the current situation in a song:

> A woollen dress and a heart free of sorrow
> Is dearer to me than a silk gown.
> A tent beaten by the desert winds
> Is dearer to me than the palatial heights.
> To ride a hard camel in the open field
> Is dearer to me than a mule's gentle pace.
> A dog barking to signal travelers
> Is dearer to me than the softness of a kitten.
> A chunk of bread in the corner of a hut

Is dearer to me than a slice of cake.
A sprightly, thin man, my cousin,
Is dearer to me than a fool, a fat man.

Time and time again, she would travel with her son into the *badiya*, the Syrian desert, where her tribe roamed about and where her son learned to hunt, ride, and write poetry. From that time on, the *badiya* became the school where the Umayyad princes learned the pure Arabic language that no one mastered better than the Bedouin. They also practiced poetry and stayed away from lax urban life.

In those days education meant learning to speak pure Arabic, to ride and swim, to be skilled with a bow and arrow. Bedouin virtues such as courage, perseverance, *sabr* (patience in difficult times), *jiwar* (respecting the neighbors' rights, generosity and hospitality), *muru'ah* (true manliness, chivalry, and keeping one's promises), as well as a habit of sleeping little, were highly-praised qualities. Those who could not afford to educate their children in the *badiya* sent them to the mosques where they were taught the Qur'an and the hadith.

The greatness of the Umayyads was especially apparent in their poetry and in their magnificent architecture, that most lasting human creation. The Bedouin now longed to give their settled way of life an outer expression of beauty. The architecture of the Umayyads expressed itself mainly in a series of large mosques, among which the most famous is the Dome of the Rock in Jerusalem (built from 689 to 692), on the site where according to the Jewish tradition, Abraham was asked to sacrifice his son Isaac. The dome was built there to symbolize the fact that Islam places itself in the succession of Abraham. Splendid mosques were built throughout the new empire as an emblem of the new independent community.

Islam also furthered the dissemination of Arabic. Unlike most Germanic victors, the Arabs did not exchange their language for that of the conquered people, but instead taught them their own, turning it into a universal instrument. Although Arabic was the language of the rulers and of Muslim revelation, its particular qualities and creative power are what enabled it to fulfill this unifying function: even writers who opposed the Arabs' militrary hegemony could not resist the strength of their language and wrote in Arabic.

There were fourteen Umayyad caliphs altogether, but the fifth caliph, Abd al-Malik ibn Marwan, who ruled from 685 to 705, is regarded as the most capable head of the whole dynasty as far as administration is concerned. His goal was to unite the great empire along three lines: to standardize, to Islamize, and to Arabicize. He started by granting Arabic the status of administrative language throughout the empire. Then he introduced a new type of coin by creating a single gold coin, the dinar, which weighed 4.25 grams of gold, and a silver coin, the dirham, which contained 2.97 grams of silver and weighed seven-tenths of a dinar. Those coins, symbols of power and identity, carried Arabic-Islamic inscriptions and with time they became the main currency of the vast realm, just like the American dollar today.

Postal services also prospered. Horses and, in desert regions, camels were used for transporting the mail. Originally intended as a service for the government, in time it also came to be used for a fee by the private sector, thus connecting people from the different provinces. Each provincial capital was supplied with a main post office and roads were built to link the various cities to Damascus, the seat of the caliph.

Today, when people think about the Umayyads in the Arab world, they associate them foremost with the transition from simple Bedouin life to settled life, with all the accompanying novelties and transformations. Yet they also remain to this date the symbol of an Arab culture in which the art of poetry was particularly cultivated and fostered, and in which the poetic tradition flourished anew.

Pre-Islamic poetry is characterized by its simplicity and by the purity of feelings shaped by the harshness of the desert, which fostered strong loyalty to the community as well as fierce individualism. A poet was the spokesman of his tribe, acting as mouthpiece, journalist, preacher, entertainer, and political representative of his people. Just as warriors defended the tribe with their swords, poets fought for the honor and the rights of their tribe with their words. And how well did Arabic and its flowing rhythm harmonize with verses!

Arabic is the most recent and most widely spread of all ancient Semitic languages, and like them it is built on a three-consonant root system. For example, if we take the root "k-t-b" which carries the idea of "writing" and we decline it in any of the fourteen different forms applicable to the three-consonant root system, the words simply flow: *kataba* (to write); *kitab* (book); *maktab* (desk); *maktaba* (bookshop); *maktub* (letter); *mukataba* (correspondence); *kaatib* (writer); *kuttab* (Qur'anic school); *kitaba* (document, written amulet); *istiktab* (dictation). Each time different sounds, mainly vowels, are added to the basic root "k-t-b." Thus rhythm and melody are already predetermined in Arabic, where aesthetic rhythm and creative melody are as important as meaning.

A *qasida* (poem) is made of seventy to eighty pairs of half verses and contains many themes: love, women, fighting, camels, horses, desert landscapes, and storms. The various themes are connected by means of the rhythm and by two half verses (a half verse is a long as a line in European poetry), which should be complete both in terms of meaning and grammar.

At the time of the Umayyads, poetry became the product of a more complex, "urban" era. The meaning of the poem became more important than the clinging of the language to the rhythm and emptiness of the desert, and the themes were henceforth divided. Political poetry and love lyric poetry developed the most. To this date, three great "political" poets remain linked with this period: Al-Achtal, of the Christian tribe of the Taghlib, al-Farazdaq, of the tribe of the Tamim, and al-Jarir, of the tribe of the Bani Kulayb, a branch of the Tamim tribe. All three practiced satire as well as eulogy, all three were born and grew up in Iraq, and all three came from Arab Bedouin tribes. This trio enjoys unique fame among the Arabs.[6]

Al-Jarir and al-Farazdaq fought with poems of abuse, *naqa'id*, and they needled each other, while al-Achtal danced alternatively to one or the other. Their most caustic poems were directed at the enemies of their tribe or those of their ruler, but they also used them against each other. They dedicated their poetry to the various rulers and wielders of power of their time, depending on who paid best. Al-Achtal was generally known as the greatest champion of the Umayyads, and he dedicated most of his poems to the caliph Abd al-Malik. He was always seen in court wearing a large cross on his breast, filling the space with his poems to the caliph's delight. He cared for no one, got drunk often, and the sharpness of his eye was reflected in his tongue. He was feared by his enemies and he inspired his people through the beauty of his poems and the refinement of his speech.

The wealth of the conquests saw the emergence of an aristocratic class, which dedicated itself to sensual pleasures such as music and dance. Poetry united with music and was recited by women. Its language became lighter, its meaning more charming. As a result of the major interest in love poems, two love (*ghazal*) schools appeared: the Hijaz school, sensual, urban, and realistic, whose most famous representative is the refreshingly erotic poet Umar bin Abi Rabi'a[7] and the 'Udhri school, which expressed the unfulfilled, melancholic-spiritual, "when-I-love-I-die" longing.

The most extreme martyr of love was the poet Qays bin al-Mulawwah, whose love for Leila—who returned his love but was forced to marry another man—drove him into madness. "My longing for love knows no cure, and when I pray I turn my face to her, even if the right direction is exactly the opposite one!" According to legend he spent the rest of his life pathetically wandering through the desert, hoping the sun would burn the memory of Leila out of his heart. The couple entered history as Majnun (the madman) and Leila and their story is even more famous in the Arab world than Romeo and Juliet in the European one.

It is to the Umayyad dynasty that Syria owes its major role in the history of the Arabs. Even today, politicians try to link to that once important position and build for Syria a leading role in the Arab world.

THE LEMON PICKER

Humor is the salt of life;
whoever is well salted stays fresh a long time.
—Oriental proverb

We usually drove to Damascus for two reasons: sightseeing and shopping, though my parents also had many friends there whom we visited time and again.

Safa' lived in the center of Damascus in a beautiful Damascene house. Like all typical Islamic houses, it was rather nondescript from the outside, but as soon as the door opened and you walked through the dark corridor, a delightful splendor greeted you inside.

Syrian architecture typically includes an inner courtyard planted with greenery, with a central fountain. Safa' bred goldfish that swam leisurely among the reeds. The summer reception room was a covered open room. Mattresses on low wooden frames lay along three sides of the room, from which you could see the courtyard and enjoy the sea breeze. All the rooms of the house were built around this courtyard. Going from one room to the next therefore meant first going into the courtyard, taking in the sun's rays, and then disappearing into another room.

Old lemon trees grew in Safa's courtyard, and they gave the largest, most yellow lemons I have ever seen. They were as big as small melons and their beauty was almost surreal. Safa' lived in this house with her mother and her two brothers. Her mother was a small, sociable woman who loved entertaining and spoiling her guests. She was very particular about her lemon juice, which she had developed into a ritual.

"If you want them to be really good, you must snip the lemons before the first light of dawn, before they are wide awake. In this way, all their blessings stay hidden underneath their skin."

Then she would carry the lemons carefully into the kitchen and start preparing them. "The worlds came into existence in the name of the All-Merciful and All-Compassionate, and in His name I sacrifice you!"

This is how she prepared the lemons for the transformation. "You must always give the living time to reach the state of surrender, otherwise it is mere cruelty," this sensitive wise woman would explain. I could see how some of the adults smirked when she spoke, but I felt deeply touched and fascinated by her. Suddenly the lemons had turned into friends willing to sacrifice themselves for our refreshment and strengthening.

Safa's mother had yet another gift, and that one never brought a smirk among the adults — quite to the contrary, they fervently begged her for it. Most of the time, she would shake her head.

"I'm not in the right mood today," she answered modestly, letting a new litany of requests wash over her.

"So be it!" she finally grinned mischievously and called to the kitchen: "*Habibti, sawwilna kahwe,* darling, make us some coffee." Moments later, the fragrant coffee was brought in, balanced on a tray. It was sipped slowly, and then the real ceremony started.

Safa's mother took the first empty cup, covered it with the small saucer, skillfully turned the whole upside down and laid it on the table for the coffee grounds to slowly run their fated way. Um Safa' folded her arms across her chest and waited. The owner of the cup waited excitedly, for soon she would find out about her destiny. Although no one really believed in coffee reading, everyone was under its spell, aroused by the hope of finding out more about the future.

After a while, Um Safa' would lean forward, lift the cup, turn it over, and peer silently inside. She turned it between her fingers and seemed to be searching for mysterious signs. Without looking up, she started speaking: "I can see four paths ahead of you. Two of them are blocked at the end; in front of the third path stands an old man who blocks the way; near the fourth path lies a white snake that protects you and means well by you. You will have to choose carefully when you stand before these paths, for only one of them will bring you success."

"I can also see a letter arriving soon, and it will change your life," she added.

The owner of the cup listened eagerly and seemed to ponder.

"It's true, Um Safa'!" came the reaction. "I have an opportunity to go over to my brother in America and study there, but my father doesn't want me to, maybe he's the old man in the cup. Or I can start working in a bank here, and I also received a marriage proposal from a very nice man, an architect. But I really don't know about the fourth path!"

And the riddle developed into a long discussion. Um Safa' gave information, but she always left something open.

"When is the letter coming, Um Safa', will it be long?"

"Soon, within the next few weeks!"

Everyone started guessing about the sender of this important letter.

If it comes, they won't need to guess, they'll know, and if it doesn't come, then they shouldn't believe in coffee reading, I thought to myself. I was much more fascinated by the atmosphere of those fortune-telling gatherings than by the actual predictions. More than the result, I loved observing the excited faces, the tensed bodies jointed in curiosity, and the continuous murmur of Um Safa's soft voice at such times.

"Whatever is meant for you will come to you, no matter how indirectly!" my grandfather had always told me, and I believed him, for he was the living proof of this attitude. He fulfilled his tasks and responsibilities, did whatever he could to succeed, and was equally satisfied when success came as when it did not.

"It was not meant for me," he would calmly say.

THE BLESSING OF BLINDNESS

Whoever stands on his toes
does not stand firmly.
Whoever walks with legs apart
does not progress.
Whoever wishes to shine
is not enlightened.
—Lao Tse (4th century BCE)

Whenever we were in Damascus, we visited the architectural jewel built by al-Walid, the sixth Umayyad caliph. Al-Walid only lived to be forty, but no one was as active in architecture as he. During his reign, the famous Umayyad mosque was built, as well as schools, and institutions for lepers, the physically disabled, and the blind. He was the first to build hospitals for chronic patients.

We had decided to visit the mosque once more. Black *abayas* were handed to all visiting women at the main entrance and then we entered the huge inner courtyard. In each corner of the courtyard stood a minaret; the northern one had once been used as a lighthouse. Those minarets would later serve as models for those in Syria, North Africa, and Spain. Birds flew over the inner courtyard and the sky extended contentedly over the huge area. We went on into the main part of the mosque and our feet sank into the soft, rich rugs.

An old man with a thick white beard sat next to a pillar, bent forward, the Qur'an open in front of him on a decorated wooden holder. He seemed so deeply absorbed in his reading that he took absolutely no notice of what went on around him. We walked leisurely through the great mosque and our eyes kept rejoicing over the magnificent mosaics, which slowly guided our gaze to the wonderful dome. I whirled and the ornaments in the dome seemed to follow me. How many people had patiently worked on this dome? But my attention kept returning to the old man.

I dared not look at him directly, so I stole toward him, apparently inadvertently, moving in smaller and smaller circles. Yet suddenly, as chance would have it, I found myself standing right in front of him. I could hear his weak voice; his breathing was labored and I had the feeling every breath he took could be his last. I bent slightly forward; I wanted to know where he was because although my eyes could see him in front of me, he seemed somewhere else altogether.

Then he lifted his head very slowly and I jumped back with a start. His eyes seemed to lie in two caves and the years had turned them into two gray oceans of fog that blinked and shimmered in the world. He was nearly blind! Was blindness a blessing, then? His whole being seemed to shine and radiate a peaceful contentment that could not be disturbed or matched by all the magnificence of the place. As calmly as he had lifted his head, he now lowered it and receded once more into this world that I could not understand.

In the meantime the others had gone to the shrine, to the grave where Hussein's head was kept. People crowded in front of the gated tomb, kissing it and softly reciting their prayers. Father pushed me so that I could touch and kiss the golden bars and then we walked slowly back to the exit of the mosque.

THE PEOPLE OF THE LONG
A'S AND E'S

In the surroundings of Damascus, most of the large lemon and orange plantations belonged to families who lived in the city. Now and then they would drive to their plantations and spend the day under the open sky. On one of those occasions, we were invited to spend the day with the Kusbari family. The Kusbaris were an old, established family clan and the family we knew consisted of three pubescent sons, a five-year-old daughter, a bearded father, a plump mother, a fat grandmother, and a stick-carrying grandfather.

The earth between the trees had been coarsely ploughed up and it was hard to walk on. Oranges hung in the trees, their orange glow almost artificial, and the sky was light blue with a few lost white clouds. The grandfather decided to go for a walk in the trees and I followed him. The strenuous walk seemed to remind him of times when hiking was easier and, as old people often do, he started leafing through his past. Yet this grandfather also seemed to be a historically aware, sensitive philosopher.

He stared at the earth, while the typical stretched E's and A's of the Syrian dialect ran from his wrinkled mouth: "*Eeeeeee, ya binteee, ed-dinyeee dawaaraaa*, verily, my daughter, life is a constant change! With its fertile land, Syria has always been a favorite wife, an eternal transit country crossed by all the major trade roads. Crusaders, Egyptians, Turks, French, all wanted her. But the worst were the French. They played us Syrians off against each other. You're a Christian, you're a Muslim, you're a Druze. They dismembered our country into four pieces, and Lebanon was one of them. *Eeeeeee*, wounds are hard to forget.

"When I was young, I first fought with the English against the Turks so that we could at last become independent—that's the way it was agreed at the time. Eeeeeee, but I only fought so that we could be ruled anew, and even worse. While I was putting my life on the line for our independence, the English and the French sat in the backrooms partitioning the Arab world between them and as a special gift they put Israel in our lap.[1] *Eeeeeeee ed-dinyee ghaddareee*, life is truly treacherous!"

The old man stood still and he checked his surroundings, apparently looking for a suitable place to sit down. He didn't seem to find one, so he walked to the next tree, turned around slowly, pushed on his hand for support, and leaned cautiously back. He bent his knees, pressing his back against the tree trunk, lost in his memories and in the injustice. Defeats apparently leave deeper marks in the human soul than victories. I watched him quietly and felt sorry that he was so sad. But a sudden bang caught my whole attention and I ran to see what it was.

The old man shouted something at me, but I was already too busy even to listen to him and I shouted a quick "I'll be back!" over my shoulder.

I ran over the plantation's narrow dirt road and arrived just in time to see a young man aiming at the sky with a big rifle. Next to him stood a boy about ten years old. He held a rope in his hand, on which hung many bird corpses. I slowly went closer, and he proudly held up the lifeless birds so that I could see them better. He extended his other hand to me and showed me a large red cartridge.

"You're shooting these little birds with those big cartridges? Why?"

The young man laughed: "They make a good meal!"

I felt he was the biggest fool I had ever met in my life.

"Those birds are not here for eating—they're supposed to sing between the trees, not be shot by cartridges almost bigger than they are."

I was deeply disturbed, but the young man laughed again, lifting his rifle to search the sky through the visor. And suddenly I understood: he actually enjoyed the killing! He enjoyed shooting those birds!

Powerless rage overcame me. I wanted to do something, but I knew that I didn't stand a chance against him. So I thought to myself, Well, if he doesn't let them sing between the trees, I'll sing even louder and warn them. I started singing at the top of my voice.

"Shshshsh!" he hissed at me, but I stuck to my plan.

He turned around, walked toward me in large steps and stood right in front of me.

He looked down at me nastily: "Shut up, *ya binit*, you girl! You're scaring the birds away from me."

I tried to answer as confidently and innocently as I could: "I'm only singing!"

"If you open your mouth once more, then..."

While he spoke, my brain whirred, desperately looking for an answer, torn between fear and stubbornness.

Then a deep familiar voice rang out: "Here you are! We've been looking for you everywhere!"

The young man immediately took one step back and suddenly he no longer seemed so big.

"Mummy, he's killing small birds!"

"Don't you know that's a punishable offense? There are hardly any singing birds left in this country!" my mother thundered.

The young man smiled again, but his smile was different now. "We were only having a little fun."

"Go now or I'll call the person in charge and you'll be in trouble!"

The two of them pushed off, but I still felt quite bad. Bigger one threatens smaller one, smaller one threatens an even smaller one, and the birds will always get killed, some place else, some other time. I followed my mother. The others were already waiting for the fragrant food. I felt as if I was sitting in a bubble of silence. I could see people moving around me, yet everything was like a silent movie.

THE SWIMMING EGG

We always went to visit an old man in Damascus by the name of Dhu Nun. He had snow-white hair and his glasses sat comfortably on his potato-shaped nose. Mr. Dhu Nun lived alone and two great passions governed his life: eating and traveling. He earned his living doing business here and there. He was a cheerful old man whose motto in life was to enjoy whatever came.

"I try to sleep as little as possible, because at the end of our days we will sleep long anyhow!"

"What does he mean, we'll sleep long?" I asked my mother.

"Some people describe death as a long sleep."

I liked his idea and I decided to do the same that very evening. Um Safa' and Mr. Dhu Nun had known each other since they were young and we often drove first to Mr. Dhu Nun to pick him up and then drive on to Um Safa's. But this time Mr. Dhu Nun wanted to come on his own and join us there.

We were sitting together, pleasantly sipping lemon juice when the doorbell rang and Mr. Dhu Nun came in with two huge bags.

"What are you bringing there?" Um Safa' asked.

But he ignored her question and trotted into the kitchen.

"For God's sake, he's got one of those crazy ideas into his head again!" she said and slipped behind him.

Voices became loud in the kitchen: "No!" "Yes!" "Why not?" "Not now!" The voices became louder and louder.

Um Safa' came out of the kitchen. "He wants to pickle vegetables. He has put it into his head to pickle vegetables now!" she cried, shaking her head.

All started laughing.

"Let him!"

"He'll make a mess of my whole kitchen again!"

"No, no," Mr. Dhu Nun's head peeked through the door. "I promise I'll tidy everything, upon my honor! Um Safa'," he added shyly, "all I need is an egg!"

At that point Um Safa' had to laugh, too.

"Why does he need an egg?" I asked, surprised.

"You may go into the kitchen and watch!" Mother answered.

I ran and stood by the door, looking inside. The little old man had put on an apron and he was busy moving to and fro. He washed a couple of glass containers, filled them with water and placed them neatly on the floor. Then he spread bags on the floor, put a pile of cucumbers on one, lemons on the other, peppers on the third, and carrots on the fourth. He took a sharp knife in one hand and in the other a bag filled with something white, and sat on the wooden stool with his legs apart. Then he spotted me.

"Come in, my child, I'll show you something beautiful!" He scooped up the white from the bag with his hand and threw it into one of the containers. As soon as it touched the water, it dissolved into nothing.

"That's salt!" he explained to me, and he repeated the process several times.

"Pass me the egg, my child!"

It lay alone on a small kitchen board. I took it carefully in my hand and gave it to him. He took the egg, examined it with a satisfied grin and put it in the salted water. "When the egg remains floating half the way up, without going up or sinking down, staying quietly as if on an invisible thread of faith and trust, then we have put in the right amount of salt," he said dreamily and contentedly.

I was totally fascinated by the egg, which hung in the water floating freely, as if by magic.

He turned his attention to the cucumbers and started cutting them in thick slices. He spoke with each cucumber as if it were his trusted ally in this venture. I felt almost embarrassed to watch him, so intimate was his talk with the vegetables. With much love he let each slice splash into the water and they fell happily to the bottom of the container.

He did the same with the other vegetables and once they were all in the containers, he covered them with a cloth and pulled an elastic band around them. "Right, now we can but wait until salt and vegetables become friends!"

"How long do we have to wait, 'ammu, Uncle?"

"In two weeks we'll have a look, we'll move the vegetables a little, and then we'll leave them alone for another two weeks. By that time some of them are already edible, but others may need another two weeks."

I looked at him wide-eyed: "So long?"

He smiled: "It's a long time for a child, but for grown-ups, especially when they're as old as I am, it's just a moment. All of life is just a single opening and closing of the eyelids."

What was that supposed to mean?—weeks are weeks, and I close my eyelids every night and open them again in the morning. Old people were nice indeed, I thought, but totally different from us.

A MODERN HAREM

Moonlight grew as the moon embraced the night,
The rose was given fragrance when she united with thorns.
—Maulana Jalaluddin Rumi

Mother loved Syrian embroidery, which was mainly found on the famous Damascus tablecloths. Syria was well-known for its textile industry, which used gold threads and manufactured brocades, curtains, and slipcovers. We wound our way through the souks to the textile shops that sold those treasures.

Syria was a socialist, secular state, yet the number of veiled women on the streets were surprisingly many.

"The veil serves as a protest, as a sign of the people's dissatisfaction with the political and socio-economic situation of the country. It is the only protest that is tolerated, because it is linked to our cultural and religious inheritance and it would be difficult to prohibit," a friend of my mother's explained.

Interestingly, socialist Syria does not have any women's organizations independent from the state, just as in some conservative Arab states. In those conservative states, such womens' groups are seen as a danger because they threaten the rigid control over women, whereas in progressive structures they are seen as putting the state at risk because they jeopardize the social consensus insofar as they might question and possibly give a different interpretation to the social goals set for the mobilization of women.

On the other hand, in Syria as in Iraq and in Tunisia, the *sharia* has been partly redefined. For example, polygamy and unilateral divorce are now more difficult (in Tunisia polygamy is totally prohibited), which gives women a stronger position.

The same friend went on explaining over coffee: "So now when a man wishes to marry a second wife, he must ask his first wife for permission and since women of the new generation usually prefer divorcing rather than living with a second wife, polygamy is becoming scarcer. I actually think it's good that polygamy wasn't totally abolished," she added, "because it takes into consideration the situation of older, traditionally educated women who may not be capable of handling life by themselves if they were to divorce because their husband marries another woman."

"But according to Islamic law, didn't women always have the right to restrict polygamy with an appropriate clause in the marriage contract?" my mother asked.

"Yes, that's right! My brother's father-in-law made him sign a statement in the marriage contract, according to which his daughter can ask for a divorce if he takes a second wife. It has always been possible but seldom done, supposedly because it wasn't proper to prescribe such things in a marriage contract. Some men might argue, 'Do you really believe I would want to keep you bound to me if you didn't want to stay with me any longer? My honor wouldn't allow that!' Yet when it comes down to it, other factors matter more than honor! In the past, those conditions were not written into the contract out of respect for the tradition, and nowadays it is the modern women in love who gives in too quickly. Romantic ideas obscure the fact that it's a marriage contract."

"I can see so many businesswomen here!" Mother said.

"Yes, the women from Damascus are known throughout the world as excellent businesswomen. There are four times more women in academic fields than in other jobs. This high representation in academia is an exceptional phenomenon of the Middle and Far East.[1] Most women graduates work in the teaching and medical professions, but also in other fields. There are women engineers, architects, physicists, accountants, and a growing number work in communications. Only recently have women started to push forward in the sales and services sector, as well as in factories. These spheres of activity used to be avoided because of the possible contact with the other sex.

"It is beneath a woman's dignity to serve strangers in public—she might as well stay at home and help her family! To be a doctor, an architect, or a teacher, that's something else. She is then her own boss and it brings prestige to her and her family. A woman will only take a simpler job if the family is poor and needs it economically. And what man would ever publicly admit that he alone can't provide for his family, unless there was absolutely no choice?" So runs the argument, and the attitude endures. Many middle-class women accept male dominance inside the family in exchange for the right to education and employment outside the home. But with the extension of schooling, the difficult economic situation in most Arab countries, and the increasing demands of modern life, often families can no longer live on a single income, and prejudice against women working in offices and sales is fading.[2]

"We come from a culture that practiced a strict separation of the sexes. This had advantages and disadvantages," a good-looking, mature lady explained to my mother. "Man ruled in the outer world, but at home it was the woman who looked after the extended family. Therefore in prosperous homes, women were not only dominated, they ruled too. Many women were therefore used to exercising authority and developed a good management sense. Once the first graduates stepped into working life, they simply transferred their experience to the outside world, without coming into conflict with their feminine identity, without needing to apologize in front of men or seek their recognition. Authority was never seen as contradictory to femininity.

"In Syria, and I believe also in other Arab countries, relations and social status are more crucial than gender when it comes to reaching high positions. But unfortunately, our patriarchal tradition can be seen in the fact that a great number of women would rather have a man as a boss!"

Mother listened with interest—she enjoyed these themes, so the lady went on.

"For most women, the greatest obstacle to a career lies in the inability to harmonize professional and family life. In the cities, the extended family is gradually disappearing, and it used to provide a wonderful, permanently available babysitting service. A woman could go to work reassured; she knew that her children were in good hands. When she came home late, she was certain a meal had been prepared and her husband wasn't sitting at home alone, grumbling and hungry. That made a big difference. Today many women have to first find suitable home help and they can't always afford it. And there are not enough nurseries."

Mother reflected and said, thinking aloud: "The best would be to combine the extended family system with individual life. Those women in the family who would rather stay at home could look after the children, and the others could pursue a career to support them financially. Two women could share a full-time job. Furthermore, there are several age groups and generations in an extended family, and many things would happen in different times, so that every woman could have a possibility to study, to train, and to enjoy motherhood..."

"You mean a modern harem?"

Both women laughed thoughtfully.

THE GREAT MASTER IBN AL-ARABI

A word is a fan—it veils and unveils at the same time.
—Ibn al-Arabi

West of Damascus, on Mount Qasiyun, lies the tomb of *ash-shayk al-akbar* (the great master) Muhyi-al-Din Ibn al-Arabi (1165–1240). While alive, he was both revered and fought against, but his influence on Islam's mystical path, Sufism, cannot be denied. Ibn al-Arabi was an ocean from which each one could drink what he wanted.

Once, I woke up in the middle of the night, my heart pounding fast. I sat up. My room was deep in darkness and my eyes could not distinguish anything. I let my head hang a little and when I looked up again, the faint moonshine had lent soft outlines to all the things around me, but it was different than usual: it was everywhere. Everything lay there peacefully, quiet and silent. I don't know what happened in my heart, but I suddenly felt things quite differently. Everything seemed so right, each object seemed to have taken exactly the place it had been allocated. The picture that hung on the wall could simply not have hung anywhere else, the pencil on the floor, in the corner, beamed confidently: "This is my place!" Such a deep harmony reigned in the room that I barely dared to breathe.

But what happened next tore my heart from my breast and made it dance naked in front of me. Everything seemed to follow a music of silence, a round dance around itself in blissful happiness, and the rhythm was surrender. I suddenly stood up and started whirling, circling around my axis between heaven and earth, one arm up and the other longing for the earth. I whirled and whirled and whirled, and if someone had asked me what happiness and meaning were, I would have answered silently, "Here and now!" I cannot remember how long it lasted, but I visited the entire world while whirling. I went to the Mongolians and to the bear caves, I became an ant and emerged as a whale, I was a child and an ancient being, both man and woman, limitless and like a dot. The most tender exhaustion took me back to bed and a poem came to my lips:

> I saw You with the eyes of my heart
> Saw the sky standing without pillars
> The stars in which my soul rejoices
> And the earth that nurtures my heart
> How could I not believe in You,
> Not praise You
> When my heart calls that You are in everything
> I see You everywhere and yet You are nowhere
> No darkness after this day
> No injustice after this day
> For I am a part of You and You are a part of me
> Oh, Beloved, let no "I" stand between us!
> Praised, You are praised,
> Light of heaven and of the worlds.

With a slight vibration throughout my body and a humming in my heart, I finally closed my eyes.

Only a few years later did I encounter Ibn al-Arabi and through his words and deep spiritual insights I came to understand what I had experienced and my heart was clarified. This great master also fascinated me because of his view on femininity.

Ibn al-Arabi was born in Murcia, Spain, where he was brought up by two holy women: 95-year-old Fatima of Cordoba and 14-year-old Nizam Ayn al-Shams (Harmony eye-of-the-sun), the daughter of a Persian traditionalist, who met him in Mecca in 598. He said of Shams: "In her spiritual activities and in her link to the Divine, she belonged to the greatest souls." She inspired him to create one of his most beautiful works, "Interpreter of the longing," in which he celebrates his real love for her while she is the focus of his divine experience. Through her the whole kingdom of Divine love was brought to his eyes.

A divine beauty also shone through Fatima, the mystical leader, who led Ibn al-Arabi to recognize the Divine through the medium of feminine beauty, and to see the feminine as the true revelation of God's mercy and creative powers. Fatima accompanied Ibn al-Arabi on his spiritual path for two years. He built her a small, low thatched hut in which he also buried her at the end of her secular life, before moving on.

I have never visited his tomb, but I cannot resist his influence. In the bustle of modern times, many people still see the tombs of the saints as tangible proofs that life has meaning, and so many pilgrims go to Ibn al-Arabi's tomb.

In order to understand Ibn al-Arabi, I offer a little insight into Islamic cosmology.

The starting point of Islamic thought is God. The first of the five pillars of Islam is the attestation: "There is no God but God and Muhammad is His messenger."[1] The fundamental principle of Islam is *tawhid*, this statement of unity: "There is no God but God." If duality exists in the cosmos, then it is linked to the One, and the One is beyond all duality.

According to Islamic terminology, the world or cosmos can be described as *al-'alam* (everything other than God), *ma siwa Allah* (without qualification in time or space). In the Islamic tradition, everything is discussed in relationship, *nisba*, to God. It is this relationship that enables one to reach a proper understanding of things, for the existence of the universe depends on this single reality.

There are two fundamental, opposite relationships in the Islamic cosmology, radically different from one another, yet complementary, for God is one single reality.

The theological view stresses that God is infinitely beyond the cosmos, *tanzih*: "God cannot be compared to anything that exists." In this view, God is totally out of His creatures' reach and beyond their understanding, an intangible reality beyond all human pursuit. Several verses of the Qur'an express this view, such as "Glory to thy Lord, the Lord of Honor and Power! (He is free) from what they ascribe (to Him)!" (sura 37/180) or more directly, "There is nothing whatever like unto Him!" (sura 42/11).

The spiritual traditions generally known as *tasawwuf*,

Sufism, hold a different viewpoint, which is also clearly present in the Qur'an. Ibn al-Arabi remarked that the theologians' God was a god whom no one could really love, for he was too distant and intangible. Yet the God of the Qur'an, of the Prophets, and of the spiritual authorities is a God who is infinitely loving and caring to His creatures. "A people whom He will love as they will love Him" (sura 5/54). God's love to His creatures brings out His creatures' love to him.

This God of mercy and love is tangible and can be understood. Therefore, to a certain extent, He is explained as similar, *tashbih*, to His creatures. We can imagine, understand, and express Him through human qualities. This view stresses that God is everywhere: "Whithersoever ye turn, there is Allah's countenance" (sura 2/115) and "We are nearer to him than (his) jugular vein" (sura 50/16).

Experts in jurisprudence, namely those Islamic authorities who present and defend the outer, legal aspect of Islam, emphasize the fact that God cannot be compared. They insist that He is a wrathful God and keep warning about hell and Godly punishment. God is a distant, domineering, and powerful ruler, whose orders must be obeyed. His qualities are those of a strict, authoritarian father. But spiritual authorities constantly refer to the words of the Prophet Muhammad, "God's compassion takes precedence over His wrath." They underline that compassion, love, goodness, and gentleness are the foundations of reality and that they always win in the end. God is above all a warm and loving mother.

It is often repeated in the Qur'an that all things are *ayat* (signs) of God and that everything reports on Divine reality. Many Islamic thinkers and cosmologists see everything in the universe as a reflection of the Divine names. Those names and characteristics represent qualities such as beauty, knowledge, and life.

When asked why God had created the cosmos, the Prophet Muhammad answered: "God says: 'I was a hidden treasure and I wanted to be recognized, so I created the Creation in order to be recognized.'" The world is the place in which the hidden treasure manifests to the creatures. Many cosmologists use words such as *dhuhur* (manifestation), and *tajalli*, (self-unveiling and revelation, shining through and beyond) to explain the relationship between God and the world.

There are thus two "types" of Divine names and the words used in the Qur'an. "God's two hands" are understood by many as a symbol of the incomparable and the similar, namely for *jalal*, majesty, and *jamal*, beauty.

It says in the Qur'an that humans are the only beings that God created with His two hands (sura 38/75)—and therefore, the only being in which all the names of God manifest. Only the human being represents a complete picture of God; all other beings show only parts of Him since they have been shaped either with one hand or the other. For example, *malak* (angels) were only shaped with God's right hand. Human beings were created in perfect harmony of both aspects of beauty and majesty. This is how *sharaf* (honor), which was given to human beings, comes to be expressed. The human being is the most perfect symbol of Divine reality. His theomorphic nature, of which so many people are ignorant, reflects the Divine qualities that only pertain to God in their perfection. God is *hay* (alive), which is why man has a life. He has will, which is why man was given a free will, and he has the quality of the word, *kalima*, of speech, which is why man has the power of language.

The reality of God, revealed through the cosmos, can be described by opposite and contrary characteristics. The whole cosmos can be described as an immense collection of opposites and God's two hands are busy shaping everything that exists: compassion and anger, sternness and gentleness, life-givers and killers, humiliation and elevation. The interactions of those names are most evident in *haraka* (constant changes and movements) and *istihala* (transformations). Nothing ever remains the same, not even for one breath. Everything needs the constant Divine replenishment because nothing exists by itself.

At every moment God is creating the universe anew, preserving it from annihilation. Every moment God creates mercy and gentleness in the cosmos, every moment Divine sternness disrupts it anew. As with breathing, the universe is created every moment. The great movement of coming and going is represented symbolically in the first part of the creed: *la ilaha* points to the emanation, the emergence of all things from the unchanging, Divine One, of "things outside Him," and *illa Allah* points to their return to Him, the eternal unity. Ibn al-Arabi saw the Divine being as a wide green ocean from which fleeting forms surface like waves before disappearing again into the bottomless depths.

Sharaf (honor), which was given to man in the cosmos to stand at the top of all creatures, also placed a great burden and responsibility on him. A frog never changes into a humming-bird, yet human beings are constantly in the process of developing. A frog—an imperfect human being—kissed by the spirit can change into a human being. Only man can be more or less human. Such is the mystery of the human fate.

Human beings have a natural goodness, for we are signs of God, yet unlike all other things, we can also become malicious if we take advantage of this extraordinary position that has been given to us. In order to be truly human, a person must first make clearly visible the good qualities that are already naturally present in the creation, in accordance with balanced guiding principles and harmony. Evil manifests itself when a person disturbs this equilibrium by acting against the Divine balance of heaven and earth. This is the only way that evil can come into the world, because human beings are the only beings who can choose. This freedom lends man a unique dignity, a central and all-embracing quality, but it also opens the door to misuse. (The only other beings who also have the possibility of free choice are the *jinns* (invisible beings who may intervene in human affairs, for good and bad), whose leader is the devil, Iblis.

According to Ibn al-Arabi, a human being is like an isthmus (*barzach*) between two oceans—God and the cosmos. Because of their all-embracing (*jam'iyya*) central role, only human beings can upset the harmony and balance that exist naturally between God and the cosmos. In the same way, only they can, through their mediating role and the fact that they are God's representatives on earth, achieve a perfect harmony and balance between God and the creation.[2]

Human beings are the axis of the cosmos around which all things turn. It is therefore our duty to fulfill our function as mediators and build peace and harmony on earth. But one must first learn to serve before one can rule. In relationship to God's incomparability and distance, a person is His absolute servant, and in relationship to His similarity and closeness, a person—the only creature formed by God's two hands—is the only one that can be *khalifa* (God's representative on earth). The combination of both leads to true knowledge of God.

The path to inner knowledge (*ma'rifa*) comprises several steps (*maqamat,* or the singular, *maqam*), to make durable progress in spiritual development. They are levels of self-knowledge and knowledge of one's own soul, for he "who knows himself knows his master."

God is always close to us, but we must first strive for this closeness. A never-ending, mutual longing was born between the Creator and His creatures: the yearning of the drop, of the individual, to dissolve into the ocean, into the whole. God's majesty and power as well as His beauty are unveiled in this ocean. God becomes the mirror in which man perceives his own reality, and in turn man becomes the mirror in which God sees His names and qualities.

The essence (*dhat*) is for Ibn al-Arabi the feminine element. *Dhat* is feminine in Arabic, so al-Arabi could sometimes talk of the "feminine Creator." To him, the woman unveils the mystery of God's compassion. Ibn al-Arabi said that since God cannot be seen separately from matter, contemplation of the True Reality is impossible without physical supports, since in His essence God does not depend on this world and He is seen more perfectly in the human being than in any other, and more perfectly in woman than in man. God's contemplation in woman is most perfect and magnificent, and in her God's creative activity is best manifested. The core of Ibn al-Arabi's commentary is that if one experiences God in the woman, one can see both the God of Majesty and Beauty; one can see Him in the active and the passive; one can see the right hand and the left. "In herself the woman concentrates the strength of every reality received, in her gathers the strength of the whole universe, therefore there is nothing stronger than her in the universe."

Ibn al-Arabi's great soul can be recognized in his words:

"Every individual soul and the followers of every religion seek salvation but since they do not know salvation, they do not know the way to it either, although each one believes himself to be on the right path. All discord between people is about the way that leads to salvation, not about salvation itself. Salvation reveals itself everywhere, like the sun; whoever perceives it believes that it is in him in its essence, so that envy and jealousy disappear from his heart."

With time, this view has become generally accepted by the Sufis. Indeed, the more they knew about God, the smaller their religious prejudice became and they understood that "the ways to God are as many as the breaths of human beings." Whoever walks the flaming ocean of love can no longer differentiate. Nevertheless, Sufis see Islam as the last and most complete revelation of Divine truth and they abide by the rites and laws of the *sharia*.

Indeed every religious system contains a form of moral code regulating the relationships between self and others. In Islam it has been revealed through the doctrine of the Divine laws of the *sharia*. The "inspiration" or "revelation" granted to the mystic has a different quality than the Divine revelation of the law.

The mystical path is often long and hard for the searcher. Times of euphoria alternate with times of darkness and loneliness in a constant inner struggle. The searcher's proper orientation at the beginning through a master is essential for success: Whoever starts in God will also end in Him.

Qualities or characteristics such as charity, honesty, patience, gratitude, and humility are the Sufi's virtues. Humility does not mean sentimental subservience. As a spiritual virtue, it means acknowledging that God is everything; it means bowing in front of oneself and in front of all creatures, for each creature carries a perfection in itself.

Man's deep need for beauty and love cannot be satisfied through luxury goods, while material charity requires an inner ethical attitude and is therefore a way of being. Man should not be charitable out of some selfless, sacrificing motives, but because in the end he himself needs charity too. Charity means to embed oneself into the great circle of giving and receiving, and to recognize that in the end the universe is but one.

In one of his essays on Islamic heresy, Peter Lamborn Wilson writes:

> Among the Sufis, purity is not achieved through ritual ablutions, faith and worship, deeds or merit, but through direct knowledge, direct experience, certainty, the drunkenness of ecstatic realisation. Only this intoxication truly cleanses the soul because one loses oneself through this "wine" to find oneself again in the heart.
>
> One loses all the dividing illusions, the dirt of a veiled consciousness, and reaches the One. That means walking naked through the bazaar [...] But if the bazaar is shocked, the scandal is the bazaar's, not the dervish's. Like a drunkard the Sufi loses his good reputation in the world because the world has lost its reputation for him. The petty bazaar stands charged with hypocrisy, the naked stands in front of God."

Indeed, on the secular level, to be abnormal means to be disturbed or mentally unwell!

The aim of Islamic cosmology is to explain the duties of human existence. Our nature gives human beings the duty to live in harmony with the Divine and to surrender (*islam*) to the ways of heaven and earth in order to reach harmony on earth and in human relationships, for the lights of Paradise and the trestles of Hell are gathered here and experienced now. Every action, every deed, bears fruit. If you plant roses, you need not worry about thistles.

Don't let the sleep of carelessness, *ghafla*, numb you in the dark. Tear the curtain open and see the lightning and comets: You must love!

KUWAIT

LIKE HOT BREWING TEA

Whoever follows a mirage is looking for water.
Whoever goes to the shore of the ocean is looking for unity.
—Sufi wisdom

Mother had an Iraqi friend whose second husband was Kuwaiti. She had often invited us to Kuwait, and one day we went. We flew to Kuwait, whose capital is also called Kuwait, which confused me a little. The wealth of that state was apparent to me from the very first moment. The airport was a white sea of marble. Everything was generously and splendidly laid out. Mummy's friend was already waiting eagerly for us.

She was a tall, austere woman whose hair was severely tied back, which made her masculine face even more angular. She had wide ankles and her long fingernails made her hands look nearly threatening. Her deep rough voice irritated me and when she came to me happily and hugged me, I felt like I was being squeezed by a compressor. Yet behind this powerful shell that Allah had given her lived a kind and sensitive heart, as patient and reliable as a desert camel.

In her overwhelming happiness, Kawthar squeezed Mother too, and violently shook Father's extended hand in both of her own. Her husband stood next to her and smiled pleasantly. His gray temples framed a voluptuous bald head and his bulging belly made another curve, which lent him a comfortable appearance. He and father went first with the luggage and the three of us followed, accompanied by Kawthar's many questions about our journey and health. Mother answered her quietly and pleasantly. We got into the car and drove off.

I had never seen such wide streets in my life, as they forced their way through the city in three or four lanes. Along the streets magnificent villas constantly came out of the sand. It all seemed bewitchingly beautiful. My eyes jumped from one house to the next and I liked each one more than the previous one. But then it came to me and I looked at the bare country; actually it was all sand, sea, and sky. The car took a sharp turn to the right and suddenly the villas were gone, replaced by more modest houses.

Soon after, we stopped in front of one of them, set foot on white sand and went inside. I wanted to take a deep breath before going inside, so I started breathing in through my nose… and at that very moment I felt a burning as if I'd poured hot brewing tea down my throat. My whole body was paralyzed with fear and pain. I pressed my hands as strongly as I could against my breast and waited for the pain to go away. My God, in Kuwait you're only allowed shallow breaths, at least during the day!

The house had a few disarrayed pieces of furniture and many, many books.

"Do you have children?" I asked our host curiously. "No, my love," my mother answered for her.

There was a short silence in the room; I seemed to have blundered into what had been a difficult life decision. Like so many immigrants from Arab countries, Kawthar was a teacher. She taught Arabic and mathematics. But Mahmoud, her husband, was a journalist and a *rawi*, a teller of fairy stories. The first story he told me was about his ancestors…

THE FAIRY TALE OF KUWAIT

Fasting and praying is great,
but to remove pride, envy, and greed from one's heart
is even better.
—Abu-l-Hasan Charaqani (Sufi master, d. 1033)

Once upon a time, a small caravan of men, women, children, animals, and household goods was on its way in the scorching heat of the Nefud desert. They belonged to the Bani Utba, a sub-tribe of the Anaza, and they had had to leave their pastures after drought fell upon them. They were heading southeast toward the Gulf, in hope of finding better living conditions. The march saw much privation. They had very little water left, and even the camels had started showing signs of fatigue. Then suddenly they saw water, a lot of water, in front of them.

"Excited, they came closer, and found themselves standing on a coast. They looked around and saw that it was a bay at the estuary of the rivers Euphrates and Tigris, north of the Gulf. They were Bedouin and the sea was foreign to them, yet it seemed somehow familiar. The space and the distance quietened the eyes just like the desert. Could their future lie in this element? The reef coast was not welcoming, though, so despite their exhaustion, they decided to march on. One step after another, slowly and laboriously, they followed the bay, heading south. Their perseverance was rewarded.

"In the distance they suddenly made out a few wretched huts. When they approached, they saw a few human beings. They were fishermen who lived in those huts. The Bedouin decided they would set up their camp there. At night, everyone gathered around the fire and Bedouin and fishermen started discussing their lives. The desert and the sea people soon realized that survival in both elements demanded the same human qualities: patience, perseverance, surrender to nature's laws, and courage.

"The fishermen showed them their boats and nets, and the Bedouin's sharp eye saw that this place could be a good harbor for the boats. 'It's the most favorable spot on the coast—everywhere else the reefs endanger navigation. It's an ideal place for a harbor and for shipping goods around the entire region,' a fisherman explained. 'For instance we could sail all the way to Africa and India, buy goods, bring them back, carry them on caravans to the inner part of the country and sell them.' 'But there's not enough grazing space for our animals, nor fertile land for us to cultivate!' an old Bedouin said. 'We'll have to change our way of life,' a young Bedouin answered. Turning to the sea, he added: 'From now on, the great water will be our second home. I'm sure that it will give us everything that we need to live.' The excited discussion went on and ideas were exchanged until the small hours of the morning.

"This is how the Bedouin started concentrating their life on the sea. They built boats and took fresh water from the river Shatt al-Arab. The clever Bedouin learned about boat building from the experienced craftsmen that they met on their way. The new settlement grew slowly and it was decided to name it Kuwait (little fort), the diminutive of *kut* (fort), after a nearby abandoned Portuguese fort. This all happened around the middle of the 18th century, when Portuguese rule in the Gulf was coming to an end.

"The al-Sabah clan was among the Bedouin who settled on the bay of Kuwait. The settlers chose the eldest from this clan as their leader. The story of this dynasty—which still rules in the Emirate of Kuwait today—begins with Sheikh Sabah, who reigned from 1756 to 1762. Sheikh Abdullah I, son of the founder of the dynasty, was a particularly gifted leader who reigned from 1762 to 1812.

"During his reign Kuwait became the most important harbor and trading place north of the Gulf. Pearl-fishing, trading, fishing, and growing dates in the fields in the estuary of the river Shatt al-Arab led to a pleasant life and a powerful al-Sabah dynasty. For more than a hundred years, Kuwait was the center of boat building in the Gulf, and it owned the most impressive merchant fleet in those waters. Kuwaitis had developed into brave seafarers and their boats were famous for their speed and safety. The vast quantities of wood needed for their construction, mostly teak, were obtained from India.

"But from the beginning the Kuwaitis also proved to be clever and skillful diplomats. The Ottoman Empire had already conquered Mesopotamia all the way to the river Shatt al-Arab in the 16th century, before taking possession of the Gulf region as far as Rub' al-Khali (the southern coast of today's Saudi Arabia). Until the 19th century, the Bedouin of the Arab peninsula were opposed to the Ottomans and there were ceaseless battles, with victory often changing sides. But the Kuwaitis sent a delegation to the Ottoman governor in Basra to avoid conflicts with their powerful neighbor from the north, and the Ottomans tolerated the new settlers.

"The next danger came from the south at the end of the 18th century, in the form of the Saudi Wahhabites. The Kuwaitis defended themselves bravely against those attacks, which still represented a constant threat when pirates brought insecurity to the seas. Kuwait then turned to the emerging political power in the Gulf region, namely Great Britain. But Great Britain was not interested in obligations, especially as this area was under the influence of the Ottomans, with whom it did not wish to enter into conflict. So the Kuwaitis turned to the Ottomans, who offered them protection in exchange for the payment of a tribute. The Ottoman governor of Basra appointed the sheikh of Kuwait as local governor, thereby bringing Kuwait under Ottoman rule. Times began to change...."

There was a break, the adults sipped their coffee and I was given my favorite drink, water-diluted yogurt with a pinch of salt. After water, this was the best remedy against thirst. The storyteller looked at me as he spoke, and I felt very important, so I listened raptly even though I couldn't understand everything.

"In the second half of the 19th century, modern British freighters started ousting the traditional Kuwaiti sailing boats—

dhows and *boums*—and this marked the beginning of the decay of boat-building."

Another sip of coffee...

"In addition, the Ottomans suddenly started to threaten Kuwait. Great Britain was now interested in limiting the influence of other states in the Gulf, for what mattered most was to secure its strategic interests by protecting the sea route to India. At this time, Kuwait held no interest from an economic viewpoint. So Great Britain promised to prevent Kuwait from being occupied by the Ottoman armies in exchange for a partial renunciation of sovereignty.[1] To the outside, Kuwait appeared to be under Ottoman rule, but in reality Great Britain had the final say. The Ottoman era came to an end with the First World War and the Arab world was divided between Great Britain and France through the 1916 Sykes-Picot Treaty. Kuwait finally fell into the hands of Great Britain.

"Now the borders to the Saudi state—created between 1902 and 1926 with British help and approval—and to Iraq were determined through the British mandate, and by 1923, the spatial definition of the Kuwaiti state was complete.

"In the thirties, when Japanese cultured pearls invaded the world market, the demand for the much more expensive natural pearls almost vanished, ruining Kuwait's second major economic activity. Until 1930 there had been some 12,000 pearl fishers, but now they were losing their jobs, while pearl merchants and emirs were deprived of a brilliant income. Bitter poverty came back to many homes. Just as strongly as Kuwait had developed and claimed its place in the Gulf, it now stagnated and returned to economic insignificance and poverty. But while people let their heads droop, fate sent them a new source of life."

The storyteller now looked increasingly at the adults. I started fidgeting and showing signs of tiredness.

"During the First World War, Great Britain had come to realize the weakness of its military apparatus because it depended on oil imports from America. It therefore focused its efforts on finding its own oil sources within the Empire, and the Gulf region became the economic center.

"From the time between the two world wars, the interests of the oil industry moved increasingly from the Western hemisphere (the United States, Mexico, Venezuela) to the

Middle East. The oil from the Middle East was abundant and of high quality, and it was closer to the European markets and cheaper to produce. The United States also started taking an interest in this region and it gradually replaced Great Britain in regional supremacy.

"When Russia quit competing for Persia, Great Britain extended its influence over the whole of that country and started obtaining the oil to cover the needs of the British fleet from Persia and from the refinery of Abadan, on the east bank of the river Shatt al-Arab. After the dismemberment of the Ottoman Empire, it also systematically extended its political control to Iraq. But this is when the competition started with the American oil companies, and after protracted disputes Great Britain and the United States agreed on a common exploitation of the Iraqi oil wells. For safety's sake, Great Britain also signed a contract with Kuwait granting it oil concessions and therefore securing potential oil wells in this country too.

"Isn't it a gift from fate that in the same decade that saw the ruin of pearl-fishing and the pearl trade a new source of life was discovered that would bring unsuspected riches?"

I couldn't tell whether the storyteller was serious or sarcastic. In any case he went on with his story.

"In 1938 oil was discovered in Kuwait. And in 1946, as the first oil from the Burgan field left the country on a British tanker, a fairy tale began, called 'when the master becomes wealthy, the servant also profits!'"

What did he mean? His voice concealed anxiety. This fairy tale seemed to be one with a sad end.

"After the Second World War, the United States managed to supplant Great Britain in the Middle East and henceforth implement their policy in the area. A new world order was born. The major intersocietal relationships such as trade, transportation, currency, and customs were governed by American interests. After fierce competition, seven groups of companies held the oil sector under firm control: five American (Exxon, Mobil, Socal, Texaco, and Gulf) and two British (Shell and BP), which were later joined by a French one.

"In exchange for the absence of US state control of the energy market, the granting of tax privileges, and an equal distribution between the different groups, the companies had to support America's foreign policy in the region. Not only that, they controlled the market and kept it stable, ensuring that there would be no over-production. For as long as the companies restricted the production of cheap oil in the Middle East, thereby artificially maintaining the need for expensive American oil, the relatively high American production costs in Texas could determine the energy prices worldwide. The reward for the companies was an additional profit gained from the difference between both production costs.

"The United States came out the absolute winner: Firstly, they protected their local oil industry; secondly, they were in a position to influence energy policy; and finally, to politically control the Middle East, since the countries depended totally on the income they received from the oil companies and were hardly allowed to examine the companies' commercial practices. The companies manipulated oil production and therefore those states' income according to political discretion—one time this government would fall, another time that one would come into power. Of course only conservative governments, pursuing American interests, were supported."

My head was buzzing, I couldn't understand much but I could see the faces of the adults, I read bitterness in my father's face, anger in my mother's eyes, and I felt that it was about injustice. Injustice, like the grown-ups always warned us against: Don't take anything away from anyone; If you want something, ask for it politely; Respect and honor your guests, for this is how you show love to all creatures; Be kind and courteous toward the smaller and weaker. Somehow this didn't reflect what the grown-ups themselves did!

The storyteller took a sip of water, leaned back and went on. "But the United States could not totally control this region, because they were also busy checking the Soviet Union and stabilizing Western Europe, among others endeavors. Class struggles and revolutions broke out in Egypt (1952–1970), in Syria (1958–1970), and in Iraq (1958–1974). These movements offered alternative development policies, thus threatening Western interests. Not only that, they tried to influence the cooperation of the oil countries with the companies and the imperialistic powers through propaganda and ideological influences.

"They also competed for leadership in the Arab world and opposed the Israeli occupation of Palestine in words and actions. The imperialistic powers could only conceive of responding to such revolutionary forces through military action. When Israel prepared its so-called 'liberation attack' against Egypt, Syria, and Jordan in the June 1967 war, it was not only looking after its own national interests, but it did those powers the greatest favor, for which they would remain grateful for a long time, because it brought an end to the socio-economic confrontations in the region."

Silence fell as the grown-ups seemed wrapped up in their own grief. Their hearts still seemed overcome by the pain, the feelings of helplessness and resignation that this war had brought about. With a little smile, our hostess tried to lift the atmosphere by passing around a tray of sweets.

"Let's not talk about politics! Instead, why don't you tell our guests about life in Kuwait!" she kindly said.

She put the tray in front of me and encouraged me to help myself, which I did quite happily.

"The face of Kuwait is changing fast. We are a small country, but one of the wealthiest in the world!" Mahmoud's voice became softer. "All our wealth comes from this black, liquid mass called oil. We sell it to the industrialized countries and then with the money we buy from them everything we need. This money has turned Kuwait into a paradise and we have created the affluent state par excellence. We don't need to pay any taxes, and medical care and education are free, as are electricity and phone service.

"Yet these privileges are limited to Kuwaitis, holders of a Kuwaiti passport; all other inhabitants of this country are excluded from nearly all social welfare benefits. And we have many foreigners in our country—more than half of the population consists of Palestinians, Egyptians, Iraqis, Syrians, Persians, Indians, and Pakistanis. At the end of the day, Kuwaitis represent a minority in their own country."

He stopped, immersed in his own world of thoughts, and then surfaced saying: "Oil is a blessing for this country. Through oil we have become one of the richest countries in the world."

THE FATE OF THE WORLD

Kawthar was quite different from her husband, and she was interested in all the mysterious fates that influence human life.

"Everything in this world is connected. Light comes from darkness and darkness comes from light. 'Up' and 'down' keep interchanging and we human beings live in-between," she would say.

"The sky with its stars and planets have a great influence on us human beings and on all the creatures on earth. The art or science that deals with the forces of the universe and tries to understand and control them is called *akham al-nujum* (the determination of the stars). For the world of the heavens determines the course of the earthly, human world. Observing the stars and planets and studying their constellations and movements explains to us what happened in the past and what will happen in the future, and thus enables us, maybe, to influence these events by writing figures and letters in specific orders. This is because the stars affect the health of the body and of the soul."

"What do you mean, they have an influence?" my mother asked while I looked at her enquiringly.

I loved the sight of the sky, the shapes of the clouds, the light of the stars on the dark cloth that covered us. I loved playing with the sunlight and magically covering the sun with my hand. But that beyond this beauty the sun could also influence our health and our bodies was something I had never contemplated. Kawthar leaned back on the mattress, turned slightly to the right and left to settle her pelvis well, and then she started explaining calmly.

"The universe is a sensitive organism, and its balance is built on the harmonious and complementary relationship between the pairs, male and female, that bring all things into existence. All outer phenomena are the reflection of an inner light, just as all diversity goes back to unity. In the same way all colors can somehow be brought back to one. Relationships between the celestial bodies and between heaven and earth throw a light on the analogies in this world and in the souls. The same qualities that appear in the stars also manifest in the bodies here on earth, which makes it possible to work out a relationship."

"I don't quite understand what you mean," said my mother, and I waited impatiently for Aunt Kawthar's next words.

"Let me explain: the human being is the most perfect creature on God's earth and just in the human body the wise people among us found all the forms that exist in the universe. They found that the wonderful shapes of the heavenly bodies, their different constellations, the movements of the planets, the manifold materials and minerals, the various planets, plants and animals, all these were related to the human body."

Aunt Kawthar's voice grew deep and soft. "There are four pillars, *arkan*, below the moonlight. They are the four mothers, *ummahat*, or four elements, and when they come together, the children, *mawalid*, or three kingdoms are born: the mineral kingdom, the plant kingdom, and the animal kingdom."

She smiled at me, and I was far too eager to return her smile, for here I was, hearing of a world that I didn't know existed and there was no way I wanted to be distracted.

"Those four elements are also found in the human body: the head, the breast, the belly, and the lower part of the abdomen all the way down to the feet."

As she spoke, her hands brushed the respective parts. "For instance the head corresponds to the element fire; it is the home of the sight and the control of the senses. The breast is in harmony with the element air because this is where breathing is formed. The belly coincides with the element water because this is where moisture lies." I suddenly felt slightly queasy thinking that my stomach was all wet inside.

But Aunt Kawthar went on speaking quietly: "The area from the lower part of the abdomen to the feet corresponds to the element earth because it rests on the earth, just like the others are built above and around the earth. Those four elements produce steam, out of which come the winds, the clouds, the rain, the plants, and the minerals. Similarly, the four elements produce vapor in the human body: mucus in the nose, tears in the eyes, saliva in the mouth. Winds originate from the belly, together with the liquids that are eliminated, such as urine. The structure of the human body is like the earth, the bones are like the mountains, the inside of the bones—the bone-marrow—is like the minerals, the belly like the ocean, the bowels like rivers, the veins like brooks, the flesh like land, the hair like plants, the front the east, the back the west, the right hand the south, the left hand the north, the breath the wind, human speech like thunder, human shouts like lightning, human laughter like daylight, human tears like rain, human despair and sorrow like the darkest night, human sleep like death, human wakefulness like life; the days of youth like spring, young adulthood like summer days, the days of maturity like autumn, and the days of old age like winter. The movements and deeds of human beings are like the movements of the planets, with birth and existence on earth like the rising stars and death like their fading."

Aunt Kawthar paused, as if to check whether her audience was really interested in what she was saying.

"Please go on," my mother said immediately.

And Aunt Kawthar went on contentedly: "When the male drop falls into the womb, together with the egg it represents the first matter or substance. When the embryo receives four layers of tissue, those represent nature and the four elements. When the different parts of the body appear, such as the head, the hands, the belly, the sexual organs and the feet, they represent the seven regions of the earth. The inner organs—the lungs, the brain, the kidneys, the heart, the gall-bladder, the liver and the spleen—represent the seven heavens."

Kawthar took a sip of cold water, put the glass down and went on talking, more softly: "The lungs are the first heaven, they represent the sphere of the moon, for the moon is the lung of the cosmos and the communicator between both worlds. There are many angels in this heavenly sphere and the angel of soft water and air is prince here. The brain is the second heaven and represents the sphere of Mercury, because Mercury is the brain of the cosmos. In this sphere too are many angels and here rules the angel responsible for learning to write, for gathering knowledge, and for mastering everyday life. His name is Gabriel and he is the second reason for human knowledge on this earth, praise to Allah! The kidneys are the third heaven and they represent the sphere of Venus, because Venus is the kidney of the cosmos. The angel of joy, happiness, and appetite rules here.

"The heart is the fourth heavenly sphere and represents the sun, for the sun is the heart of the cosmos. In this sphere dwell many angels and the angel responsible for life is the leader here. His name is Serafiel and he is the second reason for the life of the inhabitants of the earth. The spleen is the fifth heaven, and it represents Mars, for Mars is the spleen of the cosmos. The angel who rules here is responsible for angers and hardness, for striking and killing. The liver is the sixth heaven and represents the sphere of Jupiter, for Jupiter is the liver of the cosmos. Many angels dwell there and they are ruled by the angel responsible for food. His name is Michael and he is the second reason for the food of the inhabitants of the earth. The gall bladder is the seventh heaven and it represents the sphere of Saturn, for Saturn is the gall bladder of the cosmos. Azrael rules over the other angels of this sphere. He is the angel who takes the soul at the time of death."

"Why do you always say that those angels are the second reason for something, Aunt Kawthar?" I asked, astonished.

Aunt Kawthar's voice became even softer, so that mother and I had to bend forward a little: "Nature's phenomena are a sign of God, just like human souls are a sign of God. And God is the First Reason for everything that exists. The details of similarity do not matter so much as the fact that there is a correspondence. When you become a witness to God's manifestation in the cosmos, then you recognize the correspondence in all things. Astrology is the quest for the qualitative correspondence, namely the correspondence between the upper and lower worlds. The relationships between the heavenly bodies, and between heaven and earth, throw a light on the relationships that take place here on earth and within the souls.

"All things represent certain qualities, and all these manifestations ultimately flow from unity and back to the same source. Different things on different levels of reality and at different times and in different places manifest the same qualities of reality, namely unity, because everything is connected. And this is why the stars can influence the health of the soul and the body."

Aunt Kawthar closed her eyes and became silent. She was a peculiar woman. Her simplicity and her mysterious knowledge had a magical effect on me, and I found it difficult to take my eyes off her, as if I could discover further mysteries in her face, in her whole appearance.

As darkness fell and the heat relented with the sunset, we decided to go out together for a walk.

TIME IN PERSPECTIVE

The body divides society into manhood and womanhood.
— Leila Ahmed

The favorite theme of Mahmoud, Kawthar's husband, was the future of Kuwait, and the subject of women belonged to this theme.

"The Kuwaiti woman is self-confident, capable, and full of fighting spirit. She has always been the pioneer champion of women's rights in the Gulf. The first women's organization was founded in Kuwait as early as 1964, three years after Kuwait's independence. Yet to this day women don't have the right to vote in Kuwait.[1] The Kuwaiti government has withheld political rights from women, even though they contribute so much to the building of this country and the doors to higher education and professional life are open to them."[2]

We were wending our way side by side on the extremely wide pavement that edged the even wider, several-laned streets.

"Is it Monday today?" my mother asked.

With that question, Kawthar went into another dimension: "It was the Babylonians who introduced the seven-day cycle. They gave the days the names of the planets they knew. At the time there were five of them, and they called the sixth day Sunday after the sun and the seventh Monday after the moon. And from the Babylonians this division spread to the whole world."

"According to the constitution, Kuwait is a hereditary monarchy, which grants the Emir nearly unrestricted powers. The parliament has only limited authority.[3] The real meaning of those participation channels is a critical and functional outlet that enables the ruling family to harmonize its policy with the views of the increasingly important non-traditional social groups," Mahmoud went on explaining.

Our ears bounced from one subject to the next—one minute we were here on earth, the next Kawthar would take us to the stars. Somehow it was beautiful to know that life is so full!

"The Arabs divided day and night into sixteen time periods, each one lasting approximately an hour and a half. Do you know the names of those periods?" Aunt Kawthar asked me.

"I only know the five praying periods!" I answered modestly.

"Let me tell you: the division starts for us with the night. *Al-ghasaq* is the dark at the beginning of the night; *al-'atama* is the first and *al-ghalas* the second third of the night; *al-sahar* is the last third of the night, the time before dawn. It is the time of meditation and contemplation. *Al-fajr* is dawn, as you know, the time of early light and the time of the first prayer. Then *al-sabah*, the daybreak, begins, followed by the sunrise, *al-shuruq*. *Al-bukur* is the early morning and *al-duha* the morning. *Al-hajira* is noon, literally noon heat, and *al-dahira* is the middle of the day and the time of the second prayer. *Al-rawah* is the time of coming and going and *al-'asr* the afternoon, the time of the third prayer. *Al-'asil* is the late afternoon, namely the time before the sunset. The sunset is called *al-ghurub* and it is the time of the fourth prayer. *Al-'isa* is the evening and the time of the fifth and last prayer. Just as the day is divided according to hour and a half rhythms, so is sleep. It is therefore more restful for the body to sleep four times one and a half hours or five times one and a half hours, that is seven and a half hours, than eight hours because in that case you wake up in the middle of a phase. You notice it more when you sleep for a long time, yet wake up without feeling refreshed.

"Our women actually no longer need to look after anything at home. We have maids from Sri Lanka, cooks from India, nannies from the Philippines, and chauffeurs from Egypt."

"There are roughly three groups in Kuwait. First, the native Kuwaitis, descendants of the approximately 80,000 people who used to live here before the oil boom. Then the immigrants, mainly Arabs from Syria, Lebanon, Palestine, Egypt and Iraq, who have been living here for years. They're managers, teachers, consultants, and senior executives. They are mostly Muslim, like the Kuwaitis, but this is not enough to unite them. Many of them are very rich and pursue important goals for the government, yet they are not nationals and have no right to vote. The Palestinians are the largest group here. They nearly always come with their families because they would like to stay here for a long time, if not for good, since they have no country to which to return. The third group is the so-called 'immigrant workers.' They are not rich, they are not nationals, and basically they have no rights at all. In actual fact the weakest Kuwaiti female national has more rights than any male immigrant worker. And so it is that three different societies live here in Kuwait—maybe even four if you count the Europeans who come, usually on fixed-term contracts. We have become a Muslim class society and not, as our faith intends, a Muslim brotherhood nation, and this is the greatest obstacle to our political evolution."

"What do you mean?" Father asked.

"Basically we're a transition society because so far—and it won't change that soon—the political participation potential of the various population groups living in Kuwait is not clear. This situation is blocking development, especially the full application of parliamentary law. Right now the so-called parliament is only a consultative council for the ruling house."

"When you wake up in the morning, it is important for the body not to jump up immediately. You can stay in bed lying for a short while, and thank God that you may live another day, or you can consciously flow through all the parts of the body and greet them. And when you get up, it is good to roll on your side or even on your belly and to stretch out on all fours like a cat and only then to stand up," Kawthar said.

I liked that idea of stretching out like a cat.

"Do you know how it stimulates your whole body when you take a glass of water on an empty stomach first thing in the morning, and you wait to have your breakfast until forty minutes later. My father used to add four garlic cloves, which he cut in the middle and swallowed with the water. When he had reached a ripe old age, we found it difficult to overtake him when he walked. He would jump up the stairs like a gazelle and fly over the footpath!" Kawthar's gaze turned inside and she smiled softly at the thought of her father. She seemed to love and miss him very much.

Mahmoud continued: "Our greatest problem is the Kuwaiti youth who basically don't see it as necessary to take up paid employment, as their fathers are rich enough to feed them and the next generation. Women are often blamed for this lack of a sense of responsibility in the young because they leave their children's education to foreign nannies. But one could blame the fathers just as much.

"Basically we're dealing with a unique phenomenon in this country. Kuwait has practically become the richest country in the world—overnight and without any effort. And it is not easy for people to handle this properly and wisely. Fancy going to bed at night feeling hungry and when you wake up the next morning there's a chest full of gold next to you. On the gold is a rolled up letter that says: 'This gold is for you. No matter how much you use it, it will last for a hundred years and it won't run out!'

"You'll start doing good to yourself and your children and relatives, and you'll also do good to the inhabitants of your small country and change your country into a paradise. You will get people from the whole world to help you build and others to serve and spoil you and your fellow men. Good should also be done to other peoples around you, why not, this is how prestige grows and recognition, and your influence. Life should be good for all, but not equally good for all and no one apart from you and your neighbors should decide what is to be done with the gold and how it should be distributed. It is human to act in this way, but not democratic."

"What does 'democratic' mean, Uncle?"

"Democratic is when everyone can state their ideas and views concerning the distribution of the gold and then the decision is taken together for the benefit of all."

"But Kuwait is known for its liberal views," Father said.

"That's right, the small Emirate of Kuwait offered many opposition groups in the Arab countries an alternative to Beirut when they wished to escape local press censorship. Many Arab immigrants send their salary home, or take it with them when they return. This income has flowed into their country's economy and contributed to economic stability, bringing changes to the life conditions of the most remote villages. Kuwait has also supported the poorer Arab states with loans and funding. This has brought Arab oil-producing and non-producing countries closer."

"In that case, Uncle, haven't they distributed the gold well?"

Mahmoud smiled: "You are right, but Kuwaitis bought everything with their gold: everything here is imported, from bananas to flowers."

He turned to Father: "Social and material privileges have been an obstacle to local intellectual and economic efforts. Instead of developing our own industrial structures, we simply buy them! Standards of living rise, and then comes the demographic explosion. Eating habits change and our agriculture, already limited by natural conditions, is neglected, so that we depend more and more on imports, and there is no way we will avoid a dangerous food crisis.

"Moreover, advertising, worldwide mass media, and models keep pushing us into consumerism. We import masses of electric and electronic products, and tons of cars and luxury goods, and we are becoming incalculably dependent. And our cultural dependence is just as bad—if not worse. Suddenly we find ourselves covering our values and principles through Western-dominated media, and we are increasingly confronted with information, news, consuming habits, and lifestyles that are not based on our identity or interests.

"Western education and economic systems have become our models. Our capital too is controlled by the West, because we invest in Western companies and in the international banking system, instead of creating alternative, innovative development strategies in the Middle East and participating actively in local economic developments. The ensuing poverty and uniformity is not only our loss, but the whole world's.

"We are economically dependent, and politically, we are vulnerable to all world fluctuations, including on the energy markets. And those huge military budgets of ours, which are meant to protect us, don't help at all, quite to the contrary!"

Mahmoud gazed into the distance. He was a gifted, visionary story-teller.

"We need our own creative education system and we must develop our own capacities. We shouldn't bury the potential of women either—they are our mothers, our sisters, our daughters, and partners, and they make up half of our population! A man needs both legs to stand up and walk!"

Kawthar suddenly turned her head toward us and said: "If women are granted the same rights as men, then they can contribute equally to the development of the country, but as long as they are pushed aside and the doors remain closed, the myth of men's superiority will survive!"

She could see clearly in the sky, yet she knew exactly what was happening on earth.

"We do have women's organizations in Kuwait, but they are not mixed—I mean mixed between native Kuwaiti women and women from other Arab countries who have been living here for years and have integrated. And women's organizations should not only be considered charitable associations, although their work and achievements in the field of development and in the education sector are not negligible. For instance, morning classes for women to learn to read and write, centers for children after the Montessori model, or the founding of village communities in Lebanon for families and orphans according to the SOS-children's village system.

"Women's organizations should commit themselves more to the political participation of all women in Kuwait. Once we have the political rights, the others are easier to obtain. But we must learn to unite, to become one voice! The doors of education are open to both sexes and women get the same salary for the same work, but promotion and promotion opportunities are not so good."

"And how are things with respect to tradition and religion?" Mother asked thoughtfully.

"Kuwaiti women are under pressure to bear many children. The government wants them to look after their children and stay at home with them despite the nannies. Islam respects women and women should participate in family life and in the life of the Muslim community. Women must first know their rights and then fight for them, as no one will give their rights to them. Women need more rights in their personal life, for example in the marriage and divorce law."

"You are a true feminist!" Mother said laughingly to Aunt Kawthar.

"You know that we don't have such an expression, but if it means the fair division of the good on earth between man and woman, then so be it!"

We decided to walk back and I was very happy that

everyone kept silent, each wrapped up in their own dreams.

That evening Kawthar prepared *dolma*, my favorite Iraqi dish: stuffed onions, eggplants, tomatoes, and grape leaves all cooked together in one pot, and then served on a big tray. They lay next to each other, waiting to be seen by lustful eyes and snapped up by hungry fingers. Unfortunately I ate too much of the wonderful dish and had to wait for a long time before I could taste the dessert. I went early to bed that day, with my belly aching and my head buzzing. The life of grown-ups is mightily complicated, I thought as I slid into bed. If I got the chest of gold, I would distribute the gold over the whole world so that no one would hunger anymore. I was so tired. Tomorrow it was already time to go back to Beirut.

EGYPT

CAIRO, THE HEART OF EGYPT

I planned to spend the coming year in Cairo and the single thought that I would spend autumn, winter, spring, and summer, a whole year cycle, in the land of the Pharaohs, made my heart beat faster with joy and excitement. Egypt, the mother of the world, as Egyptians affectionately call their country, is for the Arab world the quintessence of musical pleasure (*tarab*), the Arab Hollywood, and also the seat of the great Islamic university of al-Azhar, the most respected theological university of the Muslim world. Nowhere in the Arab world is so much hashish smoked, nowhere is there so much dancing and singing, and nowhere are the people so devout as in this country. I planned to study Arabic, ethnology, and Islam for one year at the University of Cairo.

Before I travelled to Cairo, a friend told me: "You either love Cairo or you hate it, there's no in-between!" I wondered which group I would belong to.

The plane landed before sunrise at Cairo airport, an unimpressive new building. I pushed my suitcase on a trolley to customs with all the other passengers, was examined by a customs officer behind his windowpane, and was given my passport with a stamp and a friendly smile.

Eager porters stood outside the airport and I was happy I had only one suitcase, because just this one attracted five of them. I looked at them unobtrusively, quickly determining who had earned least that day, and decided on a friendly, slightly stooped middle-aged man. He picked up my suitcase happily, led me to a taxi, and swiftly opened the trunk with a skillful turn of the thumb.

"*Ahlan wa-sahlan fi misr!*" Welcome to Cairo! Although he said *misr* (Egypt), I would later find out, to my bewilderment, that this means Cairo too. This is how much Cairo meant to the Egyptians.

"*Ithibbi it-truhi fen, ya madam?*" "Where would you like to go, lady?"

I had to smile. Like nearly all Arab men and women, over the years I had become acquainted with this dialect from the many Egyptian films and television shows that had infiltrated the whole Arabic-speaking world. It was therefore particularly amusing to experience it live. So they really talk like they do in the movies! People moved and gesticulated in real life exactly as actors showed them in the films. During the first days, all of Cairo seemed to me like one string of movies. What great actors Egypt contains!

I was tired and at the same time excited. There was no way I could sleep.

"It would be nice to take a little tour around the city before we drive to my friends in the area of Jami' at-Tahrir, in the center of Cairo."

"*Min enayya!*" "By the light of my eye, with pleasure!" was the driver's answer. Arabic expressions are always a balm for the soul. I settled in the car, after having expressed my gratitude to the porter with a tip, and off we went. It was early and still dark, and the city was still in peaceful slumbers.

The taxi rode leisurely through the streets. A pleasantly refreshing breeze played about my face when I rolled down the window, and suddenly the call to morning prayer caught my ear. It started in one mosque and spread out. Like waves, the voices flooded over the whole city, the muezzins' calls flowing into sleeping ears and calling souls out to rise, *as-salatu hazrunmin an-nawm*. Prayer is more blessed than sleep.

The whole city vibrated under this call. Cairo was renowned for its beautiful voices, which my soul could but confirm. With the dawn prayer, every day the soul is born again, the gift of life renewed, and from the morning quietness the soul captures the strength to face the turbulence of the day. The first tea and coffee shops rolled up their shutters with loud raspings. We stopped at a teashop and the taxi driver brought me a hot, dark, sweet tea, which I slowly sipped while he exchanged morning greetings and pleasantries with the shopkeeper.

As if by magic, the city started moving and the streets slowly filled up. The all-powerful light removed the darkness and pink trails in the sky heralded the day. Cats and dogs crept about, moving knowingly into side streets and hiding spaces, leaving the city to God's highest creatures. A garbage cart pulled by two devoted, hardened donkeys rattled past, led by two teenagers.

The garbage city, which grew parallel to the dwellers' city, was the world of the poorest among the poor, a world with its own laws and codes of conduct. It was mostly attended to by children who made sure that the city was clean. They made a living from other people's garbage, where day after day they hoped to find a small treasure. A ring thrown away by mistake could change their whole lives. Cairo had many faces, and they were not all pleasant or easy to take.

With light came traffic and as we headed toward my new home, there was no trace of the comfortable flow of empty streets. One line of cars waited after the other, wildly hooting and dodging passers-by who jumped out, sleepy civil servants, small, sweetly dressed schoolgirls with inordinately large ribbons in their hair, people hiding their still-sticky sleepiness behind serious faces, others whose smiles pleaded with the drivers for understanding and consideration, hands holding on to car hoods or hitting the cars from behind when they could not get through.

Where were all these people coming from, all of a sudden? Out of every wrinkle of this overcrowded city flowed a stream of human creatures who suddenly stood on the street to participate in the daily dance of survival. I was left gasping. To survive here, one would either have to be capable of surrender, forearmed with all one's instincts, or go mad, or flee as quickly as possible. I chose the first option for the time being. My daredevil driver finally managed to drop me at the requested address.

He helped me with my suitcase to the elevator, which—as I would later find out—only operated at indefinable times, though always when the caretaker was around. Maybe the elevator's sense of duty was triggered by the sight of the caretaker, or maybe it was frightened of him. Once upstairs, I rang the bell and Um Adel opened the door. She was a chubby widow in her mid-fifties. Traces of henna covered her whitened, shoulder-length hair, and her eyes, circled by a weariness of life, expressed kindness as well as skepticism. She asked me to come in, in a slightly tired, yet friendly manner. She had been waiting for me, she explained with a mellow voice. She took me straight to the living room. Actually it wasn't a living room but a library or a reading room with two seats and a floor lamp.

Her husband was a writer who had died eighteen years earlier and left her a huge library, which dominated the modest apartment.

"Unfortunately you can't eat books," she told me later with a tired smile. "My husband spent more time in prison than outside. He was a committed communist and he held on to his life philosophy to the very end."

Um Adel had two sons, the first-born called Adel (the just), and the second Lenin, aptly translated as "the one who suffers for his father's opinions." He had already had to change jobs often because of his name. It is not always easy to live in a strict society.

Houses were Cairo's oases of calm, for as soon as you went out on the street, you were swept away by the current of the city, which spat you out only once you locked the door behind you. Um Adel left the house at seven o'clock every morning to go to work in a library, and she came back exhausted at two in the afternoon. After eating her modest lunch she would sit in her favorite armchair with a pot of Arabic coffee that she poured leisurely time and again into her small china cup. She spent a couple of hours like this, letting everyday life run from her.

During the two weeks that I lived at her place, I always left her alone in peace during that time, only joining her afterwards for a chat and a coffee.

"You know, Fawzia, I actually brought up my sons by myself, because in the eighteen years of our marriage, Abu Adel, the father of my children, was only outside prison walls for twelve years, and when he was out, he was so busy getting back in, with his articles and books, that he hardly had any time for them. But at least I had a man and protection. When he died things got worse.

"I was still young and suddenly fair game. The doorbell rang ceaselessly and marriage brokers brought me offers right and left. But I only wanted to be left in peace and to bring up my two sons. As far as I was concerned, the marriage chapter was over. It's not easy to bring up two children when you're alone and a woman, and I had to take great care of my reputation. No strange man was allowed to enter my house, and when it needed some repair, I always called the caretaker as a witness to my purity, so he could confirm my good reputation. I resolved never to invite anyone home, to avoid all possible temptation, and anyhow I didn't have time either, as I had to work because my husband had left us very little.

"But now my sons are grown-up. Lenin helps me when he can, yet I still go to work. Adel is a good boy, but he can't cope with this world. He prefers burying himself in his books, and sometimes for days on end he only comes out of his room for meals. He is currently writing for daily newspapers and he tries hard to be a journalist, but he didn't inherit his father's brilliant mind. I hope he finds a life partner who will understand him and give him the stability he needs."

Um Adel was a realistic woman with a practical mind. She didn't embellish her world, but neither was she a pessimist. She had been so busy protecting her reputation over the years, going to work and reflecting on memories and injustice that her whole life had fallen by the wayside. She had simply forgotten to live.

"I come from Upper Egypt. Soon after our wedding my husband and I came to Cairo, because he wanted to study here and he thought he could find more career opportunities. I also started studying at the Cairo University and I graduated in marketing and accounting. But then came the children and all by myself, without family support, it was difficult to reconcile the two, so I stayed at home to bring up my children.

"I have somehow fallen between two chairs: I've given up the traditional way of life in the extended family, but without managing to enjoy the modern, individual way of life. In the old days, in the country, there was no separation between 'private' and 'political,' 'domestic' and 'public.' The affairs of the community were ruled through personal relationships and despite all difficulties, women exerted a great influence.

"Through mutual visits and the hosting of guests, by preparing a great meal or a celebration, women were directly involved in events and could establish social connections, preventing or destroying them if they considered it necessary. But here in the modern city, each woman lives isolated in her small private box. Of course there are modern, Western institutions, political and cultural spheres in which they can participate, but society still demands that a woman behave according to traditional standards, by which she is also judged."

Um Adel stared ahead. I suddenly felt a heavy pressure on my breast, an unpleasant pressure that seemed as ancient as the history of womankind. I liked Um Adel, but I didn't feel much at ease in her presence. Maybe she stirred something in me that I wasn't yet ready to face. I also had the feeling that the lifelessness, which hung over her house like a cloud, threatened to overwhelm me.

I noticed that I too started to walk around the house like Um Adel, slightly stooped, shoulders dropping indifferently, probably afraid to become shrouded in the mist of the cloud which hung over me. I also laughed with Um Adel, but it was more a polite kind of laugh, planned and culturally conditioned, not lusty and spontaneous. I could understand her: she didn't forgive this society from which she felt excluded and rejected, and which gave her only solitude as a reward for the brave and honorable way in which she had mastered her life.

"I'm not bitter—I did what I had to do." She stared again and slipped into a world I couldn't see. When she came out of it, she seemed even more tired, but in that moment she also unveiled the true being that lived inside her—strong, proud, and indestructible. She was really a beautiful woman, who did not awake pity but sympathy in me.

The two weeks went by quickly. Neither of us found it difficult to say goodbye, and I thanked her for everything and promised to visit her.

EGYPTIAN ANTS,
OR THE FREE TENANTS

*When you give, give to those
who know how to use what you give.*
— Sufi wisdom

With two other students, I found a furnished flat through an agency, near Cairo University, in Dukki, an upper-middle-class quarter. I took to the flat instantly. It was spacious, with two bedrooms, a big entrance hall that also served as dining room, living room, and balcony. The kitchen was tiny and on the wretched side, and the bathroom told of better times. Still, the flat was located on the top floor and the view was pleasantly expansive.

Karin and Randa were my flatmates. Karin had come from Austria to study Arabic, and Randa was an Egyptian who lived in Europe but wanted to spend some time in her native land. They had totally different personalities. Karin was an independent young woman who wandered through the world with a look of permanent inquiry: "Who am I and what am I doing here?" Still, in her own way, she mastered wonderfully all the obstacles that stood in her path. She overlooked the nuances of life, which enabled her to focus on her goals better. I never knew quite what to make of her.

Randa was a reserved, extremely sensitive woman, afflicted by an inferiority complex, gifted with a charming irony and a sharp mind, which perceived the world and herself so clearly that it often turned into cruelty against herself. She was blessed by a sense of humor that I cherished and her loyalty and honesty opened my heart to her.

Every morning Karin jumped out of bed with a frantic jerk because she was always late for her Arabic class at the Goethe Institute. No matter how hard she tried, she never managed to get up on time. With one hand she would take a piece of bread to her mouth, hopping on one leg and sleepily struggling to get the other into her trousers, then hopping again to catch the other leg. She pulled at her tee-shirt mercilessly until all three holes were filled with the right parts of her body, then she would jump jump into one sandal, hop hop into the other, frantically search for the bag and papers scattered around the flat, and with a loud goodbye, rush outside. That was Karin's morning acrobatic performance. I must admit that I enjoyed watching her, and my oriental calm could probably be seen from the raised corners of my mouth.

Once our Austrian whirlwind had left us, Randa and I could begin our civilized breakfast, she with tea, I with coffee. We sometimes ordered a plate of *ful* (cooked fava beans, sometimes known as "the poor man's meat") from the little shop next door, sprinkled with small pieces of tomato and served with Arab bread. Each of us sat in front of her bread, took little pieces from it and, shaping it into a small ladle, dipped it into the warm *ful* before devouring it sensually with an elegant quick movement, the food disappearing swiftly into the mouth. On the days I didn't have any classes afterward, I also ate raw spring onions with it, openly relishing the thought of the awful smell, and Randa had to do the same, merely for self-protection.

Cairo was really a city bursting at the seams, with every single corner turned into living quarters. Small rooms came to life under the flight of stairs, shops no bigger than a square meter changed overnight into sleeping space for a family of five, and huts were built on the roofs to accommodate several additional families. Since most of these people had emigrated from the countryside, they often brought small livestock with them.

On our roof lived a family with their three geese, ten hens, and a sheep that was mainly active during the night. It pattered back and forth over our heads all night long. Hence this thing about counting sheep to fall asleep. I once went up to the roof to take a closer look. The view was actually wonderful from there—you could even admire the pyramids in the distance. Maybe a mountain goat would be happier up there.

The customs and practices of the country ruled on the rooftop. The women cooked over an open fire, and they fetched water in buckets from a public tap that they had discovered like a spring. They balanced the buckets on their heads or caught them between shoulder and head. They wore gaudily bright clothes and small head scarves tied at the back to cover their heads. They shouted loudly when they spoke, as if their voices still had to carry over the distant fields.

Yet my most intense encounter in those days would take place with yet another population of Cairo, one that outnumbered all the others. I discovered them for the first time one morning when I went to prepare breakfast and opened the bread bag. They had apparently woken up much earlier and were busy reconnoitering and collecting. Tiny black *namil* (ants)! The bread was past eating and Randa kindly fetched some fresh bread for breakfast.

"What are you doing?" she asked me when we had finished breakfast.

"I'm putting up a string to hang the bread bag on."

I was very proud of my brilliant idea and thought I had tricked the ants. But the people of the ants seemed to have a longer tradition and span of experience than my youthful imagination. The following day, I was greeted by long black lines creeping along my string, which led straight into the bread bag. This time I went to the shop to get the bread.

I rose to the challenge, something along the lines of Goliath against the people of the million! I found myself a big plastic bowl, filled it with water and put a tin in the middle, on which I balanced the bread bag. I went to bed satisfied.

The following morning, I woke up excited. I must have dreamed of ants, and my first steps took me to my water castle. The sight that awaited me tore my eyes wide open. My water bowl was full of dead ants, whose tiny corpses gathered into a bridge on which other ants crawled toward the bread. The bread bag had already been completely conquered. It was full of ants. They seemed to be absolutely determined fighters—I could make out the red headbands on their oval heads. We had a couple of apples for breakfast. I wouldn't have given up, had it not been for something that happened later that day.

The three of us drank some tea and decided to drive to the pyramids, to take a little walk and enjoy the sunset. It was dark when we came back home. Karin opened the door and we followed her into the flat. When she switched on the light, we discovered a sight so surprising that it nearly floored us. Our dining table had turned into a living mass of ants. I remembered that the tablecloth was red, but not a single spot of it was visible. Millions—no billions!—of ants covered the whole table and floor. We had forgotten the sugar box on the table!

Karin stood there transfixed, and Randa gave a cry. A shudder went down my back.

"What shall we do now?" croaked Randa in a hoarse and desperate voice. Never before had I experienced such a collective display of the power of purposeful beings working together. Somehow I felt fascinated and I resolved to do what had to be done. I went up to the table, extended my arm very calmly, grabbed the sugar box with a jerk, ran into the kitchen and threw it into the bin.

"Let's go to sleep—there's nothing else we can do."

We went to bed feeling rather drowsy and silent. I lay on my back, my eyes open, staring at the ceiling. A couple of hours later, I got up again and marched toward the dining table. Nothing. Not a single ant in sight, as if we had imagined them all. The red tablecloth lay innocently spread across the table, and I had to laugh.

"Fine, you can live at our place and we'll find a way for all of us to get by."

My breath filled with confident warmth. "I'll prepare a bread bag for you and another one for us, and you promise to leave us in peace." I spoke the covenant out loud into the room, so that all the ant people could hear me. I put their bread bag in the kitchen and hung ours safely on a string, for those ants who didn't know what a promise means. Henceforth there were two kinds of tenants in the flat: those who paid rent and those who lived there for free.

A PEOPLE OF POETS & BELIEVERS

Humility is to serve without making a distinction.
—Muhammad al-Razi

I went to the university four times a week. It was a wonderfully beautiful complex, surrounded with an edged lawn and shady trees. Students there came from all directions and conceptions of life and from all social classes. Each different life philosophy and social class showed essentially in their clothes and means of transportation.

The poorer would arrive in overcrowded buses, arms and legs hanging from the windows, and a few muscular travelers hanging from the doors. Many students preferred walking long distances rather than exposing themselves every day to this forced adventure. The slightly better off came to the university in collective taxis. Students who came in their own little cars belonged to the upper middle class. And then there were those who drove luxury cars, and finally those who were driven by chauffeurs. The richer the students, the more Western their style of clothes; they no longer spoke pure Arabic, but mixed in some English, or, for the particularly well travelled aristocrats, French.

The poorer students came mostly from the countryside or small towns. Their main refuge in the big city was Islam; it gave them protection and a sense of identity, and also represented to them a protest against the unjust socio-economic distribution in the country and against what they saw as the capitalist Westernization of society. Isn't every human being on a search for the meaning of life, longing to be happy, to understand oneself and to fill one's place on earth?

The lower middle class, under constant threat of ending up in poverty, held the more prosperous social classes in its mind's eye, and it tended increasingly toward politicized Islam, symbolized first and foremost by the Muslim Brothers in Egypt.

And to find out about the currently prevailing political, social, and religious trends in a Muslim-Arab society, the best way is to observe the women. Egypt was no exception. I registered at the university in Arabic linguistics, Islam, and ethnology. When I entered the lecture hall for the first time, somewhat shyly, and looked around for a seat on the benches, I noticed that the male students were seated on the right and the female ones on the left. Approximately half the women wore veils and a third of these also donned long caftan-like clothes, while most of the other veiled women wore a long skirt and a long-sleeved blouse. The unveiled women wore typically Western clothes. Since I was wearing a long skirt and long-sleeved blouse, but no veil, I didn't quite fit into any category, which left me open to several groups of people fighting for my favor. At the end of the lecture, four young women came up to me.

"*As-salamu alaykum*, oh sister in faith!"

"*Wa-alaykum as-salam wa-rahmatu llah wa-barakatuh*! And peace be with you and Allah's mercy and blessing," I answered.

My response encouraged them and brought a warm smile to their beautiful young faces, all framed with white veils that came down to their waists.

"Welcome to Egypt. Have you come here to study?"

"Yes, I'll be staying here for one year."

"How beautiful, praised be Allah," the most dynamic of them answered. "Come and we'll show you around the university."

One woman went in front of me, one behind me and two of them linked arms with me, right and left. They were coordinated and well organized.

We passed young men who gazed after us, probably wondering at my going around unveiled with those strict believing students. The four of them built an impenetrable protective ring around me and I let them lead me across the university grounds. They showed me their meeting place in front of the small mosque, an anteroom reserved for women. Immediately next to it was the very busy women's bathroom, which was obviously used by female students of all social classes. Tolerance ruled between the different groups, yet I noticed that they existed more alongside than with each other. I liked this colorful diversity and wondered how it had come to be.

Contemporary Egyptian society is the child of its earlier history. Egypt fell under the Ottoman rule at the beginning of the 16th century. Its last representative was the Ottoman viceroy Muhammad Ali. In the first half of the 19th century, Muhammad Ali began to sever the umbilical cord to the Ottoman Empire. He planned to shape Egypt into an independent, modern state, able to adopt the emerging political and economic conditions that came from the rising West. Through an absolutist reform state and an interventionist industrialization program, he wanted to catapult Egypt into modern times and bring on the country's autonomous development.

I could see Muhammad Ali in his castle, looking down over Cairo and thinking about how best to grab hold of this people and purposefully shape them according to his visions. He loved his country, and in the distance the pyramids reminded him of their magnificent past. He also strove for eternity and wanted to be remembered throughout history as a visionary ruler, who pursued his aims in a hard but just way. I pictured Muhammad Ali stroking his thick beard leisurely and reflecting:

"Most of the population is made of farmers or peasant family units. To a large extent, they can take their own decisions in terms of land, the workers they employ, the crops they choose, and how they sell their products. This is therefore the starting point. Food must clearly be in my hands, a strong military must be introduced to protect against inner and outer turbulence, and industry will guarantee this country's economic strength and independence. A radical restructuring must take place to start with, a process of socio-economic transformation, reading the country for modern times. Society must be broken up and shaped anew."

And as always throughout the history of mankind, this transformation would affect first of all the family, and consequently the women.

Muhammad Ali put production and commercialization under state control and weakened ownership of rural property; of course, in a patriarchal society, this first threatened women's property rights. The family as a production unit was partly broken up by means of forced labor, compulsory military recruitment, and expropriations of property. Toward the end of the 19th century, the state policy—defined first by Muhammad Ali and later by the British colonial administration in accordance with the requirements of capitalist penetration—had largely robbed the peasant families of their land and brought about rural waged labor. This social upheaval acted as a double-edged sword for women.

On the one hand the state development policy created a demand for a female work force in the economic and industrial sector, especially in the textile industry, which granted women a certain economic independence from the family group. It also widened their horizons and brought new knowledge. On the other hand the exodus of the men who left the villages on military duty or for employment resulted in an additional workload for the women left behind. They took on further duties, while at the same time their own work came to be seen as less worthy.

The collapse of the traditional family and gender structure with its mutual duties and entitlements to support, and the new separation between home and workplace, suddenly reduced the meaning of the work of women, which was most strongly linked to the home. It was not easy for women to come to terms with this new situation. They were given access to independent income, but suffered partial losses on the family front. For instance, a woman willing to take up employment outside the family unit to secure income for herself and her children risked being labeled a "bad" mother, and she was under threat of losing the custody of her children. On the other hand, the men's departure put women in a position to take over the traditional male guardianship of the children.

This economic pressure also threatened women's property rights, which were only legally confirmed through their relationship to father or husband. If the husband disappeared for an extended period of time because of military service and if he didn't at least send his pay home to compensate for his missing work contribution to the family economy, it could sometimes happen that his wife and children had to leave the family unit.

Muhammad Ali, you didn't think of the women! Though I believe that the consequences of state-controlled production and the resulting weakened family system were rather unintentional. Transitional phases are also a threat to women when they lead to the destruction of classical patriarchy, especially when no clear alternative can be seen on the horizon and women's access to possible new resources remains directly linked to the family structure.

In the urban areas, Muhammad Ali's policy promoted the recruitment of women for state work, in the state-owned industrial companies and the growing health and education sectors. This contributed to freeing them from the exclusive control of the family, which naturally provoked antagonistic reactions from those families.

"My daughter is supposed to work for strangers outside the house, and what's more, for money! Do I need this shame!" the head of the family would say. "Am I sick or too old to provide for her? I'm crazy to jeopardize my honor and let her work outside my protection!"

Those who benefited from modernization were mostly women from the urban upper classes, who came to enjoy, so to speak, the privileges of their class. The state's modernization policy gave them access to new training opportunities and jobs, as well as greater freedom.

"Hello, I'm Amira."

I was abruptly torn from my history of women. I looked at her wide-eyed. She must have realized that she had jolted me out of another world.

"I'm sorry to have frightened you!"

"No, not at all!" She laughed and her mouth stretched nearly from one ear to the other.

"You're not an Egyptian either, are you?"

"No, I come from Iraq, and you?"

"The Sultanate of Oman."

Amira was stunningly self-confident. When she spoke her curls kept stroking her forehead. She didn't just generously fill the space around her with her beautiful hands while talking; her whole body followed her words, sometimes to the right, sometimes to the left.

She lived together with her sister who also studied here and two servants in a private apartment in Garden City, an elegant district of the city. They had both come to Cairo to study Arabic and to return home two years later as trained Arabic teachers.

"Every Omani, man or woman, rich or poor, who wishes to study abroad receives state support and makes a commitment to work for two years in state-owned institutions at the end of the course of study," Amira proudly explained.

She was very proud of her country, with its beautiful Sultan and its Arab–African–Indian cultural blend. Although she liked Egypt and the Egyptian people very much, in truth she looked down on them a little, with their many socio-cultural and economic problems.

"To the outside, the Egyptian society is conservative and strongly Muslim, but when you look behind the scenes, it's worse here than in Europe."

"What do you mean?"

"You only need to keep your eyes open at the university. Do you know that a great many of the female students earn their keep (university fees, clothes, and personal expenses) through prostitution? Good looks and a beautiful dress are their only chance to catch a rich man. These days, diplomas don't get you anywhere in Egypt—you just remain a small civil servant, unless you study medicine or law, but how many girls manage to get the required high A level grades? And if you and your husband are small civil servants, you'll never be able to afford your own home, just nothing but daily survival.

"These days, when a suitor comes to your family, people hardly enquire about his family descent or his personality. The essential questions are: how much does he make and does he have his own home? Need is damaging and destroys true values!"

"Could it be that your viewpoint is slightly one-sided? Aren't you exaggerating when you say that the university is full of prostitutes? How are those girls supposed to marry if they're no longer virgins? And how about all the veiled students?"

Amira smiled at me: "Of course I'm exaggerating a little, but the phenomenon shouldn't be overlooked. As far as virginity is concerned, that's not really a problem. It doesn't cost much to have an operation just before the wedding or to insert a little bag full of chicken blood. Most of the time, the mothers are let into the secret and help their daughters."

Her tone became dreadfully dry: "The vagina is the tear that runs through our whole culture and the Western powers have crucified the whole country. The whole Arab world is like a woman raped—maybe that's why our men are so attached to patriarchy."

Amira looked at me challengingly and smiled: "Would you like a taste of Omani delicacies? I'd like to invite you home."

"Great!" I liked Amira's confidence and her extremely direct way with words.

I was lucky to be accepted by each of the various groups at the university, and spent my time with first this and then that one. To me they all belonged to the many souls that lie in the Egyptian breast.

Ula told me proudly that she belonged to the Muslim Sisters, something like the female counterpart of the Muslim Brothers. She was definitely the leader of her year. Ula's small round black eyes, further emphasized next to her white veil, sparkled with enthusiasm when she spoke of her faith: "With Nasser, we have experienced Arab socialism, with Sadat we've been thrown into the mechanism of the Western capitalist economy as a result of the 'open door' policy, and both directions have failed to bring just solutions for Egypt.

"We must return to our traditional values. We've become confused and disoriented because we've neglected our faith, which gives us security, a sense of direction, and spiritual support. For instance, my family was fragmented, my father was at work all day, he didn't know anything about us and neither did we about him, and my mother no longer managed to bring her children up properly in those confusing times. She didn't know what my sister was doing and my little brother spent all day playing football in the streets.

"When I went to the Muslim Sisters, I found meaning and a sense of security. I wanted to help all human beings and of course I started with my family. When I started wearing the veil, my father objected at first. But I started to talk about Islam, I prayed five times a day, I told them how a Muslim woman had to be, how many rights she had and how proud she could be.

"I told my father what it meant to be a true father to his family and he had tears in his eyes. My sister was the first who came praying with me, then Mother and Father followed. Now we're a proper family. We sit together every evening, we talk about our religion, we eat and pray together and everyone is happy. Now even my mother comes to wake me up for the morning prayer if I oversleep." Ula radiated such self-confidence as I had seldom seen in such a young woman.

One day a car came to pick up Ula from University. A beautiful woman in her thirties sat at the wheel. Her hair was covered with a neat turban that enhanced her classical reserved features. Her face looked familiar, but I couldn't place her.

Ula was very excited: "I'd like to take you with us, Fawzia!"

"Where to?" I asked, surprised.

"I'd like you to meet our sheikh. He is receiving guests today. You see the lady at the wheel? She's his wife and she'll take us to their home."

"No, I can't." I didn't feel comfortable with the idea.

"Please come with us—we'll only stay as long as you wish. By Allah, say yes!"

"All right, then."

I found myself sitting in the back of the car, both women in front of me, and the radio played Um Kalthoum.

"It's not very proper that she should sing so openly about love," Ula said.

"But who can resist Um Kalthoum?" the sheikh's wife answered with a smile.

We stopped at a house with a little front garden and I followed the two women into the anteroom. A couple of young men stole busily back and forth. They were obviously in charge of the guests' well-being, greeting them, taking them to a large hall and getting them tea and coffee.

"We are all guests on God's earth," said the sheik's wife.

I noticed a gray-bearded, bulky man who completely filled the seat on which he sat. A few young men were also seated in the room. The sheikh and his wife greeted each other easily and pleasantly, and you could immediately feel that there was obviously a great love between them, based on mutual respect.

"I've brought guests."

"Everyone who comes is welcome!" answered the sheikh, looking straight at Ula and me.

Ula shook with joy. She felt in good hands here and she felt honored to be a part of this Muslim community.

Silence.

The sheikh was apparently used to people coming to him with concrete questions and he wanted to give his guests time.

Ula had a question. "Is it right for a woman to work outside the house?"

The sheikh smiled. He seemed pleased by the question. "A woman has the right to work outside the house if respectability is maintained in the workplace. But she is not obliged to work because it is the man's first task to provide for the family. However, if she works, she must get equal pay for the same job. But not every woman is capable of fulfilling both her family and professional obligations. If she can't manage both, she should renounce the latter."

He added: "The family represents the unity of society and both man and woman must fulfill their family responsibilities in accordance to their specific and natural abilities in order to bring up the next generation. Man and woman are different but equal. A woman who understands her role is the key to a just society based on the principles of a true Islam. A woman is not a weak creature—she is the model of society. Whoever wishes to discover the secret of the progress or decline of a people should examine the influence of the woman on the character of her men."

His wife sat there with pride and dignity, and her look said that she knew what he was talking about. He was a practiced speaker who spoke clearly and without beating about the bush, yet everything was open when he spoke. I didn't know whether I felt comfortable or not. You couldn't reject this sheikh lightly, yet he failed to open my heart. I was surprised that he didn't comment on the fact that I wasn't wearing a veil.

I decided to ask a question: "What are the Muslim Brothers?"

Without pausing he started talking immediately: "The founder of the Egyptian Muslim Brothers was Hasan al-Banna. In one of his letters he wrote: 'Our duty as Muslim Brothers is to work toward transforming ourselves, our hearts, and souls by connecting them to God, and then to organize our society in such a way that it is capable of being a virtuous community that commands good and prohibits wrongdoing, and then the good state will come from society.'"[1]

"We want a just order, a Muslim state that takes up the modern challenges while remaining committed to our traditional Muslim virtues and laws, and upholding community sharing and the solidarity of the patriarchal family. It is not right that the poor majority should live off beans while the privileged take quick flights to go shopping in Paris."

He was right—that is not fair. But what happens when the Muslim Brothers and Sisters take over the state before they have transformed their hearts and souls? Will it be better for the people then?

I signaled to Ula that I wanted to leave and she excused us, saying we still had a lecture to attend.

"You are always welcome here. My wife also studies at the university," and then he turned to me: "I hope you will find a good Muslim for a husband, and that you will then wear the veil like a good Muslim woman!"

There it was, the comment, and I got angry. I thought, then smiled, "If my heart and soul connect with God, His mercy will certainly envelop me."

I CAN'T FORGIVE HIM

I'm engaged!" With those words Karin burst contentedly into the flat. "Pardon?" came out of both our mouths. Randa and I looked at each other, and then at Karin again. "When did it happen, and who is he?"

We didn't know whether to rejoice or be angry at our flatmate for getting engaged without any ado, leaving us all this time in the dark. But it seemed perfectly normal to Karin. That woman would always surprise me with the way she acted and with her philosophy of life.

"I met him at the Austrian embassy."

"Have you met his family?" Randa asked.

"He lives with his mother and sister, and he works at the embassy."

"Yes, and what else?"

"He's 35, he's a Copt[1] and very attractive. I'm moving in with them until the wedding!"

Randa and I exchanged amazed looks again.

"Well, when are you moving?"

"Right now, I'm just packing my bags!"

And truly, before our confusion abated, she had packed her luggage and disappeared with a "I'll be in touch in a few days!"

"She's crazy," were Randa's first words after silent minutes. "I hope she doesn't regret it," she added softly. Plans were already taking shape in my head.

Accomplished facts must be dealt with by swift, concrete steps. "I'll go down quickly to the rental agency. We need a new place, as we can't afford this one by ourselves."

And four days later we were sitting in a new flat. We were very lucky because we liked the first flat we were shown so much that we didn't have to look further. The flat was not in an elegant area and it was rather run-down, but it was on the top floor.

We followed the estate agent upstairs. He was an old man wearing an old, dark gray *galabija* (long cotton gown). He opened the door with one turn of the key and a strong push, and there, to our surprise, we found ourselves standing in a small square open area, its floor covered with ornate tiles. Beautiful, I thought. Then he shuffled to the door that led to the actual flat—a living room with old seats, a bedroom with three beds and a window overlooking the river Nile, a tiny kitchen, a sink, and a small shower room with an earth-closet. Everything was run-down.

"Does anyone have a view of the courtyard?" was my first question.

"No, you are quite undisturbed."

"How much is it?"

"90 guineas."

"75 and we take it."

He reflected. "All right. The flat belongs to a lady who comes at the end of every month to collect the rent."

I was pleased that the flat belonged to a woman and saw it as a good omen.

"Your neighbors are a nice family. The woman will certainly help you if you need anything. Come, I'll introduce you!"

We followed him to our new neighbors' flat. They also had a courtyard, but bigger. The flat consisted of two large, adjacent rooms leading off from the courtyard.

"*Ya Sattar*,[2] Um Hasan, *ya* Um Hasan, your new neighbors have come to see you," he shouted.

And there came Um Hasan, stooped under the weight of a big plastic bowl full of soapy water. Her hair was stuffed under a headscarf, her features mild but stiff. And her eyes were two large dried-out oceans. She seemed old although her sturdy body spoke to the contrary.

When she saw us, she put the bowl on the floor, quickly

wiped her hands on her apron and came to us, her hand extended in a friendly gesture.

"*Ahlan wa-sahlan, hallat il-baraka, tfaddalu, tfaddalu*, welcome, blessing has come with you, please, please!" she said invitingly, her arm beckoning. "*Tisrabu eh, shay willa 'ahwa*? What may I offer you, tea or coffee?"

"Sorry, Um Hasan, but we have to get our things, it will be for another time!"

"*May sihish*," she replied, outraged. "But that won't do, do us the honor!"

"Fine, a glass of water for your sake!"

She disappeared busily and returned with three glasses of fruit juice. We drank and promised to be in touch as soon as we had moved in.

"May the Lord lighten your path and protect you!" she called after us.

We settled in quickly and my favorite place became the courtyard, where I studied, sunbathed, and in the evenings took out my mattress to fall asleep under the stars. Every night they were a little different than the night before and I enjoyed going to sleep feeling protected by them. I started longing for the night. In the morning I would start yearning for the stars that whispered their stories to me every night, in a language beyond words. Randa preferred sleeping inside, as she was afraid to sleep on the floor. "That's where all the cockroaches are creeping around!" she would say, her whole body shaking at the very thought. I didn't like them either, but I didn't think they would creep into my bed.

One day Um Hasan's daughter knocked on our door: "Abla Fawzia, my mother would like to invite you both for lunch. She's made stuffed zucchini."

I had to laugh, no one had ever before called me *abla*—a form of polite address for older women, somewhat like "aunt." (Teachers are given this title in Egypt.) I gladly accepted. A little later, Randa and I appeared at Um Hasan's. She greeted us happily and took us to one of their rooms. I shyly looked around. The room was carpeted with large plastic mats, the mattresses stacked up in a corner and in another corner stood a frayed cupboard with little scraps of paper stuck in the cracks to hold the wood together.

"*Ahlan wa-sahlan, nawartu*! Welcome, you have brought light to my home" Um Hasan said.

"*Allah inawwir 'aleki, ya um hasan*!" we answered politely.

She went out and returned with a tray full of stuffed zucchini that she put on the newspapers spread out on the floor. We sat around the tray. Um Hasan held a zucchini toward each of us and we bit in politely. It wasn't very tasty but her joy at our visit made up for this. Then a little boy crept in with snot running into his mouth. I couldn't take my eyes off him and I found it difficult not to throw up.

"This is Sayyid, my youngest one," Um Hasan said. "He's sick." She didn't mean a cold or a cough, but mentally sick.

Sayyid crept closer to me and his mother wanted to shoo him away, but I gestured to say it was okay. The throttling in my throat mixed with compassion for Sayyid. I knew that look, the same look had accompanied me throughout my childhood. Dunja, my cousin, appeared in front of my eyes and my hand stroked Sayyid's thick black hair. Sayyid grimaced a grin and saliva ran out of the corners of his mouth.

"Have you been to a doctor?"

"It's written all over his face and no one can change fate," Um Hasan answered. She took her apron and wiped the snot and saliva away. "I don't want to complain, praise and thanks to Allah, whatever He may decide."

Then a part of her soul burst open and she started talking: "When I was fourteen, my father married me to the son of my uncle on his side. On the wedding day, the women came, they held on to my shoulders and in front of my father's eyes, my cousin sat down between my spread legs, shivering, with sweat running down his forehead.

"'Do it, otherwise I'll do it!' my father hissed when he saw him falter. My cousin looked at me and I could read in his eyes, 'Forgive me, cousin, I have to do it!'

"Then he jabbed inside me. I felt a burning pain between my legs. My cousin's finger had penetrated me and moved roughly to and fro until the hymen was torn and warm, and sticky blood flowed out of me. When he removed his finger, the white cloth he had tied around it was stained with blood. Father was satisfied. He leaned on his thick fighting stick, which he would have turned against me to smash my head, if blood had failed to come out. The women tore the air with their loud trills. Their honor was safe and the wedding feast could begin.

"But I could not come to terms with this humiliation. I knew many girls in our region had gone through the same experience, but they seemed to cope with it better, and get over it with time, but my nature was not so light. I could not look at him, I couldn't stand him being near me. My whole body started shaking the minute he approached me and I cried. I couldn't stop crying. How often he apologized to me! How often he repeated that he was forced to act in this way—tradition, my father. Once he collapsed and cried like a child in front of me, but I couldn't feel anything, I couldn't forgive him. He had failed to protect me, he had left me at the mercy of a cruel world.

"After three months—imagine, three months—I let him come to me. Then came Hasan and life took its course. Then it was Ali, Nafisa, Fatma, and Zahra, and finally little Sayyid. Out of all the children, Abu Hasan is most attached to him. It was Sayyid who brought us together, me and my husband, and who healed the wound between us. Abu Hasan is a good man, he can't help it. We all have our excuses. I don't want to complain—it's just that I'm unhappy about my life. It comes and goes without me knowing how I can really live as a woman."

The three of us women sat there in silence, with aching bellies and dreary thoughts. No one felt like eating any longer. Nafisa brought some tea, but I felt as if I couldn't spend one more minute sitting there. My head was buzzing and nausea spread like a sticky mass all over my body. But I had to say one thing: "May Allah protect Sayyid!"

"May your words go straight from your lips to Heaven's gate," Um Hasan answered with a smile. She had shared her wounds with others for the first time and it did her good.

LET US DECIDE FOR OURSELVES

In spiritual matters, associate with those who are above you,
and in worldly matters with those who are less blessed than you.
— Muhammad al-Sulami

Lecture: Arab literature! It was announced that today's subject would be four short stories by Tawfiq al-Hakim, one of the most famous Egyptian writers. Tawfiq usually wrote plays and philosophical treatises. It was exciting to know that this 90-year-old man was still alive—it gave the lecture an inspired flavor.

When I entered the room, I saw Ula and her friends bunched around someone. It was Najwa, and she was wearing the veil. Only yesterday she had appeared with flowing black hair, and suddenly she was sitting there, veiled. It confused and fascinated me. How people can change! I went to her. I had taken a liking to her from the very first day. She was a quiet, reserved young woman, whose eyes always beamed with kindness. The other veiled women congratulated her. Once they had progressively withdrawn, I couldn't hold back any longer:

"Why have you put on a veil?" the question burst out.

"You know, Fawzia, it makes things easier. I leave home every day—in the morning I attend lectures, in the afternoon I work in a bookshop. On the way I'm often pestered and spoken to cheekily, and the neighbors have already asked my parents why they let their daughter study and work and spend all day outside the house.

"With the veil, I have my peace. It proves that I'm a virtuous girl and that my intentions are honorable. I no longer need to steal shyly through the streets, but I can show myself in public with my head held high, my mind set at ease."

Najwa was happy about her decision and I could well understand her. She was the first woman in her family to lead her life outside the house, and she was trying to combine traditional values and modern requirements.

Fadwa, a resolute young university colleague, saw things totally differently. "I know myself whether I am virtuous and my deeds honorable. I don't need to prove it to those around me with a veil. I have the same right to education and jobs as men, and if men can't cope with seeing me without a veil, they should look at the floor! We need equal rights in our society. A bird needs two equally strong wings to fly well!"

I could understand her well, but Fadwa's social position was not at all the same as Najwa's. She came from a prosperous family, had her own car (which enabled her to move in public without being disturbed), and her family could afford both from a social and financial point of view to support their daughter in her individual development.

Fadwa and Najwa both studied the same subject. Najwa would probably marry after her degree and work if the financial situation demanded it; otherwise her education would enable her to bring up her children "well." Even if she didn't work, her education would bring a new dimension into her family. On the other hand, Fadwa would have the possibility to study for a Master's degree, maybe even a doctorate. Her education and her parents' social connections would then secure her a high position before she looked for an appropriate partner.

When the lecture came to an end, we went out into the lawn where Hala and Maha joined us.

"We can't live without our families," Maha explained. "The family gives protection and security, but it also expects obedience and conformity. We don't have a state that offers protection or social safety; we have the family, the clan, the religious community. We don't need any freeing of the individual—we need family emancipation. To be alone and without protection should not be the price to pay for freedom."

"We have many problems in Egypt. We live under pressure around the river Nile, our vital line of communication, and every nine or ten months there is another million people. Who is supposed to feed them all? It seems impossible to govern Egypt. You know, we don't just have a state crisis, we also have one inside the family. With Nasser we had socialism, then capitalism with Sadat, and now with Mubarak we have a tactician who tries to maneuver astutely between internal and external political pressures."

Hala studied anthropology. She was a delicate young woman, intent on seeing life clearly. "The future is uncertain and there are also changes and shifts within the family. The shift from the extended family to the nuclear family, the shift from the housewife to the professional wife. Survival becomes always more difficult, one income per family is no longer sufficient, the millionaires' club grows while poverty spreads. Is it therefore surprising that people should remember their religion and their tradition and see the solution in a true Muslim order?"

"You know, basically we've only experienced a pseudo-modernization," Maha said. "We have adopted Western concepts that don't meet our needs and they haven't helped us much. Our position as women has indeed partly changed, our participation in education and work has increased, yet the relationships within the family have been maintained. Many women accept man's power within the family in order to pursue their education and work. It is true that there has been a socio-economic transformation, that the modern state has extended to areas that were previously under the control of the family and religious communities. But for us women it hasn't just brought advantages—quite to the contrary. The traditional informal power strategies in which women participated extensively are disappearing and the new alternative life forms cannot be implemented. No wonder that many women see the restoration of traditional patriarchal structures as an opportunity to regain their protection and dignity."

"That means we want a free Muslim woman, not a free Western woman," said Fadwa, "but for that we need more social freedom, more equality within the family—that is to say a reform of the family law. We need a balanced family to create a balanced society. The West is flooding us with consumerism and with its life philosophies, which fascinate some of us, while causing others to doubt themselves or feel inferior. Our cultural identity is under threat. All social classes are busy with the West."

"The West doesn't just flood us with its goods, it also meddles in our affairs," Hala added. "And we women have suffered most from that interference. Thanks to the colonial powers, the veiling of women turned into a political issue and the veil came to be seen as *the* sign of oppression. But was wearing a miniskirt or not ever an essential issue among Western women's movements? The colonial policy was to free poor Arabic women from oppression and backwardness. What did it bring us, apart from the fact that women's movements and women's rights are constantly linked to colonialism?"

"The same is happening now with the cutting," Fadwa added. "In 1979, cutting the clitoris was declared illegal by the Egyptian government. At that time there was a conference on the subject of cutting, and Egyptian doctors, nurses, journalists, lawyers, theologians, and representatives from various women's organizations—consisting of both men and women—declared this practice unhealthy, degrading, and dangerous. All along the river Nile, it is performed by Muslim and Christian women alike. The old women cut the young ones! It is an ancient tradition. The education of the families against this practice worked very well and progress was made.

"But then the West started interfering, and this led to confusion and a certain act of defiance. Can't they let us decide for ourselves in peace!"

"That would undermine their legitimacy as moral guardians and defenders of human rights!" Maha said with an ironic smile. She turned her head. "Come on, let's go!"

THE RACE WITH THE SPHINX

The fragrance of sincerity is closest to the scent of Paradise.
—Sufi wisdom

The closer we came to the terminus, the more the bus emptied. After the unbelievable crush that would have raised pity among sardines, this was nearly like being born again. Whoever had survived so far could be sure that they would make it in life!

Every meter brought us closer to the majestic pyramids, and I forgot about the squashed journey. The discomfort seemed ephemeral and banal next to these symbols of human will, greatness, and imagination. I left the bus with a sigh of relief and a happy jump and went straight to the Bedouin who awaited the tourists with their horses and camels.

"Greetings to you, O daughter of my tribe!"

Abu al-Hawl came to me enthusiastically in his usual big, hurried steps. He was the most loveable crafty devil of all Egypt. His head reached my shoulder, and I was myself only 5 foot 6 inches—with heels. He had a small wrinkled face, in which two dark cherries, a flattened nose, and a crooked mouth had found their place. When he laughed—and he often laughed—the three became distorted and made an indefinable symbiosis. His appearance culminated with his name, or rather the name he had given himself: Abu al-Hawl, the father of the sphinx. Somehow the name was apt. He mumbled and whispered when he spoke, and whatever he meant was most of the time a mystery to me. Yet somehow we seemed to understand each other in the ether of the words, on a level that neither of us could quite grasp.

"Is Antar free?"

"He's ready and waiting!" came his friendly answer.

I remember the first time when I met the Bedouin around the pyramids and I ran into Abu al-Hawl. He would not let me ride alone. "That won't do, there must be a guide with you, such is the law here, otherwise we'll be in trouble with the tourist police."

I agreed sullenly, as I wanted to be alone, far from the hustle and bustle of the city. I wanted to lose and find myself again in the sand dunes, but I understood him and maybe it was better that way, at least the first time. I was given a young brown mare and Abu al-Hawl took the stallion Antar.

We rode at a walk slowly past the powerful pyramids. I saw the open space of the desert in front of me and my heart started pounding wildly, I felt the palms of my hands becoming wet and my whole body stiffening. My excitement reached the mare and her nostrils widened, and I breathed in the fragrance of freedom. Beloved desert, home of the soul, your daughter is here. Neither law nor politeness could hold me back. I spurred on my horse, holding her back at the same time with the reins; her muscles tensed and she started prancing. I pressed my thighs even more, my Bedouin blood rose up in me, together with the ancient knowledge of the art of merging man and horse.

"You see those dunes over there, behind the valley? If I can reach them before you, next time you'll let me ride alone!"

Abu al-Hawl looked at me, and then in the direction I pointed. He could only agree; this I knew. Here was a foreign young woman challenging him, and on top of that on his horse and in his profession. He laughed a little embarrassedly. I spurred the mare a little more, and she started prancing sideways. I gave in to the reins a little, to assess her strength, and she wanted to climb. I pushed her down gently with the reins and hummed softly. She pricked up her ears, now she was perfectly collected and ready.

"*Mwafiq*, okay!"

He had hardly spoken the words when I gave her the reins and pushed with my thighs. What a joy! We both shouted with delight and off we went. Abu al-Hawl galloped in parallel, some eight yards away. I kept my eyes on him while feeling the muscles of my horse under me. There was no doubt; he was an experienced rider. He sat on his horse like a rolled up little bundle, holding the reins in one hand, his other palm beating the horse's back. We galloped over the plain and he passed me, beaming with joy. He too had been longing for a race.

Suddenly he disappeared, swallowed by the desert. A little later I reached the edge of the slope and saw him again. Now that he felt he was well ahead, casualness overcame him with the nearing of the dunes, and I could tease out our reserves in peace. I leaned forward as far as possible, so that my head disappeared under the mare's mane, my mouth touching her soft, powerful neck. I made a shrill sound and abandoned the reins to her, holding them as softly as silk threads so that she had the required support without impairing her movements.

She reacted instantly, stretching her neck. The muscles of her legs blossomed. She felt the unity between us just as I did, and as we galloped together, her hooves didn't seem to touch the ground. Again and again I spurred her on, at times breathing into her ear, at times making a shrill sound. Abu al-Hawl was overtaken and in the last few meters we both shouted the shrill Bedouin call.

We arrived nearly at the same time, and he laughed, impressed.

"I'm your brother Samir and I live with my family over there in the valley. You, your family, and friends are welcome any time."

I thanked him very politely, happy that from now on I could ride alone. Being a stranger everywhere did have its advantages. Although I had to fight for my position every time, I also enjoyed a certain freedom to do as I pleased.

THE GHOST OF THE PYRAMIDS

Understandably, the pyramids were always swarming with tourists. Camels and horses were hired out—click!—a picture on a camel in front of the pyramids looks nice in any photo album. Guides tramped through the surrounding tombs with interested groups of tourists, Egyptians sat close to their wives, licking ice-creams, excited school classes came from all corners of the country, young hitchhikers settled down for a while, sitting on the ground, contemplating the pyramids, and in between, young boys sold nuts and policemen in blue uniforms patrolled conscientiously. A colorful, lively picture. Again and again, throngs pushed into the gigantic stone masses of the pyramids.

I stood in front of the overcrowded entrance to the pyramids with a few friends and thought to myself: I'd love to be alone once in the pyramid and let the old world affect me without jeans and cameras appearing by my side. But this seemed impossible. But nothing is impossible, and Allah—praise to Him—fulfilled my wish. All of the sudden the electricity went out and the guards of the pyramids explained that unfortunately no one was to enter the pitch-black pyramid for the next two hours, the risk was too high… danger of stumbling!

The guides translated and disappointed tourists turned round and climbed back down.

I went up to the guard: "*As-salamu alaykum*, I'd like to go into the pyramid!" I said innocently.

"I'm sorry, daughter, you can't, it's pitch-black. The electricity went out!"

"Can't I go inside all the same—I can't come another day!" came the small white lie.

"Unfortunately, I can't authorize you, I'm responsible for security, but"—he said this more to placate me—"if you have a couple of candles, I'll let you in."

He said this with a quiet, cheeky smile around his lips. Of course he suspected that I didn't have any candles with me.

I was going to turn away, disappointed, when a young boy appeared out of nowhere holding candles in his hand. Before he could say anything, they were in mine, a couple of coins in his hand, and the guard's quiet smile was playing on my lips. As a man of honor, he had to keep his promise. I had exactly seven candles in my hand and there were six of us. I pressed one candle into each of my friends' hands and put the last one into my bag. "Take good care of yourselves!" the guard shouted, slightly worried, before we disappeared into the entrance.

My God, was it dark inside, absolutely dark, and as quiet as befits a tomb. "The whole pyramid to ourselves!" we giggled happily. We climbed the steep wooden platforms and slowly pulled ourselves up. A large room awaited us. Here, in an empty stone sarcophagus at the end of the room, the pharaoh was supposed to have rested. In the candlelight, the room was majestic and eerie. One of us lay down in the sarcophagus, arms crossed on her breast the way the pharaohs did, and stayed there motionless.

"A crazy feeling, to lie there under so many tons of stone!"

The middle of the pyramid was marked by a hole in the room's center. We made a circle around it, letting the quiet and timelessness of this pyramid stream over us. Here everything seemed to stand still, cut off from the outside world. Only the present moment lived in the vacuum of history. Were the high priests conducting their rituals outside, or the Bedouin invading? Was Napoleon passing by on his white horse or was Abdel Nasser's voice coming out of the radio? Everything was possible, inside and outside, and everything was but a passing moment. Only the dripping candles made us feel how time went by.

"Let's go back!" one of us said in a deep voice.

We were on our way out, curious to find which era awaited us, when I caught sight of an opening sealed with wooden boards. I bent down and made out a little room. Overcome by an adventurous curiosity, I started to shake the boards. "Leave it, maybe it's dangerous," my friend said a little fearfully.

"I want to know what's behind, come and help me!"

Together we managed to remove the wooden boards. Ducking, we blinked inside. It was a narrow airshaft, big enough to crouch inside. We crawled inside wordlessly and closed the opening in the door.

"What now?"

That I didn't know either.

All of a sudden, we heard approaching voices. "Blow out the candles!" We listened, and the voices came closer. It was a man and a woman, speaking French. Apparently they too had been given permission to enter the dark pyramid. They came closer and closer to us, and suddenly the rogue in us woke up.

"Hooooooo, hooooooo…" we started humming softly.

It went quiet outside.

"Did you hear that?" the woman asked her husband.

"What am I supposed to have heard?"

"Well, the humming!"

They listened carefully, and of course we didn't make a sound.

"You're only imagining things!" he replied confidently and they walked on.

"Hooooooo, hooooooo…" the sound came again.

Agitated dialogue outside, suppressed giggles in the airshaft where we could hardly contain ourselves. And then: "Hooooooo, hooooooo…"

"Now, can you hear it now?" I imagined the upset woman nervously tugging at her husband's shirt.

"Stop it, it's absolutely quiet in here!"

They went on and the man spoke soothingly to his wife, and while he was talking the sound came: "Hooooooo, hooooooo…"

"Be quiet, listen, just listen!" Her voice shook slightly with anger and despair. They were standing just in front of our hiding place.

I think at that moment their relationship was put to the test. We did the woman a favor and repeated very softly: "Hooooooo, hooooooo…"

"Yes, I can hear it!" the man finally confirmed. She seemed to breathe a sigh of relief, better frightened than crazy.

"Who is there?" he asked, nervous but unafraid.

That was a mistake because suddenly our imagination soared: "*wen inta far'on, far'on ta'al 'indi*! Where are you, Pharaoh, Pharaoh, come to me!" I whispered softly in Arabic. I think two of us said it.

The couple mumbled something about... ghosts, curses, and souls... and then the boards shook as they hurriedly fled for the exit.

"What a shame, I wanted to shake the planks!" my friend said. "They wouldn't have survived that! Come on, let's go out too, this place gets really uncanny with time!"

We lit the candles, pushed the wooden door aside, and climbed down carefully.

"Those two won't forget their visit to the pyramids so soon! It was a bit mean, that's true, but it was so much fun!" We could but agree.

Just before we reached the entrance, the electricity came on and dreadful neon lights illuminated the tomb. "Am I happy that we could experience it in the dark!"

The visitors were already streaming in, but the French couple was certainly not among them.

THE TREASURE CHEST OF PATIENCE

Don't search for the chains of knowledge,
but rather for the freedom of being.
—Sufi wisdom

The heart of Cairo is Khan al-Khalili, the city's huge bazaar. It starts near the former Egyptian opera house, which burned down in the 1970s, and extends all the way to the venerable al-Azhar University. If you like human throngs, shopping, haggling, and losing yourself in the din, in the scents and colors of this world, you have found your home here. Should an extraterrestrial being land on our planet and wish to gain a quick insight into humanity turned upside down, I would recommend Khan al-Khalili.

Randa and I decided to go there one day after breakfast. I loved this human labyrinth and my heart jumped with joy at the idea while hers contracted in fear. She was afraid of that many people and felt they stole the air she breathed, but she came for my sake.

We wound our way past the book bazaar next to the Khan al-Khalili directly into the heart of the big bazaar. I opened all my senses to this theater of life. We started in the main streets, but then the small alleys drew us in, and the gold bazaar appeared in front of us.

"Look how beautiful those earrings are!" Randa loved as much as I those *fellahs'* earrings, thick crescent moons hanging on hooks. We went on and came to the herb bazaar. The shops were filled to the ceiling with herbs, mysterious mixtures, ointments and spices, and they promised a cure for every disease.

Our noses led us to the scent bazaar. Young men stood at the door, catching clients and leading them into the shops, in a firm yet friendly way.

"Let's go inside!" I whispered to Randa. "Only for a short while!"

We sat on comfortable leather seats and looked around. Everywhere stood bottles filled with various colored liquids. The owner greeted us and apologized at the same time. He wanted to finish explaining the scents to two tourists. They must have been in the shop for quite a while, for the couple smelled so intensely of every possible fragrance that you could have taken them with you as perfume bottles.

"The French buy the essences for their famous perfumes from us, they process and then sell them at a hundred times the price," the merchant explained.

The tourist couple nodded politely, and we both nodded. As Arabs we knew that we always delivered the raw material for everything.

"There are three categories: A, B, and C. The A fragrance is very expensive, the C is not good enough for you. I would therefore suggest the B category." The couple nodded again, and so did we—it couldn't hurt. Tea was served, the couple nodded thankfully and so did we, by now out of habit, and also solidarity. The merchant was very happy with our supporting role. The couple bought more than they had intended. When they hesitated over one fragrance, we nodded and smiled, and they bought it.

The merchant was so happy he would have loved to give us a job immediately. Since we both wore *galabijas*, and I had wrapped a transparent black scarf around my head, we both looked very authentic and decorative. Another group of tourists was dragged into the shop and the merchant asked whether he could quickly attend to them before devoting himself fully to us. We nodded our permission. The tourists looked around the shop enthusiastically and gave us an equally interested look.

"Look at those beautiful Egyptian women," they said in English.

They were Americans on an adventurous trip to Egypt. They grinned at us politely and naively and we nodded back, dignified and majestic, as befits a millennium-old civilization greeting a two-century-old culture. The merchant started again his stories about the scents and their qualities, and the Americans listened raptly. They kept nodding, but we decided to remain sphinx-like and mysterious. It worked, for they too bought many scents, bewitched by the haze of our majesty.

"Come, let's go!" No sooner said than done. The merchant was inconsolable, but we promised to return.

We turned into a dark alley, and there she was sitting: All wrapped in black, she held one hand in her lap while the other clasped the crimson hose of a hookah. Her big, heavy eyes were bordered by thick layers of black kohl and she wore heavy golden ear-pendants. Her lips were a sensual black-blue and clouds of smoke came out of her noble nose. We came closer and pressed past, voicing faint greetings.

"*Rayhin fen, ya banat*? Where are you going to, girls?" Her words huffed at us.

We turned around, and without moving her head, she looked at us through the corner of her eyes.

"We're taking a little walk!"

"The world is full of dangers and deceit! *Sallu 'an nabi*, praise the Prophet and sit down with me." We looked at each other and decided to accept her invitation.

"Ya Hasanen, bring two chairs and three teas!"

"*Hadir ya m'allima*! Aye, aye, o boss!" was the answer. Chairs and tea appeared.

"I may be an old woman, but I understand the world well," she started, the fumes of the hookah swirling around her. "Human beings stumble over bones and skulls and at the same time they sing the songs of false pride and lying greed. Everything races and hurries after a bite of bread. They're all running without knowing where and imperceptibly life goes by. Drink from each day as if it were the last and then entrust it to the night so that the clarity of the next morning can greet you as you awaken."

Had we chanced upon a wise or a crazy woman? Why did she speak in riddles, and why to us? I wanted to say something in reply, but she waved me aside, bored. She wasn't interested in words. When we put the tea back on the tray, she released us from her presence with a *allah ma'kum*! May God be with you. I surrendered my thoughts to confusion and for a while we walked speechlessly side by side.

The alley became more and more narrow and winding, and suddenly we were standing in a cul-de-sac, and my confusion hit a wooden screen before dissolving with a jolt.

"What is this?" Randa's delicate fingers touched the screen. "It's beautiful workmanship—look how finely everything is shaped!"

I nodded and a movement caught my eyes. In a small apartment shaped like a cave, three old men sat stooped around a heavy table.

"Come!"

We went cautiously toward them and stood at the door while our curiosity peeped inside. They held tweezers in their old horny hands and turned them to the right and to the left, bouncing and then pressing down. I couldn't see anything but those tweezers.

Barely looking up, the old men invited us in. The old hand opened and I saw a tiny star inside. It was so small that I had to bend down to recognize it clearly. I looked at the old face, astonished.

"The little star is made of sixteen pieces," the old man explained. "Each piece is added to the next until the six point star is finished."

My attitude showed I was still amazed.

"Patience is the key to happiness," he said with a smile. "We are among the last few craftsmen of this art. The days of haste have caught up with all of us. But—praised be Allah—the wind has not yet blown in this little corner. One must pay immediate attention to the present moment before it changes into the past. One shouldn't allow oneself to deal with any other time than the moment in which one finds oneself, but that requires patience and modesty," he said with a smile.

I could hardly bear in my body the precision with which they worked. I had to turn away, but I felt a strong attraction to this concentrated moment. For a second I felt how the moment extended, swallowing past and future. A heaviness on my shoulders that I hadn't noticed seemed to dissolve, like a back ache after a good massage, and lightness and light-heartedness surrounded me. We took our leave from that treasure chest of patience with grateful thanks.

A few steps later I broke my sandal-strap and I would have tripped, had Randa not caught me skillfully.

"What's the matter with you?"

"I'm running after the future!" I answered almost as a joke.

We walked slowly, with me hobbling slightly, back to the main street, and there I saw a young *fellah* woman who sold plastic mules. I decided to buy a pair of mules with huge garish yellow flowers. My feet rejoiced under the flowery magnificence and Randa congratulated me on my kitschy taste.

We arrived in Darb al-Ahmar, one of Cairo's poorest residential districts in terms of money, but certainly the wealthiest in stories. The windows of the old low houses were all open and passers-by shared scraps of the various family stories. We wandered down the street as if walking past a film.

"You're not from here, have you lost your way?" there came a voice.

We looked up and she beckoned in a friendly way. "You're welcome to a coffee, please come up!"

"Come, why not!" I said to Randa and she agreed immediately, which was quite unusual for her.

The woman stood outside the front door, already waiting for us. She looked cute in a candy-pink negligee, high plush mules, her thin black hair slightly combed back. Her sweet smile was a perfect match to her appearance.

"Please come in!"

The flat kept up with the charming colors: the living room had been painted in dark pink, her bedroom, which she showed us proudly, in light pink, and in the middle stood a voluptuous large bed, with a picture of a hissing leopard hanging above it. She trotted into the kitchen on her plush mules, soon returning with the coffee. The bittersweet taste of loneliness hung in this flat, which no young blood had entered for a long time.

"My husband and I have been living in this house for two years already," she told us, "we come from Alexandria. There's only the two of us but we're happy. We came here to have our peace—our families in Alexandria wouldn't give us any. They always wanted my husband to take a second wife because I can't have any children, but we love each other and we're happy with our destiny," she said with a sweet smile.

We took our leave after the coffee.

"Please come again!"

We promised we would come again one day. Back on the street, I remembered that a university colleague lived nearby and we decided to visit her. I stopped a young man and asked him whether he knew where Fatma Awad lived. He thought a little and then pointed toward a run-down, two-story house. "But I don't know which floor!"

We thanked him and walked to the house. A crowd of children came to meet us in the entrance hall, squealing and shrieking wildly. On the first floor, we asked a pregnant woman for Fatma and she showed us the adjacent door.

The door was open, so we called inside, "Does Fatma Awad live here?" A young man appeared. Yes, but she wasn't here right now. A small, elderly woman with a headscarf tied at the back showed herself. She was Fatma's very pregnant mother. When she caught me looking at her belly, she gave a tired smile. She invited us in and we sat on a worn-out sofa on which several children were already seated. They were all staring at a little television set, the only luxury article in the whole house. The air was stale and the small windows could not bring in enough light or fresh air. The young man puffed pointlessly and senselessly at his cigarette.

I could barely stand the confinement. If Fatma didn't turn up soon, I would have to think up an excuse and disappear. But then she arrived, clean and neat as usual, not seeming a part of this family at all. When she saw us, I immediately noticed that she was embarrassed that we had discovered her family, her intimate life. But she pulled herself together and greeted us, slightly nervously.

"We were in the neighborhood and we wanted to pay you a little visit!"

Fatma didn't quite know what to do with us. "Unfortunately, we have to leave now, would you like to come with us for a while?" She was grateful for the offer.

We walked a little ways down the street in silence. Thoughts whirled in Fatma's head. She wanted to say something to justify herself but she didn't know how. "My mother loves children," it suddenly exploded from her. "She thinks she can prove her youth and femininity in this way, and my father is proud that he can still have children." I didn't know how to answer her. Maybe her mother longed for more attention, attention that women in the poorer classes were only given during pregnancy. Maybe she thought she could justify her existence in the world in this way. Or maybe she didn't think anything. Life is the way it is.

I felt sorry for Fatma. She had other dreams and she didn't want to have anything to do with this world of her mother's. I admired her for studying under such difficult circumstances and making her way in the world. I imagined her in the stairwell, studying with her books on her knees. I imagined her shooing away her brothers and sisters, to read at least one sentence in peace. Doesn't one weave the future with the deeds of the past, creating the garment that one wears as if it were one's own skin?

Don't let dark worries limit your soul; in reality we are beyond all limitations, I wanted to tell her. Don't distance yourself from your mother out of fear, for no creature is separate from the other, and if you can greet all of life, then you no longer need to remain within the limited world of your own understanding, you become free to climb up, to grow, to demand your birthright and fully occupy your place. I wanted to say how much I admired her, how much I believed in her, but I remained silent. Fatma accompanied us until we reached the outskirts of her area and when she looked at me as we parted, I saw that she was asking me to keep her family secret to myself. I kissed her on the cheek as softly as I could to reassure her. Your dreams are well preserved, Fatma.

THE MOST BEAUTIFUL PEOPLE

When she moves, the thousand-year-old history of her people swings in her hips. What is femininity? What a question with this appearance, with these movements, with this knowing smile and sublime gait, with this strong suppleness and this wise composure. She broke a wound open in me whose sweet pain wrapped itself around my heart. My soul was squashed between invisible fingers and my spirit shouted: Who are you? Her veil swirled calmly around her face, and time stood still. She was veiled and if she had removed her veil—what agony!—I would have burned in no time. Which face but the divine, time and again shining in His creatures.

I saw her in a street in Luxor. As is customary in that region, she was dressed all in black. The veil that framed her face was embroidered with small emerald-colored pearls whose shimmering was reflected in her eyes. She went purposefully through the world; her alluring, shining eyes looked straight ahead without wavering. That was good, for I was certain she could bewitch the world with one look. I came exactly from the opposite direction and the minute my soul caught sight of her, Luxor became a magical city. Before I could free myself from the spell, she was already gone.

I looked for her over the next few days, and although I was disappointed not to see her again, I was also happy, because the second is not like the first. I had come to Luxor with a group of friends and together we wanted to visit the Valley of the Kings and Queens on the other side of the river Nile. Luxor was an old Egyptian city, in which the descendants of pharaohs and Bedouin lived together miraculously. People here were tall and slender with a complexion called *qamhi* (wheat-colored) in Arabic, a mixture of lush earth and sunlight taken out at just the right time from the divine oven.

Men covered their heads by wrapping a long cloth several times around. They wore warm-colored *jalabiyas* and always carried a long, strong stick, which they used to defend themselves, to drive donkeys, and as venerable support while walking. The men and women in this region were the most beautiful people I had seen so far, and what was most beautiful about them was their dignified stance and their dark, sparkling eyes.

The sun shone down intensely on the earth, but we decided to visit the Valley of the Kings despite the sweltering heat. This is how we went to the *corniche*, the main avenue along the river bank. One luxury hotel followed the other. Inside, you spurned the surroundings, as you could just as well have been in New York or New Delhi. "Comfortably familiar for rich tourists!" said my class-aware girlfriend.

We walked leisurely to the ferry, jumped aboard and waited until it filled up. It floated slowly to the other bank, over the powerful river. Once we arrived, the passengers disappeared in all directions and we waited for something, not knowing quite what to do next. Our answer came, in the shape of four donkeys with their young guides.

"Would you like to go to the Valley of the Kings?"

We agreed happily and jumped on the donkeys, landing with a plump. Off we went. The earth was green along the bank of the Nile, with reeds and light green tangled grass. Two huge statues suddenly appeared in the middle of the reeds. The long wait had somewhat eaten them away. They stared forever in the distance, their gaze stern and fixed. Our donkeys continued; they seemed to know their way better than all the others.

"We can only bring you this far. Walk on a little more, and you will be in the Valley of the Kings."

We jumped down from the donkeys, the young boys gave them a slap, and they disappeared into the tall grass.

"Don't your donkeys get lost?"

"The donkeys live free—when you need one, you catch it, ride the distance and then let it go. We all share them!"

Whenever people do something right and decide wisely in their lives, a pleasant feeling warms up one's belly.

So we continued on foot. The valley was not really that close. The sun's rays blazed down on us and the green band along the river Nile disappeared completely into the desert sand, two or three isolated bushes, and then only more sand. A narrow asphalt street appeared and, to our joy, a taxi. We jumped inside to drive to the Valley of the Kings modern style. We saw many sandy hills, and in between the hills stole sightseeing-crazy groups with their guides.

As we drew closer, we spotted openings in the different hills into which the groups kept disappearing. Tutankhamun surfaced in our minds, the famous young pharaoh who died when he was eighteen, supposedly from leukemia. We decided to discover the various tomb openings without a guide. When we came to the first one, we looked inside and saw an apparently endless wooden staircase leading downwards. We went down, slowly and in a dignified way, as befitted the surroundings. The temperature changed instantly. It was pleasantly cool inside and the tomb was filled with a strange smell. I remembered how many of the explorers had died of mysterious illnesses soon after discovering these tombs. Was that smell still effective?

Once we were down, we were speechless. We hadn't expected anything so beautiful and magnificent! The tomb was actually a hall whose walls were decorated all over with Pharaonic scenes and hieroglyphs. From one wall the Pharaoh and his wife stared straight at me with their big, black bordered eyes. I had to look away ashamed—after all, this was their tomb I was entering unasked.

We went back up the steps, and walked about, following other people up and down the hills. I kept looking around me, and every curve seemed to hide a tomb yet undiscovered. It would be great to chance totally intuitively upon the tomb of a Pharaoh. Just as in the old films, you fall into a hole, walk a few steps in the dark and suddenly find yourself standing in front of mountains of sparkling jewels and gold coins. Or else, a wall breaks down, clouds of dust, no view and then mysterious bronze statues, altars of pure gold and poisoned cult objects… Oof! With all my mental film directing, I had nearly fallen into a real hole.

But the truth is, people still hope to find new tombs. Excavations continue to this day.

I would have quite liked the next tomb as living quarters, so harmonious were its oval shape and old rose hue. It was, like the first, decorated with scenes and hieroglyphs. But this tomb seemed much softer, more feminine and alive. We stood there for a long time, savoring the huge egg-shaped room. I was filled with those two tombs, but we had to visit yet another, the tomb of Tutankhamun, the only one that had escaped looting and whose treasures are now resting—or rather, being disturbed!— in the Egyptian museum.

So we went to his tomb. My God was it tiny and simple! We felt quite confused. If this small tomb had contained so many treasures, how many must have been inside the others... quite beyond anyone's imagination! Tomb looters needed no poison to lose their mind. Poor Tutankhamun, what a destiny! You died at eighteen, you weren't a gleaming personality, and you didn't make any outstanding contribution to your kingdom. Yet centuries later they discover you and you live on, most famous of all the pharaohs. You really managed to find a new life on earth after your death!

And now down to the Valley of the Queens! It wasn't far; we reached it after walking for half an hour. Strangely enough, hardly anyone was there. Only three people walked about—no comparison to the swarming Valley of the Kings! We crept into the graves, which were small and beautiful. Isis and Osiris greeting us everywhere! Pleasant, beautiful graves had been built for the queens. I felt angry that now, too, the kings' graves received greater attention and care than the queens', which were obviously more neglected. We looked at a few more graves before walking back to the river Nile.

THE STICK DANCE

I n the heat of midday we walked slowly for two hours along a desert road until we finally spotted the green of fertile country. We went into the greenness and soon reached a village. The whole village was made of small mud huts that must have looked the same at the time of the Pharaohs. Nothing to remind us of our own century. The heat meant that not a single human being was to be seen—only a couple dogs were lying lazily in the shade of the huts. They didn't even find it necessary to bark at us. People who walk about in such a heat can't intend any danger.

So we went on and discovered a canal surrounded by overhanging trees. We decided to stop there, unpacked our provisions, ate and drank a little and dozed off. Then we heard a rustling noise. A couple of bushes moved and suddenly four men were standing in front of us. They gave us a sharp look, and they carried big sticks in their hands. For a minute the six of us held our breath. My head buzzed, I knew these moments when a gesture or a word can either make the situation dangerous or enriching.

"*Tfaddalu, mish min maqamkum, tfaddalu*! Welcome, have a share although it is not worthy of you!"

Faces immediately relaxed, the four men threw themselves on the ground and sat crossed-legged next to us. The spell was broken! We introduced each other and they helped themselves politely. The four men came from a nearby village and they had been observing us for quite a while. We told them about our excursion and they nodded knowingly. The Valley of the Kings and Queens belonged to the tourists, but this was their territory. The men relaxed visibly, and so did we, especially after they had smoked a few hashish cigarettes, which they kindly offered us.

"What do you use the sticks for?" I wanted to know.

"For everything, for fighting and for dancing!" one of them answered with a grin. To our delight, the eldest asked the two younger ones to give us a demonstration. They jumped up, lifted their heavy sticks up in the air, crossed them and started to prance and hit each other's stick. From below, in the dazzling yellow sunlight, the earth swirling up, the two men in their proud turbans and flowing caftans seemed like two giants from another world who kept approaching each other, whirling, crouching down to jump up again and escape, dancing away from the other's deadly blows.

They sat down again, sweating and smiling, and we chatted a little longer. Then one of them whistled and to our surprise a donkey appeared, followed by another two. They held them by the tail until two of us were seated on each donkey, and accompanied us to the ferry. While we were crossing the river, the sky became progressively pinker and the Nile country prepared itself softly for the night.

DESERT REVELATION

He met a woman on the sea shore and he asked her:
"What is the end of love?"
And she answered: "You fool, love knows no end!"
And he asked: "Why?"
She said: "Because the Beloved knows no end."
—Dhu'n-Nun (d. 860)

It was in the Egyptian desert that I truly realized for the first time that we live on a planet. I felt it in my body. The desert is like the ocean. Its moods and power rule over the people who live in it. Its majestic quietness and its endlessness tempt human beings into contemplation.

Five of us decided to ride into the desert for a few days. Two of Randa's cousins who lived in Alexandria had promised us this journey a while ago, and the time had come. Soon after dawn the three of us women—Karin had decided to join us—stood next to the jeep, filling it with our luggage. Karin, Randa, and I sat in the back, and slender Ahmad sat in the front next to round Mamduh. We drove past the sleeping pyramids and headed toward Fayyum, the first large oasis.

My God, how beautiful Fayyum was! The *fellahs* walked leisurely with their water buffalos to their fields as the young girls drove the goats and sheep. Tall, slender palm trees, dust-covered bushes, and gaping irrigation channels formed the scenery, and everything appeared magically hazy in a soft filtered light. A dusty wind made its obligatory rounds through the oasis. Nothing had changed here throughout the centuries. Mamduh knew the *'umda* (mayor) of Fayyum and he wanted to pay him a short visit. We drove to a yellowish building, in front of which men stood dressed in the traditional costume. Deep, sky blue *jalabiyas* and light-colored turbans. Here men moved with the belief that masculinity was the God-ordained measure of all things.

Mamduh disappeared into the building and after a while he came out with a bunch of men. I knew this was the beginning of endless polite greetings. Magnanimity, generosity, and hospitality were a point of honor—they reflect the nobility of the human mind and who better than the Arabs at mastering them.

One of the men came to the jeep: "You can't just drive on like that. Now that you have set foot on our soil, you have to stay three nights, this is what the law of hospitality says!"

Now we started with our part of the politeness formula: "We would love to, but we really can't... we promise, another time... circumstances really don't permit this time..."

Time and again, our excuses were interrupted by the kind man's protestations.

In the end Mamduh won by swearing on his honor to return soon, and allowing them to fill the whole trunk of the car with treats: boxes full of oranges, freshly baked bread, goat's cheese, smoked sausages, fresh water, dates. Only when it came to the live ducks did Mamduh protest... now we could lose ourselves comfortably in the desert for a whole month. Waving madly, we left Fayyum and headed for Dakhla, the next oasis.

I couldn't believe my eyes! The desert we were driving through was covered with natural, God-ordained sand pyramids. Had the pharaohs seen them here before they built them? My eyes drank in their majesty; I wanted to impress them forever in my heart. They were indeed a confirmation that everything rests in Unity. Truly nothing on this earth is separate from the other but through the distance generated by fear.

I put my arms around the two women next to me, overwhelmed by the call of my soul, which spread over the whole world. In that moment they were my family, the home for which my tired brow longed; everything was true in that moment. Whatever the future would make of this truth was irrelevant. In that minute only that truth existed and I was allowed to experience it. I hadn't noticed in the least how darkness had swallowed the light in a single kiss and spread out its mystery.

"Let's camp here!" said Mamduh.

It did him good to be the leader of the small group. He took a turn to the right and parked the jeep between two dunes. Swiftly and skillfully, the men erected a little tent for us women. We rolled out our sleeping bags inside. Then I heard her voice... *"ashukku fika li'anni ashukku fi nafsi wa-anta minni..."* I doubt you and thus I doubt myself for you are a part of me... The voice attracted me like a current. Mamduh and Ahmad sat next to a little fire and the tape recorder was next to them. I ran and stared at it as though Um Kalthoum herself was sitting in it, singing. I felt so grateful and happy that they'd brought it. Is there anything more beautiful on this earth that to listen to Um Kalthoum in the middle of the desert under a starlit sky?

I blinked when I came out of the tent the next morning. The sun had already taken up the whole sky. How had I gone into the tent yesterday, how had sleep kept me under its spell for such a long time? Karin and Randa woke up too.

"Good morning! Come, the day started a long time ago!" Mamduh and Ahmad were sitting in the shade of the jeep drinking coffee. Black coffee, a couple of warm oranges, and we resumed our journey.

We approached the next oasis, where a lifeless collection of four-story buildings bordered the road left and right, as inviting as dried-up porridge.

"What's that?"

"Those are the state-supported residential projects, meant to persuade the Bedouin to adopt a settled way of life, and to attract the people from the valley of the Nile in order to counterbalance overpopulation and extend the cultivated areas. But Egyptians feel it to be a punishment to leave the Nile, so despite all the financial support and enticements, cultivation of new land progresses very slowly," Ahmad explained, who was always well informed about developments and projects in the country.

"It was Nasser who started these projects, but as you see, it hasn't been very successful!"

The Bedouin around these residential blocks seemed to use the houses as pantries and the upper floors as an ideal place to hang clothes to dry in the wind. They themselves lived in front of the houses, which provided pleasant shade and protected them from the heat of the sun.

Before we could penetrate into the Libyan desert, we had to go through a checkpoint. Our papers were taken, checked, and returned cheerfully. We drove several hours through a monotonous stone desert before reaching Dakhla. This oasis comprised several clay houses, and a small Isis temple, but apart from that nothing of interest. We drove to an irrigation system where small children played, and got out of the jeep to stretch our legs while Mamduh drove to the only gas station in the oasis to fill the tank.

The children looked at us curiously, and then a little girl came over. When she found out that we spoke Arabic, she ran away and returned soon after with two men.

"Welcome, welcome, we didn't know that you're Arabs! Usually only foreigners come by!" While they spoke, the flies of the oasis danced around them, and also seemed to enjoy us very much.

The men apparently took no notice of them. When Karin tried to chase them away with her hands, I whispered to her: "Stay quiet, because through this movement you exhibit qualities that aren't appreciated here!" She stopped. Only later, after we had been invited for tea, when we sat back in the car, did she ask: "What did you mean about qualities?"

"The difference between a Muslim—or an Arab as we say here—and a foreigner is that the first can sacrifice himself whereas the latter wants to take over everything with his hand!"

She thought about it for a while and then she had to laugh. We all laughed and we felt happy that she was with us.

The journey continued through the desert and I slowly felt myself turning into a grain of sand that had lost itself on the backseat of the jeep. The air became softer. We came to a village, drove to the main square, and stopped near the village coffee-house. Four little old men were sitting in front of it, leaning on their walking sticks, their eyes half closed as they let the wind tickle their gray beards. When they heard the car engine, they lifted their eyelids a little before letting them drop listlessly again.

Mamduh had a friend who came from the village and he wanted to visit his family. He got out of the car and sat next to the men. He greeted them with a loud voice to make sure they would hear him, asked them how they were, inquired about their health, and they answered in quite a detached fashion.

"I'm looking for the house of Hasan Mustafa al-Malihi."

"Who is he looking for?" they asked each other. "Speak louder, my son!"

"The house of Hasan, Mustafa's son," one of them answered, who had picked it up.

"Oh, Mustafa's little son. Whose daughter did he marry?"

"Ali's daughter. Ali, Muhammad's son, the one who saved the goats in the valley in that year when it rained so much."

"Oh, yes, wasn't beautiful Nafisa, may the Lord have mercy on her soul, his wife?"

"Yes. Nafisa—no one could run up the hill faster than her."

"Yes and no one could aim better than her with the little stones!" A couple of dark little teeth appeared in the old man's mouth. "There's not one boy in the village who hadn't got at least one of her stones in his head!"

The memories of younger days blew over their dried out bodies like a dewy breeze, turning dryness into fertility. But the breeze vanished as suddenly as it had sprung up and each man lost himself again in the blur of his confused thoughts.

The youngest of them suddenly stood up: "Come with me, I'll take you to his house!"

We got out of the car and followed him obediently. He walked surprisingly fast and his knees gave in skillfully to the familiar curves of the earth.

We passed a large square between the houses. A rostrum stood there with a few chairs in front of it, and a couple of men carefully carried something bulky that they put down carefully on the rostrum.

"Devil's work!" muttered the old man and we recognized the village television.

"Only brings destruction and bad manners, confuses our women and steals the young men's hearts!"

His step quickened, as if he was fleeing from the demon's ether.

We climbed up a little hill where a couple of houses stood close to each other. He went to a wooden door that stood ajar.

"*Ya allah*!" he shouted loudly and we waited. He clapped: "*ya ahl li-llah*!" O, children of Allah!

A faint woman's voice rang out: "There's no one here!" By that she meant that no man was at home.

"A friend is asking about your son Hasan."

"Greetings to him and blessed be he, may Allah preserve
and protect him. Hasan isn't here!"

"Please give him my greetings, *ya 'amma*, o my brother's
sister, my name is Mamduh!"

"God be with you, my son!"

The whole conversation had taken place without our
setting eyes on her. I had a feeling of oppression in my breast
and it pressed to the innermost of my soul. Was this the voice
of the granddaughter of Nafisa, the beautiful stone thrower,
who was hiding behind the gaping door? I wanted to run inside
to bring her out, so that she could show herself with pride and
confidence. And although as a woman I could have entered
easily, I didn't. I longed for the openness of the desert and the
pressure on my chest only eased once my eyes saw the desert
again.

We drove through a soft sand desert and although the day
already bowed deeply in front of darkness we decided to keep
driving. We were completely silent in the jeep, dozing off while
Mamduh drove on heroically. He seemed in a rush, as if racing
with an invisible opponent. Maybe it was also the natural rush
of youth expressing its urge to live through speed.

Ahmad tried to persuade him to take a break but Mamduh
wouldn't give in. "It's not a good place to stop here," he said,
"it's too dangerous, there are military stations and training
camps everywhere."

We drove and drove and our bottoms grew stiff under the
poorly upholstered seats of the jeep.

"That's enough, Mamduh, you have to stop otherwise
you'll have an accident because you're tired!"

Mamduh kept driving and the atmosphere in the jeep
became tense and uncomfortable.

"Stop right now!" we shouted aggressively. Angrily giving
in to his fatigue and our pressure, good-natured Mamduh
turned the jeep left from the track and stopped soon after.

"Fine, let's have some sleep!" he muttered. Each of us tried
to find the best sleeping position and we were gone.

There was knocking, far in the land of dreams. There was
knocking and I didn't feel like opening the door. It knocked
again—the knocker could wait until tomorrow. There was
knocking everywhere. What a nuisance! I opened my eyelids in
annoyance.

Five pairs of men's eyes stared through the windowpanes. Alertness flashed through my limbs and woke up the others too. Mamduh rolled down the window.

"What are you doing here! Where do you come from!" thundered one of the men.

Looking between the heads I took stock of the situation: we had spent the night on the maneuver area of the barracks. Well, if worse came to worst, they'd hang us as spies. I decided to surrender to my destiny, but Karin and Randa were shaking me nervously, apparently possessed by a strong need to go on living.

I sat upright and joined in the discussion between the men, Mamduh and Ahmad. Only with life can you oppose people drilled in killing and defending.

"*Ya ahl il-cher*, o people of the good, it's very simple, we had been visiting relatives and we wanted to go back to Cairo when my sister suddenly felt unwell and complained about nausea. Allah help us, we got scared and we stopped immediately... May Allah grant you strong descendants, too!"

The morning sun dawned on their faces. "Why didn't you say so right away! Fetch some water, quickly! Please come out and have a rest! Check if everything is okay with their jeep!" We thanked them profusely, they apologized inordinately, and off we went. Thus the tender pulse of inspiration flows between life and death.

"The Egyptians are *tajjibin* (good-hearted people)," Mamduh mumbled.

We had been travelling for five days and in our youthful haste we had covered large distances, but some parts of our body had had enough. We decided to drive back to Cairo.

On the way back, we stopped in the night for a short while. We got out of the car, taking some cheese and a few oranges. I leaned against the jeep to revel once more in the sight of the desert. The sand hills curved softly in the moonshine. Moonshine... I looked into the sky and was suddenly overwhelmed by the mystery of the worlds. The gates of my soul opened and I was led into the limitless space where yesterday and tomorrow unite silently in the rhythmic pulse of the endless moment. My arms gave into the weight of the pieces of orange and cheese and fell into my lap. Wings seemed to grow from my shoulders, opening my breast to its limits and filling it with a deep sigh. My breast felt crimson, sated, round, full, and limitless, and I realized that everything was as it should be. I sighed once more, then got into the jeep and closed my eyes gratefully to sleep.

TA'MIYYE AND KUSHARI,
OR HOW A PEOPLE SURVIVE

The days of the worlds may be counted,
yet there is no end to the wonders of the heart.
—Sufi wisdom

I ran down the stairs. We needed bread, cheese, tea, and sugar. I walked down the street, as usual without paying any attention to what went on around me, when suddenly the red of a cut melon beckoned. It was sitting on the tip of a whole hill of melons sold by an old man on a wooden cart. Sweet, watery, refreshing fruit. I decided to take one home.

From the outside, they all looked the same, but how was I supposed to guess about the inside from their external appearance?

"Ammi, choose me a small juicy one to the best of your knowledge and belief."

The old man went to the melons and inspected them all before picking one. He knocked on one cheek, then on the other, lifted the melon to his ear, shook it slightly, examined the stalk, and pulled it a little. "This one's good!"

I nodded in agreement and he put it carefully on the scales. I paid and took it under my arm. Then I walked to the baker's, which I could smell in the distance. I went down to the basement where the baker stood in front of the oven's deep opening. He held a long wooden stick whose flat end was like the palm of a big hand. There were hundreds of small flat round pastry loaves, which he put in threes on the flat end of the stick and skillfully pushed to the back of the oven where other loaves waited to be taken out.

"*Ya'tik il-'afiya*, may Allah grant you life strength, I'd like a pound of *'esh*."

Bread is the most important food for Egypt's poor and they call it lovingly *'esh* (life). The Egyptian people can put up with a lot, but when the state considers lifting the state-subsidized bread prices, even good-natured Egyptians take to the streets in protest.

Loaded with melon and bread, I went to the *gam'iyya* (co-operative) and joined the line. I was lucky—there weren't so many people there today. These co-operatives, which sold rationed quantities of food to the country's poor, kept Egypt alive and preserved it from chaos. About 90 percent of the country cannot live without these subsidies. Since Sadat, food supplies had become a monopoly.

In this country, there was a silent agreement between the state and the lower classes: "I provide you with relatively high quality food at prices that all can afford, and in exchange you stay away from politics and let me rule in peace!" After the *gam'iyyas* there is nothing for a long time, and then come the modern supermarkets with the imported goods that only the highest classes can afford. I was happy that in the meantime I had mastered the Egyptian dialect so well that I could go easily shopping in the *gam'iyyas*, because Randa and I could not have survived without them.

There were almost only women in the line, strong women full of fighting spirit, artists of life who had learned to support their family patiently under the most difficult circumstances. Just as in the old times, when village women would gather around the fountain to chat, share their worries and encourage each other, now they met at the *gam'iyya*. Many of them knew each other, and they knew the sellers, who always kept a bag of sugar or lentils tucked away in a corner for their favorite clients.

"*Iz-zayyik ya um mohammad*, how are you, o Um Mohammad, is your son doing better at school?"

"How is your toothache, have you been to the dentist yet?" one woman asked.

"She's Ali's widow, and she's looking after her three little children by herself now," a woman whispered behind me to her friend.

"May Allah help her!" was the answer.

"What are you going to cook today? Will you let us have a taste?" the seller joked while pressing two tins of tomato purée in the woman's hands.

"*Min 'eneyya, ya abu sa'd*! By my eyes, o Abu Sa'd!" the old woman smiled.

"She fought against her husband's whole family to be able to keep her children after the divorce and now, with Allah's help, she has already married two of her daughters," a woman explained, turning her head toward the old woman.

The various feminine *kismets* (destinies) of this country stood at the *gam'iyya*, each woman carrying her own like a she-wolf who did in life what had to be done. Those women endured difficulties and oppression, making the best out of hardship. Each of them whispered her story to the wind they called destiny in these parts. It was my turn and I bought tea, sugar, yellow cheese, and a bag of lentils. My thoughts stayed with them as I wandered slowly home.

In the 1960s Nasser had given women the opportunity to obtain qualified training and jobs thanks to his educational and vocational policy, which was focused on the middle and lower classes. Education was free from primary school all the way to university, and the state guaranteed jobs to both sexes and equal pay for equal work.[1] Laws were enacted for the protection of mothers, and child-care centers were built in all workplaces that had at least a hundred women on staff. Women started seeing and defining themselves differently; they were participating actively in the construction of their society.

Of course, it was clear to many of them that although they had become economically independent from their families, which they could even support, they had become dependent on the state. But the state did not touch the internal patriarchal family structures. Had women gained liberation or a double burden? Father-state outside and physical father or husband at home?

My thoughts buzzed like flies. I chased them away and precisely because I chased them, they came back in an even denser swarm. Nasser wanted an Arab socialism and he had either locked up or locked out the Islamists. Then came Jehan and Anwar Sadat who wanted an open Western capitalist line, and now the left-wing was locked up or locked out, and the Islamists tolerated or integrated.

Sadat had first flirted with the Islamists, but when they became too influential, he flirted with secular forces instead. Did he want to please everyone, this *rayyis*, president, who behaved in a fatherly way? He, or rather his wife Jehan, launched a campaign to reform civil law.

Women's situation within the family improved. The divorce law was modified, polygamy made more difficult. A woman could divorce her husband if he married a second wife. A woman with children was entitled to the house in which she had lived during the marriage and she got forty percent of her husband's income for three years. If she had been married to the same man for more than fifteen years, she would receive alimony for life or until she married again. Her daughters stayed with her until they married and her sons until they were fifteen, provided she was not "unfit."

But at the beginning of his presidency Sadat had addressed women's civil rights in the Constitution in such a way that they could find themselves at the mercy of male politics.[2] Mubarak, the Egyptian Arab Republic's third president, further refined the policy of integration and exclusion to preserve his own power, and the issue of women's rights was always the bait used to that end. Civil law was revised; hard edges were smoothed down; and men were favored in the public sector. Mubarak trimmed Nasser's and Sadat's reforms to suit his goals.

But the women in the *gam'iyya* were hardly concerned by all that, for divorce and polygamy were seldom a issue to them. They could not afford one or the other since they and their husbands were too busy fighting for their daily survival. The pill existed—it was just about free at the pharmacy—but having children still served as a way of safeguarding the future. They were still a guarantee that the husband would not marry again. They were a divine blessing, the pride of life, and they brought external prestige.

One of the most significant and influential reformers was Muhammad Abduh (1848–1905), who supported the improvement of women's position in his role as Egypt's Grand Mufti, which he took over in 1899. In Abduh's view it was Islam and not the West that had first awarded women full human equality. Traditions and practices such as polygamy and divorce went back to centuries of misinterpretations and deviations in Islamic societies. He wanted to improve the position of women through education, by making polygamy and divorce more difficult and by putting an end to all practices that encouraged division.

Progress and modernity were not in contradiction with Islam, as long as man used his reason and moral responsibility to bring them into harmony. Changes toward modern civilization were even prescribed by Islam, and religion was a friend of science, encouraging man to explore the mysteries of existence. Nevertheless, man needed to respect fixed truths and rest his moral life and conduct on them. How much education and inner maturity this required! May Allah's mercy be with you, Muhammad Abduh!

"What's the matter with you?"

Without quite realizing, I had arrived home.

"Oh nothing, Randa. I'm just thinking about our life."

THE EMIRATES

ABU DHABI, THE FATHER OF
THE GAZELLE

I finally made it! After spending months trying to get a visa, I finally received my entry permit. The difficulty had come from the fact that I wanted to travel alone, and although I had received an invitation from a local family, an Arab woman wanting to travel without male protection aroused suspicion. On the flight to Abu Dhabi, I could already feel the cosmopolitan atmosphere of the country.

Veiled women sat on the plane wearing *burqas*, gleaming face masks behind which dark eyes watched. With their masks and black veils, they seemed to belong to another world. They were a fascinating sight and only politeness kept me from spending the whole time observing them. I wondered how they ate, since the mask hid most of the mouth. As I would find out later, they in fact had a very elegant way to eat.

There were also many unveiled women on the plane, whose origin could easily be determined by their clothes and behavior. The Lebanese women were dressed in the most Western fashion. Their hair slightly backcombed and delicately lightened, they wore the shortest and tightest clothes. When they spoke their gestures took up a lot of space, and when they brought cups to their lips they never failed to extend their little finger like a tiny antenna. They seemed very self-confident yet fragile.

It so happened that all Egyptian women were veiled. They wore a specifically Egyptian creation as head cover, from which they could be recognized from miles away. Egyptian women love all sorts of caps and imaginative headgear. No other country boasts so many veil variations as Egypt. On the plane, their caps were artistically combined with cloths hanging around the neck and fastened to the cap by pins decorated with mother of pearl. One of them wore a gold-embroidered headband over her veil; another had draped it on one side, as in the Arab films of older days.

The two Iraqi women on board were unveiled. They behaved in a distinctly intellectual way, sitting with stern expressions and discussing a book recently published. They were dressed in very plain, buttoned-up blouses and knee-length skirts. They were probably teachers or university professors.

I also discovered a bewitchingly beautiful Syrian woman. Her behavior was extremely feminine, adorned with charming little gestures. Her voice was sweet and she kept her lips very soft, so that they could delicately stretch with each word she spoke.

Classification was much easier with the men. Some wore *jalabas* and white, or perhaps red and white, *kufiyas* on their heads; others were dressed in Western suits. Oh, and some wore those famous safari suits, the favorite summer clothes of Middle Eastern men when they do not wish to wear a *jalaba*. The safari suits, which always come in shades of beige and green, consist of tight-fitting, short-sleeved, shirt-like jackets with large buttons and nondescript trousers of the same color. They must be extremely comfortable, for no man in the whole Middle East ever looked good in them.

Nothing enhances more the beauty of a dark-eyed, dark-skinned man than a white *jalaba* with a white *kufiya* and *igal*. Any hint of a bulging stomach disappears behind the cool robe, which stretches out the stature; the *kufiya* disguises any hint of baldness, as it plays about the face in an interesting, distinguished fashion, with the black *igal* the finishing touch. Such clothing has a cooling effect and flows lightly and obediently with each movement. A man looks as elegant sitting on the floor as in an armchair. Why any man would choose to squeeze into a Western suit despite the heat is simply beyond me.

The plane landed and we were greeted by the sight of a very beautiful airport. It was huge and had been built in the shape of a tent, held up in its center by a powerful column. I stood in the hall, totally fascinated. The tent was decorated with green, white, and blue tiles, and it radiated a modern oriental mood. Modern technology and tradition combined in this wonderful architecture. I had nothing to declare and I soon came out with my luggage, immediately spotting Uncle Sabri and Aunt Adeline. They waved, I waved back, and the three of us grinned.

Uncle Sabri was an old friend of my father's. Their mothers had been friends and now their friendship extended to the third generation. Uncle Sabri had been married to Adeline, a lively American, for more than 25 years and they had two sons. The elder was born in Baghdad, but for socio-political reasons the younger had come into this world in the United States.

Both my aunt and uncle were known as an active, socially committed, and fun-loving couple. Whenever political problems arose between Iraq and the United States, Uncle Sabri would spend days only talking grumpily to his wife, while shouting abuse at the Americans at the top of his voice without even deigning to glance at her. Adeline felt hurt to be constantly identified with and made responsible for the politics of her country, but she took it patiently. She knew her husband's violent temper well and after so many years she had learned that waiting and ignoring his pained outbursts was the quickest way to let him calm down. This may be the reason why she was so intent on striving for peace and understanding between East and West. At the end of the day her marriage and peace at home depended on it.

She was actually much smarter than he, for she had managed to strengthen and develop in their sons the Arab side that she so loved in her husband, while at the same time sharpening their American vision and orienting their education toward that powerful country, so that they could benefit from both sides of their inheritance.

We got into the car and drove toward Abu Dhabi City. I gaped as we drove through the streets. Never before had I seen such magnificent streets, and I was so surprised by all the surrounding greenery that it nearly frightened me. So this is what it looks like to use wealth properly, I thought, and my heart fluttered in joy and gratitude for Allah's blessing over this country. It looked like the land of milk and honey. Everywhere lay beautiful villas, palaces even, and always gardens, gardens in the middle of the desert. Was there no poverty here? Had man really managed to create a peaceful, equitable paradise in this little corner of the earth? Could it be that not greed but goodness and a willingness to share had won here? I didn't want to ask questions yet and I surrendered to the beauty of the moment, savoring the splendid surroundings. The ancient human yearning for justice, beauty, and love spread like a balm through my veins.

The car took a turn and entered the garage of a flat-roofed house that lay hidden behind tall trees. We got out and a pleasant breeze surrounded us. It was January, the sky was blue, and the sun shone on us softly and graciously. We entered the house.

It was a comfortable home, with pictures by Arab painters on the walls. I caught sight of a beautiful, old wooden chest. A comfortable blue sitting area beckoned to me and I sat down. The house was furnished in Western style and only the pictures, the chest, and a couple of ornaments showed that the Arab world also lived in this house. Muhhi, a delicate dark man with lively eyes, brought refreshing drinks. He smiled pleasantly.

"Muhhi is our famous Indian cook. He has been with us for fifteen years already and he is now part of the family," Adeline explained. Why famous, I would soon find out.

I had come to Abu Dhabi planning to write about Bedouin women, their customs, ceremonies, and language. I wanted an interesting and enjoyable subject for my thesis, one which touched me as a woman.

"It won't be easy to get into contact with local families. There are many foreigners here who have been doing business with the locals for twenty years, and yet they have never been invited to meet their families. The high proportion of foreigners in this country where the natives account for less than 25 percent of the population has contributed to the fact that people are particularly keen to protect the intimate area of the family from foreign influences," Adeline explained to me. "We'll help you as best we can to take the first step. But whether or not they will accept you is entirely in your hands — especially since you want to record their voices on tape! This will definitely not be easy!"

I fell into a slight panic; had I travelled all this way to return, maybe, with blank tapes? But my joy at being here and discovering a new world kept me from feeling depressed by Adeline's words.

"Food is ready!" announced Muhhi, and we went to the table. I was surprised to see that the countless dishes were all Iraqi; I had rather figured they would be Indian. But I should have known that after so many years, Uncle Sabri would have taught Muhhi all the Iraqi dishes. After tasting almost everything, I understood why Muhhi was famous: no Iraqi woman could have prepared better or tastier dishes. I wondered at Aunt Adeline's and Uncle Sabri's relatively slim figures!

"Many friends have already tried to steal Muhhi away, but he has stayed with us faithfully. He will only cook for others when there is a celebration, and earn some extra money in this way."

"I have bought myself a piece of land in Pakistan and I'm having a house built—it will soon be ready," Muhhi explained contentedly.

"One more year, and he'll be back in his homeland. But maybe we can convince him to stay for another year," said Uncle Sabri, winking at him.

Muhhi looked at the floor, slightly shy, moving his chin to and fro.

"This afternoon the owner of the house will come to collect the rent for the next six months. It will be a good opportunity for you to ask a few questions about the life of the locals, and to get a feeling of the language," Uncle Sabri said. He was a practical-minded, action-oriented man and I was grateful to him for those qualities.

"Doesn't the house belong to you?" I asked, somewhat surprised. It was a simple house, and compared to the villas I had seen on the way, quite modest. I was sure that they could have afforded it.

"Foreigners are not allowed to own any property in Abu Dhabi. It is true that the country is now full of foreigners, because they were and are still needed for development and education purposes, but they are not allowed to take root forever. It's not easy because the young generation, our sons for example, were brought up here; they feel at home, and more connected to this country than to their country of origin. But everybody knows they will have to leave one day. You come here, you work hard, you make a better living than anywhere else in the world, and then you leave with a full purse. This is how it's supposed to be, but there's nothing you can do against the affections of the heart."

Uncle Sabri was a clever businessman who had sensed very early on the unique opportunities in the Gulf and he was among the first to emigrate here. Back in the 1970s, he had tried to convince my father to try his luck here, but Father could not imagine trading his beloved brightly lit Baghdad for bare sand dunes, even with the prospect of a lot of money. After Uncle Sabri had used his powers of persuasion for a long time, my father finally declared himself ready to take a look at Abu Dhabi. He came, stayed for two weeks, and left again.

"Do you know what your father told me at the time? That there's no place is the world worthier of living and dying than Baghdad! Yet he would have had great opportunities here," Uncle Sabri added, shaking his head slightly.

I smiled shyly.

After lunch we all had a rest, I in my new guest room with light yellow curtains and a green carpet, Adeline and Sabri in the opposite, blue-shaded bedroom. The air conditioning whirred and my eyelids slid over my eyes.

I must have slept, for Aunt Adeline—she loved to be called "Aunt"—woke me with her sweet American accent: "Tea's ready, come and sit with us!"

"I'm coming!" I jumped out of bed and took a quick shower. There was no need for hot water—the cold water was warm enough. I enjoyed the flow for a few minutes. I dried myself quickly and put on a long, flowery black and white skirt with a matching blouse. While I was combing my hair, Aunt Adeline called again: "Where are you? The tea is getting cold!"

I felt as if I were at home, for my mother would have said exactly the same thing. The older we get, the more impatient we become with time. All the same, I decided to put on some make-up before I appeared.

My sweet smile made amends for their wait. I sat between Aunt and Uncle on the sofa while Muhhi poured the tea.

"Tell me, Uncle Sabri, how was life here in Abu Dhabi when you first arrived?"

Uncle Sabri seemed to remember everything, for he immediately started talking:

"When we arrived here at the beginning of the 1970s, Abu Dhabi was one huge building site, the biggest in the world. Before they discovered oil, this region was one of the poorest in the world. When the first oil tanker left the coast, life changed so dramatically that even I sometimes can't believe it. A team of French architects was appointed to design a new city. Before that, hardly anything was here—no streets, no houses. The only large building was the sheikh's fort and you can still see that today, shining white amid the roses and the palm trees. Back then it was the color of sand and it towered in the middle of nowhere, surrounded by clay or palm huts where the people lived.

"I came to Abu Dhabi to head the management of the newly built Hilton hotel in the al-Ain oasis. The oasis lies at the foot of Hadjar mountain, some 150 kilometers east of Abu Dhabi, toward the Omani border. A few years earlier, I think it was in 1966, a motorway had been built between Abu Dhabi City and the al-Ain oasis. We spent the following six years in al-Ain—or rather at the Hilton hotel, because there wasn't much else and it was the major meeting point.

"I remember very well the overheated faces of businessmen who had come from all over the world to make their fortunes. There was a gold-diggers' atmosphere. Greedy and sweaty, they sat with their red heads in the hotel halls, their files full of projects, sales catalogs, old dreams and new hopes, waiting to be granted an appointment with Sheikh Zayid, the ruler of Abu Dhabi. Al-Ain was actually his favorite residence and where he was most likely to be found. Many businessmen became very wealthy; many went home empty-handed, only to be replaced by new ones. This went on for years.

"In the meantime, Abu Dhabi was growing and growing. Clay huts were pulled down by bulldozers and replaced with villas, schools, administrative buildings, streets, airports, everything that belongs to a modern city. It was like a set change in the theater. The audience watches as walls disappear to make room for new ones, the emptiness suddenly fills up, gardens and alleys materialize. And before they even fully realize, they're in another world, another time, and all this speed has left them breathless. Local people hardly had time to adapt. As if through a time machine, they were hurled from the centuries-old quiet rhythm of simplicity into the twentieth century."

The door bell rang. "Ah, that must be the owner, Abu Faraj." Uncle Sabri stood up to open the door.

A powerful dark head set on a bulky body came in, white teeth flashed and a voice far too soft for that body said: "*As-salamu alaykum!*"

"Welcome, Abu Faraj. How are you, my friend, and how is your family?" Uncle Sabri greeted him.

So this was Abu Faraj. Uncle Sabri introduced us and explained to him that I had come to Abu Dhabi to interview women from the different local tribes. Abu Faraj gave a friendly nod with his powerful head. The men sat down and I went to Aunt Adeline.

"I didn't know that the men were so dark in this region," I told her shyly.

"Abu Faraj actually comes from Africa. He was brought over here at the time of the slave trade. But he is a free man now, a full member of the tribe he used to serve, and he carries the name of the tribe like all the others."

"What's the name of his tribe?"

"He belongs to the Dhawahir, who live mainly in the al-Ain oasis."

I felt slightly uncomfortable to be intruding in the intimate sphere and story of this man, but I had come here to understand. Sensitive Adeline felt my shyness.

"Abu Faraj is a good-natured, simple man, whose wisdom comes from life experience. He has become very wealthy and if he trusts you, he will certainly invite you to meet his family. Accept the invitation without declining first, as the Arab custom would have it." Adeline had lived long enough with the Arabs to know the nuances in manners. I thanked her for this advice, for as she had rightly guessed, I would have declined first.

I joined the two men.

"Abu Faraj, would it be possible to talk a little about life in Abu Dhabi? I know too little about the customs and traditions here, and maybe you could give me a little introduction."

Abu Faraj looked straight at me for a moment with his small shiny eyes, then flashed his white teeth again and nodded: "Glad to help if I can!"

"May I also record you?"

Surprised, Abu Faraj looked at Uncle Sabri questioningly.

"She needs it in order to record the dialect of this region," Uncle Sabri said soothingly.

"If that is so, fine!"

Happily I fetched my tape recorder and its big microphone. It was really intimidating—how would I ever get people here to relax and speak in front of this thing!

I sat next to Abu Faraj, greeted him again as the Arab

custom demands, and pressed the record button. I chose to ask general questions and to progress cautiously, so that he had a chance to retreat whenever he no longer wished to speak. I asked him how Islamic feasts were celebrated here, where weddings took place, as well as the names for men and women's clothes. Abu Faraj started talking very softly, watching the tapes turn and turn. Then suddenly the moment came when he forgot about the machine and spoke freely.

When his voice grew stronger, I asked him about his family.

"I have six children. My eldest son is preparing his 'A' levels and next year it will be my daughter's turn. Neither my wife nor I can read or write, but all my children will be able to."

"Praised be Allah!" I answered.

Abu Faraj looked at me and giggled, "My wife now attends morning adult classes. The state started offering evening classes for women, but it didn't work; now they offer morning classes and she goes three times a week, together with another two women from the neighborhood. She felt embarrassed that her youngest daughter could read and write, and she couldn't understand anything."

"This is the voice of a proud father and husband, may Allah keep your family in good health!" I replied with a smile.

"You must come and visit us, my wife would enjoy it, and she can tell you much more than I!"

I was very grateful to him for his trust and his kindness.

"I'd love to come—it would be an honor for me to get to know your family, Abu Faraj!"

He stood up, promised to call to set a date, and took his leave. I had taped my first conversation and looked confidently to the future.

I NO LONGER KNOW WHERE I AM

Aunt Adeline pulled out all the stops. She called girlfriends and acquaintances and did her best to set up meetings for me with local women. Her efforts were touching and although I felt deeply grateful to her, at the same time I could observe her with detachment, as though this concerned someone else.

At last she came to me beaming with joy and shared her triumph: "We are invited to a local family this afternoon. One of my girlfriends advises some women of the al Bu Falah clan, the ruling family. She spoke with them and they agreed: We can go, and you can try your luck!"

Keenly excited, I prepared my tapes and put them into a bag with the tape recorder. Would they agree? Would they give me information? Would I be able to record their voices?

Forget the questions—just let things come, I told myself.

Aunt Adeline and I sat in the car and drove off past the beautiful villas, the thousand yards of black water-hoses with an opening next to each plant, out of which water flowed everyday at the push of a button. Water came from the sea and was processed in huge desalination plants. Desalinated water served many other purposes, except drinking. One had to buy bottles of drinking water and one liter cost nearly as much as a liter of gasoline, if not more.

Adeline knew her way around Abu Dhabi; she darted skillfully and purposefully to our destination until we turned into the courtyard of a magnificent, delicately yellow palace. There was no other word for that splendid building. We stepped out and a man—given his tender features, his flat nose and golden brown complexion, he must have come from the fertile Philippine islands—opened the door and invited us courteously in.

We walked in, in a leisurely way. Inside too, everything was in soft yellow hues. The furniture was Italian, expensive, solid yet surprising simple. Many women stood around, some from India, others from the Philippines, and several locals. All local women had taken off their *burqas*, the face-masks typical of this region, and their *abayas* (black capes), revealing their faces and their colorful, splendid, sparkling, flowing robes. It was a wonderful sight. They looked like bright birds of paradise. Their features betrayed neither dislike nor sympathy. They watched us calmly, almost indifferently.

Adeline went and shook hands with all of them, and I followed suit. Limp hands were extended to me, their pressure nearly that of the dying. I did not feel comfortable at all. Indian and Philippine staff stood one step behind the local women and Adeline greeted them with a nod. I decided to do the same.

Then a woman in her fifties made her appearance, and beside her a woman dressed in European clothes, her hair slightly bleached. The latter was the only one who beamed and from whose face one could tell where one stood. Although I did not know her, her expression felt comfortably familiar.

"Hello Adeline, how are you?"

She came slowly toward us so as not to overtake the woman of the house, who was definitely the fifty-year-old woman. Adeline and I approached to meet them.

"This is my friend Adeline. She has an Iraqi husband and she's been living here for seventeen years." The woman inspected Adeline and extended her hand in greeting.

"And this," she stretched her arm toward me, "is her friend who has come to Abu Dhabi to collect information about the women here."

I found the introduction highly unsuitable and for a moment I felt like a little spy. The woman nodded indifferently. Somehow none of her movements seemed to belong to her; she breathed and moved her lips, but she did not seem present. Was this the epitome of boredom or renunciation of the world, or simply arrogance? Or was it supposed to express dignity and nobility? I could not understand.

We all followed her into a spacious room. Comfortable armchairs with thick armrests were lined along the walls, but she sat on the floor while Adeline's friend sat in an armchair next to her. For the first time I felt a link and I sat on the floor too, a few meters away from her. I put the bag behind me, where my tape recorder waited impatiently.

As soon as we were seated, two Indian women appeared carrying large trays filled with tea cups. The other women sauntered slowly toward us and sat down in armchairs. Tea was served and we all sipped it dutifully. Then came a tray with sweets that must have come from a Lebanese confectioner because I knew them all. They could not be specialities from the Gulf. I looked unobtrusively at Adeline's Lebanese friend. She sat there quite pleased with herself, bending forward to whisper something into the ear of the woman of the house, or to listen to her. She clearly exerted a strong influence on her.

There was not much talking in this get-together. You either whispered with your neighbor or kept exchanging traditional greetings and polite phrases. I was getting nervous: time was passing and I had not had the slightest opportunity to steer the discussion toward my request. I intuitively felt that the visit would be over soon. If I were to achieve anything, it would have to be now.

Suddenly the woman of the house suddenly turned toward me and asked, "What would like to know about Abu Dhabi?"

I was so taken aback that I would rather have answered "Nothing at all." Thank God it did not come to that.

"If you would do me the honor, I'd like to hear something about how life used to be here."

I seemed to have touched on a sore point.

"Aaaaaah," came the deep sigh. "Before everything used to be simple and small. We were a community. Now when I leave home, I no longer know where I am. If I want to visit my sons or daughters, they put me in a car and they drive me through streets and places that I have never seen before. I sit there, lost, and wait until they come and take me out of the car.

"Everything is alien, everything is new, everything keeps changing. I don't know Abu Dhabi any longer. Abu Dhabi is no longer Abu Dhabi. Everything is made of stone, hard and opaque."

She spoke like an old woman whose time was past, whose principles and lifestyle no longer belonged, who could only drink tea, visit her children, and wait. So her Lebanese friend counseled her and helped her gain at least some orientation so that she could face this new world with a modicum of dignity and knowledge.

I was happy that she had spoken, and I followed her with all my senses, taking in her tension, her heavy gaze, her limp hands, and her lost heart. I heard her speak that dialect that was still foreign to me, and at the same time I felt myself growing tense inside. The tape recorder, I must record her, I need her voice on tape. I knew it would not be easy, but I had to do it.

"May I tape your words on the tape recorder?"

She looked at me and the other women in the room looked at her with a sudden alert curiosity. Older people were models to be observed and to which one adjusted one's behavior. I dared not move. It felt like a long time, although only a few moments must have gone by.

"No," she said firmly and coldly, "you can take notes, but no tape-recorder!"

Adeline looked at me sadly and compassionately. It would be more difficult than we had thought.

I felt my hope break inside. Was it not to be? Was I not to do this work, was it not meant for me? But I knew this pessimistic side of mine and I was not ready to give in. Not yet!

BEDOUIN IN THE PALACE

The door opened and he walked in confidently. Before I turned around, I had already felt the peculiar strength that came from him. The air seemed to become instantly colder and my neck muscles tensed expectantly. I gave myself time, I wanted to fill my ears with his voice before my eyes discovered his face.

"*As-salamu alaykum*, Aunt Adeline!"

"Greetings to you, Qutayba!"

I turned around as slowly as I could, feigning disinterest but tense with anticipation. He was tall, his slender body casually widening into broad shoulders. I lifted my head to see his face and my hopes were not disappointed. He had dark, nearly shoulder-length hair, and his chin was covered by a well-groomed beard. I examined his brown eyes carefully. They gazed indifferently at the world; nothing seemed to move his cold heart. From the very beginning I knew he was a lost soul in this world, yet this may be precisely what attracted me.

Adeline started the conversation in her sweet, direct way: "Qutayba knows many local business people through his work. He'll certainly be able to help us, won't you, Qutayba?"

Qutayba looked at us with his cool gaze and answered pleasantly: "Sure, we'll do that. I'll speak to my friend today and ask him if you can visit his mother. He belongs to one of the most important families in this country, and once you have started with her, it'll be easy for you to get to know all the other women in the family."

He said it with such confidence and certainty, as if it were the easiest thing in the world. I must admit, his words filled me with confidence too, and I waited expectantly to see how things would develop.

The very next day when were having our afternoon tea, a horn tooted outside. A few minutes later, Qutayba appeared. He greeted everyone before turning to me: "We can go, I've arranged everything for you!"

I looked at him incredulously. Aunt Adeline was very satisfied. She smiled happily and spurred me on: "Go on, make yourself ready. Now is your big chance!"

I hesitated inside but I jumped up and put on a new *jalabiya*, tying my hair and covering my head with a black transparent shawl bordered with gold thread embroidery. This is how the younger generation dressed in Abu Dhabi, while married women and members of the older generation wore an additional *burqa*, a sort of small mask that covered the face, with a long black opaque veil on top of it. With the prevailing heat around here, it was a miracle that the women could wear it all! Members of the ruling house pulled a black scarf over their faces so that they were completely hidden from sight. I packed my tape recorder in the bag, together with a notebook, a few pencils, and a couple of boxes of chocolates.

I enjoyed adapting myself to the clothing rules, especially when they were so comfortable. When I came out of the room, Qutayba looked at me wide-eyed but he did not say a word. Fine, I thought to myself.

I said goodbye, Uncle Sabri and Aunt Adeline wished me all the best, and I went with Qutayba to his red sports car, feeling slightly nervous. We sat down and he sped off.

"I told them you're my cousin—it makes things easier," said Qutayba after a while.

I nodded. My shyness crept up my limbs and I kept trying to push it away.

"I can't do more than introduce you," Qutayba went on slightly coolly. "The rest is in your hands. But they won't give you more than one chance, so use it well!"

Thank you very much, I wanted to tell him. Just what I

wanted to hear. Like a taut elastic band, I felt torn between two familiar worlds: the world of confidence (*everything will be all right*) and the world of doubt (*I'll never make it*).

We came to a wide street into which Qutayba darted like an arrow before suddenly braking, turning left, and stopping in front of a giant gate behind which stood three villas.

"Here we are! Good luck then!" I looked at Qutayba wide-eyed, my heart pounding.

"Aren't you coming in with me?" I asked with a hint of despair.

"No, I'm not invited. Anyway today is women's day at the Mazruíi family. Only women are allowed in."

I swallowed.

"Where am I supposed to go?"

"To the house in the middle, that's where the mother lives. Just knock, they're expecting you. I'll come and pick you up in two hours."

I got out of the car with a heavy heart, wondering whether my project wasn't absolute nonsense. But there I was—I had been given the opportunity to enter a world almost completely sealed off to strangers. Without turning back, I went to the middle house and rang the bell. The door opened and a surprised but smiling Philippine woman greeted me. My God, I had forgotten to ask about the mother's name, so I had no choice but to introduce myself and say "I am expected."

She invited me in. There I stood, while she went down the long corridor and disappeared through a door. I wanted to leave but I forced myself to stay. Soon after she reappeared and invited me to follow her.

I followed her slowly to the door. It opened on eight women of different ages sitting on mattresses on the floor and looking at me with their big eyes. They all wore colorful *jalabiyas* and their heads were covered with black transparent veils. Some also wore the typical masks. The scene seemed nearly unreal, as if exotic, inordinately large, colorful birds had gathered in one small room.

They stood up and I shook hands with all of them before sitting down.

"Greetings to you, welcome," one of them said to me.

She was the eldest woman in the room. Her face was smooth and beautiful and her eyes looked clever and sceptical. "So you have come to write about our life?"

This direct question crept awkwardly under my skin. It was true in a way, but I would not have worded it so dryly.

"I'd like to write about the women's dialect in Abu Dhabi"—I wanted to say no more. The big bag with the tape recorder seemed to betray me. The time had not come to mention it. Suddenly the Philippine help appeared with a vessel full of incense. It gave off clouds of thick smoke and in no time the room was filled with the intense sweet fragrance. I took it in with a deep breath and instantly felt its relaxing effect.

The vessel was handed to the eldest woman. She held it with both hands, then took it in her left hand, waving the smoke into her face with her right hand, time and again, in a fan-like motion. Her eyes closed and her nostrils widened, absorbing the precious smoke. Then she moved the vessel to the right side of her face, under the veil, near the ear, and let the smoke go up. She repeated the movement on the left side. When she was finished, she passed the vessel on to the woman next to her who did exactly the same, like a mirror. I lowered my head a little and watched eagerly.

When my turn came, I knew the movements as if I had practiced them all my life. Still, excitement overcame me once the idea turned into action. I took the clay vessel in both hands and let myself soak in the fragrance. All the pores of my face seemed to open to the incense. What a beautiful way to greet a guest! Slightly dazed, I passed it on with a gentle smile. I felt my back soften and my nerves relax.

A small round person appeared. She was in her mid-fifties, with a smile that took up her whole face. Nice, I thought to myself. I felt how the atmosphere changed and the women's hands grew excited. So this was the friend's mother, whom Qutayba had told me about. A few women stood up and kissed her, some on the tip of the nose, others brushing her shoulders with their lips, to the sound of repeated greetings. I stood up too and kissed her as all the others did, albeit on the cheeks, as I was used to.

"Greetings to you!" she said to me in a friendly voice, and sat down. Without shame she asked into the room: "And who is that?" I felt the heat flow through my cheeks.

"She has come to write about the women here. That's all we know." I would rather have sunk into the floor, but instead I remained seated, in full view.

"Well, why not! Write down! Do you have a pen and paper?" was her friendly reply. Now I had to come out with the truth, now or never. "I would like to record the women's traditions, rituals, and various ceremonies. The language is very important and I can't write as quickly as you speak."

To emphasize my words, I took out my by now uncomfortably large tape recorder. All eyes turned to it and I too found it very ugly. Her head turned away and words bounced out of her lips: "Recording? Never!" There I was sitting with my device, alone and an outcast. If only the floor could open and swallow me, or a *jinn* of some description materialize and take me away!

Instead, coffee was served. The golden thermos flask was shaped like an old Arab coffee-pot and the small china cups piled up. Both were handed to the youngest woman in the circle. She stood up and poured half a cup for the first woman. The woman took it, swallowed the coffee in one gulp, and gave the cup back to the young woman. She poured again, handed it to the same woman, once more she drank the liquid with a single gulp, and then she elegantly swung the cup quickly this way and that, before handing it back. The young woman now went to the next, who drank three times before waving the cup back and forth. So this was the sign that one had enough.

When my turn came, I took the cup, but before I brought it to my lips, an intuition came to me and I turned to the mother and handed her the cup. For a moment the room was silent. All followed the scene without a word. She looked at me for a minute, then she extended her arm, took the cup from my hand, and drank.

Laughter and voices filled the room. I heard scraps of different conversations. "She has good manners!" "Polite and generous!" "Where did you say she comes from?" "Yes, she's dressed discreetly, like us!"

One gesture can change the whole world. I was amazed. After she had drunk her coffee and the full cup was handed to me again, I was again surprised by the taste. This was no normal coffee. It was a mixture of cardamom, herbs, and a little coffee. But it livened the senses wonderfully.

The mother spoke: "You may record, but you must promise that no foreign man will hear the tape."

No man—how could I promise that? I didn't want to lie. In my heart I promised to do my best, but I decided not to answer.

Silence is also a form of acceptance. I'll never forget this, mother of Qutayba's friend.

"What would you like to know?"

I decided to start carefully. My eyes wandered in the room and then came a thought. "Please tell me how you used to weave your carpets in the old times."

She seemed pleased by the question and the words tumbled from her lips. I switched my recorder on and silently pushed the microphone toward her.

She seemed to recall her own youth because she told such a lively story that I could see the picture clearly in front of me. Two women, each sitting at one end of the loom, pulling the thread through, then handing it to a child who jumps up and takes it to the other woman, who in turn pulls the thread through and gives it again to the child, who runs back to the first woman. All the while they sing in rhythm, old, timeless songs about life; about the desert flowers springing up from the barren soil like small wonders in the rainy season, catching a quick sight of the world before departing as unexpectedly; about the sound of ankle bells and the camels' gentle gaze.

It was beautiful to dive into this old world and when I looked around, I saw nostalgic joy on the women's faces. I had succeeded in connecting them through this recording and their hearts beat in unison. A soft contented smile played on my lips.

"You must stay for dinner," Mother said.

"Oh, no, I really can't, I'm being picked up in a moment."

"You're staying. Is Qutayba picking you up?"

"Yes."

"How is he related to you?"

"He is my cousin," I lied. Well, somehow it could be true and I didn't want to complicate things.

"When he comes, my son will invite him to join the men in the *majlis* (guest reception room) and he will eat with them."

We all stood up and went into the big corridor. We all sat on the floor and a large dish filled with fruit was served. Those once so competent women didn't have much left to do. The cooks cooked, the helpers cleaned, the nannies looked after the children, and the women were left to cultivate their social contacts and have more children.

With a sudden swing the door opened and a fat little woman came in, greeting us loudly from far off, puffing and panting and carrying something dark in her arms. When she came closer, I saw that it was a small goat and before I had overcome my surprise, she had already put the animal in Mother's lap, laughing and saying: "A present for you!" Mother burst out laughing too and gave the goat to one of the Philippine girls, who carried it away. I laughed inside. Bedouin will be Bedouin, even when they live in palaces. This discovery left me somehow appeased and happy—the old endures even in the new.

The fat woman sat down panting and she stared at me questioningly. Mother satisfied her curiosity: "She's a friend and she has come to write a little about our customs."

I was grateful for her answer, but she would not be free of the fat energetic woman so quickly.

"Why does she want to write about our customs?" she asked directly.

The question suddenly seemed to interest the other women, too. I felt that my whole project depended on my answer.

"I would like to write about the language and the customs of the women here. I'd like to demonstrate that the language spoken by the women is much older and more archaic than that of men."

The fat woman looked at me a little nonplussed, then she laughed loudly and started talking with Mother about other things that I couldn't quite understand. I found it difficult to understand the dialect. Many sounds were still foreign to my ear and there were many expressions that I had never heard before, but I decided to use my nights to study it.

Four large steaming trays were brought in. One after the other, the women stood up and washed their hands thoroughly. I wondered how those who wore a face mask would eat. Would they remove it or was there a special method that I didn't know yet? The trays were laid on the floor and a huge mountain of rice with vegetable and meat pieces appeared in front of me.

The women gathered around the trays in fours. Each woman leaned on her left hand, wrapped her legs under her body, and extended her hand after saying the *bismillah*. Those who wore the traditional mask would delicately push it forward with the fingers of their left hand, while eating with the right hand. The rice grains were elegantly scooped up with the index and middle fingers, lifted and shaped into small rolls in the palm of the hand. The rolls then landed in the mouth with an elegant sweeping movement, whereby the women took great care to keep their mouth as clean as possible. The small vegetable pieces were eaten with the rice, the meat torn in small morsels and eaten separately. It was extremely sensual and I enjoyed sharing a meal in such a wonderful way.

The dish was spiced with salt and dried limes, which gave it an edge. Later the women told me it was called *makbus*. After the meal, we washed our hands once more. Coffee was served again and soon after came the incense vessel again, this time signaling that visiting time was over. All those gestures without words, without awkwardness, and all knew what they had to do. I thanked them for everything and we agreed that I would come back in a few days. I met Qutayba outside.

"You must have made a good impression if you are invited again!"

I smiled contentedly.

MY LIFE LIES IN THE STARS

Zainab—in my mind I always called her "the mother"— promised to take me to another local family. She would visit her school friend and I could have a chat with the mother. Now we sat in the big comfortable car and the driver took us to them. He turned off the main street and we rode through unpaved roads. The houses were not as elegant as those on the main streets. We went past a school and the driver had to stop because the street was crowded with loud children in their light blue smocks pouring happily out of school. In the whole world children enjoy the end of school.

Soon the street cleared up and we could drive on. We turned into one unpaved street after another until finally we stopped in front of a modest house. A little girl stood next to the entrance and Zainab shouted at her from the car to call Haya. The girl disappeared, a little afraid. The person we wanted appeared immediately.

"Who—Zainab? Greetings on you, welcome, welcome! What an honor!" I could tell from the way Zainab was greeted that she came from a nobler family than the one she was visiting.

Haya showed us into the living room and the sight that awaited us brought a smile to my lips. The television was on and in front of it sat a woman with a plump back, her behind comfortably spread on the floor. She sat with her back to us and watched with rapt attention. A camel race was on and she spurred on the camels with heavy hip movements and loud interruptions.

"Mother, we have visitors. Zainab and her friend have arrived!" Um Abdallah turned around and a wide smile immediately shone in her face, which had already experienced much in life.

"*Hallat il-baraka*, blessing has appeared. *Ahlan wa sahlan, ahlan wa sahlan*, welcome, welcome!" She wanted to get up and pressed her arms heavily against the floor to lift up her weight.

"Please, Auntie, stay seated, don't strain yourself!" Zainab said.

We kneeled down next to her and greeted her.

"Oh dear, these knees won't obey me any more!" Um Abdallah rubbed her knees with her hands. "Come and sit next to me, children!" I felt that this woman carried a full heart and that her heart sat on her tongue.

Zainab looked at me and I spoke as if on cue. "Um Abdallah, I'd like to ask you to tell me a little about your life. I'm collecting stories about the customs and ceremonies of Abu Dhabi." She looked at Zainab, who smiled.

"I'd be glad to. What would you like to hear?"

"I have a tape recorder with me, may I record your words?"

Again she looked at Zainab, who answered: "She needs those tapes for her studies, Auntie."

"Oh, I see, for her studies, well then, fine!"

She was such a loving and simple soul, she warmed my heart. So I put my tape recorder on the floor in front of Um Abdallah and she straightened up as best she could in front of it. "What should I say?"

"Just tell me a little about yourself, whatever you like."

She waggled a little back and forth, sighed deeply as if she was looking back on her life and with that sigh reminiscing about its difficulties, disappointments, and hardships.

"I am Um Abdallah of the tribe of the Qubaysi," she said in a voice heavy with experience, sounding much deeper, much older than before. With her tone my face became quite serious and my body turned to her imperceptibly.

"Ours was a hard life. My husband is also my cousin. He was a pearl-diver and we lived in Abu Dhabi. Every summer he would go to sea with the pearl-diver fleet while I stayed home alone with the children for months on end. Abu Dhabi was not the way you see it now. A few mud huts, without water or electricity.

"During the first years of my marriage I did not get any children. I would always lose them in the first months of pregnancy. Sorrow filled my belly every time. I kept trying to cure my belly and my arms with the *wasim*. Small, narrow iron rods are heated on an open fire and then applied to specific parts of the body. Look, can you see the scars?" She showed me her forearms. "But it didn't help. After three years, I went to a woman who did the wasim on my belly and this is how Abdallah came to this world. Then it took another few years until Haya came, and then Masud, and finally, very late, little Zwena.

"Life was hard. To get water, we would dig our own wells and carry the water in *girbas* (water-bags made of goat's skin). We carried the water bags on our heads over long distances. The water from those fountains was a little salty so we cooked the rice without salt. Some merchants would bring water from outside, from Qatar or so. They sold it down at the harbor, where those who had money bought the sweet water. In high summer most people left Abu Dhabi to spend two or three months at the al-Ain oasis. They travelled on camels and it took them approximately a week to get there. But I stayed with my children in Abu Dhabi while my husband went pearl-diving."

We heard someone cough and Um Abdallah called: "Just come in, Abu Abdallah, Haya's friends have come for a visit!"

In came a small, thin, old man in a white *jalabiya*. His brown face looked like old leather and his stoop expressed modesty and humility. He greeted us, we greeted him back, and then he crouched down on the floor. "Abu Abdallah, tell them about the pearl-diving, tell them!" his wife asked him.

The old man looked up: "It was a long, a very long time ago. The main season for pearl-oysters, *gos al-kabir*, was from May to September. The water was particularly warm then and we could dive deep without freezing, because pearl-oysters settle between six and thirty meters down. The work was very bad for our health and also very dangerous.

"Each of us divers was equipped with a horn peg, *ftam*, which served to protect the nose and which we wore at the end of a string around our neck, with leather thimbles, *chubat*, to protect our fingers because the oysters clutched energetically when they were dethroned from the pearl beds, and with a *diyin*, a pearl-diving basket which we tied around our waist. We would stand on a stone tied to a *yida* (rope), pinch the horn-peg on our nose and glide down the rope, feet first. We often came up half-suffocated, emptied our baskets on the deck, and repeated the exercise for days and months. We managed to remove some ten oysters during the one- to two-minute dive, then we would pull on the rope to signal the *seb* (rope attendant on the pearl boat) that we wanted to be pulled up. We opened the oysters the following day because it was easier then.

"The *nochada* (captain) was in charge of the pearls. Some of them were sold at sea to the pearl dealers, and the rest went to the pearl market. The sheikhs, captains, and dealers made a very good living, but we divers didn't. We kept having to borrow money from the captain so that we were nearly always in debt. Many divers had to start again, year after year, although they were already tired and old, because they owed the captains and thus carried a rope around their neck.

"The divers seldom made a good income, unless they found such a precious *dana* (pearl) that the captain acquitted and rewarded them. Once I was lucky—I found a huge black pearl. It saved my life because I was already at the end of my strength and I wouldn't have survived another season.

"Because of their debts, if the main season had failed to bring the desired yield, the captain could force his divers to set off once more. We called this *gos il-barid*, the cold pearl-diving season, because the water was no longer so warm and the divers suffered even more. They often wore *sharbas*, a sort of diving suit made of thin cloth, to protect them from the jellyfish that surface during that season. Sometimes divers died but they had no choice if they wanted to keep their families from starving.

"With the money they received, the divers would buy food for the whole year—rice, flour, dates. Sometimes the money was enough to buy a piece of material, out of which their wife would sew some garments for everyone in the family. If the food ran out, the diver had to go to the captain to borrow some money and then he was in the noose once more and the circle started anew."

The old man paused. He seemed exhausted—his eyelids drooped and his breathing was flat. Zainab seemed depressed because, although she obviously knew about the pearl-diving season, it was the first time that she heard about the pearl-divers' hard life. She belonged to the tribe of the Mazruíi, who had always been prosperous merchants and therefore knew little about that part of her country's history. I was also touched by his story, but I wanted to know more. There had to be another side.

"Please tell us how you got your bearings at sea and how you spent the night."

"Hundreds of boats went to the *gos al-kabir*," he made a wide gesture with his hand, as if he could see them on the horizon. "The *sirdal*, the leader of the pearl-diving fleet, led the way on his *boum*. A *boum* is a sailing boat with two or three masts. It can carry between 100 and 400 tons. Those boats were once the major means of transportation in the Gulf and in the Arabian Sea, all the way to the African coast. When we sailed far from the coast, we would orient ourselves by the stars, which shone down on us at night."

A fleeting smile played on his lips. He went silent, thought for a while and said: "I have an old map with drawings of the stars. I'll go and get it!"

Suddenly the quiet old man became quite cheerful and his excitement gave his slight body more space and volume. Haya brought a bowl of fruit and Um Abdallah started peeling and slicing the fruit for us. She fed us personally, a sign of great respect. "Abu Abdallah knows many stories and songs. Ask him to sing you a few. He does it so rarely and I love hearing them!" Um Abdallah looked at me pleadingly and I promised her I would try.

He soon returned holding a rolled up paper in his hand. He unrolled it very carefully and a strange picture of dots, lines, and circles appeared. "Those are the *banat na'ish*, the girls with the long hair (the Great Bear), and those the *thrayya*, the rich ones, far away from the wet earth (the Pleiades). This is the *mughib* star, which shows the sailor the western cardinal point, and that one the *yah* star, which shows the sailor the northern cardinal point. And this here is the *ghbesha*, the last star that rises before dawn." As he explained, his fingers wandered along the map as if following letters in a book. It was beautiful to watch him and his words made the nondescript map come alive for us.

"At night we would sing our old songs, no one could remember where they came from, to us they were as old as the stars above us. The stars and the songs were our life strength on the dark, black sea."

"Let us hear your songs, Abu Abdallah!" I asked spontaneously, now that his soul could feel the dark ocean again.

He did not hesitate. His words rose from the distance, to the rhythm of the rope puller, rhyming with the waves, from the depth of the sea and into the friendly sky. He stopped miraculously at the same time as my tape.

"*Ma gassart, ya abu abdallah, ma gassart*! You have given generously, Abu Abdallah, generously and richly!" I took the tape out and turned to Um Abdallah. "You have your husband's poems here, please keep them in memory of our meeting." Um Abdallah took the tape and pressed it against her heart.

"Thank you," she whispered, putting it into her bra.

Moments later we left the family of the tribe of the Qubaysi. I had been given precious gifts and I now longed to go back home for an afternoon nap.

THE HOUSE OF BIRTH

We were traveling on the wide, luxurious motorway toward the al-Ain oasis, the largest and most important oasis in Abu Dhabi. It was Ramadan, the month during which no Muslim should eat, drink, or smoke from dawn until dusk. Thanks to the air-conditioning I hardly felt thirsty, despite the heat. I enjoyed the soft dunes along the motorway, up and down like the gentle curves of a full feminine body. Trees had been planted and they seemed a little lost, barely withstanding the sublime solitude of the desert. I filled my eyes with this emptiness and it felt good not to see any man-made building.

We were on our way to visit two girlfriends and a house of birth. One of the friends, who headed the house of birth, was Aunt Adeline's, and the other was Lina, my school friend from Beirut who had been living in al-Ain for six years with her husband and their two children.

Lina had spontaneously left school to marry her cousin, who managed a booming paper shop in al-Ain. We had all been very sad when Lina told us about her decision, only a few weeks before her wedding.

"Don't you want at least to finish school before you marry?" we all stormed at her.

"No, I don't want to be in school anymore. I don't like studying—I'd rather marry and go away. See the world! Be free!"

I remembered her words and, after so many years, I was quite curious and excited to find out how she was.

Al-Ain was a proper city, generously laid out with many islands of greenery around which the traffic circled, and beautiful, well-tended grass verges between the streets. It took us a while to find the house of birth. We parked right next to a small house with a tiny front garden. Aunt Adeline switched off the engine, and a big round woman with thick glasses and a bloated face had already come out. She was obviously very happy to see Adeline, and both exchanged greetings, while Adeline kept apologizing for being late.

"I was already worried, but everything's fine now," Adeline's friend said. She was a self-sacrificing, hard-working woman, one of those angels on earth who had decided to put their life at the service of others.

"Hello, Fawzia — I've heard so much about you already. You couldn't find a better person than Adeline to help you in your work!" I knew Adeline had adopted me and my project long ago, and we were part of her list of ambitious goals.

"Where are your suitcases? You must be totally exhausted! Well, it won't be long now until the sunset, *ramadam karim*!"

"*Allah akram*!" we answered.

Since during the month of Ramadan you cannot offer your guests anything, you say instead: "The month of Ramadan is generous in its gifts" and the answer is: "Allah is even more generous!" Although as a Christian Aunt Adeline did not fast, she kept away from food out of solidarity, only drinking a little water when she thought no one could see her.

We carried our bags inside. It was a simply, even sparsely, furnished house where everything seemed very impersonal. Whoever lived here did not set great store on personal belongings. It reminded me of those furnished beach houses you can rent for a few days anywhere near the Mediterranean. Funny how a house in the middle of the desert could radiate a sea atmosphere. I had already noticed that Adeline's friend did not come from the Emirates. But where was she from?

"You speak wonderful English!" I said, for she had been speaking English with Adeline all along.

"No wonder — I'm half American, half Syrian!" she said moving her nose in such a way that her glasses danced to and fro.

I couldn't help smiling.

"If you're not too tired, we could go to the house of birth right now, and you can look at everything. Maybe we're lucky and you can even do a few recordings."

"That would be very nice!" I was already standing near the door with my tape recorder. Faced with such enthusiasm, poor Aunt Adeline had no choice but to come with us.

We wandered over to the house of birth, a long, flat building about 400 meters away. Adeline's friend opened a door in the lower part of the building, behind which extended a long corridor with many doors on both sides. With its ochre shade, its simple wooden doors, and its roofless parts, where a few pigeons could be seen, it seemed to be alive and breathing.

"Come, let's see how this woman is—she gave birth to a little girl yesterday." Adeline's friend opened the door, went inside, and soon came back, inviting us in and saying "We may visit her!"

To my astonishment, within was a comfortable traditional living room with carpets, mattresses, and upholstered furniture. The light was dimmed and in a corner stood a small wooden cradle. Six women sat in the room and I couldn't make out who the mother was, for they all wore their traditional clothes. Nothing indicated that one of them had given birth to a human being yesterday. I shook hands with every one of them, and kissed them on the cheeks, muttering congratulations, and it was only through one's slightly weaker hand pressure that I recognized the young mother. Her eyes seemed a little tired, but very awake and content.

We sat down, but I couldn't resist for long—I wanted so much to see the little one. The door opened and three women came in. I looked up and my eyes discovered a moon. This is what you call a human being with a special charisma and an unusually beautiful face, because the moon, *qamar*, is different from all the other celestial bodies: it reflects the divine sunlight. The woman who had just entered had the sweetest face one could ever imagine. One of the two women who came with her had a thin and stringy build, like most desert Bedouin women, a longish face and strong hands. The other was heavy and round. She let herself fall on the mattresses with a loud sigh.

"Oh dear, I'm hot!" she moaned, lifting her *kandora* (dress) and using it as a fan.

All the women laughed. "Where is your husband?" the women teased her.

"Not far away, I hope!" she answered with a giggle.

"Will you make it until the evening?"

"I'm not sure!" she said, throwing herself backward and moaning rhythmically.

Again they all giggled.

"We've brought you *jadi*," she said, changing the subject. She lifted the lid of the pot they had brought and an appetizing smell wafted out, filling our nostrils and pressing down our abdomens. *Jadi* was the dish given to a woman after birth. It was made out of camel's milk, chicken, and a special mix of spices.

"Tomorrow I'll bring you *harut*," another woman said. *Harut* is a drink made of milk and various strengthening spices. Like *jadi*, it helps the exhausted mother regain her strength.

The young mother expressed her thanks and took the pot. She didn't want to eat now in front of the others out of respect for our fast. Suddenly the baby moved and all attention spontaneously focused on the cradle. One woman stood up and picked up the little bundle from the bed. A black mop of frizzy hair appeared. With his body wrapped in cloth, the baby looked like a worm. I couldn't resist any more and stood up. With a "*bismillah*" she handed me the little being.

"*Mashallah*," I muttered, as I looked at the face of a little woman. You always say *mashallah* (Whatever God wills happens) when you see something beautiful, both to express your admiration and to protect the beauty against jealous feelings. The little one had intense black eyes that stood out even more with the black kohl. Her fluffy black hair framed her small mature face in a charming fashion. In that instant I felt as if I could see her whole life in front of me, as if her whole destiny were already written, invisibly, in her small bundled body. How much of it could she still influence, how much could she change its course? What is written on the forehead will surely be seen by the eye, an Arab proverb says. Was it really so?

A faintness came over me, together with a deep feeling of calm. I must have stood there with the little being for a long time for I suddenly heard voices call me back: "She must love children very much!"

I shook myself awake inside and handed the little one to her mother with a heavy heart. She began to breastfeed her. A few women said goodbye, and we were invited into a small adjoining room by the beautiful woman who turned out to be the mother's sister. There was a carpet and a few mattresses here too.

We sat down and the beautiful woman brought a casket. She went out and returned moments later with an incense vessel and burning coals, put it on the floor and took out a few small discs and sandalwood sticks. She rubbed the little sheets between her soft fingers and as soon as they touched the coals, they gave out a heavy scented smoke.

My hungry body took the scent in through all pores like a dried-out body absorbs water.

"What is it?" I asked, slightly dazed by the intensity.

"Homemade incense," the beautiful woman answered. "We boil the bark of aloe wood, black or white nutmeg, amber oil, acacia resin, rose oil or rose water with sugar and a little water, until everything is well-mixed and then we shape the mixture into small discs and let them dry in the sun."

She was not only beautiful, but also sensitive and clever in the way she moved her beautiful hands to accompany her words and looked at you unobtrusively. I enjoyed her presence. She felt like a rose and I wondered whether she was married and whether her husband too recognized her inner beauty. One of the women put the casket in the middle and she opened it carefully. Several small bottles with yellowish, brownish, and transparent liquids appeared.

"Those are various scents that we like to use," she explained as she took one of the bottles, opened it and spread some of it on my hand. It was a sweet, heavy fragrance that smelled strongly of amber.

"May I record your explanations on tape?" I asked spontaneously, and I was happy that they allowed me to do so without much discussion. We sat together for an hour or so, while the women explained the fragrances, and every time they would rub a little of it either on the hand, the clothes or the veil, behind the ears or on the forehead. Finally the beautiful one took a little bottle in her hand and explained.

"This is the *mchammariya*. They say it is the most precious fragrant essence and it is mainly used at weddings." She opened the bottle and went on: "It is made of aloe oil, saffron oil, and amber. We use it to perfume the head veil, the hair, and the back of the earlobe."

While she spoke, she rubbed some behind my earlobes and wiped her hands along my veil. I thanked her a little shyly. When we finally stood up, I felt like a walking perfume box.

We said goodbye and thanked them for their hospitality.

Adeline's friend walked with us through the building. "The rooms are arranged to make the women feel at home. Visitors may come any time and stay overnight, in accordance with the tradition in these parts. The women may cook if they wish, and they usually stay here for three or four days so that they can rest before returning home and resuming their occupations.

"Young mothers are really spoiled in this country, aren't they?" Adeline asked.

"Yes, that's true. Our country is small but very rich and it has a small population of approximately 300,000. Women here usually have two to three children, and they get strong support from the state." I pricked up my ears—only two to three children? That was very few by Middle-Eastern standards.

"Sheikh Zayed, the ruler of Abu Dhabi, is trying to encourage women to have more children by giving each newborn baby an allowance. In addition, every child who attends school—which is free in any case—receives a grant, and the same applies to university."

"And yet so few children?"

Adeline's friend adjusted her glasses. "It's because of the salt lump. Once you've used it two, three times at most, women become sterile."

"What is this salt lump?"

"Salt is mixed with a couple of herbs and made into a sort of big pessary. It is inserted into the vagina on the second day after birth and it's supposed to help the womb cleanse itself and pull together. They call it *milha*."

We walked on and came out the building through another door. In front of it was a small market, where women sold all sorts of jewelry. I went through the rows and looked around. Different types of incense were being offered, as well as henna and henna patterns to stick on and copy. Small bundles of the silver or gold thread embroideries that the women sewed on their clothes. I took one of those ornamental bundles in my hand and looked at it closely. The seller watched me behind her mask.

"Would you like to know how it's made?" I nodded.

She turned around and reached for an unusual stand with an

oval cushion on top of it. The stand looked like two cones placed on top of each other, the bottom one upside down, and the other supporting the little oval cushion.

"*Kajuja!*" she explained, pointing at the stand. "*Musida*," she added, touching the cushion.

Seven silver threads were fastened with needles on the cushion. She took three threads in each hand, holding two of them between her fingers while her thumb and index fingers secured the middle thread. Then she started skillfully tying the threads together until they formed a thick band with an interesting pattern. She worked calmly and quickly. I watched her, fascinated.

After a while she stopped and said: "*Heee*, and this is how the *talli* is made!" The *talli* was an ornamental braid made of narrow metallic threads, usually silver or gold. I bought it, thanked her, and walked on.

I was hot and felt thirst tugging at my body. I had to sit down, so I found a large rock in the shadow of the house of birth, sat on it, and looked idly around. A soft breeze rose and accompanied my gaze. Palm trees were scattered here and there, small sand dunes. Everything seemed as though it had been spontaneously painted, and everything felt right.

I was happy to be there. I enjoyed listening to all those new things, yet with each new knowledge I felt stranger to myself, as if I no longer knew where I belonged. Where does the other begin and where does the familiar end? Sitting in the shade near the house of birth, I felt overcome by the closeness of life and death. As women, we are all connected with the knowledge that death is the shadow, the other side of birth; such is the price that women pay for the honor of being able to give life. I looked at the walls of the house of birth. How much joy and gratitude, how much suffering and pain had they already witnessed? As a woman, I was part of this cycle and I carried it within me.

A tender, silent sadness suddenly came over me. I felt my heart beat in the rhythm of the sister drums of bliss and solitude. My body seemed to perceive memories alive deep inside my belly, beyond the reach of reason. So I sat there and let my thoughts drink from my inner fountain, while the hunger fed on my nerves. I stood up and silently called for Aunt Adeline.

"Here you are!" She was coming around the corner with her friend. "Sama suggested we go and break our fast with a local family. You could visit Lina tomorrow."

"You'll see, they are a really lovely family, the woman of the house has a very special daughter, I'd love you to meet her!"

Why not? I hadn't seen Lina in years—one more day would not make much difference. So we went to the car and drove slowly through narrow dusty streets. Sama stopped in front of a wide gate, hooted a few times and a guard opened it. We were greeted on both sides by large, well-kept bushes with heavy flowers. After Sama parked the car, we followed her to a covered terrace. When the woman of the house saw us, she stood up and came to us. She greeted Sama warmly and Sama explained who we were, after which we, too, were warmly greeted.

Especially during Ramadan, everybody enjoys entertaining guests. To share one's meal is seen as a gift of God. The lady of the house was a small round woman with tiny sparkling eyes and a noble demeanor. I took an instant liking to her. Three guests were on the terrace and we greeted them before we sat down on the carpet.

"How are things in the house of birth?" the lady of the house asked.

"Everything is going well, *alhamdulillah*, praised be Allah," Sama answered. While they chatted, I let my eyes roam. I saw three clay jars tied with strings to a beam. They swung quietly next to each other, reminding me of my childhood, when we used to hang the water jars in the same way. Despite the heat, the water would stay pleasantly cool thanks to the gentle wind playing around the jars, and its taste simply could not be compared to any refrigerated water.

"And where is your daughter?" Sama asked.

"She's at university, she should be back any minute."

"And how is she?"

The small round woman sighed. "Hiba really is my problem child. She's different from all her brothers and sisters, simply different from girls her age."

I listened intently. How different? I wondered.

"She doesn't care about nice clothes or gold jewelry, she's not interested in marriage. Yet the best families have asked for her hand. I really don't know what I should do with her!" She sighed again.

Hiba had just arrived and I understood immediately what her mother meant. She had about her an intensity seldom found in people, especially those as young as she was, and a gaze that one could not hold for long. She wore a very simple long dress void of any ornament, and her hands were bare, without any jewelry or henna decorations. Even the black transparent scarf on her head did not have the usual golden strip that made women's face sparkle.

On the other hand, Hiba had no need for this ornament. She went to her mother and kissed her hand, and I noticed the special love that her mother felt for her in her heart. She recognized the jewel that was her daughter, but found it difficult to connect it with social expectations. The sorrow of many a mother. She stroked her head lovingly and I could just about see the exchange of their souls. The sight moved me deeply. It was so intimate that I had to look away. A love declaration between mother and daughter.

Hiba turned to the other three women and kissed their hands while looking modestly at the floor. She came to us, kissed Sama and Adeline on the cheeks and then she moved toward me. She held her hand, I gave her mine and without pulling it even slightly to her, she bent toward me with her whole body and kissed me. She shamed me with her humility. Hiba sat down and looked at the floor.

"You see what I mean," her mother started in a worried, yet loving tone. "She wears no jewelry, no rings, no chains, no henna ornaments on hands or feet, nothing. She refuses everything."

"Oh Mother, you know that I'm not interested in those things. I don't like them and definitely not the henna paintings."

"Yes, but a girl who is old enough to marry has to look after her appearance," her mother countered. "Or doesn't she?" While she spoke, she looked for confirmation and support among the women present.

"Let her be the way she is, Um Khaled," one of the women answered, who seemed to be a close family friend. "Your daughter is worth a hundred girls, her smile alone enchants more than enough!"

"And anyhow, Mother, you know that I'm not interested in marriage."

"You see, is that the way a reasonable girl should answer?" Um Khaled sighed.

"I'd rather stay with you," Hiba said smiling at her mother.

"Oh, daughter, what am I supposed to do with you? I'd love to keep you with me, but this is the way things are in life—a daughter marries and starts her own family. I won't be here forever."

There was silence for a moment and every woman seemed to retreat into her own world, examining the decisions she had made in her life, the right ones and the wrong ones. Was this really the only way for a woman? Were there not other possibilities, could a woman not experience different ways of life?

After a while, Sama spoke, the woman who had chosen for herself the way of a single woman: "Your daughter is young and she is now in the middle of her studies. Give her time, give her the possibility to make a mature and clear choice. She is clever and strong enough for that. And time will help her."

Hiba stood up. "I'm going to pray, Mother, please excuse me."

"I'm coming with you." I stood up and followed her into an empty room laid with carpets.

She stood in the middle of the room and started her prayer. I stood a little behind her and watched her for a few moments. How beautiful she was, and how devotedly she absorbed herself in her prayer! Then I started my prayer and it bound with hers, invisible threads seemed to appear between us, my kneeling down, touching the floor with my forehead, everything seemed to move by itself. My body was linked with the movements of her body while my spirit, freed from my body, hovered limitlessly in the room, prancing between beauty and majesty. I stood up with a sweet taste in my mouth.

We went back to sit with the women and chatted for a little while. Hiba hardly took part in the conversation, and I didn't feel like talking much either. I enjoyed being with her; I did not want anything else. Soon two servants spread a tablecloth in the adjoining room and the meal was served in small dishes. We slowly filled our stomachs with water and food. As usual in the summer, two-thirds water and one-third food. In the winter, it was the other way around: two-thirds food and one-third liquid.

Hiba ate little. She did not seem to care about food, whereas we were quite absorbed by the meal. Once it was over, the women stood up one after the other, washed and performed the sunset prayer. We went back to the terrace, drank tea together and had a little rest. Sama, Aunt Adeline, and I took our leave.

I looked into Hiba's eyes for a long time. We both smiled.

"Good luck, Hiba!"

"God be with you, Fawzia!"

I never saw her again.

A DAEMON IN THE DESERT

When I entered she was sitting huddled between her daughters, grandchildren, nieces, and family friends. I noticed her immediately, because her small but expressive movements and her penetrating gaze were those of a free soul who had never adapted to the settled way of life and the narrowness of city walls.

She hardly looked up when I approached, but her nostrils widened like a young foal's, breathing in the vibrations, the mood, and only then did she lift her head to take in the new sight with her eyes. I sat down next to her, keeping the distance commanded by respect, and I absorbed the scent of her, letting her vibrations play about my senses. I felt my neck relax and enjoyed sitting next to her.

Since the women knew each other quite well and I now belonged to the so-called inner circle, I could come to my actual theme quite quickly. I unpacked my tape recorder and put it in front of me. The machine and microphone always seemed importune and awkwardly large to me. Zainab, her granddaughter who had become a dear friend, leaned toward me: "By all means, you can ask my grandmother, she will be happy to tell you." I smiled gratefully at her.

"Hajja," I started. This was the polite way to speak to a mature or elderly woman. It is actually used to address women who have been on a pilgrimage to Mecca. Since this life-changing voyage is usually undertaken after the fortieth year of life, older people are given this title out of respect. "Would you tell me something about your life, about your childhood, about the way life used to be?"

The old woman looked at me and then at the tape recorder. "What is this?"

"It's a tape recorder, Grandmother, it will record your words," Zainab answered.

"And then everyone can hear my words? Men too?" she asked.

"Only people to whom I will play it," I answered shyly.

She thought about it, holding her head to the side.

Then I had an idea. While the women talked among themselves and I explained a little about my work, I pushed the recording key, then rewound and said: "Hajja, listen!" I pressed the play button and out tumbled the women's voices, their giggles, my words, the words of the old woman, and Zainab's explanations. The old woman shrunk back a little in surprise, but when she heard the giggles, she had to join in.

She sat there quite excited and listened attentively. "But this is my voice, and this is Zainab's, that's us!" she said excitedly. The machine went silent. "The speaking iron has talked like we do!" she said thoughtfully, but with curiosity and without rejection. She reflected quickly. "I'll tell you and the speaking iron, but you must promise that no man will hear my voice."

I thought it over. Could I make such a promise? Would I be able to keep it? I would store the tape carefully. "Yes, I can promise you, Hajja!" We were both satisfied.

"Zainab, great-granddaughter, how old am I now?"

"About 75, Grandmother."

"We were Bedouin and we lived next to the Liwa oasis. My tribe owned many camels, and palm groves too. During the hot months, the men went to Abu Dhabi for pearl-diving while women, children, and old men stayed behind. We looked after the camels and the palm trees. It was hard work to care for everything. We were thrown back on our own resources for many months, with the children, the camels, the palm trees, and the old people. And when the men returned, they brought us food and presents, material for a *kandora* (dress), a shawl, maybe a ring, depending on how the pearl-diving season had gone."

It was not easy for me to follow her words, because she still spoke the pure old dialect of this region, free from the influence of the outside world through television or radio. No Egyptian or Lebanese words had stolen into her language. I also noticed how Zainab had to ask about some expressions that she didn't know. This woman spoke with the words of a time gone by.

"Grandmother, do tell us your first experience with the car!" Zainab asked.

"Ha!" Grandmother reared up. "I was alone in the desert, gathering wood. I was a young girl, much younger than Zainab now, about ten years old. I discovered the strangest tracks in the sand. They didn't belong to any animal that I knew and they were not human either. They were long, long, as long as an endless snake. Like two snakes. My heart stopped, my whole body shook. And suddenly, out of nowhere came a camel litter. But it moved without a camel and its noise was deafening. Horrified, I threw down my bundle of wood and ran as fast as I could, back to my tribe, to the camp. "A daemon, a giant daemon is on its way! I saw it with my own eyes! A daemon, a daemon!" I kept shouting until everyone came out of the tents.

The whole tribe stood there. And suddenly the daemon was there for all to see. It stopped in front of us and out came two men, people like us. But one of them was pink and had a thin, white-yellow fur on his head, so light, lighter than our camels' hair. The other was a Bedouin from another tribe. He greeted us and explained to our tribe leaders about the daemon and the pink man. I'll never forget that experience, not as long as I live."

Everyone laughed. They all knew the story, but they loved hearing it again. The old woman had to giggle, too. "Now my children and grandchildren drive me around in this kind of thing. The English have filled the country with them. They even use them for the *tuluh* celebration."

I listened intently. "What is a *tuluh* celebration?"

"The celebration that takes place forty days after the birth of a child."

"Can you tell us about it?" I asked, full of hope.

"Yes, please, Grandmother, tell us!"

Grandmother was in the best of moods. It was so sweet to watch her bending over the microphone when she spoke, as if the speaking iron would not hear her otherwise.

"We grind saffron, the most precious and costly of all spices, and we take the child out and show it to the people. The mother stays away from people with her child for forty days. She does not see any stranger. It is a time of quiet and adaptation to the new life. So on the fortieth day we have the *tuluh* celebration. We cook a big pot and we bake unleavened bread. We distribute the bread to the children. Then they run together and shout: 'Oh, Abbod, follow us! Oh, Abbod, follow us!'—or whatever is the newborn's name. The baby is washed on that day. We wash him on the feet of a young woman blessed with luck. A woman whose brothers stand behind and protect her, whose mother and father are alive and who has a prosperous life. They have all been washed on these feet of mine, like this..." She put her legs together and stretched them out.

"So the women grind saffron and fennel seeds for the *tuluh* celebration. They burn incense and then they eat together. There is usually rice, meat, and milk. Sometimes an animal is also sacrificed on that day. After the child has been washed, he is laid on sour dough, then bathed, dressed anew, wrapped up, and put in the cradle.

"Then the men bring shotguns and hang them over his head. They also bring the cartridge-belt and the dagger, which they put next to the sleeping child's head. A camel is brought and put next to him. These days, most of the time they bring a car and they put the child next to the car. All these things are done so that the child does not become a weakling. Everyone wants him to be brave and grow into a good man. After the *tuluh* celebration, the child is a member of the community. He now belongs to life."

"Is it the same with a girl?" I asked.

"With a girl, we look for a woman whose qualities and ways we like. Of course she too must have many men who stand behind her, who strengthen her, protect her, and fight for her rights. Then the girl is laid on her feet and she is given the same name as the woman. The woman says her blessings and enumerates the good qualities over the young baby girl, such as courage, compassion, generosity, contentment."

Grandmother's eyelids began to close. She was getting tired and all this bending over the microphone had played a part in it. It was time for me to leave. After a cup of cardamom coffee, I said goodbye and promised to return.

THE MYSTERY OF THE HAWK

Would you like to go visit Lina now?" We were back at Sama's and I still felt full of energy. The two ladies seemed a little tired already, but my self-sacrificing Aunt Adeline volunteered her services, as she always did. "I'll take you there."

During the month of Ramadan, most people stay up later than usual, and it is customary to visit them after the breaking of the fast.

"If you don't mind, I'll stay here," Sama said.

I called Lina and told her we were coming. She was very excited, and so was I. I was looking forward to seeing my old school friend again. So we sat in the car and drove off. On the way, we saw long lines of cars parked in front of the mosques. The mosques were overflowing with people who were praying the special Ramadan prayer, *tarawih*. There was a very special atmosphere in the air, a mixture of quietness and excitement.

After several unsuccessful attempts, we finally found Lina's house. It was light and inviting, and I was happy to see that things were going well for my friend. Aunt Adeline wanted to go home right away, so we said goodbye in the car and I promised to call her later. I went up the stairs to the entrance door, rang the bell, and immediately heard footsteps. Lina had hardly changed. Her beautiful jet-black hair was cut shoulder-length and set off her face wonderfully.

Lina, at last! We fell into each other's arms and laughed and giggled as if only a few moments had passed since our daily bus trips to school. I pushed her away a little and looked into those black eyes I knew so well. It was a little like coming home, closer to the innocent games, closer to giggling for no reason, closer to secretly copying homework in the school bus, closer to the worry-free soul of childhood, closer to Lebanon. I had been gone so long.

"Are you well?"

Lina nodded and happiness filled her eyes, covering them with a wet film. My eyes filled with tears too, and we went inside arm in arm, laughing. How surprised I was when I saw a little Lina and a younger boy come to us.

"Here is Dina and here is Sami!" she said in that sweet Lebanese dialect of hers that already sounded almost foreign to me.

"Mummy, mummy, who is this woman?"

I suddenly saw Lina with different eyes as she spoke reasonably and calmly to her children. "This is my friend from school!"

So Lina had become a mother. This is when I became aware of the time that had elapsed since our childhood. Life is a river, it never stops flowing and nothing remains the same. So what does one hold on to for strength? I find my hold in growth, in deeper understanding, in the unfolding of the heart. I shuddered inside and I felt I had made an inner jump, my awareness widening in that moment.

"Come, Fawzia, let's go into the kitchen and prepare something to drink!"

The children ran ahead and the familiarity that goes with relationships rooted in childhood allowed us to drop all etiquette and social norms.

"How are you, Lina? Are you satisfied?"

Lina smiled. "He is a good man!" she answered. We drank cool orange juice and took our glasses into the sitting room. It was light and comfortably furnished, Mediterranean-style, with cozy armchairs and sofas, small tables and floor lamps. A jar filled with sweets and a bowl overflowing with various brands of cigarettes sat on a side table for the guests. Just as was customary in Lebanon.

"Sami is doing well with his business of books and paper. He is a clever salesman and has contracts with al-Ain University. They order all their paper from him."

"How long do you plan to stay in Abu Dhabi?" I knew that foreigners were only granted limited residence permits in the Emirates.

"Of course we'd rather go back to Lebanon, but the civil war is not over yet, so we are thinking of going to Canada for a few years to get Canadian citizenship. It makes life easier, because opportunities are limited when you hold a Lebanese passport, and we would like our children to grow up without expulsions. But tell me about yourself: what are your plans, and what are you doing here in al-Ain?"

I didn't want to give her a full answer. I had never been too fond of talking, and in any case words only ever conveyed my thoughts in part. Whenever I spoke, it left an aftertaste of misunderstanding in my mouth. Over the years, this had turned me into a good listener. When I listened, I did so with my whole being and nearly always felt like I was receiving a gift. "I came because I wanted to become acquainted with the people here, to experience their stories and their life, and maybe widen my understanding."

Lina laughed. "Oh, Fawzia, you'll never change!"

I looked at her, somewhat puzzled. "What do you mean?" I replied in a small voice.

"But it's true, isn't it? One either needs to ask you very precise questions or else—and that's even better—none at all, right?"

Now I had to laugh, too. It felt good to find my old friend again. "Lina, what would you say about coming with me to visit local women? If I know you, you've probably never been to their homes."

Lina looked at me wide-eyed. "You want me to come with you? But why?"

"Because I think it would be good for you to know a little more about the people here. After all, you're living in their country."

"But I don't understand them at all, and they're so different!" she cried, somewhat confused.

"That's precisely why!" I said, grinning at Lina coyly, and she knew that it was settled. "I'll call Aunt Adeline, maybe she feels like joining us."

"What, now?"

"It's the best time—it's Ramadan and nobody's sleeping anyway!" I called Aunt Adeline and although she sounded sleepy, she wanted to come along.

An hour later, the three of us were sitting in the car, driving to a family from the Manasir tribe whose menfolk were famous for their bravery and for being the best warriors in the whole region. They had been living in harmony with the ruling tribe for decades already and had often fought by their side. Sama had given me the address of that family and they were already expecting us when we reached their modest house. You could really rely on Sama, May Allah bless and protect her!

The mistress of the house invited us in. She was a thin reed of a woman. Her hands were wrinkled and her face only carried with difficulty her eyes, which expressed her disappointment in life. Yet she spared no politeness, hurrying to get us some coffee and sitting down at our feet. I wanted to sit next to her but I knew Lina would never sit on the floor, so I too stayed on the sofa.

The coffee cups floated in a bowl of water. She took out one cup, filled it with coffee and handed it to us. Lina took it and looked at the water in the bowl.

"Do you think the water is clean?" she whispered.

Without answering, I took my cup and drank the coffee. Aunt Adeline also drank hers and Lina finally took the cup to her lips.

We had barely finished drinking our coffee when the woman stood up and brought a bowl full of apples. I knew how expensive apples were in this part of the world. They came mostly from Syria and only wealthy households could afford this kind of luxury. Our hostess started peeling the apples, cutting them into slices and handing them to us. Although she knew that we would surely never eat all of them, she peeled all the apples, as a sign of hospitality and to honor her guests. She was truly among the givers on this earth. I felt how difficult it was for Lina to be there. She was probably counting the minutes, but I couldn't take that into account just then.

"We have come to drink from your knowledge. Could you tell us a little about your life here?"

Without quite looking at me, she said, "I'm no good at telling!"

I was slightly taken aback and unsure as to how to reply. "Maybe you could tell us a little about the wedding tradition?"

She said nothing.

I tried again: "Or about the celebrations in your country?"

"We celebrate after Ramadan, and there's the big feast after the pilgrimage, otherwise there are no celebrations."

She hadn't told me anything new, since those celebrations exist in the whole Muslim world. I was beginning to give up and Lina started fidgeting on the sofa. I looked out through the door, hoping to find some inspiration. Nothing seemed to spur this woman into talking, yet I did not believe she could possibly be so empty that she had nothing to tell about her world.

Something moved outside, in the glow of the lamp. I peered and made out something like an enormous cage with a dark, elongated figure inside, as long as a human arm. Our hostess noticed my eyes and without saying much, she called: "Hasan, come, our guests would like to see the *shahin*!"

A man in his thirties appeared instantly. He had dark curls, a nondescript face, and tired eyelids. His back was slightly stooped and, like his mother, he did not seem to have drunk from the fountain of happiness. He mumbled some greetings and invited us to follow him.

You could tell Lina was happy to get up, and Aunt Adeline smiled that sweet smile of hers. Despite being a woman of few words, our hostess was quite perceptive of what was happening around her. I thanked her for everything and we headed for the cage. Hasan opened it and immediately started speaking to it. The hawk instantly turned its head toward him. It seemed to know him well, for it made no attempt to flee. On the contrary, it went directly to his arm, sitting on it as quietly as though it were a familiar, trusted branch.

Hasan nestled his head against the hawk's, and they greeted each other like soul mates. I felt deeply moved by the sight of such total surrender in friendship of those two completely different beings.

Suddenly our hostess stood next to us and in a voice that wasn't much used to speaking, she explained: "The hawk is a free bird, as wild and free as the desert. Humans need to be very patient and very clever to catch a hawk. He will fight for his freedom and use his strong, sharp claws and his pointed beak. One can only get close to him by protecting oneself with a *mingala*, a leather hawk glove.

"During the first weeks, the eyelids of the *shahin* are sewn together, so that he no longer perceives anything from the outside world. His only link is the voice of the human being who caught him. Day and night, he speaks to the *shahin*, telling him about his life, his worries and his dreams, and his new life. He feeds him the choicest meat, and after a while, he touches his feathers. The hawk learns to feel at home on his companion's arm, and to understand the warmth of a human being. Then comes the time when his eyes are opened, a delicate moment for both the *shahin* and his companion.

"Again, the soothing voice of the teacher weaves the link between the two beings. Will the hawk bear the sight of a human being so close to him? That is the test of the master's quality and greatness. Now the hawk is tied with a rope, and upon one single word from his master he flies away, upon another word he is brought back. Time and again, master and hawk repeat this routine, time and again the hawk returns with the call and the rope.

"After a protracted period, intensive and exhausting for both of them, there comes a day when the rope is removed. Now the hawk is as free as he was at the beginning of his journey with the human being. Now only his longing for his teacher's voice brings him back, the friendship which came to be between their souls, because the hawk is a soul bird and only the soul brings him back."

The voice of our hostess faded. Hasan did not look at us, but he did something which to me was much more beautiful: he turned around, taking a hawk glove from a corner. As if on cue, I stretched out my arm, Hasan put the glove on it and then he sat the hawk on my arm.

My arm shook under the weight of this proud, noble bird, and at first we both looked the other way. I stretched my arm out as far as I could, afraid of his crooked and pointed beak. Despite the leather glove, I could feel his sharp claws digging into my bones. Time stood still. I didn't want to carry on, but the bird did not make the slightest move to return to Hasan.

I had to overcome my fear; I had no choice but to trust this being. I slowly turned my ringing head toward him. He turned his, and I recognized him. The moment was over, and the bird went up on Hasan's arm. What had taken Hasan months, the hawk had done in one moment. My arm fell down limply. Aunt Adeline tore the air with her "Wonderful, wonderful how you held the hawk!" Lina was tired and happy to leave, and I had been allowed to touch the mystery of the hawk. The taste of gratitude played on my lips like nectar in a beehive. Um Hasan was a great hostess indeed!

BEDOUIN ON THE ISLAND

I had heard so much about the Bedouin women on the islands, especially on the island of Dalma, and I longed to go there. How did they live? What language did they speak? I decided to go and visit them, but it was not so easy because it is almost impossible to drive to the tiny bridge where small fishing boats leave for that island. To start with, no one knows when the boats leave, and not everyone is allowed to go there, Uncle Sabri explained to me patiently.

"There has to be a way," I answered calmly, looking at him with such conviction that he immediately knew I would drive there by myself, with a hired car if need be, unless he did something. Apparently he would not take any chances.

"There certainly is," he replied thoughtfully. "Give me a little time and I'll find out." I was satisfied.

A few days later, Uncle Sabri came through the door grinning mischievously. I was about to listen to my recordings and transcribe the conversation into a notebook. The draft alone that came in with him told me that something interesting had happened. I looked at him and my face lit up.

"You've made it, haven't you?"

Somewhat puzzled, he answered: "You can go to Dalma! I've managed to get you a special authorization, only you won't be going by car, but on board the army plane, which takes supplies to the island every fortnight. You'll be the only passenger."

I swallowed. This was a surprise.

"When do I leave?" I asked casually.

"The plane takes off at 6:30 AM from the military airport. We have to be on time."

Whenever you have a strong wish and that wish is meant to be, things tend to happen faster than you even wanted them to. Excitement overcame me, crawling all the way up my spine and settling happily in my pounding heart. My mind was already busy planning. What should I take with me? What would I do on the island? Who should I turn to? Where would I sleep? On an island you simply can't leave whenever you wish.

"How long am I allowed to stay and where should I go?"

"The plane stays overnight, which means you'll have two days on the island. I have the name of a woman who will help you on the island, Sheikha al Bu Falah—that's all I was told."

"Fine by me. Thank you for everything, Uncle Sabri!"

I stood up and kissed him affectionately on the cheek. I knew how much he loved me and that reward was worth all the trouble he had taken.

I got up shortly before sunrise, had a quick shower, put on my *jalabiya*, said my morning prayers, had a bite to eat, and I was ready. Uncle Sabri drove me to the military airport. The day hadn't broken when we arrived and I felt like a spy on a mission, incognito in the dark, a scarf around my head, clutching a small travel bag in one hand, and the bag with my recording equipment in the other. Just the picture!

The pilot and another soldier, a friend of Uncle Sabri's, were waiting for us at the airport. The nose of the plane was open and several soldiers were loading bags and crates. "The trip won't be very comfortable, but we're not going far," Uncle Sabri's friend said. Once loading was complete, they led me into the plane.

On each side was a long bench on which parachute jumpers usually sat. Brown cloth belts hung down everywhere. "You must tie yourself up, otherwise you'll be flying through the plane when we take off!" So I put the belt on. Uncle Sabri looked at me with mild concern.

"Don't worry, Uncle—everything will be all right."

We parted with those words.

They got off and the nose was closed, and suddenly it was very dark inside. I sat among the many crates and bags, waiting for take-off. And what a take-off it was! Everything shook and the engines were so loud I couldn't feel my own fear. Yet as soon as we were up in the sky, everything went quiet and when the first sun rays appeared, I started enjoying my strange situation.

I looked out of the small round windows and saw the sea below. It lay there, blue and peaceful, and I felt mellowed by its beauty. Parachute jumping was definitely not for me. I don't think anyone could ever convince me to jump out of a plane unless they just shoved me. I felt completely alone, and yet the plane was flying—there had to be someone else on board. And the door to the pilot's cabin opened.

"Is everything okay?" he asked.

"Yes, great!" I shouted back over the din of the engines.

The door closed again. There I was sitting in an army plane in my light *kandora* (dress), a scarf, and light shoes. How much of this country's riches is invested in military equipment, a field that has nothing to do with us women. This world doesn't need weapons—it needs more knowledge.

The plane took a sharp turn to the left, then to the right. I felt my stomach tickle my throat and then the island was below us. We soon landed in the small airport. Landing was just as overpowering as taking off and I really had to clutch at my seat. The monster opened its mouth.

"*Hamdillah ala salatitsh*, Praised be God that you arrived safely," said the pilot, who had already opened the nose from outside.

I went down on wobbling knees. How lovely the old, dusty earth felt beneath my feet after that turbulent flight high up in the sky! A small building stood next to the landing strip and a few men hurried toward us from its shadow. They greeted us and disappeared immediately into the plane to unload the goods. I looked around. Small dunes were everywhere, and in the distance I could see a couple of buildings.

"I'm looking for Sheikha al Bu Falah," I told the men.

"She'll be here soon," one of them said. "She always comes to get the mail." Indeed, a few minutes later, a green jeep arrived, a young woman with a strong gaze sitting at the wheel. She stopped near the plane, rolled the window down, said her greetings and waited for the bag to be brought to the car.

She waited like a queen, without bothering to get out of the jeep. Her olive-colored skin, narrow angular features, and large black eyes spoke of her Bedouin origins. I walked slowly toward her and introduced myself. Her face became immediately more friendly. She opened the door, stepped down, and greeted me warmly. I explained briefly what I had come for and asked for her help.

She thought for a short moment and said: "I'll take you to my aunt, I'm sure you can stay there. But come in, I'll show you around the island to start with."

Happy and grateful for this gift, I got into the jeep and we left with the mail. We first went into the city center, although such a word was hardly adequate for the two rows of small shops where sleepy-eyed shopkeepers sat with their goods. At the end of the souk stood the island's main mosque, and behind it the school.

After this little tour, Sheikha turned around and drove into the residential area. That too consisted of two blocks of low, very simple houses. All the doors stood wide open and you could easily see inside. Here a woman sat leisurely stirring a large pot. In the next house, a man sat near the door, his limp hand ceaselessly pulling a string to activate the palm fan on the ceiling. Everything seemed bathed in the infectious haze of timelessness. Sheikha stopped in front of one of the houses. We got out and went through the open door.

"Samiha! Where are you?"

"Here I am!" A woman in her mid-forties hurried toward us, wiping her hands on her apron.

"Peace be with you, Samiha! I brought you a guest."

"Welcome, welcome, Sheikha's guests are also mine, welcome!"

I felt touched and a little ashamed—touched by the lightness of her heart and ashamed of my intrusion.

"My husband is travelling and there are no men in the house at the moment—you can move freely here!"

She led the way into her *majlis*, the guest reception room, traditionally fitted with rugs, mattresses, and cushions to lean on. *Majlis* literally means "meeting and sitting space" and hers was in shades of blue, lined with simple rugs. I put my bag into a corner and suddenly felt extremely tired. I sat down, leaned my head slightly back and closed my eyes. I always get tired when I'm on an island, although our whole earth is actually an island.

Samiha's head appeared: "Please come, a modest meal awaits you!"

"Allah's gifts are always great," I answered, standing up slowly like an old woman tired of living.

So much goodness can be oppressive at times. But hunger soon lightened me and I ate heartily with Samiha and Sheikha. "How many children do you have, Samiha?"

"Allah gave me four daughters."

"May Allah keep them in good health for you and may they grow up in your warmth!"

The door opened and a tender eight-year-old boy peeked in. "Should I buy something for you, Mummy?" he asked confidently.

"No, thank you my child, I don't need anything right now. Just go and play, and come back for dinner!"

I looked at Samiha with astonishment. She understood instantly and said with a smile: "Omar is not my own son. My neighbor had five sons and not a single daughter, so we exchanged. She's bringing up one of my daughters and I have been given a son."

I marveled at this brilliant solution. Two women made each other happy and each of them could rest assured that the other would do her utmost, because they had exchanged what is most precious to any mother.

"I guess you'd like to speak to different women," Sheikha ventured.

I liked this practical, quick-thinking woman, and I felt I could talk with her quite openly about everything. "Sheikha, I have to tell you, I would like to record the women. Do you think it would be okay?"

"If you travel with Sheikha, everything is possible, she is the absolute queen on the island," Samiha replied with a smile. "She's one of the few who can read and write, so she knows all our secrets. She reads our letters to us, and the newspapers too, and for us women she is the link to the world beyond the island. She is a noble being and keeps everything in her heart. Never has a wrong word passed her lips, never has she exploited what she knows."

Sheikha listened to those words as though they related to someone else. Only by looking at her very closely could I see how grateful she was for the great praise. A new figure appeared at the door. A most beautiful sixteen-year-old girl came to us swaying her hips.

"Peace be upon you! Samiha, I heard you had guests so I thought I'd come by!"

"Welcome, welcome, Moza, please sit down with us and help yourself," Samiha answered politely.

"No, no, my husband is due back soon and I'd like to greet him!"

"Moza married only a fortnight ago. This time, she wedded her rich cousin."

I looked at Moza. This time? Had she been married before despite her young age?

My face was an open book to the Bedouin woman's sharp eye. "Yes, I've been married twice already. The first time I was twelve, the second time I was fourteen, and now I'm sixteen and it's the third time!"

There was no end to my amazement and it must have shown. Samiha explained. "You see, it's quite common on the island. We marry often, and since most of us are related it doesn't matter in the slightest."

I was fascinated by this island. Moza disappeared, her footsteps light and swift, and my eyes followed her for a long time.

"Fawzia, why don't you have a rest, I'll come to pick you up when the sun is lower on the horizon," Sheikha said. And so it was. At the end of the afternoon, Sheikha turned up in her jeep and we drove away.

"Where are we heading?"

"To the beach!"

Sheikha drove slowly and skillfully. I enjoyed sitting next to her. I savored the gentle breeze on my face and when we stopped the drive felt almost too short. We got off next to a large, flat sandy bay.

"This is the most famous beach on the island of Dalma. Before they discovered oil, Dalma was already one of the major islands in this region. Water has always been abundant here and so the island was the place where pearl divers stopped over to rest.

"They would come to this beach on their boats, buy water, and barter or sell some of their pearls. A representative of the ruler in Abu Dhabi also lived here and he collected the tax on the pearls, approximately 2.5 percent of their total value. When the pearl industry declined, several pearl-fishing communities settled down on the island, and when the riches from the oil came in the 1970s, houses were built, and later schools so that the young generation can now read and write.

"We also have a small hospital, and transportation to and from the island is free. But we still prefer staying on our island." She spoke softly about her island. Her knowledge was ancient and it was beautiful to listen to her. "Come, I'll take you to a couple of old women—they can tell you things!"

We stood up and went. Sheikha stopped near the many identical mud houses where two old women greeted us very warmly. The encounter was a total fiasco. Both sisters kept talking simultaneously, interrupting each other, jumping from one theme to the next, so that in the end I simply switched off the tape recorder, relaxing and observing the torrent of words, the deep breath intake before each new avalanche, the waving gestures, the flowing robes, the mutual pushing and shoving.

After about an hour, we tore ourselves away. Sheikha and I laughed for a long time in the car after that encounter. Although I felt tired, we decided to make one more visit, to a lady from the ruling family, Um Fahd.

She too lived simply and her noble origins could not be detected from her garments, but from her posture and from the generosity that surrounded her forehead. She was a thin, small woman who had matured with life. Many stories had nestled in the wrinkles of her forehead and around her eyes. She spoke slowly and softly. I asked her to tell me about the wedding traditions.

"If they want the girl, they go to her father, have coffee together and eat, and then they say: 'We come to you with good intentions!' 'Welcome!' says the father, 'I am at your command! If you want my son, you may have him!' This means that they may ask for anything. 'No, no, by God, may Allah keep you in good health, we are asking God and you for the girl!' The father then says: 'The blessing has come, welcome to you from the beginning of your journey until you arrived here. There is no difference between us. You only need to say your wish once without raising your voice, for everything comes to fruition, even with a low voice. If I was to give my daughter away as a gift, I would give her to you!' This was how the Arabs spoke in the old times.

"Then a sheep is sacrificed and cooked with wheat. The women and the men from both families all ear together. The dowry is discussed, and how much gold the bride should receive in earrings, necklaces, and rings, according to the groom's wealth. And then there is the bride's wedding attire.

"The women gather before the wedding to bathe the bride and rub her body with *kafur* (a mixture of pulverized eucalyptus leaves, rose leaves, and oil), paint her hands and feet with henna, and rub her hair with *mhalab* (nutmeg, saffron, and other fragrances). She is dressed beautifully, with an embroidered pantaloon, a long dress, a transparent black veil with a gold border. The women sing and tell her about the first night. They prepare her, encourage her and take her fears away. In the afternoon, they all take her solemnly to the groom.

"When the next morning comes, they knock on the door, and the girl comes out. The groom bathes and dresses, goes to her parents and says: 'May you be blessed, blessed!' And the neighbors and friends call back: 'You were blessed and made happy. Blessed, blessed, o groom, blessed, o groom!' 'May Allah's blessings be upon you!' the groom answers. 'How is the girl?' they ask. He says: 'I call her a virgin—God has created no human being like her!' He praises her with words or poems. All the women—relatives, neighbors, and friends—fetch the girl, pamper her, bring her breakfast, dress her anew, and take her back to the groom. Both of them shut the door until noon."

The old woman spoke slowly, as if she could see her own weddings again, and the many others she had known in her lifetime, ancient rituals carried out for generations and generations, so that all became part of those memories. Time and again she paused and watched the circling tape.

"Come noon, they knock on the door and tell the groom that lunch is ready. He gets up and eat, while they fetch the girl. Together the women eat with her before taking her back. The bride and groom lay together again until the late afternoon. Then the women return, knock on the door, and shout: 'Open the door!' Again they fetch the girl.

"All this to and fro is especially for the bride, to soften the breaking away from her own family and to pave the way to her new life. One moment she is with her husband, the next with the women in her familiar surroundings. One moment she tastes from the first, one moment from the second, thus linking the new and the old, the strange and the familiar, until they unite into one life.

"The time comes for the girl to be dressed in all her finery. Her clothes have been taken near the incense, on the *midchana* (clothes stand), so that the fragrance of the incense accompanies her. The women also bring the gold she has received from her husband. The jewelry is examined and passed around the women's circle, admired and praised by each of them. Rings for the *chinsir* (little finger), rings for the *shahid* (index finger), *marami* for the middle finger, for the ring finger, and for the thumb. Sometimes there is also a *chaff*, a hand jewel adorning the whole hand with chains and linked to five rings. The bride also receives *dlal* (gold chains), or a *setami* (a heavy gold chain adorned with gold coins), *tarshiyas* (earrings), and maybe also *hyul* (toe rings), and more.

"If the groom is poor, all the women collect their jewelry. I give mine, you give yours, and the neighbor gives hers. Everything is gathered into a cauldron that they take to the bride. It is important that she should not want. Every woman who has some gold must give it to the bride for the seven-day visiting and viewing period. The bride may wear the jewelry day and night. This is as important as the *zakat*, the alms tax that we Muslims pay every year.

"Then the women make up the bride with *chihil*, kohl, and *bdaha*, a powder made of rose petals. They cover her with a transparent veil and she sits on an elevated seat so that she may be seen by all, and everyone comes to see her. That is the tradition. They lift her, they sit her, they spread her hair, they watch and admire her. And they keep calling: 'Blessed, blessed be the bride!' The bride goes from one woman to the other, and she blesses each one of them. Together they have coffee, they eat and then they go, and other people come. The wedding lasts for seven days and they all come to see the girl. This is the way of our weddings."

"You have been generous and candid in your giving!" I said when she was finished. "I thank you!"

When I looked at my tape recorder, I realized with horror that it had died on me. I shook it and tried to move the tape with my fingers. Nothing. Here on the island there was no way I could find anyone to repair it. I leaned my buzzing head on my hands. I had no choice but air my thoughts and sharpen my memory, the way the Bedouin used to in those days when they would remember and recite poems with several hundred verses, after hearing them only once. Not remembering words, but pictures and atmospheres, and letting the words flow.

The following day, I decided to go back to Abu Dhabi. Sheikha helped me with everything. Although I hardly remember the journey back, I have been carrying Um Fahd's story in my heart to this very day.

IRAQ

THE CENTER OF THE EARTH

[1] AH, *anno Hegirae*, in the year of Muhammad's Hegira

[2] Fleischhammer 185.

A BLUE SHOE DAY

[1] Harun al-Rashid, the fifth Abbasid caliph, reigned from 786 to 809. All in all, there were 37 caliphs, some of whom only reigned for a few months. Harun's conquests were legendary and his reign the height of the Arab Golden Age.

[2] It was founded by the Abbasid caliph al-Mansour (who reigned from 754 to 775).

[3] The important of Arabic science lies in the fact that the Arabs actively drew upon the knowledge of the Greeks, the Persians, the Byzantines, the Indians, and brought it all together, translated it into one language and synthesized all the information and perspectives into a vital whole.

[4] The Persian name—the God-given—also reminds us that Islamic civilization had evolved from the historical connection between Arabianism striving for progress and the old civilized people of Persia (Heller 36).

[5] The religion of the Yazids includes elements taken from both Christianity and Islam. They believe that the world was created by God, but that it is guarded by a hierarchy of subordinate beings, and that people achieve perfection in the course of many lifetimes (see Hourani 236).

[6] In March 1933 in a confidential memorandum.

I'M THE QUEEN!

[1] The real Zubayda had set up a whole infrastructure to exert her influence. She had her own palace guard of young men and girls who carried her letters and messages (see Walther 80).

[2] In the Qur'an, women's clothing is mentioned in two verses: "Say to the believing men that they should lower their gaze and guard their modesty; that will make for greater purity for them; And Allah is well acquainted with all that they do. And say to the believing women that they should lower their gaze and guard their modesty; that they should not display their beauty and ornaments except what (must ordinarily) appear thereof; that they should draw their veils over their bosoms and not display their beauty except to their husbands, their fathers, their husbands' fathers, their sons, their husbands' sons, their brothers or their brothers' sons, or their sisters' sons, or their women, or the slaves whom their right hands possess, or male servants free of physical needs, or small children who have no sense of the shame of sex; and that they should not strike their feet in order to draw attention to their hidden ornaments..." (sura 24/30–31). And, "O Prophet! Tell thy wives and daughters, and the believing women, that they should cast their outer garments over their persons (when abroad): that is most convenient, that they should be known (as such) and not molested... . " (sura 33/59). (Translation from *The Meaning of the Holy Qur'an*, 'Abdullah Yusuf 'Ali, 1422 AH/2001 CE, Amana Corporation).

[3] "Oh Consorts of the Prophet! Ye are not like any of the (other) women: If ye do fear (Allah), be not too complaisant of speech, lest one in whose heart is a disease should be moved with desire: but speak ye a speech (that is) just. And stay quietly in your houses, and make not a dazzling display, like that of the former Times of Ignorance..." (sura 33/32-33). (*The Meaning of the Holy Qur'an*, 'Abdullah Yusuf 'Ali, 1422 AH/2001 CE, Amana Corporation).

[4] Rabi'a Al-Adawiyya was an emancipated slave, born in Basra in 714 or 717. She was famous for her ascetic life and her infinite love of God, compared to which nothing in this world mattered. She became a model for future female mystics.

[5] Nearly throughout the Middle East and in southwestern Asia, women tend toward the elite professions, even today. In Iraq women make up approximately 24 percent of the engineers, physicists, or other specialized technical fields, 31 percent of doctors, and 15 percent of accountants (ILO: *Year Book of Labor Statistics*, Geneva 1979). This high representation in academic fields is special to this region. Women from the middle and upper classes either choose a highly respected profession or they prefer to stay at home. Non-academic jobs are avoided because they lack prestige, they bring undesirable contact with the opposite sex, and they offer lower salaries. The only exceptions are in the food, textile, and tobacco industries. Positions that imply contact with the public in shops, hotels, and restaurants remain mostly male domains. Office employees—like women in other non-academic fields— often leave once they get married, unless the economic situation does not permit, because women prefer staying at home instead of slaving themselves to death in jobs void of any opportunity for promotion (see Minai 226).

THE RIVER TIGRIS

[1] The name Tigris comes probably from ancient Persian, where tigra means "arrow," which aptly describes its fast, mountain-river flow. The source of the river Tigris lies in Turkey, in Eastern Taurus. It is 1,850 kilometers (1,150 mi) long, mostly (1,400 km) in Iraqi territory. Five tributary rivers flow into the Tigris from the Zagros mountains in northern Iraq.

[2] Three-quarters of the Iraqi population is Arab. The second largest ethnic group is the Kurds, followed by the Turkmens, the Armenians, the Assyrians, and the Cherkess. 50 percent of the Iraqi population is Shiite and 35 percent Sunni, out of which 5 percent are Kurds from the north. The others are Kharijites and Christians.

[3] The urban architecture of a "traditional" Muslim city is characterized by three key elements: the city is divided into clearly separated areas, in accordance with religious, ethnic, and clan membership; the architecture guarantees segregation of the sexes and the privacy of family life; finally, business and residential areas are clearly separate.

[4] Gamal Abdel Nasser, Egyptian president and Arabic national symbol (died in 1970).

[5] *Al-ud*, an instrument made of assembled thin wooden boards. *Al-ud* literally means "the wood" in Arabic. When the word migrated to the West, *al-ud* turned into the Old Provençal *laut*, then into the Middle French *lut*, then into the English *lute* (13th century).

[6] Abu Yusuf Yaqub al-Kindi (d. 866) was a famous Arabic philosopher and doctor. He tried to bring the Greek philosophers—Plato, Aristotle, and Plotin—in harmony with the Islamic faith. Al-Kindi defined *falsafa*, the Arabic word for philosophy, derived from the Greek, as: "Knowledge of things as they really are, according to human capacity." Truth is universal, and as a result religious and philosophical truths are in harmony.

[7] "In the Middle Ages much was made of the four humours; phlegmatic, sanguine, choleric, and melancholic (phlegm, blood, bile, black bile). [...] The four humours were also types of personalities or temperaments: phlegmatic (calm, stolid temperament, unemotional); sanguine (benign and gentle, cheerful, optimistic); choleric (easily angered, bad-tempered, irritable); melancholic (named for a daughter of Saturn, is also called saturnine)." From Paul Calter's *Squaring the Circle: Geometry in Art & Architecture* (Key College Publishing, January 2003).

[8] Al-Mutawakkil ibn al-Mutasim (847–861), grandson of Harun al-Rashid.

[9] Zalzal (d. 791) was an *ud* virtuoso who played at the court of the Abbasid caliph al-Mahdi (775–85). Caliph al-Mahdi was particularly famous for his love and patronage of music. Muhammad Abd al-Wahhab (d. 1995) was a great Egyptian composer and singer. He combined Western and traditional Arabic music in a song category called *ughniyya*, which enjoys great popularity from Morocco to Iraq.

[10] Abu Nasr al-Farabi (874–950) whose book *kitab al-musiqa al-kabir* (The great book of music) covers themes such as the science of tones, intervals, tetracords, octaves, the different musical instruments and compositions, and the influence of music on the human soul and body.

[11] "You ask me what the meaning of music is. To carry the listener into a spiritual experience, to embody this experience, to give it an audible form; to make the breast vibrate, to transform the soul and to move the heart toward reality. In other words, to lose oneself and to find oneself back in the heart, such is the goal." (Rosina-Fawzia Al-Rawi)

SINDBAD'S HERITAGE
[1] A boy who goes on errands for a few pennies.

KARBALA' AND NAJAF
[1] A *kufiya* is a scarf worn by Arab men, which comes either in white, black and white or red and white, and an *igal* is the black band of rope used to hold the *kufiya* in place.
[2] Ali's son with another woman whom he married after the death of the Prophet's daughter.

NONE OF OUR WOMEN SIT AT HOME
[1] Historians and writers confirm that there were in the 12th century in Baghdad women lawyers, doctors, civil servants, and university teachers. But later, when law and order collapsed, when it came to plundering, to the formation of armed gangs and to political *coups d'etat*, women could no longer leave their homes without being accompanied and protected, and they had to retreat from public life.
[2] Dr. Malka al-Saati investigated the obstacles to birth control at the beginning of the 1970s in Baghdad. She came to the conclusion that women who could barely read did not use the existing facilities, even when they were available to them. Family planning centers are hardly equipped for those women's specific problems. Patients who cannot refresh their memory with written instructions forget the details of the presentation given by the social workers on the pill and pessary, and they don't use them properly. The personal relationship, to which the poorer classes, attached to tradition, give so much importance, is often missing from the Western-style, businesslike technocrats, and this is the major obstacle. In addition, many patients who are not used to remembering exact dates and times forget their appointments. (From *Family Planning: The Difficulties Facing Implementation in Iraq*. Dissertation, Baghdad University, 1973).

UNEVEN SISTERS
[1] From an outer perspective, the difference between Sunna and Shia lies in the succession of the Prophet Muhammad as leader of the community after his death. It can be said that the separate existence of both Muslim communities — Sunna and Shia — started when the Prophet came to the end of his earthly existence, for it was precisely then that the differing conceptions started with respect to his succession. A small group was of the opinion that this function should remain within the family of the Prophet. They supported Ali, the Prophet's nephew and son-in-law, who, according to their view, was meant for this role. However, the distinction between Sunna and Shia cannot be reduced to a political difference. Sunni Islam saw the "successor" of the

Prophet as its *chalifa* (caliph) only in terms of his official power as leader of a newly founded community, whereas the Shiites believed that the "successor" also had to be the guardian of his esoteric knowledge. To them, the "succession" also entailed a spiritual function, which comprised the esoteric interpretation of the revelation and the legacy of the esoteric teachings of the Prophet. The right to the succession of the Prophet is therefore the exclusive responsibility of his family and of those who follow the family of the Prophet, *ahl al-bayt*, as the source of inspiration and direction for the understanding of the Qur'anic revelations conveyed by the Prophet. The members of his family are the channel through which the teachings and the blessing strength, *baraka*, of the revelations reach the Shia.

[2] All four schools handle all legal issues, from the most complex succession questions to the smallest details of the proper way to pray. All four schools were based on the Qur'an and on the *sunna*, the tradition of the Prophet, and they recognised the *ijma'*, the agreement of jurists on one point or another as a condition for introducing innovations in jurisprudence.

[3] The Hanafites of Abu Hanafi (d. 767); the Malikites of Malik ibn Anas (d.795); the Shafiites of al-Shafei (d. 820), and the Hanbalites of Ahmad ibn Hanbal (d. 855). The Hanbalite school had the fewest followers, and its center remained in Egypt and Syria for a long time. The Shafiite school counts most of its followers in Egypt and to a certain extent in Syria. The Malikite school totally dominates North Africa and its followers represent the most homogenous group. The Hanafite school is widespread in Turkey, in the Eastern part of the Arab world, and on the Indian-Pakistani subcontinent.

[4] Abd al-Rahman Jami, "the seal of Persian poets," (d. 1492) describes the difference between the ascetic and the true mystic as follows: the ascetics observe the beauty of the hereafter in the light of faith and certainty and they despise the world: yet they are still veiled by one sensual pleasure, namely the thought of paradise, whereas the true Sufi is shielded from both worlds through the vision of eternal beauty and intrinsic love.

[5] In the Arabic language, feminine gender is ascribed to the sun and masculine gender to the moon.

LEBANON

THE LAND OF INFINITE POTENTIAL

[1] *Um* means "mother," so Um Isam means Isam's mother, a title given to a woman after she has borne a son. If she only bears daughters, she is then named after the name of her eldest daughter — for example, Um Dina — or she is given the name of a fictitious son, and becomes, say, Um Ismail, although the wish to have an Ismail has not been fulfilled.

[2] Beit ed-Din (literally, "the house of religion") is a village high in the mountains of Lebanon, surrounded by fruit trees, olive orchards, and vineyards. It is one of the most beautiful villages in Lebanon. Its inhabitants are mostly Druze. Its famous palace, a beautiful example of Middle Eastern architecture, was built on a steep cliff, overlooking a deep bay, and it belonged to Emir Beshir (1788–1840).

[3] Deir al-Qamar, "the Monastery of the Moon," is a village peopled mostly by Maronites.

[4] A baking tray on which is placed a bent metal plate called a *saj*. The thin pastry is beaten against this hot plate where it stays for approximately three minutes until golden brown. Then the bread is taken off and wrapped in fabric to keep it fresh and soft. The art of preparing this bread, *chubz marquq*, is passed from mother to daughter and it requires much practice and skill.

THE ETERNAL FLOW OF THE OCEAN

[1] France had always seen itself as the protector of Christian minorities—Maronites, Chaldeans, Nestorians, and others—and tried to increase its influence through them.

[2] In 1943, during the National Pact, it was verbally agreed that the Lebanese president would always be a Maronite, the Prime Minister a Sunni Muslim, the speaker of the House of Representatives a Shiite Muslim, and so on.

LEBANESE DEATH DANCE

[1] The occupation lasted 22 years. It was only at the beginning of 2000 that the Israeli army retreated under the pressure of the attacks carried out by Hezbollah partisans.

LEBANON'S COLORFUL WOMEN

[1] For example, women represent 90 percent of bank employees, but there is not a single woman bank director (see Khouri).

[2] This constitutional document aimed at restricting the president's powers, achieving equal percentage among parliamentary representatives of the Muslim and Christian populations, eliminating denominationalism in the state machine and implementing economic and social reforms.

SYRIA

GREAT SYRIA

[1] Al-Hakim (996–1021) was the sixth Fatimid king in Egypt. This eccentric young ruler saw himself as embodying the Divine nature. From the very beginning, his disturbing, unpredictable behavior, his nightly walks, and later his extreme asceticism dismayed those around him. In order to purify the mores of society, he took a whole series of draconian measures such as prohibiting all fermented foods and public festivities, persecuting astrologers, forbidding men to go out at night and women to go out at all, and prohibiting the manufacturing of women's shoes. When al-Hakim started subjecting himself to the strictest demands of devoutness and losing all interest in the government, he multiplied the alms and rode everywhere on a donkey. At this point in time, two Persians appeared who spread the teaching that al-Hakim embodied Divine reason, God's highest incarnation outside his inexpressible being. Although al-Hakim encouraged this movement, the remaining followers are only one group that we call to this day Druze

(duruz), after al-Darazi, who proclaimed the divinity of al-Hakim.

[2] Mu'awiya I. Ibn Abi Sufyan reigned from 661–680 in Damascus.

[3] A vegetable that looks like spinach, but with a milder taste. Only found in the Middle East, it is cooked with onions, chicken, or meat and served with rice.

[4] After Persia and Syria, Egypt and then the whole Maghreb, all the way to the Atlantic coast, were conquered under the Umayyads. In the opposite direction, the region east of Chorasan to the river Oxus was conquered, and the first Muslim advances into northwest India started.

[5] After the death of the Prophet Muhammad, the four "righteous" caliphs: Abu Bakr (632–634), Umar ibn al-Khattab (634–644), Utman ibn Affan (644–656), and Ali ibn Abi Talib (656–661). The quarrels between caliphs Ali and Mu'awiyya led to the splitting of the Muslim community into Sunnis and Shiites, the murder of Ali, and the beginning of the Umayyad dynasty (661–750) in Syria.

[6] Al-Farazdaq (approximately 640–728) was court poet to Abd al-Malik, the fifth Umayyad caliph, and later to his sons. Al-Jarir (d. circa 729) was court poet to al-Hajjajs, the governor of Iraq during al-Malik's reign. Al-Achtal (circa 640–710) was the great poet at the court of the Umayyads in Damascus.

[7] Umar bin Abi Rabi'a (circa 643–712) came from a noble family from Mecca. He was the first Arabic poet to turn the erotic *qasida* into a separate love poem. His poems were easy to sing and reflected contemporary tastes, so they were very successful.

THE PEOPLE OF THE LONG A'S AND E'S

[1] The 1916 so-called Sykes–Picot agreement in which the British and the French divided up the formerly Ottoman regions between themselves.

A MODERN HAREM

[1] In Latin America, educated women are more or less equally divided into academic and non-academic senior positions (Minai 226).

[2] In Saudi Arabia, they thought of alleviating the labor shortage by widely switching office staff to women so as to free the men for physically demanding activities. (From *al-Raida*, a women's magazine, in 1979).

THE GREAT MASTER IBN AL-ARABI

[1] The other four pillars of Islam are as follows: (2) To pray five times a day; (3) To give alms to the poor, (4) To fast during the month of Ramadan, and (5) For those who are able, to go on pilgrimage to Mecca at least once.

[2] Humanity here does not mean humanity as it is on earth, but those qualities that are *potentially* present in this and similar species, in different worlds, qualities of a centering, all-encompassing, vicegerent, and isthmus-like nature. Only in such "humans" is the Divine portrait reflected to the whole.

KUWAIT

THE FAIRY TALE OF KUWAIT

[1] This treaty was signed in 1899 between Kuwait and Great Britain and initially kept secret. The partial renunciation of sovereignty meant that Kuwait needed Great Britain's approval to receive representatives of foreign powers and that any territorial cession to foreigners could only take place with Great Britain's agreement.

TIME IN PERSPECTIVE

[1] Women were granted the right to vote in 2003. Men and women have the right to vote across the Arab world—in Lebanon, Syria, Jordan, Palestine, Iraq, Egypt, Yemen, Algeria, Tunisia, Morocco, Sudan, and Libya.

[2] When in 1981 some Kuwaiti members of parliament appealed for women's political rights, they were refused in the name of protecting "traditions and customs." It would take more than two more decades for women to be granted voting rights.

[3] In 1963, parliamentary elections were held to elect the 50 members of the National Council. All male Kuwaiti citizens could vote provided they were over 21 years of age and could read.

EGYPT

A PEOPLE OF POETS AND BELIEVERS

[1] Quoted from Sami Zubaida, "The Quest for the Islamic State: Islamic Fundamentalism in Egypt and Iran," L. Caplan, ed. *Studies in Religious Fundamentalism* (New York, 1987), 25–50.

I CAN'T FORGIVE HIM

[1] The Copts are one of the most ancient Christian communities in the Middle East. They represent approximately 10 percent of the Egyptian population.

[2] Al-Sattar: the Shrouder. One of the names of the Divine. It is pronounced upon entering a house to give the women of the house a chance to veil themselves, that is, to prepare themselves for a visit.

TA'MIYYE AND KUSHARI, OR HOW A PEOPLE SURVIVE

[1] The 1962 National Charter (a charter that served to reorganize the country's political and constitutional life) proclaimed: "Women must be considered equal to men and therefore they must shake the remaining ties that impede their freedom of movement in order to be able to provide a constructive and fundamental contribution to the shaping of life." (Ahmed 209).

[2] Constitution of 1971, Art. 11: "The state guarantees a balance and agreement between the duties of a woman toward her family on the one hand, and toward her work in society and her equality to man in the political, social and cultural areas on the other hand, provided that the laws of the Islamic *sharia* are not broken" (Kreile 314).

BIBLIOGRAPHY

Abu-Lughod, Janet L. "The Islamic City. Historic Myth, Islamic Essence, and Contemporary Relevance," in *International Journal of Middle Eastern Studies* 19 (1987).

Ahmed, Leila. *Women and Gender in Islam*. New Haven and London 1992.

Badeau, John S., et al. *The Genius of Arab Civilization: Source of Renaissance*. London 1983.

Barthel, G., et al. *Geschichte der Araber*, vol. 6. Berlin 1982.

Butt, Gerald. *The Arab World: A Personal View*. London 1987.

Chittick, William C. *The Sufi Path of Knowledge: Ibn al-Arabi's Metaphysics of Imagination*. New York 1989.

Fleischhammer, Manfred, ed. *Altarabische Prosa*, Leipzig 1991.

Glubb, John Bagot. *A Short History of the Arab Peoples*, London 1969.

Gundert, W., A. Schimmel, and W. Schubring, ed. *Lyrik des Ostens*. München 1965.

Heller, Erdmute. *Arabeske und Talismane. Geschichte und Geschichten des Morgenlandes in der Kultur des Abendlandes*. München 1992.

Hourani, Albert. *The History of the Arab Peoples*. Second Edition, 1991.

Ibn al-Arabi. *Fusus Al-hikam. Das Buch der Siegelringsteine der Weisheitssprüche*, übersetzt von Hans Kofler, Graz 1970.

Khouri, Ghada. *Women in Lebanon. The Role of Sectarianism and Patriarchy in the Struggle for Equal Rights*. Washington, DC 1997.

Khoury, Adel T. *Abtreibung im Islam*. Cibedo-Dokumentation Nr. 11, 1981.

Kreile, Renate. *Politische Herrschaft, Geschlechterpolitik und*

Frauenmacht im Vorderen Orient. Pfaffenweiler 1997.

Minai, Naila. *Schwestern unterm Halbmond. Muslimische Frauen zwischen Tradition und Emanzipation*, 3. Aufl., München 1991

Murata, Sachiko. *The Tao of Islam*, New York 1992.

Nasr, Seyyed Hossein. *Three Muslim Sages*. Cambridge, Massachusetts 1963.

_____. *Ideal und Wirklichkeit des Islam*, München 1993

Ruthven, Malise. *Seid Wächter der Erde. Die Gedankenwelt des Islam.* Frankfurt/Main, Berlin 1987.

Scholl-Latour, Peter. *Allah ist mit den Standhaften. Begegnungen mit der islamischen Revolution*, Frankfurt/Main, Berlin 1991.

Schimmel, Annemarie. *Mystische Dimensionen des Islam. Die Geschichte des Sufismus.* Köln 1985.

Stanek, Norbert. *Irak, Land zwischen Tradition und Fortschritt.* Wien o.J.

Steinke, David. *Irak.* München 1989.

Walther, Wiebke. *Women in Islam.* Leipzig 1981.

Wilson, Peter Lamborn. *Skandal. Essays zur islamischen Häresie.* Wien 1997.

Wohlfahrt, Eberhard. *Die Arabische Halbinsel.* Frankfurt/Main 1980.